# THE PENGUIN BOOK
# OF
# CANADIAN SHORT STORIES

Edited by
Wayne Grady

Penguin Books

Penguin Books Canada Limited, 2801 John Street, Markham, Ontario, Canada L3R 1B4
Penguin Books Ltd, Harmondsworth, Middlesex, England
Penguin Books, 40 West 23rd Street, New York, New York 10010, U.S.A.
Penguin Books Australia Ltd, Ringwood, Victoria, Australia
Penguin Books (N.Z.) Ltd, 182-190 Wairau Road, Auckland 10, New Zealand

First Published 1980
Reprinted 1981, 1983, 1984, 1985, 1987, 1988

This collection copyright © Penguin Books Canada Ltd, 1980
Introduction and biographical notes copyright © Wayne Grady, 1980
All rights reserved

The Acknowledgements on pp. vii-viii constitute
an extension of this copyright page
Manufactured in Canada by Webcom Limited

CANADIAN CATALOGUING IN PUBLICATION DATA

Main entry under title:

The Penguin book of Canadian short stories

ISBN 0-14-005673-4

1. Short stories, Canadian (English)°
I. Grady, Wayne.

PS8319.P46          C813′.0108          C80-7618-4

PR9197.32.P46

# CONTENTS

# PREFACE

ALTHOUGH short stories have been with us since Gilgamesh and the Book of Ruth, most theorists of the genre agree that the modern or literary short story was invented simultaneously by Edgar Allan Poe (1809–1849) in the United States and Nikolai Gogol (1809–1852) in Russia: in the words of Dostoevsky, 'We all spring from Gogol's "Overcoat."' In Canada we were writing short fiction before we wrote novels: *The History of Emily Montague* (1769) by Frances Brooke is generally recognized as the first Canadian novel, but it *is* epistolary, and it is not a far imaginative leap from composing letters to fictional friends to writing fictional letters to newspaper editors. As David Arnason has noted in his *Nineteenth Century Canadian Stories*, the Canadian short story can be considered as 'the development of the Letter to the Editor as a specialized literary form.' It was in such newspapers and magazines as the *Acadian Recorder*, in which Thomas McCulloch's 'Stepsure Letters' appeared in 1821, Joseph Howe's *Novascotian*, which first published Haliburton's Clockmaker series in 1837, and John Lovell's *Literary Garland*, which carried Susanna Moodie's 'Canadian Sketches' in 1847, that the modern Canadian short story was conceived.

From its conception in pioneer journalism the Canadian short story inherited in turn its most characteristic feature: a realism so intimate and natural that what it describes is often mistaken for real life. Robert McDougall, in his introduction to the New Canadian Library edition of *The Clockmaker*, informs us that 'when Haliburton visited England in 1838, Lord Abinger is reported to have raised himself on one elbow from a sick-bed long enough to ask the author if it was not true (as he firmly believed) "that there is a veritable Sam Slick in the flesh now selling clocks to the Bluenoses."' Similarly, Stephen Leacock's 'Sunshine Sketches' of small-town Ontario, first published in the Montreal *Star* in 1912, were so transparently modelled on the town of Orillia—to the point of using real names—that Leacock's biographer, David M. Legate, asserts that the humourist 'was extremely lucky to escape legal actions,' and certain prudent alterations were made in the book edition. And the 'semi-autobiographical' nature of works by such contemporary authors as Mordecai Richler, Margaret Laurence, and Alice Munro is often emphasized by critics, and sometimes by the authors themselves: Hugh Hood, for example, has referred to certain of his stories as 'semi-documentaries.'

The Canadian short story as a literary art form wasn't born, however, until 1896, with the publication of Duncan Campbell Scott's *In the Village of Viger*. If one thinks of Gogol and Poe as the twin parents of the modern short story—Poe representing the imaginative, fantastic side of the family, Gogol sticking closer to earth—then Scott's collection of ten realistic short stories about the residents of an ordinary French Canadian town is the salient indication of the branch the Canadian story was to follow. In that sense, at least, Canadian literature has had more in common with Russian literature than with American literature. *In the Village of Viger*, as a series of thematically linked short stories, looks back to Gogol's *Evenings Near the Village of Dikanka*—though with obvious nods in passing to Flaubert and de Maupassant—and ahead to Leacock's *Sunshine Sketches of a Little Town*, Margaret Laurence's *A Bird in the House*, and Alice Munro's *Who Do You Think You Are?* Scott is what the genealogists would call a gateway ancestor.

Since then the short story has developed into Canada's healthiest and most versatile literary genre. Collections of short stories regularly masquerade as novels. Several of our novelists—Morley Callaghan and Hugh Garner, for example—are better known abroad for their short stories than for their novels. And many of our best writers write virtually nothing but short stories: Mavis Gallant, Norman Levine, Alice Munro, W. D. Valgardson, and others. And by interpreting for us the complexities of human life, by helping to bring the unarticulated soul of an entire community into sudden and radiant being, the short story can be said to have assumed a social responsibility left vacant by poetry since the late 1950s. It is to reflect the dominant notes in this progression that the following twenty-eight stories have been chosen.

W. G.

# ACKNOWLEDGEMENTS

'The Last Cannon Ball' by Joseph Marmette, translated by Yves Brunelle, reprinted by permission of Harvest House, Montreal.

'The Perdu' reprinted from *Earth's Enigmas* by Sir Charles G. D. Roberts by permission of The Canadian Publishers, McClelland and Stewart, Toronto.

'Paul Farlotte' by Duncan Campbell Scott is reprinted with the permission of John G. Aylen, Ottawa.

'The Marine Excursion of the Knights of Pythias' by Stephen Leacock is reprinted by permission of The Bodley Head, from *Sunshine Sketches of a Little Town* by Stephen Leacock. Reprinted by permission of The Canadian Publishers, McClelland and Stewart, Toronto.

'The Boat' by Frederick Philip Grove, from *Tales From the Margin: Selected Stories of Frederick Philip Grove*, by Desmond Pacey (ed.), McGraw-Hill Ryerson Limited. Reprinted by permission of A. Leonard Grove.

'Mist Green Oats' reprinted from *The Last Day of Spring: Stories and Other Prose* by Raymond Knister, selected and introduced by Peter Stevens, by permission of University of Toronto Press © University of Toronto Press 1976.

'A Cap for Steve' from *Morley Callaghan's Stories*, Macmillan of Canada, reprinted by permission of the author.

'Ghostkeeper' by Malcolm Lowry © 1975 by Margerie Bonner Lowry, reprinted by permission of Literistic, Ltd.

'The Satellites' by Gabrielle Roy, translated by Joyce Marshall, reprinted by permission of the author.

'The Legs of the Lame' from *The Legs of the Lame and Other Stories* © Hugh Garner 1976, reprinted by permission of McGraw-Hill Ryerson Limited.

'Bernadette' reprinted from *My Heart Is Broken* by Mavis Gallant, by permission of the author.

'By a Frozen River' is from *Thin Ice* by Norman Levine, (Wildwood House, 1980 and Deneau & Greenberg, 1979), reprinted by permission of the author.

'To Set Our House in Order' from *A Bird in the House* by Margaret Laurence, reprinted by permission of The Canadian Publishers, McClelland and Stewart, Toronto; and Macmillan of London.

# The Penguin Book
## of
## Canadian Short Stories

# Thomas Chandler Haliburton

THOMAS Chandler Haliburton was born December 17, 1796, in Windsor, Nova Scotia. In 1815 he graduated from King's College, and in 1820 he was admitted to the bar. After six years as a lawyer in Annapolis Royal he became that riding's MLA in the legislative assembly in Halifax. In 1829 he succeeded his father as a judge in the Inferior Court of Common Pleas, where he remained until the position was abolished in 1841, at which time he was elevated to the Supreme Court of Nova Scotia. He retired from the bench in 1856, moved to England, married Sara Harriet Owen and, in 1859, became the Tory member for Launceston. He died on August 27, 1865, at Isleworth, Middlesex, England.

This may sound an unlikely biography for the man who, according to William Dean Howells, dominated American humour for three generations. While living in Halifax as an MLA, Haliburton became associated with 'The Club,' a group of young writers who contributed to Joseph Howe's newspaper, *The Novascotian*. In 1835 and 1836, Haliburton wrote 22 satirical instalments for Howe, which the latter published in 1836 as *The Clockmaker; or, The Sayings and Doings of Sam Slick of Slickville*.

As a politician Haliburton angered his fellow Tories by criticizing Nova Scotians for failing to recognize the economic realities of post-war depression, and for wasting their talents on political and religious squabbling instead of getting down to the practical affairs of running a colony. As a writer he created two complementary characters, Sam Slick and the Squire, each of whom possesses qualities Haliburton admired and disliked. The Squire is quintessentially English: educated, generous, well-mannered; but at the same time rigidly conservative, snobbish, and obstructive. Sam Slick, the Yankee clockmaker who plies his trade throughout Nova Scotia, is industrious, practical-minded, and shrewd; he is nonetheless intolerant, ethically suspect, and profit motivated. Haliburton wanted Nova Scotians to select the best qualities from each, in order to run the province on a firm economic basis without sacrificing the vital thread of civility that connected them with the mother country.

# THE CLOCK MAKER

I HAD heard of Yankee clock pedlars, tin pedlars, and Bible pedlars, especially of him who sold Polyglot Bibles (*all in English*) to the amount of sixteen thousand pounds. The house of every substantial farmer had three substantial ornaments: a wood clock, a tin reflector, and a Polyglot Bible. How is it that an American can sell his wares at whatever price he pleases, where a blue-nose would fail to make a sale at all? I will enquire of the Clockmaker the secret of his success.

'What a pity it is, Mr *Slick*,' (for such was his name), 'what a pity it is,' said I, 'that you, who are so successful in teaching these people the value of *clocks*, could not also teach them the value of *time*.'

'I guess,' said he, 'they have got that ring to grow on their horns yet, which every four-year-old has in our country. We reckon hours and minutes to be dollars and cents. They do nothing in these parts but eat, drink, smoke, sleep, ride about, lounge at taverns, make speeches at temperance meetings, and talk about "*House of Assembly.*" If a man don't hoe his corn, and he don't get a crop, he says it is all owing to the Bank; and if he runs into debt and is sued, why he says the lawyers are a curse to the country. They are a most idle set of folks, I tell you.'

'But how is it,' said I, 'that you manage to sell such an immense number of clocks (which certainly cannot be called necessary articles) among a people with whom there seems to be so great a scarcity of money?'

Mr Slick paused, as if considering the propriety of answering the question, and looking me in the face, said, in a confidential tone, 'Why, I don't care if I do tell you, for the market is glutted, and I shall quit this circuit. It is done by a knowledge of *soft sawder* and *human natur*. But here is Deacon Flint's,' said he, 'I have but one clock left, and I guess I will sell it to him.'

At the gate of a most comfortable looking farm house stood Deacon Flint, a respectable old man, who had understood the value of time better than most of his neighbours, if one might judge from the appearance of every thing about him. After the usual salutation, an invitation to alight was accepted by Mr Slick, who said he wished to take leave of Mrs Flint before he left Colchester. We had hardly entered the house before the Clockmaker pointed to the view from the window and, addressing himself to me, said, 'If I was to tell them in Connecticut there was such a farm as this away down east here in Nova Scotia, they wouldn't believe me. Why, there ain't such a location in all New England. The Deacon has a hundred acres of dyke'—'Seventy,' said the deacon, 'only seventy'—'well, seventy; but then there is your fine deep bottom, why I could run a ramrod into it.'

'Interval, we call it,' said the Deacon, who, though evidently pleased at this eulogium, seemed to wish the experiment of the ramrod to be tried in the right place.

'Well, interval if you please (though Professor Eleazer Cumstick, in his work on Ohio, calls them bottoms) is just as good as dyke. Then there is that water privilege, worth three or four thousand dollars, twice as good as what Governor Cass paid fifteen thousand dollars for. I wonder, Deacon, you don't put up a carding mill on it: the same works would carry a turning lathe, a shingle machine, a circular saw, grind bark, and—'

'Too old,' said the Deacon, 'too old for all those speculations—'

'Old,' repeated the Clockmaker, 'not you; why you are worth half a dozen of the young men we see now-a-days. You are young enough to have'—here he said something in a lower tone of voice which I did not distinctly hear; but whatever it was, the Deacon was pleased. He smiled and said he did not think of such things now. 'But your beasts, dear me, your beasts must be put in and have a feed'; saying which, he went out to order them to be taken to the stable.

As the old gentleman closed the door after him, Mr Slick drew near to me, and said in an undertone, 'That is what I call "*soft sawder*." An Englishman would pass that man as a sheep passes a hog in a pasture, without looking at him; or,' said he, looking rather archly, 'if he was mounted on a pretty smart horse, I guess he'd trot away, *if he could*. Now I find—' here his lecture on '*soft sawder*' was cut short by the entrance of Mrs Flint. 'Jist come to say good bye, Mrs Flint.'

'What, have you sold all your clocks?'

'Yes, and very low, too, for money is scarce, and I wished to close the concarn; no, I am wrong in saying all, for I have just one left. Neighbour Steel's wife asked to have the refusal of it, but I guess I won't sell it; I had but two of them, this one and the feller of it, that I sold Governor Lincoln. General Green, the Secretary of State for Maine, said he'd give me fifty dollars for this here one—it has composition wheels and patent axles, it is a beautiful article—a real first chop—no mistake, genuine superfine, but I guess I'll take it back; and beside, Squire Hawk might think kinder harder, that I did not give him the offer.'

'Dear me,' said Mrs Flint, 'I should like to see it, where is it?'

'It is in a chest of mine over the way, at Tom Tape's store. I guess he can ship it on to Eastport.'

'That's a good man,' said Mrs Flint, 'jist let's look at it.'

Mr Slick, willing to oblige, yielded to these entreaties, and soon produced the clock—a gawdy, highly varnished, trumpery looking affair. He placed it on the chimney-piece, where its beauties were pointed out and duly appreciated by Mrs Flint, whose admiration was about ending in a proposal, when Mr Flint returned from giving his directions about the care of the horses. The Deacon praised the clock, he too thought it a handsome one; but the Deacon was a prudent man, he had a watch, he was sorry, but he had no occasion for a clock.

'I guess you're in the wrong furrow this time, Deacon, it ant for sale,' said Mr Slick. 'And if it was, I reckon neighbour Steel's wife would have it, for she gives me no peace about it.'

Mrs Flint said that Mr Steele had enough to do, poor man, to pay his interest, without buying clocks for his wife.

'It's no concarn of mine,' said Mr Slick, 'as long as he pays me what he has to do. But I guess I don't want to sell it, and beside it comes too high; that clock can't be made at Rhode Island under forty dollars. Why it ant possible,' said the Clockmaker, in apparent surprise, looking at his watch, 'why as I'm alive it is four o'clock, and if I haven't been two hours here—how on airth shall I reach River Philip to night? I'll tell you what, Mrs Flint, I'll leave the clock in your care till I return on my way to the States—I'll set it a-going and put it to the right time.' As soon as this operation was performed, he delivered the key to the deacon with a sort of serio-comic injunction to wind up the clock every Saturday night, which Mrs Flint said she would take care should be done, and promised to remind her husband of it, in case he should chance to forget it.

'That,' said the Clockmaker as soon as we were mounted, 'that I call *human natur!* Now that clock is sold for forty dollars—it cost me just six dollars and fifty cents. Mrs Flint will never let Mrs Steel have the refusal—nor will the Deacon learn until I call for the clock that having once indulged in the use of a superfluity, how difficult it is to give it up. We can do without any article of luxury we have never had, but when once obtained, it is not *in human natur* to surrender it voluntarily. Of fifteen thousand sold by myself and partners in this province, twelve thousand were left in this manner, and only ten clocks were ever returned—when we called for them they invariably bought them. We trust to *soft sawder* to get them into the house, and to *human natur* that they never come out of it.'

## Susanna Moodie

SUSANNA MOODIE was born in Suffolk, England, on December 6, 1803, into a family that came to be called 'the literary Stricklands.' Her sisters Elizabeth and Agnes were the authors of *Lives of the Queens of England*; another sister, Catherine Parr (later Traill), wrote *The Backwoods of Canada* in 1836; and her brother Samuel wrote *Twenty-Seven Years in Canada West* (1853).

In 1831 Susanna married Lieutenant J. W. Dunbar Moodie, a half-pay officer who had been wounded at Bergen-op-Zoom. A year later the couple emigrated to Canada, eventually settling on an uncleared farm in Douro, north of Peterborough. While her husband, who had been appointed Captain of the Militia, was away helping to quell William Lyon Mackenzie's 1837 rebellion, Susanna began to write, and from 1839 to 1851 she was the principal contributor to the important literary magazine *The Literary Garland*, edited in Montreal by John Lovell. In 1847 she published five 'Canadian Sketches' in the *Garland*, and in 1852 these sketches and others were gathered into two volumes and published in England as *Roughing It in the Bush*. The following year her *Life in the Clearings*—an account of her years in Belleville, whence she and her husband, now Sheriff of Hastings County, moved in 1840—also appeared in England. When her husband died in 1869 Susanna moved to Toronto, where she died on April 8, 1885.

Moodie's Canadian sketches are closer to the anecdote or tale than to the short story proper, but they represent an important step toward the late-nineteenth century revival of interest in the genre. They were written to be read independently, they usually revolve around a single event or a unique feature of pioneer life, and they often move toward a tentative definition of the Canadian character. As W. D. Gairdner has observed, 'Traill describes mostly exteriors, surfaces. . . . Moodie, however, is curious as to the motivating force of character. Through an often exaggerated description of exterior detail we proceed to speculation on inner life. . . . For her, description is equivalent to an exploration of character." (*Journal of Canadian Fiction, 1972*).

8

# BRIAN, THE STILL-HUNTER

It was early day. I was alone in the old shanty, preparing break-fast, and now and then stirring the cradle with my foot, when a tall, thin, middle-aged man walked into the house, followed by two large, strong dogs.

Placing the rifle he had carried on his shoulder in a corner of the room, he advanced to the hearth, and without speaking, or seem-ingly looking at me, lighted his pipe, and commenced smoking. The dogs, after growling and snapping at the cat, who had not given the strangers a very courteous reception, sat down on the hearth-stone on either side of their taciturn master, eyeing him from time to time, as if long habit had made them understand all his motions. There was a great contrast between the dogs. The one was a brindled bulldog of the largest size, a most formidable and powerful brute; the other a staghound, tawny, deep-chested, and strong-limbed. I regarded the man and his hairy companions with silent curiosity.

He was between forty and fifty years of age; his head, nearly bald, was studded at the sides with strong, coarse, black curling hair. His features were high, his complexion brightly dark, and his eyes, in size, shape, and colour, greatly resembled the eyes of a hawk. The face itself was sorrowful and taciturn; and his thin, compressed lips looked as if they were not much accustomed to smile, or often to unclose to hold social communion with any one. He stood at the side of the huge hearth, silently smoking, his eyes bent on the fire, and now and then he patted the heads of his dogs, reproving their exuberant expressions of attachment, with—'Down, Musie; down, Chance!'

'A cold, clear morning,' said I, in order to attract his attention and draw him into conversation.

A nod, without raising his head, or withdrawing his eyes from the fire, was his only answer; and, turning from my unsociable guest, I took up the baby, who just then awoke, sat down on a low stool by the table, and began feeding her. During this operation, I once or twice caught the stranger's hawk-eye fixed upon me and the child, but word spoke he none; and presently, after whistling to his dogs, he resumed his gun, and strode out.

When Moodie and Monaghan came in to breakfast, I told them what a strange visitor I had had; and Moodie laughed at my vain attempt to induce him to talk.

'He is a strange being,' I said; 'I must find out who and what he is.'

In the afternoon an old soldier called Layton, who had served during the American war and got a grant of land about a mile in the rear of our location, came in to trade for a cow. Now, this Layton was a perfect ruffian; a man whom no one liked, and whom all feared. He was a deep drinker, a great swearer, in short, a perfect reprobate; who never cultivated his land, but went jobbing about from farm to farm, trading horses and cattle, and cheating in a pettifogging way. Uncle Joe had employed him to sell Moodie a young heifer, and he had brought her over for him to look at. When he came in to be paid, I described the stranger of the morning; and as I knew that he was familiar with every one in the neighbourhood, I asked if he knew him.

'No one should know him better than myself,' he said; ''tis old Brian B—, the still-hunter, and a near neighbour of your'n. A sour, morose, queer chap he is, and as mad as a March hare! He's from Lancashire, in England, and came to this country some twenty years ago, with his wife, who was a pretty young lass in those days, and slim enough then, though she's so awful fleshy now. He had lots of money, too, and he bought four hundred acres of land, just at the corner of the concession line, where it meets the main road. And excellent land it is; and a better farmer, while he stuck to his business, never went into the bush, for it was all bush here then. He was a dashing, handsome fellow, too, and did not hoard the money either; he loved his pipe and his pot too well; and at last he left off farming, and gave himself to them altogether. Many a jolly booze he and I have had, I can tell you. Brian was an awful passionate man, and, when the liquor was in, and the wit was out, as savage and as quarrelsome as a bear. At such times there was no one but Ned Layton dared go near him. We once had a pitched battle, in which I was conqueror; and ever arter he yielded a sort of sulky obedience to all I said to him. Arter being on the spree for a week or two, he would take fits of remorse, and return home to his wife; would fall down at her knees, and ask her forgiveness, and cry like a child. At other times he would hide himself up in the woods, and steal home at night, and get what he wanted out of the pantry, without speaking a word to any one. He went on with these pranks for some years, till he took a fit of the blue devils.

"'Come away, Ned, to the ———— lake, with me," said he; "I am weary of my life, and I want a change."

"'Shall we take the fishing-tackle?" says I. "The black bass are in prime season, and F— will lend us the old canoe. He's got some capital rum up from Kingston. We'll fish all day, and have a spree at night."

"'It's not to fish I'm going," says he.

"'To shoot, then? I've bought Rockwood's new rifle."

"'It's neither to fish nor to shoot, Ned: it's a new game I'm going to try; so come along."

'Well, to the ———— lake we went. The day was very hot, and our path lay through the woods, and over those scorching plains, for eight long miles. I thought I should have dropped by the way; but during our long walk my companion never opened his lips. He strode on before me, at a half-run, never once turning his head.

"'The man must be the devil!" says I, "and accustomed to a warmer place, or he must feel this. Hollo, Brian! Stop there! Do you mean to kill me?"

"'Take it easy," says he; "you'll see another day arter this—I've business on hand, and cannot wait."

'Well, on we went, at the same awful rate, and it was mid-day when we got to the little tavern on the lake shore, kept by one F—, who had a boat for the convenience of strangers who came to visit the place. Here we got our dinner, and a glass of rum to wash it down. But Brian was moody, and to all my jokes he only returned a sort of grunt; and while I was talking with F—, he steps out, and a few minutes arter we saw him crossing the lake in the old canoe.

"'What's the matter with Brian?" says F—; "all does not seem right with him, Ned. You had better take the boat, and look arter him."

"'Pooh!" says I; "he's often so, and grows so glum now-a-days that I will cut his acquaintance altogether if he does not improve."

"'He drinks awful hard," says F—; "may be he's got a fit of the delirium-tremulous. There is no telling what he may be up to at this minute."

'My mind misgave me too, so I e'en takes the oars, and pushes out, right upon Brian's track; and, by the Lord Harry! if I did not find him, upon my landing on the opposite shore, lying wallowing in his blood, with his throat cut. "Is that you, Brian?" says I, giving him a kick with my foot, to see if he was alive or dead. "What upon earth tempted you to play me and F—such a dirty, mean trick, as to go and stick yourself like a pig, bringing such a discredit upon the house?—and you so far from home and those who should nurse you."

'I was so mad with him, that (saving your presence, ma'am) I swore awfully, and called him names that would be ondacent to repeat here; but he only answered with groans and a horrid gurgling in his throat. "It's choking you are," said I; "but you shan't have your own way, and die so easily either, if I can punish you by keeping you alive." So I just turned him upon his stomach, with his head down the steep bank; but he still kept choking and growing black in the face.'

Layton then detailed some particulars of his surgical practice which it is not necessary to repeat. He continued,

'I bound up his throat with my handkerchief, and took him neck and heels, and threw him into the bottom of the boat. Presently he came to himself a little, and sat up in the boat; and—would you believe it?—made several attempts to throw himself into the water. "This will not do," says I; "you've done mischief enough already by cutting your weasand! If you dare to try that again, I will kill you with the oar." I held it up to threaten him; he was scared, and lay down as quiet as a lamb. I put my foot upon his breast. "Lie still, now! or you'll catch it." He looked piteously at me; he could not speak, but his eyes seemed to say, "Have pity upon me, Ned; don't kill me."

'Yes, ma'am; this man, who had just cut his throat, and twice arter that tried to drown himself, was afraid that I should knock him on the head and kill him. Ha! ha! I never shall forget the work that F—and I had with him arter I got him up to the house.

'The doctor came, and sewed up his throat; and his wife—poor crittur!—came to nurse him. Bad as he was, she was mortal fond of him! He lay there, sick and unable to leave his bed, for three months, and did nothing but pray to God to forgive him, for he thought the devil would surely have him for cutting his own throat; and when he got about again, which is now twelve years ago, he left off drinking entirely, and wanders about the woods with his dogs, hunting. He seldom speaks to any one, and his wife's brother carries on the farm for the family. He is so shy of strangers that 'tis a wonder he came in here. The old wives are afraid of him; but you need not heed him—his troubles are to himself, he harms no one.'

Layton departed, and left me brooding over the sad tale which he had told in such an absurd and jesting manner. It was evident from the account he had given of Brian's attempt at suicide that the hapless hunter was not wholly answerable for his conduct—that he was a harmless maniac.

The next morning, at the very same hour, Brian again made his appearance; but instead of the rifle across his shoulder, a large stone jar occupied the place, suspended by a stout leather thong. Without saying a word, but with a truly benevolent smile that flitted slowly over his stern features, and lighted them up like a sunbeam breaking from beneath a stormy cloud, he advanced to the table, and unslinging the jar, set it down before me, and in a low and gruff, but by no means an unfriendly voice, said, 'Milk, for the child,' and vanished.

'How good it was of him! How kind!' I exclaimed, as I poured the precious gift of four quarts of pure new milk out into a deep pan. I had not asked him—had never said that the poor weanling wanted milk. It was the courtesy of a gentleman—of a man of benevolence and refinement.

For weeks did my strange, silent friend steal in, take up the empty jar, and supply its place with another replenished with milk. The baby knew his step, and would hold out her hands to him and cry 'Milk!' and Brian would stoop down and kiss her, and his two great dogs lick her face.

'Have you any children, Mr B—?'

'Yes, five; but none like this.'

'My little girl is greatly indebted to you for your kindness.'

'She's welcome, or she would not get it. You are strangers; but I like you all. You look kind, and I would like to know more about you.'

Moodie shook hands with the old hunter, and assured him that we should always be glad to see him. After this invitation, Brian became a frequent guest. He would sit and listen with delight to Moodie while he described to him elephant-hunting at the Cape; grasping his rifle in a determined manner, and whistling an encouraging air to his dogs. I asked him one evening what made him so fond of hunting.

''Tis the excitement,' he said. 'It drowns thought, and I love to be alone. I am sorry for the creatures, too, for they are free and happy; yet I am led by an instinct I cannot restrain to kill them. Sometimes the sight of their dying agonies recalls painful feelings; and then I lay aside the gun, and do not hunt for days. But 'tis fine to be alone with God in the great woods—to watch the sunbeams stealing through the thick branches, the blue sky breaking in upon you in patches, and to know that all is bright and shiny above you, in spite of the gloom that surrounds you.'

After a long pause, he continued, with much solemn feeling in his look and tone,

'I lived a life of folly for years, for I was respectably born and educated, and had seen something of the world, perhaps more than was good, before I left home for the woods; and from the teaching I had received from kind relatives and parents I should have known how to have conducted myself better. But, madam, if we associate long with the depraved and ignorant, we learn to become even worse than they are. I felt deeply my degradation—felt that I had become the slave to low vice; and in order to emancipate myself from the hateful tyranny of evil passions, I did a very rash and foolish thing. I need not mention the manner in which I transgressed God's holy laws; all the neighbours know it, and must have told you long ago. I could have borne reproof, but they turned my sorrow into indecent jests, and, unable to bear their coarse ridicule, I made companions of my dogs and gun, and went forth into the wilderness. Hunting became a habit. I could no longer live without it, and it supplies the stimulant which I lost when I renounced the cursed whisky bottle.

'I remember the first hunting excursion I took alone in the forest. How sad and gloomy I felt! I thought that there was no creature in the world so miserable as myself. I was tired and hungry, and I sat down upon a fallen tree to rest. All was still as death around me, and I was fast sinking to sleep, when my attention was aroused by a long, wild cry. My dog, for I had not Chance then, and he's no hunter, pricked up his ears, but instead of answering with a bark of defiance, he crouched down, trembling, at my feet. "What does this mean?" I cried, and I cocked my rifle and sprang upon the log. The sound came nearer upon the wind. It was like the deep baying of a pack of hounds in full cry. Presently a noble deer rushed past me, and fast upon his trial—I see them now, like so many black devils—swept by a pack of ten or fifteen large, fierce wolves, with fiery eyes and bristling hair, and paws that seemed hardly to touch the ground in their eager haste. I thought not of danger, for, with their prey in view, I was safe; but I felt every nerve within me tremble for the fate of the poor deer. The wolves gained upon him at every bound. A close thicket intercepted his path, and, rendered desperate, he turned at bay. His nostrils were dilated, and his eyes seemed to send forth long streams of light. It was wonderful to witness the courage of the beast. How bravely he repelled the attacks of his deadly enemies, how gallantly he tossed them to the right and left, and spurned them from beneath his hoofs; yet all his struggles were useless, and he was quickly overcome and torn to pieces by his ravenous foes. At that moment he seemed more unfortunate even than myself, for I could not see in what manner he had deserved his fate. All his speed and energy, his courage and fortitude, had been exerted in vain. I had tried to destroy myself; but he, with every effort vigorously made for self-preservation, was doomed to meet the fate he dreaded! Is God just to His creatures?

With this sentence on his lips, he started abruptly from his seat and left the house.

One day he found me painting some wildflowers, and was greatly interested in watching the progress I made in the group. Late in the afternoon of the following day he brought me a large bunch of splendid spring flowers.

'Draw these,' said he; 'I have been all the way to the ——— lake plains to find them for you.'

Little Katie, grasping them one by one, with infantile joy, kissed every lovely blossom.

'These are God's pictures,' said the hunter, 'and the child, who is all nature, understands them in a minute. Is it not strange that these beautiful things are hid away in the wilderness, where no eyes but the birds of the air, and the wild beasts of the wood, and the insects that live upon them, ever see them? Does God provide, for the pleasure of such creatures, these flowers? Is His benevolence gratified by the admiration of animals whom we have been taught to consider as having neither thought nor reflection? When I am alone in the forest, these thoughts puzzle me.'

Knowing that to argue with Brian was only to call into action the slumbering fires of his fatal malady, I turned the conversation by asking him why he called his favourite dog Chance?

'I found him,' he said, 'forty miles back in the bush. He was a mere skeleton. At first I took him for a wolf, but the shape of his head undeceived me. I opened my wallet, and called him to me. He came slowly, stopping and wagging his tail at every step, and looking me wistfully in the face. I offered him a bit of dried venison, and he soon became friendly, and followed me home, and has never left me since. I called him Chance, after the manner I happened with him; and I would not part with him for twenty dollars.'

Alas, for poor Chance! he had, unknown to his master, contracted a private liking for fresh mutton, and one night he killed no less than eight sheep that belonged to Mr D—, on the front road; the culprit, who had been long suspected, was caught in the very act, and this *mischance* cost him his life. Brian was sad and gloomy for many weeks after his favourite's death.

'I would have restored the sheep fourfold,' he said, 'if he would but have spared the life of my dog.'

My recollections of Brian seem more particularly to concentrate in the adventures of one night, when I happened to be left alone, for the first time since my arrival in Canada. I cannot now imagine how I could have been such a fool as to give way for four-and-twenty hours to such childish fears; but so it was, and I will not disguise my weakness from my indulgent reader.

Moodie had bought a very fine cow of a black man, named Mollineux, for which he was to give twenty-seven dollars. The man lived twelve miles back in the woods; and one fine, frosty spring day (don't smile at the term frosty, thus connected with the genial season of the year; the term is perfectly correct when applied to the Canadian spring, which, until the middle of May, is the most dismal season of the year) he and John Monaghan took a rope, and the dog, and sallied forth to fetch the cow home. Moodie said that they should be back by six o'clock in the evening, and charged me to have something cooked for supper when they returned, as he doubted not their long walk in the sharp air would give them a good appetite. This was during the time that I was without a servant, and living in old Mrs —'s shanty.

The day was so bright and clear, and Katie was so full of frolic and play, rolling upon the floor, or toddling from chair to chair, that the day passed on without my feeling remarkably lonely. At length the evening drew nigh, and I began to expect my husband's return, and to think of the supper that I was to prepare for his reception. The red heifer that we had bought of Layton came lowing to the door to be milked; but I did not know how to milk in those days, and, besides this, I was terribly afraid of cattle. Yet, as I knew that milk would be required for the tea, I ran across the meadow to Mrs Joe, and begged that one of her girls would be so kind as to milk for me. My request was greeted with a rude burst of laughter from the whole set.

'If you can't milk,' said Mrs Joe, 'it's high time you should learn. My girls are above being helps.'

'I would not ask you but as a great favour; I am afraid of cows.'

'*Afraid of cows!* Lord bless the woman! A farmer's wife, and afraid of cows!'

Here followed another laugh at my expense; and, indignant at the refusal of my first and last request, when they had all borrowed so much from me, I shut the inhospitable door and returned home.

After many ineffectual attempts I succeeded at last, and bore my half-pail of milk in triumph to the house. Yes! I felt prouder of that milk than many an author of the best thing he ever wrote, whether in verse or prose; and it was doubly sweet when I considered that I had procured it without being under any obligation to my ill-natured neighbours. I had learned a useful lesson of independence, to which in after-years I had often again to refer.

I fed little Katie and put her to bed, made the hot cakes for tea, boiled the potatoes, and laid the ham, cut in nice slices, in the pan, ready to cook the moment I saw the men enter the meadow, and arranged the little room with scrupulous care and neatness. A glorious fire was blazing on the hearth, and everything was ready for their supper; and I began to look out anxiously for their arrival.

The night had closed in cold and foggy, and I could no longer distinguish any object at more than a few yards from the door. Bringing in as much wood as I thought would last me for several hours, I closed the door; and for the first time in my life I found myself at night in a house entirely alone. Then I began to ask myself a thousand torturing questions as to the reason of their unusual absence. Had they lost their way in the woods? Could they have fallen in with wolves (one of my early bugbears)? Could any fatal accident have befallen them? I started up, opened the door, held my breath, and listened. The little brook lifted up its voice in loud, hoarse wailing, or mocked, in its babbling to the stones, the sound of human voices. As it became later, my fears increased in proportion. I grew too superstitious and nervous to keep the door open. I not only closed it, but dragged a heavy box in front, for bolt there was none. Several ill-looking men had, during the day, asked their way to Toronto. I felt alarmed lest such rude wayfarers should come tonight and demand a lodging, and find me alone and unprotected. Once I thought of running across to Mrs Joe and asking her to let one of the girls stay with me until Moodie returned; but the way in which I had been repulsed in the evening prevented me from making a second appeal to their charity.

Hour after hour wore away, and the crowing of the cocks proclaimed midnight, and yet they came not. I had burnt out all my wood, and I dared not open the door to fetch in more. The candle was expiring in the socket, and I had not courage to go up into the loft and procure another before it went finally out. Cold, heart-weary, and faint, I sat and cried. Every now and then the furious barking of the dogs at the neighbouring farms, and the loud cackling of the geese upon our own, made me hope that they were coming; and then I listened till the beating of my own heart excluded all other sounds. Oh, that unwearied brook! how it sobbed and moaned like a fretful child; what unreal terrors and fanciful illusions my too active mind conjured up, whilst listening to its mysterious tones!

Just as the moon rose, the howling of a pack of wolves, from the great swamp in our rear, filled the whole air. Their yells were answered by the barking of all the dogs in the vicinity, and the geese, unwilling to be behind-hand in the general confusion, set up the most discordant screams. I had often heard, and even been amused, during the winter, particularly on thaw nights, with hearing the howls of these formidable wild beasts; but I had never before heard them alone, and when one dear to me was abroad amid their haunts. They were directly in the track that Moodie and Monaghan must have taken; and I now made no doubt that they had been attacked and killed on their return through the woods with the cow, and I wept and sobbed until the cold grey dawn peered in upon me through the small dim windows. I have passed many a long cheerless night, when my dear husband was away from me during the rebellion, and I was left in my forest home with five little children, and only an old Irish woman to draw and cut wood for my fire, and attend to the wants of the family, but that was the saddest and longest night I ever remember.

Just as the day broke, my friends the wolves set up a parting benediction, so loud, and wild, and near to the house, that I was afraid lest they should break through the frail windows, or come down the low, wide chimney, and rob me of my child. But their detestable howls died away in the distance, and the bright sun rose up and dispersed the wild horrors of the night, and I looked once more timidly around me. The sight of the table spread, and the uneaten supper, renewed by grief, for I could not divest myself of the idea that Moodie was dead. I opened the door, and stepped forth into the pure air of the early day. A solemn and beautiful repose still hung like a veil over the face of Nature. The mists of night still rested upon the majestic woods, and not a sound but the flowing of the waters went up in the vast stillness. The earth had not yet raised her matin hymn to the throne of the Creator. Sad at heart, and weary and worn in spirit, I went down to the spring and washed my face and head, and drank a deep draught of its icy waters. On returning to the house I met, near the door, old Brian the hunter, with a large fox dangling across his shoulder, and the dogs following at his heels.

'Good God! Mrs Moodie, what is the matter? You are early abroad this morning, and look dreadful ill. Is anything wrong at home? Is the baby or your husband sick?'

'Oh!' I cried, bursting into tears, 'I fear he is killed by the wolves.'

The man stared at me as if he doubted the evidence of his senses, and well he might; but this one idea had taken such strong possession of my mind that I could admit no other. I then told him, as well as I could find words, the cause of my alarm, to which he listened very kindly and patiently.

'Set your heart at rest; your husband is safe. It is a long journey on foot to Mollineux, to one unacquainted with a blazed path in a bush road. They have stayed all night at the black man's shanty, and you will see them back at noon.'

I shook my head and continued to weep.

'Well, now, in order to satisfy you, I will saddle my mare and ride over to the nigger's, and bring you word as fast as I can.'

I thanked him sincerely for his kindness, and returned, in somewhat better spirits, to the house. At ten o'clock my good messenger returned with the glad tidings that all was well.

The day before, when half the journey had been accomplished,

John Monaghan let go the rope by which he led the cow, and she had broken away through to the woods, and returned to her old master; and when they again reached his place, night had set in, and they were obliged to wait until the return of day. Moodie laughed heartily at all my fears; but indeed I found them no joke.

Brian's eldest son, a lad of fourteen, was not exactly an idiot, but what, in the old country, is very expressively termed by the poor people a 'natural.' He could feed and assist himself, had been taught imperfectly to read and write, and could go to and from the town on errands, and carry a message from one farm-house to another; but he was a strange, wayward creature, and evidently inherited, in no small degree, his father's malady.

During the summer months he lived entirely in the woods, near his father's dwelling, only returning to obtain food, which was generally left for him in an outhouse. In the winter, driven home by the severity of the weather, he would sit for days together moping in the chimney-corner, without taking the least notice of what was passing around him. Brian never mentioned this boy— who had a strong, active figure; a handsome, but very inexpressive face—without a deep sigh; and I feel certain that half his own dejection was occasioned by the mental aberration of his child.

One day he sent the lad with a note to our house, to know if Moodie would purchase the half of an ox that he was going to kill. There happened to stand in the corner of the room an open wood box, into which several bushels of fine apples had been thrown; and, while Moodie was writing an answer to the note, the eyes of the idiot were fastened, as if by some magnetic influence, upon the apples. Knowing that Brian had a very fine orchard, I did not offer the boy any of the fruit. When the note was finished, I handed it to him. The lad grasped it mechanically, without removing his fixed gaze from the apples.

'Give that to your father, Tom.'

The boy answered not—his ears, his eyes, his whole soul, were concentrated in the apples. Ten minutes elapsed, but he stood motionless, like a pointer at a dead set.

'My good boy, you can go.'

He did not stir.

'Is there anything you want?'

'I want,' said the lad, without moving his eyes from the objects of his intense desire, and speaking in a slow, pointed manner, which ought to have been heard to be fully appreciated, 'I want ap-ples!'

'Oh, if that's all, take what you like.'

The permission once obtained, the boy flung himself upon the box with the rapacity of a hawk upon its prey, after being long poised in the air, to fix its certain aim; thrusting his hands to the right and left, in order to secure the finest specimens of the devoted fruit, scarcely allowing himself time to breathe until he had filled his old straw hat, and all his pockets, with apples. To help laughing was impossible; while this new Tom o' Bedlam darted from the house, and scampered across the field for dear life, as if afraid that we should pursue him to rob him of his prize.

It was during this winter that our friend Brian was left a fortune of three hundred pounds per annum; but it was necessary for him to return to his native country in order to take possession of the property. This he positively refused to do; and when we remonstrated with him on the apparent imbecility of this resolution, he declared that he would not risk his life, in crossing the Atlantic twice, for twenty times that sum. What strange inconsistency was this, in a being who had three times attempted to take away that which he dreaded so much to lose accidentally!

I was much amused with an account which he gave me, in his quaint way, of an excursion he went upon with a botanist, to collect specimens of the plants and flowers of Upper Canada.

'It was a fine spring day some ten years ago, and I was yoking my oxen to drag in some oats I had just sown, when a little, fat, punchy man, with a broad, red, good-natured face, and carrying a small black leathern wallet across his shoulder, called to me over the fence, and asked me if my name was Brian B——? I said, "Yes; what of that?"

'"Only you are the man I want to see. They tell me that you are better acquainted with the woods than any person in these parts; and I will pay you anything in reason if you will be my guide for a few days."

'"Where do you want to go?" said I.

'"Nowhere in particular," says he. "I want to go here and there, in all directions, to collect plants and flowers."

'That is still-hunting with a vengeance, thought I. "Today I must drag in my oats. If tomorrow will suit, we will be off."

'"And your charge?" said he. "I like to be certain of that."

'"A dollar a day. My time and labour upon my farm, at this busy season, is worth more than that."

'"True," said he. "Well, I'll give you what you ask. At what time will you be ready to start?"

'"By daybreak, if you wish it."

'Away he went; and by daylight next morning he was at my door, mounted upon a stout French pony. "What are you going to do with that beast?" said I. "Horses are of no use on the road that you and I are to travel. You had better leave him in my stable."

'"I want him to carry my traps," said he; "it may be some days that we shall be absent."

'I assured him that he must be his own beast of burthen, and carry his axe, and blanket, and wallet of food upon his own back. The little body did not much relish this arrangement; but as there was no help for it he very good-naturedly complied. Off we set, and soon climbed the steep ridge at the back of your farm, and got upon ———— lake plains. The woods were flush with flowers; and the little man grew into such an ecstacy that at every fresh specimen he uttered a yell of joy, cut a caper in the air, and flung himself down upon them, as if he was drunk with delight. "Oh, what treasures! what treasures!" he cried. "I shall make my fortune!"

'It is seldom I laugh,' quoth Brian, 'but I could not help laughing at this odd little man; for it was not the beautiful blossoms, such as you delight to paint, that drew forth these exclamations, but the queer little plants, which he had rummaged for at the roots of old trees, among the moss and long grass. He sat upon a decayed trunk, which lay in our path, I do believe for a long hour, making an oration over some greyish things, spotted with red, that grew upon it, which looked more like mould than plants, declaring himself repaid for all the trouble and expense he had been at, if it were only to obtain a sight of them. I gathered him a beautiful blossom of the lady's slipper; but he pushed it back when I presented it to him, saying, "Yes, yes; 'tis very fine. I have seen that often before; but these lichens are splendid."

'The man had so little taste that I thought him a fool, and so I left him to talk to his dear plants while I shot partridges for our supper. We spent six days in the woods, and the little man filled his black wallet with all sorts of rubbish, as if he wilfully shut his eyes to the beautiful flowers, and chose only to admire ugly, insignificant plants that everybody else passes by without noticing, and which, often as I had been in the woods, I never had observed before. I never pursued a deer with such earnestness as he continued his hunt for what he called "specimens."

'When we came to the Cold Creek, which is pretty deep in places, he was in such a hurry to get at some plants that grew under the water that in reaching after them he lost his balance and fell head over heels into the stream. He got a thorough ducking, and was in a terrible fright; but he held on to the flowers which had caused the trouble, and thanked his stars that he had saved them as well as his life. Well, he was an innocent man,' continued Brian; 'a very little made him happy, and at night he would sing and amuse himself like a child. He gave me ten dollars for my trouble, and I never saw him again; but I often think of him, when hunting in the woods that we wandered through together, and I pluck the wee plants that he used to admire, and wonder why he preferred them to the fine flowers.'

When our resolution was formed to sell our farm and take up our grant of land in the backwoods, no one was so earnest in trying to persuade us to give up this ruinous scheme as our friend Brian B—, who became quite eloquent in his description of the trials and sorrows that awaited us. During the last week of our stay in the township of H ——— he visited us every evening, and never bade us good-night without a tear moistening his cheek. We parted with the hunter as with an old friend; and we never met again. His fate was a sad one. After we left that part of the country he fell into a moping melancholy, which ended in self-destruction. But a kinder or warmer-hearted man, while he enjoyed the light of reason, has seldom crossed our path.

# Joseph Marmette

JOSEPH-ETIENNE-EUGENE Marmette was born in St-Thomas de Montmagny, Canada East, in 1844. He studied at Regiopolis College, Kingston, before entering the law school of Laval University in Quebec City. In 1866 his first novel, *Charles et Eva*, was serialized in *La revue canadienne*, and was reprinted as a book in 1945. In 1867 he was hired as a clerk in the Quebec Provincial Treasury. In 1882 he was made a charter member of the Royal Society of Canada, and from 1883-87 he lived in France on the staff of the Canadian Agent General, researching documents in the French Archives relating to the Public Archives of Canada. He died in Ottawa in 1895 while working on his autobiography, *À travers la vie*, which was completed by the poet Louis Fréchette and published later that year.

Marmette was one of Quebec's most prolific writers of historical romances. He wrote '*Le dernier boulet*' in 1885, while living in Paris and steeping himself in early Canadian history, but he also seems to have been influenced by his contemporaries. 'The Last Cannon Ball' (translated here by Yves Brunelle) contains strong elements of realism and the anti-war fervour reminiscent of Guy de Maupassant and other French writers of the period. But, unlike many of his French models, Marmette ends his story not in despair or resignation, but with hope. As Brunelle remarks, the story 'is meant above all to show the tragedy of defeat and ultimate survival in spite of it.'

# THE LAST CANNON BALL

*Translated by Yves Brunelle*

AT MIDDAY on May 15, 1760, the highway between Beauport and Quebec City offered the strangest and saddest spectacle you would want to see. On the roadway, broken in many places by the fight between the spring and passing winter, through puddles, in muddy ruts where they sank to their knees, a long line of human beings were laboriously making their way to the city. Bent to the ground, stooping under heavy burdens, pulling or pushing small handcarts loaded with provisions, they were moving like lost souls, staggering at almost every step on the road that had become a quagmire.

There was not a horse or another beast of burden left to haul the carts or to carry the food. It had been a long time since the last horse on the Beaupré shore had been requisitioned in the service of the King of France or massacred with the cattle by the soldiers of the King of England. Two great monarchs taking a hand in it, you can understand that it did not take long to ruin these simple people! So, the only beasts of burden left were old men, too old to bear arms, and women and children less than fourteen years old. As for the young men and mature men too who had survived the recent campaigns, who had not stayed behind on the battlefield at Monongahela, Choueguen, William-Henry, Carillon, Montmorency, the Plains of Abraham or Sainte-Foye, the few survivors from among our militia men—hardly three thousand of them—were showing their devotion, their sublime folly by laying siege to Quebec, with three or four decimated regiments who were putting it on the line for King Louis XV, nicknamed the Beloved, who did not give a rap for them.

After the September 13 battle, in which he had unfortunately not been able to take part, Chevalier de Lévis, having immediately gone to Montreal to organize the last-ditch resistance, had returned in the spring to the walls of the capital, where, with fewer than six thousand men lacking everything and exhausted by forced marches through melting snow, he had overwhelmed the seven thousand rested and well-fed English troops. Frightened, Murray had taken refuge in the city, to which the French general now laid siege, since April 29, with an army of fewer than six thousand men. For siege pieces our people had only fifteen poor cannons, the biggest of which was a twelve-pounder. And there was so little ammunition that each of these pieces could fire no more than twenty shots in each twenty-four hour period. The supplies picked up on the way down from Montreal to Quebec had been exhausted several days before. After devouring the few victuals gathered from the inhabitants of Sainte-Foye, Lorette, and Charlesbourg, the army, already weakened by the losses of the last battle, were now to see the spectre of famine extend its skeleton-like hand over the battlefield, when M de Lévis bethought himself to requisition in their turn the people of Beauport and Ange-Gardien. Although the Beaupré shore had been laid waste the year before, although its inhabitants had lost everything, homes, crops, furniture and cattle, and had—after having had to live for several months like wild animals in the bush—to find shelter through the winter like Indians on the edge of the woods, these hapless people must still have something to eat, since they had not yet died of starvation! Well, M de Lévis had not hesitated to ask for this last bite of food from these unfortunate people whom we saw carting all the foodstuff they had left to the French camp. These sublime, poor people were carrying the viaticum to the brave men who were ready to die waging the last battle. It is true that for all of them, to die seemed the least thing they could do, and each prepared for it without murmur, quite simply, with a stoicism born of the uninterrupted succession of misfortunes.

And while these heroic beggars were dying for their king, His Majesty Louis XV was spending happy days in the golden apartments of Versailles, with the beautiful Marquise de Pompadour, who was delighted that the loss of Canada could wipe the frown off her royal lover's brow.

What a heart-rending sight were these weakly beings turned into beasts of burden travelling long distances over atrocious roads to feed the remnants of an army which the court had left to die with such unpardonable indifference!

Wheezing under the heavy loads borne too long or the strain of plodding through deep mud, these poor creatures moved on without stopping, lest they lack the strength to set off again. Thus it was in that glorious time: those who could not fight helped in their way those who placed their bodies as the last rampart of the nation.

A cripple led the convoy, harnessed to a small cart. He was about sixty, but still spry, of military bearing when he straightened up. But just then he was bent over, drawing the cart, his wooden leg boring into the ground at every step; this made his hips sway painfully, and it would have worn him down long ago had he not had steel muscles and an iron will. But his harsh breathing, the hair stuck to his temples, his perspiring face all gave evidence of great effort.

Behind the cart and pushing it with both hands—but not with much strength—came a twenty-year-old woman, the old man's daughter-in-law. And in the cart, on top of rabbits and partridges stacked haphazardly, the woman's child lay in his swaddling-clothes. Poor creature, only a month old, conceived amidst tears the previous July between two battles, one our second-last victory and the other an unmitigated disaster.

Jacques Brossard, the child's father, a militia man attached to a navy company called to arms in early spring, had left his family at Ange-Gardien. Only a few weeks after the troops had set up camp at Beauport, Brossard saw his father and his wife arrive, forced to flee before the English forces and to leave behind their little house and everything they owned in the world. A few days later, in August, Brossard was taken to Quebec, to serve with the rampart artillery. They had not seen him since. Was he still alive; had he been killed in the September 13 battle; or was he among those who in turn were laying siege to the capital? The hapless ones did not know. Having spent the most terrible winter at Ange-Gardien, which the enemy had evacuated, in a shanty built of branches by the old man on the site of their house, which Montgomery's soldiers had burned down; having given birth to her child in a hovel meaner than the stable where Christ was born, this weak woman and this lame old man had taken advantage of the occasion of the convoy to go and find out if the dear absent one was still alive. You can imagine that no amount of weariness would stop them from getting there, to those hills which have remained famous since the supreme game was played on which the fate of a whole nation depended.

As they came nearer, the booming of the cannons on the heights became more audible. But the roar came more frequently from the city, the English firing ten times for every shot from our side. On the ramparts overlooking the plain, there was a flash at every moment, followed by a large puff of sulfur-coloured smoke that leaped, stopped, twisted on itself, then rose slowly, whitening as it went into space.

The convoy reached the temporary bridge the French had laid across the St. Charles River the previous summer. Left intact by them in the hurried retreat of September 13, and kept by the English who, according to Knox, maintained a guard there through the winter until the arrival of the French troops, this flying bridge had suffered somewhat from the spring break-up. But General Lévis had had it repaired enough to allow the convoy to cross. It goes without saying that our troops controlled not only the Plains of Abraham and Sainte-Foye but also all the space between the last houses of Saint-Roch, which were then bunched around the Commissariat, and the General Hospital, the enemy being entrenched in the city. To attack the defensive walls from the rear, one of our five small siege batteries was even set up on the left bank of the St. Charles River.

On the city side, a redoubt stood at the end of the flying bridge. A troop of Frenchmen was on guard duty there. When the old man at the head of the convoy came within earshot, someone called from the redoubt:

'Eh! Monsieur Brossard, is that you?'

The voice seeming familiar, the old man shielded his eyes to be able to ascertain who was addressing him.

'Is that you, Jean Chouinard?'

'Yes, sir.'

'So,' and the old man's voice began to quaver, 'you'll be able to give me news of my boy?'

Behind the old man the young woman was shuddering with anxiety, as a leaf shakes in the wind.

'Your son is up there on the hillock, on duty with the first battery you'll meet on the way.'

'Ah!' the old man said with a deep sigh of relief.

'Thank God!' the young woman said.

'Let's go then,' the invalid added as he set off swinging on his wooden leg. The rest of the convoy followed, because it was up there, to headquarters, that the supplies were to be taken.

The road they were on wound through fields, approximately where Saint-Roch and Saint-Sauveur meet now, and went up Sauvageau Hill.

From where they were walking the people in the convoy could see distinctly to the left the houses of the city, many of which, burned down by the English during the first siege, raised their blackened chimneys to the sky like hopeless, fleshless arms, while the shattered windows looked like lifeless eyes. Above, the sky was sad, sunless, where low clouds mingled with the thick powder smoke rising from the plain and from the ramparts. And now after every artillery volley they could hear the raucous roar of cannon balls overhead howling of death.

It was four o'clock when the convoy reached the crest of the hill. To the left, some eight hundred yards from the walls, was the besiegers' camp. Behind the earthen breastwork swarmed a wretched army of less than six thousand desperate men who, with fifteen inadequate cannons, persisted in shelling a place defended by a hundred and fifty large-calibre pieces. And for two weeks now each of these men had had to fight and live on a ration of a quarter of a pound of meat and half a pound of bread a day.

The English artillery was roaring. Its projectiles fell thick and fast like hail and plowed the soil up to two miles beyond the French camp. As the people in the convoy would have been too exposed if they had continued along the brow of the hill, the General sent men to meet them to pick up the supplies they were bringing.

Once relieved of his load, Old Man Brossard asked the officer commanding the party for permission to push on to the nearest battery where his son was.

At that very moment a ball landed a hundred feet away, causing a shower of rocks and dirt to fall on the people from the convoy, mostly women and children, who panicked and ran to take shelter on the side of the hill.

'You see what you are exposing yourselves to?' the officer said to Brossard, who with his daughter-in-law and a few others had remained.

'Bah! Lieutenant, I'm well acquainted with cannon balls,' the invalid said showing his wooden leg.

'One more reason to save the other one, my good man.'

'I've only one regret,' the old man went on, striking his chest, 'and that is that it didn't hit me there! There are a lot of sad things I wouldn't have had to see.'

'You insist then?'

'Yes; I would like to embrace my son one more time.'

'Go ahead, then.'

The old man started off, hopping on his wooden leg. His daughter-in-law made to follow him.

'But not you,' the officer said, taking her arm.

'His son is also my husband,' she said.

'All right, go ahead, but at your own risk,' the Lieutenant said, shrugging his shoulders.

The young woman followed the old man, her child clasped to her heart. This one had no idea of the dangers of war, as he pressed his lips to his mother's breast, unconsciously drawing life in the midst of death. For they were walking over freshly filled graves of unfortunate men recently killed. And above them, around them, insatiable death bellowed its sinister shriek.

Still they reached the rear of the first battery unscathed. But when they wanted to go beyond that point they were stopped. They stated their business.

'Good people,' the sentinel said, 'you must realize that this is not at all a safe place. That's the seventeenth man killed today that you see being carried away over there.'

'Oh! tell me,' the young woman exclaimed, 'is Pierre Brossard . . . ?

She could not go on, the words died in her throat.

'Pierre Brossard?' the soldier answered. 'I saw him on duty by his piece ten minutes ago.'

'Oh! sir, let me see him, I beg of you.'

'I'm sorry, good people, but I can't do anything. But there's the captain; ask him.'

A flash of joy crossed the old man's face.

'Pardon me, commandant,' he said to the officer who was walking by absent-mindedly; 'don't you recognize me?'

'Well, Brossard! What the devil are you doing here? You're no longer fit for duty!'

'Alas no, Captain! But I have taken advantage of the supply convoy to try to see my son from whom we have had no news since last fall. And this is his wife. You won't turn us back, will you?'

'He is on duty by his piece, and things are hot where he is, I'm telling you!'

'Oh! please, sir!' the young woman whispered in her sweetest voice.

'Come along,' said the officer as he led them to the embrasure in the breastwork behind which Gunner Brossard's piece stood. Spotting another gunner who was taking a break seated on a pile of balls, the Captain said:

'Noel, take Brossard's place, so that his father and his wife can have a visit with him. Eh! Brossard, come over here!'

The artilleryman who was about to light the fuse turned around. At the sight of his wife and his father, his face turned white under the layer of gunpowder that covered it in part, and for a moment he had to lean on the gun-carriage so as not to stagger.

'Come on,' the officer said. 'Noel will take your place.'

There were three frenzied shouts that were drowned by a nearby report, then embraces and kisses.

After the first effusions, the gunner realized how dangerous their position was, and he hastened to lead them nearer the breastwork. He made his wife sit down on the ground where the wall was thickest. The old man refused to do so: it would not do for him to lower his head before English cannon balls—that would be to pay them too much respect.

You can guess what was said among these three loved ones whom cursed war had kept apart. Simple words but so accented by beatings of the heart and so emphasized by the indescribable fondness of their looks that it would be impossible to convey their poignant expression.

'And this little one . . . ?' the soldier said with tear-filled eyes.

Between two cannon shots, the child had fallen asleep at his mother's breast and was smiling, his dainty mouth partly open showing a few drops of milk.

'It's true, you don't know him yet, but he is our child. You remember . . . ?'

'Yes . . . ' he answered.

'Kiss him, Pierre.'

He bent over, cautiously took the little being made of his blood into his rough hands and kissed him on the cheek. The soldier's powder-stained beard left two black spots on the child's face, which made all three of them laugh.

'Is it a boy?' he asked.

'Yes.'

'Good!'

'Yes!' grumbled the old man, 'so he can be cannon fodder like us!'

There was silence among them, for these poor people well knew how horrible war is for the lowly whom glory crushes under its chariot.

'Well,' the old man went on, 'may he live in better times than these! For years now those who were lucky enough to die before us have been a source of envy.'

The day was ending. The old man was the first to notice it.

'Daughter,' he said, 'it's time we went. They won't put up with us much longer; you know that bread and meat are scarce here, and we are useless mouths.'

Noticing that the very idea that they had to leave was disturbing his son, he added to distract him:

'I see they are going to fire your piece. Ask the man who is holding the match to let me set it. It will remind me of the old days when like you I was an artilleryman.'

Pierre moved towards the cannon with his father and spoke to the soldier, who handed the match over to the old invalid.

'Gladly, veteran,' he said; 'you'll enjoy this.'

At the command, 'ready to fire!' the old man straightened up as in the old days.

'Fire!' the officer shouted.

The cannon roared and recoiled. But at the very same moment a ball coming from the city struck the piece, carommed, cut the old man in half and shattered his son's chest. The old man dropped, while Pierre, struck on the side, spun around and fell at his wife's side, spraying her with his blood.

Struck with terror she had first remained motionless and voiceless. Then with an inhuman scream she fell on her husband's body. His heart torn out, he was stretched out on his back, his eyes wide open. The child had slipped out of his mother's arms and lay wailing nearby in the blood of his grandfather and of his father.

As people rushed towards the pitiful group—war is merciless— the bugle sounded.

'Hold your fire!' the officer ordered.

The Adjutant came running:

'Spike your guns,' he yelled, 'and get ready to retreat! You have half an hour to bury your dead!'

M de Lévis had just learned that, badly outnumbered, Vauquelain had had our last ships smashed by the English. Heaven had torn away our last hope.

As night was approaching, the dead of the day were thrown helter-skelter into a hastily dug shallow grave. They dropped down with a dull thud, one on top of the other, their blood mixing in a last holocaust for France.

Around the gaping hole, a group of crying men bent over, silent as ghosts. Out in the front rank, his surplice standing out against the blurred shadows, a priest was softly blessing the martyrs. At his side, supported by a grey-bearded sergeant, Gunner Brossard's wife was staggering under the weight of her grief.

Finally, earth was thrown over this jumbled mass of corpses, and that was the end for them here below.

Above, in the darkening sky, a flight of crows whirled, croaking mockingly over the field crammed with the flesh of the victims of two battles. In the meantime, in the distance, on the city ramparts where the artillery had quieted down, the victors, informed of the loss of our ships, were shouting triumphantly in the falling night. Vultures and crows joined their discordant voices before pouncing on the remains of the vanquished.

The obsequies over, the sergeant who held her up tried to pull the widow away from the edge of the grave now filled in, where the wretch seemed to be able to see still the one who was forever asleep in the land of the brave. But she was resisting.

'Poor lady, you can't stay here,' he said; 'the retreat has started.'

She nodded but did not move.

'Where do you live?'

'At Ange-Gardien,' she muttered.

'How are you going to get back there?'

'I don't know. Before they killed my husband and his father, they burned down our house. I have nothing left in the world.'

'What about your child?' the priest said in a deep voice.

'Ah! that's true!' the mother exclaimed taking her son into her arms.

'Sergeant,' the chaplain said, 'take her to the first houses at Sainte-Foye. Surely she will find a refuge there until she can return to her friends.'

A few moments later, the rearguard that covered the retreat turned its back on the city and set off in turn on the darkened road to Sainte-Foye. Supported by her guide, the young mother moved with them carrying her son.

This soldier's widow who was carrying an orphan in her arms

and who, bending under the burden of grief and pain, was moving into the night of the unknown, was the symbol of French Canada vanquished by numbers and fate. At that terrible hour, it seemed we were through as a race. And yet, thank God! we are the posterity, numerous and hardy, of that French orphan abandoned in North America.

At the present time, when some tub-thumpers dare dream out loud for our annihilation, it may be appropriate to recall what we were . . . and what we are today.

# Isabella Valancy Crawford

ISABELLA Valancy Crawford was born in Dublin, Ireland, on December 25, 1850, the sixth child of Dr. Stephen Dennis Crawford. Shortly thereafter the family emigrated, first to Wisconsin and then, in 1858, to Paisley, in Canada West. The family moved often; in 1863 to Lakefield (near the Stricklands), and again in 1870 to nearby Peterborough. Dr. Crawford, who was reputed to have been 'a heavy drinker, but very clever if sober,' died in 1875, and Isabella's sister Emma Naomi died of consumption a year later, at the age of 22. Isabella and her mother moved to Toronto in 1879, where they lived, apparently in a series of cheap rooming houses, on the pittance Isabella earned by publishing poems and short stories in such daily newspapers as the Toronto *Evening Telegram* and the *Globe* (in which the following story appeared on September 4, 1886). Five months later, on February 12, 1887, Isabella died of a heart attack—she was 36—and was buried in Peterborough.

One cannot praise Crawford without first noting the flaws in her poetry and prose—the ambiguous use of imagery, the tendency to push Romantic sentiment into melodrama in order to appeal to popular taste. But, for a woman living in provincial, Victorian Ontario, Crawford was well-read, intelligent, and displayed a frankly sexual imagination (see John Ower's essay, "Crawford and the Penetrating Weapon," presented at the Crawford Symposium in May 1977). Some of her lyrical poems, such as 'Said the Canoe' and 'The Dark Stag,' are among the best of her time, and her prose marks an important phase in the development of the short story. In an article that appeared in the *Journal of Canadian Fiction* in 1973, Dorothy Livesay refers to Crawford as 'Tennyson's daughter,' and at the Crawford Symposium, Elizabeth Waterston expanded on that reference: commenting on Tennyson's move to the domestic idyll, Waterston called it 'a late development of the Laureate's conviction that the poet should move from his palace of art to the "vale" of ordinary life.' As this story of Crawford's indicates, a parallel movement toward realism was occurring in the short story, and Crawford was part of it.

# EXTRADITED

'OH, SAM! back so soon? Well, I'm glad.'

She had her arms round his neck. She curved serpent-wise in his clasp to get her eyes on his eye.

'How's mammy?' she asked, in a slight panic. 'Not worse, is she?'

'Better,' returned Sam; he pushed her away mechanically, and glanced round the rude room with its touches of refinement: the stop organ against the wall of unplastered logs, the primitive hearth, its floor of hewn planks.

'Oh yes! Baby!' she exclaimed, 'you missed him; he's asleep on our bed; I'll fetch him.'

He caught her apron string, still staring round the apartment.

'Where's Joe, Bess? I don't see him round.'

Bessie crimsoned petulantly.

'You can think of the hired man first before me and Baby!'

'Baby's a sort of fixed fact. A hired man ain't,' said Sam, slowly. 'Mebbe Joe's at the barn!'

'Maybe he is, and maybe he isn't,' retorted Bessie sharply. 'I didn't marry Samuel O'Dwyer to have a hired man set before me and my child, and I won't stand it—so there!'

'You needn't to,' said Sam, smiling. He was an Irish Canadian; a rich smack of brogue adorned his tongue; a kindly graciousness of eye made a plain face almost captivating, while the proud and melancholy Celtic fire and intentness of his glance gave dignity to his expression. The lips were curved in a humorous smile, but round them were deeply graven heroic and Spartan lines.

'Sure, darlin', isn't it you an' the boy are the pulses of my heart?' he said, smiling. 'Sure Joe can wait. I was sort of wonderin' at not seein' him—that's all. Say, I'll unhitch the horses. They've done fifteen miles o' mud holes an' corduroy since noon, an' then we'll have supper. I could 'most eat my boots, so hurry up, woman darlin', or maybe it's the boy I'll be aitin', or the bit of a dog your daddy sent to him. Hear the baste howlin' like a banshee out yonder.'

'It's one of Cricket's last year's pups,' cried Bessie, running to the wagon. 'Wonder Father spared him; he thinks a sight of her pups. My! ain't he a beauty; won't Baby just love him!'

She carried the yelping youngster into the house while Sam took the horses to the barn, a primitive edifice of rough logs standing in a bleak chaos of burned stumps, for 'O'Dwyer's Clearing' was but two years old, and had the rage of its clearing fires on it yet. The uncouth eaves were fine crimson on one side, from the sunset; on the other a delicate, spiritual silver, from the moon hanging above the cedar swamp. The rude doors stood open; a vigorous purple haze, shot with heavy bars of crimson light, filled the interior; a 'Whip-Poor-Will' chanted from a distant tree like a muezzin from a minaret; the tired horses whinnied at a whiff of fresh clover and rubbed noses in sedate congratulation. Sam looked at the ground a moment, reflectively, and then shouted:

'Hullo, Joe!'

'Hullo, Sam!'

By this time Sam was stooping over the wagon tongue, his rugged face in the shadow, too intent on straps and buckles to glance up.

'Back all right, you see, Joe,' he remarked. 'How's things gettin' along?'

'Sublimely,' said Joe, coming to his assistance. 'I got the south corner cut—we've only to draw it tomorrow.'

'I never seen the beat of you at hard work,' remarked Sam. 'A slight young chap like you, too. It's just the spirit of you! But you mustn't outdo the strength that is in you for all that. I'm no slave-driver; I don't want your heart's blood. Sure, I've had your sweat two long years—an' the place shows it—it's had your sense an' sinews, so it had. I'll never forget it to you, Joe.'

Joe's tanned, nervous face was shaded by the flap of his limp straw hat. He looked piercingly at Sam, as the released horses walked decorously into the barn.

'Go to your supper, Sam,' he said. 'I'll bed them. I venture to say you're pretty sharp-set; go in.'

'I'll lend a hand first,' returned Sam. He followed the other into the barn.

'It's got dark in here suddenly,' remarked Joe. 'I'll get the lantern.'

'Don't,' said Sam, slowly. 'There's something to be spoke about betwixt you an' me, Joe, an' I'd as lieve say it in the dark; let the lantern be—I'd as lieve say it in the dark.'

'A thousand dollars!'

Bessie rose on her elbow and looked at her sleeping husband. Slumber brought the iron to the surface instead of melting it, and his face became sterner and more resolute in its repose. Its owner was not a man to be trifled with, she admitted as she gazed, and watching him she shivered slightly in the mournful moonlight. Many of her exceedingly respectable virtues were composed mainly of two or three minor vices: her conjugal love was a compound of vanity and jealousy; her maternal affection an agreement of rapacity and animal instinct. In giving her a child, nature had developed the she-eagle in her breast. She was full of impotent, unrecognized impulses to prey on all things in her child's behalf. By training and habit she was honest, but her mind was becoming active with the ingenuity of self-cheatery. She held a quiet contempt for her husband, the unlearned man who had won the pretty schoolmistress; and, hedged in by the prim fence of routine knowledge and imperfect education, she despised the large crude movements of the untrained intellect, and the primitive power of the strong and lofty soul. He muttered uneasily as she slipped out of bed. The electric chill of the moonlight did not affect her spirit—she was not vulnerable to these hints and petitions of nature. She crept carefully into the great rude room, which was hall, parlour, and kitchen. The back log, which never died out, smouldered on the hearth. A block of moonlight fell like a slab of marble on the floor of loose planks which rattled faintly under her firm, bare foot. The wooden benches, the coarse table, the log walls, started through the gloom like bleak sentinels of the great Army of Privation. She looked at them without disgust as she stole to the corner where her organ stood. She sang a silent little hymn of self-laudation.

'Some women would spend it on fine fallals for their backs or houses,' she thought. 'I won't. I'll bank every cent of it for Baby. Money doubles in ten years. A thousand dollars will grow nicely in twenty—or I'll get Daddy to loan it out on farm mortgages. I guess Sam will stare twenty years hence when he finds how rich I've got to be. I'm glad I know my duty as a parent. Sam would never see things as I do—and a thousand dollars is a sight of money.'

She groped on the organ for her paper portfolio, an elegant trifle Joe had sent to the city for, to delicately grace her last birthday; its scent of violets guided her. She took from it a paper and pencil, and standing in the moonlight scribbled a few lines. She dotted her 'i's' and crossed her 't's' with particularity, and was finicking in her nice folding of the written sheet. Her cool cheeks kept their steady pink; her round eyes their untroubled calm; her chin bridled a little with spiritual pride as she cautiously opened the outer door.

'It's my clear duty as a parent and a citizen,' she thought, with self-approval. 'The thousand dollars would not tempt me if my duty were not so plainly set before me; and the money will be in good hands. I'm not one to spend it in vain show. Money's a great evil to a weak and worldly mind, but I'm not one for vain show.'

She looked up at the sky from under the morning glories Joe had thoughtfully planted to make cool shadows for her rocker in the porch.

'It will rain tomorrow. So I'll not wash till Friday; I wonder will that pink print Sam fetched home turn out a fast colour; I'll make it up for Baby; he'll look too cunning for anything in it, with those coral sleeve links Joe gave him. I hope he won't cry, and wake Sam before I get back.'

He did not. As she had left him she found him on her return, a little snowy ball curled up against his father's massive shoulder, the beautiful, black, baby head thrust against the starting sinews of the man's bare and massive throat. When choice was possible. Baby scrambled into the aura of the father—not of the mother. Sam stirred, started, and yawned.

'What's up, Bess?' he asked sleepily.

'I went to the well to draw fresh water,' she replied, folding her shawl neatly on the back of a chair. 'I was wakeful and thirsty—the night is so hot.'

'Guess that consarned pup worried you with his howlen',' he said. 'I don't hear him now—hope he won't get out of the barn— but that ain't probable—Joe shut him in, right enough; you should have sent me to the well, girl darlin', so you should.'

Bessie picked out a burr which she felt in the fringes of her shawl, and said nothing. She was strictly truthful, so far as the letter of truth went; she had gone to the well and had drawn a bucket of cool water from that shaft of solid shadow. What else she had accomplished she decidedly had no intention of confiding to Sam. She slipped into bed, took the baby on her arm, and kissed his pouting lips.

'God bless the darling,' she said with her pretty smile.

'Amen,' said Sam earnestly. 'God come betwixt every man's child an' harm.' Bessie dosed off placidly, the child on her arm. Sam lay staring at the moonlight, listening, thinking, and grandly sorrowing.

There was the unceasing sound of someone tossing feverishly on a creaking bedstead, the eternal sound of heavy sighs resolutely smothered.

'He ain't sleepin' well, ain't Joe,' thought Sam. 'Not even though he knows Bessie an' me is his friends, true as the day. Guess he ain't sleepin' at all, poor chap!

'The consarned pup is gone,' remarked Sam disgustedly as he came in to breakfast. 'Guess he scrambled up to the hay gap and jumped out. Too bad!'

'He's safe enough,' said Joe. 'He probably ran for home. You will find him at your father's on your next visit, Mrs O'Dwyer. Dogs have the homing instinct as well as pigeons.'

'Yes, I guess he went back to Pa,' said Bessie. Her colour rose, her eyes flashed. 'Do put Baby down, Joe,' she said sharply, 'I don't want—that is, you are mussing his clean frock.'

Joe looked keenly at her.

'I understand,' he said, gently. He placed the child tenderly on the rude lounge, which yet was pretty like all Bessie's belongings, and walked to the open door.

'I think I'll straighten things a bit at the landing,' he said. 'Piner's booms burst yesterday and before the drive reaches here it's as well to see to the boats—those river drivers help themselves to canoes wherever they come across them.'

'Just as you say, Joe,' said Sam, gravely. 'I've never known your head or your heart at fault yet.'

Joe gave a long, wistful look of gratitude, and went out. He did not glance at Bessie, nor she at him.

'Bess, woman,' said Sam, 'what ails you at Joe?'

'You know well enough,' she said placidly. 'He's free to stay here; I don't deny he's working well; though that was his duty, and he was paid for it. But he shan't touch my child again. No parent who understood her duty would permit it; I know mine, I'm thankful to say.'

Her small rancours and spites were the 'Judas' doors' through which she most frequently betrayed herself. She had always faintly disliked Joe, before whom her shabby little school routine, her small affectations of intellectual superiority, had shrivelled into siccous leaves. She would assert herself now against Sam's dearly loved friend, she thought, jealously and with an approving conscience, and it was her plain duty to tear him out of that large and constant heart, she was pleased to feel.

Sam's face changed, in a breath, to a passionate pallor of skin; a proud and piercing gloom of anger darkened his blue eyes to black; he looked at her in wonder.

'What's all this, woman?' he demanded, slowly. 'But it's never your heart that's said it! Him that gave the sweat of his body and the work of his mind to help me make this home for you! Him that's saved my life more nor once at risk of his own young days! Him that's as close to my heart as my own brother! Tut, woman! It's never you would press the thorn in the breast of him into his heart's core. I won't demane myself with leavin' the thought to you, Bessie O'Dwyer!'

He struck his fist on the table; he stared levelly at her, defying her to lower herself in his eyes.

She smoothly repaired her error.

'I spoke in a hurry,' she said, lifting the baby's palm, and covering Sam's lips with its daintiness. 'I feel hurt he had so little confidence in me. I wish him well; you know that.'

Sam smiled under the fluttering of the child's palm upon his lips; he gave a sigh of relief. 'Be kind to him, Bessie darlin',' he said. 'Shure our own boy is born—but he isn't dead yet: the Lord stand betwixt the child an' harm! An' there is no tellin' when he, too, may need the kind word and the tender heart. Shure I'm sorry I took you up in arnest just now.'

'I spoke in a pet,' said Bessie gently. 'I remember, of course, all we owe to Joe—how could I forget it?'

'Forgettin's about the aisiest job in life,' said Sam, rising. 'Guess I'll help Joe at the landin'; he's downhearted, an' I won't lave him alone to his throuble.'

Bessie looked after him disapprovingly.

'Trouble indeed! I thought Sam had clearer ideas on such points. The notion of confounding trouble with rightdown sin and wickedness! Well, it's a good thing I know my duty. I wonder if Pa has any mortgage in his mind ready for that money? It must be a first mortgage; I won't risk any other—I know my responsibility as a mother better than that.'

'Why, man alive!'

Sam was astonished; for the first time in his experience of Joe, the latter was idle. He sat on a fallen tree, looking vacantly into the strong current below him.

'I'm floored, Sam,' he answered, without looking up. 'I've no grit left in me—not a grain.'

'Then it's the first time since I've known you,' said Sam, regarding him with wistful gravity. 'Don't let the sorrow master you, Joe.'

'You call it sorrow, Sam?'

'That's the blessed an' holy name for it now,' said Sam, with his lofty, simple seriousness, 'whatever it may have been afore. Hearten up, Joe! Shure you're as safe at O'Dwyer's Clearin' as if you were hid unther a hill. Rouse your heart, man alive! What's to fear?'

'Not much to fear, but a great deal to feel,' said Joe. 'Am I not stripped of my cloak to you—that's bitter.'

'The only differ is that I'm dead sure now of what I suspicioned right along,' said Sam. 'It's not in reason that a schollard an' a gentleman should bury himself on O'Dwyer's Clearin' for morenor two years, unless to sconce shame an' danger. Rouse your sowl, Joe! don't I owe half of all I have to your arm an' your larnin'? When this danger blows past I'll divide with you, an' you can make a fresh start in some sthrange counthry. South Americay's a grond place, they tell me; shure, I'll take Bessie an' the boy an' go with you. I've no kin nor kith of my own, an' next to her an' the child it is yourself is in the core of my heart. Kape the sorrow, Joe; it's the pardon of God on you, but lave the shame an' the fear go; you'll do the world's wonder yet, boy.'

Joe was about three-and-twenty, Sam in middle age. He placed his massive hand on the other's bare and throbbing head, and both looked silently at the dark and rapid river: Joe with a faint pulse of hope in his bruised and broken soul.

'Piner's logs'll get here about tomorrow,' said Sam at last. 'Shure it's Bessie'll be in the twitteration, watchin' the hens an geese from them mauraudtherin river drivers. I wish the pup hadn't got away; it's a good watch dog his mother is, an' likely he'd show her blood in him—the villain that he was to run away with himself like that. But liberty's a swate toothful, so it is, to man or brute.'

The following day, Bessie having finished her ironing and baking with triumphant exactness, stood looking from the lovely vines of the porch, down the wild farm road. She was crystal-clean and fresh, and the child in her arms was like a damask rose in his turkey-red frock and white bib. A model young matron was Mrs O'Dwyer, and looked it to the fine point of perfection, Sam thought, as he glanced back at her, pride and tenderness in his eyes. She was not looking after his retreating figure, but eagerly down the farm road, and, it seemed to Sam, she was listening intently. 'Mebbe she thinks the shouting of them river drivers is folks comin' up the road,' he thought, as he turned the clump of cedar bushes by the landing, and found Joe at work, patching a bark canoe. As usual he was labouring fiercely as men rush in battle, the sweat on his brow, his teeth set, his eyes fixed. Sam smiled reprovingly.

'Shure, it's all smashed up; you'll have her, Joe, again she's mended,' he remarked, 'more power to your elbow; but take it easy, man! You'll wear out soon enough.'

'I must work like the devil, or think,' said Joe, feverishly. 'Some day, Sam, I'll tell you all the treasures of life I threw from me, then you'll understand.'

'When a man understands by the road of the heart, where's the good of larnin' by the road of the ears?' said Sam, with the tenderest compassion. 'But I'll listen when it's your will to tell, never fear. Hark, now! don't I hear them rollickin' divvils of pike pole men shoutin' beyant the bend there?'

'Yes; Piner's logs must be pretty close,' answered Joe, looking up the river.

'They'll come down the rapids in style,' said Sam, throwing a chip on the current. 'The sthrame's swift as a swallow and strong as a giant with the rains.'

They worked in silence for a while, then Joe began to whistle softly. Sam smiled.

'That's right, Joe,' he said, 'there's nothing so bad that it mightn't be worse—there's hope ahead for you yet, never fear.'

A glimmer of some old joyous spirit sparkled in the young man's melancholy eyes, to fade instantly. 'It's past all that, dear old friend,' he said. As he spoke he glanced toward the cedar scrub between them and the house.

'Here comes Mrs O'Dwyer with the boy,' he said, 'and Sam, there are three men, strangers, with her.'

'Shanty bosses come to buy farm stuff,' said Sam. He turned on Joe with an air of sudden mastery.

'Away with you down the bank,' he said. 'Into the bush with you, an' don't come out until you hear me fire five shots in a string. Away with you!'

'Too late, Sam,' said the other, 'they have seen me.'

'What's all this, Bessie?'

Bessie wiped the baby's wet lips with her apron.

'These gentlemen asked to see you, Sam. I guess they want some farm stuff off us for Piner's Camp. So I brought them along.'

She looked placidly at her husband; the baby sprang in her arms eager to get to his friend Joe, whose red flannel shirt he found very attractive.

'Potatoes or flour?' asked Sam curtly, turning on the strangers.

'Well, it ain't neither,' said one of them—he laid his hand on Joe's wrist. 'It's this young gentleman we're after; he robbed his employer two years back, and he's wanted back by Uncle Sam. That's about the size of it.'

There was nothing brutal in his look or speech; he knew he was not dealing with a hardened criminal: he even felt compassion for the wretched quarry he had in his talons.

'He's in Canada—on British soil; I dare you to touch him!' said Sam fiercely.

'We have his extradition papers right enough,' said one of the other detectives. 'Don't be so foolish as to resist the law, Mr O'Dwyer.'

'He shan't for me,' said Joe, quietly. He stood motionless while the detective snapped one manacle of the handcuffs on his wrist; the steel glittered like a band of fire in the sun.

The child leaped strongly in Bessie's arms, crowing with delight at the pretty brightness. She was a little off her guard, somewhat faint as she watched the deathly shame on the young man's face which had never turned on her or hers but with tenderness and goodwill. Her brain reeled a little, her hands felt weak.

Suddenly there was a shriek, a flash of red, a soft plunge in the water. Joe threw his arms open, dashing aside the detectives like straws.

'Don't hold me—let me save him!' he cried.

Sam could not swim; he stood on the bank holding Bessie, who screamed and struggled in convulsions of fright as she saw her child drowning. Joe rose in the current, fighting his way superbly towards the little red bundle whirling before him. One of the detectives covered him with a revolver.

'Try to escape and I'll shoot,' he called out, 'understand?'

Joe smiled. Escape to the opposite shore and leave Sam's child to drown? No; he had no idea of it. It was a terrible fight between the man and the river—and the man subdued it unto him. He turned back to shore, the child in his teeth, both arms—one with the shining handcuff on it—beating the hostile current with fine, steady strokes.

Another moment and he would be safe on shore, a captive and ashamed.

He spurned the yellow fringes of the current; he felt ground under his feet; he half rose to step on the bank. Then there rose a bewildering cry from Sam and the men watching him; he turned and saw his danger.

With one sublime effort he flung the child on the bank, and then with the force of a battering ram the first of Piner's logs crashed upon him. It reared against him like a living thing instinct with rage, and wallowing monster-like led its barky hordes down the rushing stream, rolling triumphantly over a bruised and shattered pigmy of creation, a man.

'Extradited, by ginger,' said one of the detectives, as the groaning logs rolled compactly together over the spot where Joe had gone down.

Before the men departed, Bessie, with the baby on her arm, in a nice clean frock, found opportunity to ask one of them a momentous question. 'Do you think, he being dead, that I shall get any of the reward promised for his arrest? Only for me sending that note to Pa tied round the pup's neck, you would never have found him away back here, you know.'

'I guess not,' replied the detective eyeing her thoughtfully. 'You're a smart woman, you are, but you won't get no reward all the same; pity, ain't it?'

'It's a shame,' she said, bursting into a passion of tears. 'It don't seem that there's any reward for doing one's duty; oh, it's a downright shame.'

'Best keep all this tol'ble shady from that man of yours,' said the detective, meditatively. 'He ain't got no idee of dooty to speak of, he ain't, and seein' he was powerful fond of that poor, brave, young chap as saved that remarkably fine infant in your arms, he might cut up rough. Some folks ain't got no notion of dooty, they ain't. You best keep dark, ma'am, on the inspiritin' subject of havin' done your dooty an' lost a thousand dollars reward.'

And Bessie followed his advice very carefully indeed, though she always had the private luxury of regarding herself as an unrewarded and unrecognized heroine of duty.

# Sir Charles G. D. Roberts

SIR CHARLES G. D. Roberts was born in Douglas, New Brunswick, on January 10, 1860. His father was rector of Westcock from 1861–74, when the family moved to Fredericton. After graduating from the University of New Brunswick, Roberts became headmaster of Chatham Grammar School, published his first book of poetry in 1880—*Orion and Other Poems*, which Roy Daniells has called 'a landmark in this country's literary history'—and married Mary Fenety. In 1885 he moved to Toronto to help Goldwin Smith edit *The Week*, but after a few months his nationalist temperament clashed with Smith's annexationist sympathies, and Roberts returned to Nova Scotia to teach English at King's College. There followed, as Roberts later wrote, 'perhaps the most fruitful ten years of my life,' culminating in 1893 with his seventh book of verse and in 1894 with his first book of short stories, *The Raid from Beauséjour*. The following year he resigned from King's College to become a freelance writer. Eighteen months later he left his wife and family and moved to New York, where he became assistant editor of the *Illustrated American*. He did not return to Canada until 1925, after living in Paris and London and serving in the Canadian Overseas Forces during World War I. In 1926 he was president of the Toronto branch of the Canadian Authors' Association. He was knighted for his services to Canadian letters in 1935, and he died in Toronto on November 26, 1943.

Roberts published fifty-six books during his lifetime, among them twenty-one books of short stories, mainly animal stories—a subgenre he pioneered. He always considered himself a poet, however, and his critics have tended to agree with him. Desmond Pacey, in his *Creative Writing in Canada* (1952), concedes that 'Roberts' stories are good as long as he confines himself to portraying the lives of animals and the environment in which they move, but once he introduces human characters his touch falters and the wildest melodrama results.' But 'The Perdu,' reprinted here from *Earth's Enigmas* (1896), has a haunting subtlety of environment that transcends and outlasts the admittedly peripheral plot.

# THE PERDU

To THE passing stranger there was nothing mysterious about it except the eternal mystery of beauty. To the scattered folk, however, who lived their even lives within its neighbourhood, it was an object of dim significance and dread.

At first sight it seemed to be but a narrow, tideless, windless bit of backwater; and the first impulse of the passing stranger was to ask how it came to be called the 'Perdu.' On this point he would get little information from the fold of the neighbourhood, who knew not French. But if he were to translate the term for their better information, they would show themselves impressed by a sense of its occult appropriateness.

The whole neighbourhood was one wherein the strange and the not-to-be-understood might feel at home. It was a place where the unusual was not felt to be impossible. Its peace was the peace of one entranced. To its expectancy a god might come, or a monster, or nothing more than the realization of eventless weariness.

Only four or five miles away, across the silent, bright meadows and beyond a softly swelling range of pastured hills, swept the great river, a busy artery of trade.

On the river were all the modern noises, and with its current flowed the stream of modern ideas. Within sight of the river a mystery, or anything uninvestigated, or aught unamenable to the spirit of the age, would have seemed an anachronism. But back here, among the tall wild-parsnip tops and the never-stirring clumps of orange lilies, life was different, and dreams seemed likely to come true.

The Perdu lay perpetually asleep, along beside a steep bank clothed with white birches and balsam poplars. Amid the trunks of the trees grew elder shrubs, and snake-berries, and the elvish trifoliate plants of the purple and the painted trillium. The steep bank, and the grove, and the Perdu with them, ran along together for perhaps a quarter of a mile, and then faded out of existence, absorbed into the bosom of the meadows.

The Perdu was but a stone's throw broad, throughout its entire length. The steep with its trunks and leafage formed the northern bound of it; while its southern shore was the green verge of the

49

meadows. Along this low rim its whitish opalescent waters mixed smoothly with the roots and over-hanging blades of the long grasses, with the cloistral arched frondage of the ferns, and with here and there a strayed spray of purple wild-pea. Here and there, too, a clump of Indian willow streaked the green with the vivid crimson of its stems.

Everything watched and waited. The meadow was a sea of sun mysteriously imprisoned in the green meshes of the grass-tops. At wide intervals arose some lonely alder bushes, thick banked with clematis. Far off, on the slope of a low, bordering hill, the red doors of a barn glowed ruby-like in the transfiguring sun. At times, though seldom, a blue heron winged over the level. At times a huge black-and-yellow bee hummed past, leaving a trail of faint sound that seemed to linger like a perfume. At times the landscape, that was so changeless, would seem to waver a little, to shift confusedly like things seen through running water. And all the while the meadow scents and the many-coloured butterflies rose straight up on the moveless air, and brooded or dropped back into their dwellings.

Yet in all this stillness there was no invitation to sleep. It was a stillness rather that summoned the senses to keep watch, half apprehensively, at the doorways of perception. The wide eye noted everything, and considered it—even to the hairy red fly alit on the fern frond, or the skirring progress of the black water-beetle across the pale surface of the Perdu. The ear was very attentive—even to the fluttering down of the blighted leaf, or the thin squeak of the bee in the straitened calyx, or the faint impish conferrings of the moisture exuding suddenly from somewhere under the bank. If a common sound, like the shriek of a steamboat's whistle, now and again soared over across the hills and fields, it was changed in that refracting atmosphere, and became a defiance at the gates of waking dream.

The lives, thoughts, manners, even the open, credulous eyes of the quiet folk dwelling about the Perdu, wore in greater or less degree the complexion of the neighbourhood. How this came to be is one of those nice questions for which we need hardly expect definitive settlement. Whether the people, in the course of generations, had gradually keyed themselves to the dominant note of their surroundings, or whether the neighbourhood had been little by little wrought up to its pitch of supersensibility by the continuous impact of superstitions, and expectations, and apprehensions, and wonders, and visions, rained upon it from the personalities of an imaginative and secluded people—this might be discussed with more argument than conclusiveness.

Of the dwellers about the Perdu none was more saturated with the magic of the place than Reuben Waugh, a boy of thirteen. Reuben lived in a small, yellow-ochre-coloured cottage, on the hill behind the barn with the red doors. Whenever Reuben descended to the level, and turned to look back at the yellow dot of a house set in the vast expanse of pale blue sky, he associated the picture with a vague but haunting conception of some infinite forget-me-not flower. The boy had all the chores to do about the little homestead; but even then there was always time to dream. Besides, it was not a pushing neighbourhood; and whenever he would he took for himself a half-holiday. At such times he was more than likely to stray over to the banks of the Perdu.

It would have been hard for Reuben to say just why he found the Perdu so attractive. He might have said it was the fishing; for sometimes, though not often, he would cast a timorous hook into its depths and tremble lest he should lure from the pallid waters some portentous and dreadful prey. He never captured, however, anything more terrifying than catfish; but these were clad in no small measure of mystery, for the white waters of the Perdu had bleached their scales to a ghastly pallor, and the opalescence of their eyes was apt to haunt their captor's reveries. He might have said, also, that it was his playmate, little Celia Hansen, whose hook he would bait whenever she wished to fish, and whose careless hands, stained with berries, he would fill persistently with bunches of the hot-hued orange lily.

But Reuben knew there was more to say than this. In a boyish way, and all unrealizing, he loved the child with a sort of love that would one day flower out as an absorbing passion. For the present, however, important as she was to him, she was nevertheless distinctly secondary to the Perdu itself with its nameless spell. If Celia was not there, and if he did not care to fish, the boy still longed for the Perdu, and was more than content to lie and watch for he knew not what, amid the rapt herbage, and the brooding insects, and the gnome-like conspiracies of the moisture exuding far under the bank.

Celia was two years younger than Reuben, and by nature somewhat less imaginative. For a long time she loved the Perdu primarily for its associations with the boy who was her playmate, her protector, and her hero. When she was about seven years old Reuben had rescued her from an angry turkey-cock, and had displayed a confident firmness which seemed to her wonderfully fine. Hence had arisen an unformulated but enduring faith that Reuben could be depended upon in any emergency. From that day forward she had refused to be content with other playmates. Against this uncompromising preference Mrs Hansen was wont to protest rather plaintively; for there were social grades even here, and Mrs Hansen, whose husband's acres were broad (including the Perdu itself), knew well that 'that Waugh boy' was not her Celia's equal.

The profound distinction, however, was not one which the children could appreciate; and on Mrs Hansen lay the spell of the neighbourhood, impelling her to wait for whatever might see fit to come to pass.

For these two children the years that slipped so smoothly over the Perdu were full of interest. They met often. In the spring, when the Perdu was sullen and unresponsive, and when the soggy meadows showed but a tinge of green through the brown ruin of the winter's frosts, there was yet the grove to visit. Here Reuben would make deep incisions in the bark of the white birches, and gather tiny cupfuls of the faint-flavoured sap, which, to the children's palates, had all the relish of nectar. A little later on there were the blossoms of the trillium to be plucked—blossoms whose beauty was the more alluring in that they were supposed to be poisonous.

But it was with the deepening of the summer that the spell of the Perdu deepened to its most enthralling potency. And as the little girl grew in years and came more and more under her playmate's influence, her imagination deepened as the summer deepens, her perception quickened and grew subtle. Then in a quiet fashion, a strange thing came about. Under the influence of the children's sympathetic expectancy, the Perdu began to find fuller expression. Every mysterious element in the neighbourhood— whether emanating from the Perdu itself or from the spirits of the people about it—appeared to find a focus in the personalities of the two children. All the weird, formless stories—rather suggestions or impressions than stories—that in the course of time had gathered about the place, were revived with added vividness and awe. New ones, too, sprang into existence all over the countryside, and were certain to be connected, soon after their origin, with the name of Reuben Waugh. To be sure, when all was said and sifted, there remained little that one could grasp or set down in black and white for question. Every experience, every manifestation, when investigated, seemed to resolve itself into something of an epidemic sense of unseen but thrilling influences.

The only effect of all this, however, was to invest Reuben with an interest and importance that consorted curiously with his youth. With a certain consciousness of superiority, born of his taste for out-of-the-way reading, and dreaming, and introspection, the boy accepted the subtle tribute easily, and was little affected by it. He had the rare fortune not to differ in essentials from his neighbours, but only to intensify and give visible expression to the characteristics latent in them all.

Thus year followed year noiselessly, till Reuben was seventeen and Celia fifteen. For all the expectancy, the sense of eventfulness even, of these years, little had really happened save the common inexplicable happenings of life and growth. The little that might be counted an exception may be told in a few words.

The customs of angling for catfish and tapping the birch trees for sap had been suffered to fall into disuse. Father, it seemed interesting to wander vaguely together, or in the long grass to read together from the books which Reuben would borrow from the cobwebby library of the old schoolmaster.

As the girl reached up mentally, or perhaps, rather, emotionally, toward the imaginative stature of her companion, her hold upon him strengthened. Of old, his perceptions had been keenest when alone, but now they were in every way quickened by her presence. And now it happened that the great blue heron came more frequently to visit the Perdu. While the children were sitting amid the birches, they heard the *hush! hush!* of the bird's wings fanning the pallid water. The bird, did I say? But it seemed to them a spirit in the guise of a bird. It had gradually forgotten its seclusiveness, and now dropped its long legs at a point right over the middle of the Perdu, alighted apparently on the liquid surface, and stood suddenly transformed into a moveless statue of a bird, gazing upon the playmates with bright, significant eyes. The look made Celia tremble.

The Perdu, as might have been expected when so many mysteries were credited to it, was commonly held to be bottomless. It is a very poor neighbourhood indeed that cannot show a pool with this distinction. Reuben, of course, knew the interpretation of the myth. He knew the Perdu was very deep. Except at either end, or close to the banks, no bottom could be found with such fathom-lines as he could command. To him, and hence to Celia, this idea of vast depths was thrillingly suggestive, and yet entirely believable. The palpably impossible had small appeal for them. But when first they saw the great blue bird alight where they knew the water was fathoms deep, they came near being surprised. At least, they felt the pleasurable sensation of wonder. How was the heron supported on the water? From their green nest the children gazed and gazed; and the great blue bird held them with the gem-like radiance of its unwinking eye. At length to Reuben came a vision of the top of an ancient tree-trunk just beneath the bird's feet, just beneath the water's surface. Down, slanting far down through the opaline opaqueness, he saw the huge trunk extend itself to an immemorial root-hold in the clayey, perpendicular walls of the Perdu. He unfolded the vision to Celia, who understood. 'And it's just as wonderful,' said the girl, 'for how did the trunk get there?'

'That's so,' answered Reuben, with his eyes fixed on the bird. 'But then it's quite possible!'

And at the low sound of their voices the bird winnowed softly away.

At another time, when the children were dreaming by the Perdu, a far-off dinner-horn sounded, hoarsely but sweetly, its summons to the workers in the fields. It was the voice of noon. As the children, rising to go, glanced together across the Perdu, they clasped each other with a start of mild surprise. 'Did you see that?' whispered Celia.

'What did you see?' asked the boy.

'It looked like a pale green hand, that waved for a moment over the water, and then sank,' said Celia.

'Yes,' said Reuben, 'that's just what it looked like. But I don't believe it really was a hand! You see those thin lily-leaves all about the spot? Their stems are long, wonderfully long and slender. If one of those queer, whitish catfish, like we used to catch, were to take hold of a lily-stem and pull hard, the edges of the leaf might rise up and wave just the way *that* did! You can't tell what the catfish won't do down there!'

'Perhaps that's all it was,' said Celia.

'Though we can't be sure,' added Reuben.

And thereafter, whensoever that green hand seemed to wave to them across the pale water, they were content to leave the vision but half explained.

It also came to pass, as unexpectedly as anything could come to pass by the banks of the Perdu, that one dusky evening, as the boy and girl came slowly over the meadows, they saw a radiant point of light that wavered fitfully above the water. They watched it in silence. As it came to a pause, the girl said in her quiet voice—

'It has stopped right over the place where the heron stands!'

'Yes,' replied Reuben, 'it is evidently a will-o'-the-wisp. The queer gas, which makes it, comes perhaps from the end of that dead tree-trunk, just under the surface.'

But the fact that the point of light was thus explicable made it no less interesting and little less mysterious to the dwellers about the Perdu. As it came to be an almost nightly feature of the place, the people supplemented its local habitation with a name, calling it 'Reube Waugh's Lantern.' Celia's father, treating the Perdu and all that pertained to it with a reverent familiarity befitting his right of proprietorship, was wont to say to Reuben—

'Who gave you leave, Reuben, to hoist your lantern on my property? If you don't take it away pretty soon, I'll be having the thing put in pound.'

It may be permitted me to cite yet one more incident to illustrate more completely the kind of events which seemed of grave importance in the neighbourhood of the Perdu. It was an accepted belief that, even in the severest frosts, the Perdu could not be securely frozen over. Winter after winter, to be sure, it lay concealed beneath such a covering of snow as only firm ice could be expected to support. Yet this fact was not admitted in evidence. Folks said the ice and snow were but a film, waiting to yield upon the slightest pressure. Furthermore, it was held that neither bird nor beast was ever known to tread the deceptive expanse. No squirrel track, no slim, sharp foot-mark of partridge, traversed the immaculate level. One winter, after a light snowfall in the night, as Reuben strayed into the low-ceilinged kitchen of the Hansen farmhouse, Mr Hansen remarked in his quaint, dreamy drawl—

'What for have you been walking on the Perdu, Reuben? This morning, on the new snow, I saw foot-marks of a human running right across it. It must have been you, Reuben. There's nobody else round here'd do it!'

'No,' said Reuben, 'I haven't been nigh the Perdu these three days past. And then I didn't try walking on it, anyway.'

'Well,' continued Celia's father, 'I suppose folks would call it queer! Those foot-marks just began at one side of the Perdu, and ended right up sharp at the other. There wasn't another sign of a foot, on the meadow or in the grove!'

'Yes,' assented Reuben, 'it looks queer in a way. But then, it's easy for the snow to drift over the other tracks; while the Perdu lies low out of the wind.'

The latter days of Reuben's stay beside the banks of the Perdu were filled up by a few events like these, by the dreams which these evoked, and above all by the growing realization of his love for Celia. At length the boy and girl slipped unawares into mutual self-revelations; and for a day or two life seemed so materially and tangibly joyous that vision and dream eluded them. Then came the girl's naïve account of how her confidences had been received at home. She told of her mother's objections, soon overruled by her father's obstinate plea that 'Reuben Waugh, when he got to be a man grown, would be good enough for any girl alive.'

Celia had dwelt with pride on her father's championship of their cause. Her mother's opposition she had been familiar with for as long as she could remember. But it was the mother's opposition that loomed large in Reuben's eyes.

First it startled him with a vague sense of disquiet. Then it filled his soul with humiliation as its full significance grew upon him. Then he formed a sudden resolve; and neither the mother's relenting cordiality, nor the father's practical persuasions, nor Celia's tears, could turn him from his purpose. He said that he would go away, after the time-honoured fashion, and seek his fortune in the world. He vowed that in three or four years, when they would be of a fit age to marry, he would come back with a full purse and claim Celia on even terms. This did not suit the unworldly old farmer, who had inherited, not in vain, the spiritualities and finer influences of his possession, the Perdu. He desired, first of all, his girl's happiness. He rebuked Reuben's pride with a sternness unusual for him. But Reuben went.

He went down the great river. Not many miles from the quiet region of the Perdu there was a little riverside landing, where

Reuben took the steamer and passed at once into another atmosphere, another world. The change was a spiritual shock to him, making him gasp as if he had fallen into a tumultuous sea. There was the same chill, there was a like difficulty in getting his balance. But this was not for long. His innate self-reliance steadied him rapidly. His long-established habit of superiority helped him to avoid betraying his first sense of ignorance and unfitness. His receptiveness led him to assimilate swiftly the innumerable and novel facts of life with which he came all at once in contact; and he soon realized that the stirring, capable crowd, whose ready handling of affairs had at first overawed him, was really inferior in true insight to the peculiar people whom he had left about the Perdu. He found that presently he himself could handle the facts of life with the light dexterity which had so amazed him; but through it all he preserved (as he could see that those about him did not) his sense of the relativity of things. He perceived, always, the dependence of the facts of life upon the ideas underlying them, and thrusting them forward as manifestations or utterances. With his undissipated energy, his curious frugality in the matter of self-revelation, and his instinctive knowledge of men, he made his way from the first, and the roaring port at the mouth of the great river yielded him of its treasures for the asking. This was in a quiet enough way, indeed, but a way that more than fulfilled his expectations; and in the height of the blossoming time of his fifth summer in the world he found himself rich enough to go back to the Perdu and claim Celia. He resolved that he would buy property near the Perdu and settle there. He had no wish to live in the world; but to the world he would return often, for the sake of the beneficence of its friction —as a needle, he thought, is the keener for being thrust often amid the grinding particles of the emery-bag. He resigned his situation and went aboard an up-river boat, a small boat that would stop at every petty landing, if only to put ashore an old woman or a bag of meal, if only to take in a barrel of potatoes or an Indian with baskets and bead-work.

About mid-morning of the second day, at a landing not a score of miles below the one whereat Reuben would disembark, an Indian did come aboard with baskets and bead-work. At sight of him the old atmosphere of expectant mystery came over Reuben as subtly as comes the desire of sleep. He had seen this same Indian—he recognized the unchanging face—on the banks of the Perdu one morning years before, brooding motionless over the motionless water. Reuben began unconsciously to divest himself of his lately gathered worldliness; his mouth softened, his eyes grew wider and more passive, his figure fell into looser and freer lines, his dress seemed to forget its civil trimness. When at length he had disembarked at the old wharf under the willows, had struck across through the hilly sheep-pastures, and had reached a slope overlooking the amber-bright country of the Perdu, he was once more the silently eager boy, the quaintly reasoning visionary, his spirit waiting alert at his eyes and at his ears.

Reuben had little concern for the highways. Therefore he struck straight across the meadows, through the pale green vetch-tangle, between the intense orange lilies, amid the wavering blue butterflies and the warm, indolent perfumes of the wild-parsnip. As he drew near the Perdu there appeared the giant blue heron, dropping to his perch in mid-water. In almost breathless expectancy Reuben stepped past a clump of red willows, banked thick with clematis. His heart was beating quickly, and he could hear the whisper of the blood in his veins, as he came once more in view of the still, white water.

His gaze swept the expanse once and again, then paused, arrested by the unwavering, significant eye of the blue heron. The next moment he was vaguely conscious of a hand, that seemed to wave once above the water, far over among the lilies. He smiled as he said to himself that nothing had changed. But at this moment the blue heron, as if disturbed, rose and winnowed reluctantly away; and Reuben's eyes, thus liberated, turned at once to the spot where he had felt, rather than seen, the vision. As he looked the vision came again: a hand, and part of an arm, thrown out sharply as if striving to grasp support, then dropping back and bearing down the lily leaves. For an instant Reuben's form seemed to shrink and cower with horror—and the next he was cleaving with mighty strokes the startled surface of the Perdu. That hand—it was not pale green, like the waving hand of the old, childish vision. It was white, and the arm was white, and white the drenched lawn sleeve clinging to it. He had recognized it, he knew not how, for Celia's.

Reaching the edge of the lily patch, Reuben dived again and again, groping desperately among the long, serpent-like stems. The Perdu at this point—and even in his horror he noted it with surprise—was comparatively shallow. He easily got the bottom and searched it minutely. The edge of the dark abyss, into which he strove in vain to penetrate, was many feet distant from the spot where the vision had appeared. Suddenly, as he rested, breathless and trembling, on the grassy brink of the Perdu, he realized that this, too, was but a vision. It was but one of the old mysteries of the Perdu; and it had taken for him that poignant form because his heart and brain were so full of Celia. With a sigh of exquisite relief he thought how amused she would be at his plight, but how tender when she learned the cause of it. He laughed softly; and just then the blue heron came back to the Perdu.

Reuben shook himself, pressed some of the water from his dripping clothes, and climbed the steep upper bank of the Perdu. As he reached the top he paused among the birch trees to look back upon the water. How like a floor of opal it lay in the sun; then his heart leaped into his throat suffocatingly, for again rose the hand and arm, and waved, and dropped back among the lilies! He grasped the nearest tree, that he might not, in spite of himself, plunge back into the pale mystery of the Perdu. He rubbed his eyes sharply, drew a few long breaths to steady his heart, turned his back doggedly on the shining terror, and set forward swiftly for the farmhouse, now in full view not three hundred yards away.

For all the windless, down-streaming summer sunshine, there was that in Reuben's drenched clothes which chilled him to the heart. As he reached the wide-eaved cluster of the farmstead, a horn in the distance blew musically for noon. It was answered by another and another. But no such summons came from the kitchen door to which his feet now turned. The quiet of the Seventh Day seemed to possess the wide, bright farmyard. A flock of white ducks lay drowsing on a grassy spot. A few hens dusted themselves with silent diligence in the ash-heap in front of the shed; and they stopped to watch with bright eyes the stranger's approach. From under the apple-trees the horses whinnied to him lonesomely. It was very peaceful; but the peacefulness of it bore down upon Reuben's soul like lead. It seemed as if the end of things had come. He feared to lift the latch of the well-known door.

As he hesitated, trembling, he observed that the white blinds were down at the sitting-room windows. The window nearest him was open, and the blind stirred almost imperceptibly. Behind it, now, his intent ear caught a sound of weary sobbing. At once he seemed to see all that was in the shadowed room. The moveless, shrouded figure, the unresponding lips, the bowed heads of the mourners, all came before him as clearly as if he were standing in their midst. He leaned against the door-post, and at this moment the door opened. Celia's father stood before him.

The old man's face was drawn with his grief. Something of bitterness came into his eyes as he looked on Reuben.

'You've heard, then!' he said harshly.

'I know!' shaped itself inaudibly on Reuben's lips.

At the sight of his anguish the old man's bitterness broke.

'You've come in time for the funeral,' he exclaimed piteously. 'Oh, Reube, if you'd stayed it might have been different!'

# Duncan Campbell Scott

DUNCAN Campbell Scott was born in Ottawa on December 2, 1862. His father was an itinerant Methodist minister, and though the family lived precariously, Scott later described himself as having been 'brought up by indulgent parents whose influence was ever for the best in letters, music, and in art, and who encouraged every evident talent.' After leaving Wesleyan College in Stanstead, Quebec, and lacking the funds for medical school, Scott entered the department of Indian affairs in Ottawa as a copying clerk. Ten years later he was elevated to first-class clerk, and he built the house at 108 Lisgar Street in which he was to live for the rest of his life.

In 1883 the poet Archibald Lampman began working at the Post Office in Ottawa. He and Scott became friends, and it was Lampman who encouraged Scott to begin writing. In 1887 Scott began publishing some of the stories in *Scribner's Magazine* that would later be gathered in *In the Village of Viger* (1896). In 1893 his first book of poetry, *The Magic House*, was published in Ottawa. In 1913 he became the deputy superintendent general of his department, and he retired in 1932. He published altogether six books of poetry and three of short stories, the last of which, *The Circle of Affection*, appeared a few months before his death on December 19, 1947.

The direct, pared style of the stories in *In the Village of Viger*, and their naturalistic examination of real people in real situations, provided the first breath of the modern spirit in the Canadian short story. But 'Paul Farlotte' is more than an exercise in style. On one level it is about the conflict between Farlotte's longing for the old country and his responsibility to the new. In its larger implications, the madness in Viger reflects the material and moral decay of Victorian society. In 1922, Scott contrasted 'our modern mood' with Matthew Arnold's 'soul weariness,' stating that 'the modern feels no sickness of soul which requires a panacea of quiescence; he is aware of imperfections and of vast physical and social problems, but life does not therefore interest him less but more.'

# PAUL FARLOTTE

NEAR THE outskirts of Viger, to the west, far away from the Blanche, but having a country outlook of their own, and a glimpse of a shadowy range of hills, stood two houses which would have attracted attention by their contrast, if for no other reason. One was a low cottage, surrounded by a garden, and covered with roses, which formed jalousies for the encircling veranda. The garden was laid out with the care and completeness that told of a master hand. The cottage itself had the air of having been secured from the inroads of time as thoroughly as paint and a nail in the right place at the right time could effect that end. The other was a large gaunt-looking house, narrow and high, with many windows, some of which were boarded up, as if there was no further use for the chambers into which they had once admitted light. Standing on a rough piece of ground it seemed given over to the rudeness of decay. It appeared to have been the intention of its builder to veneer it with brick; but it stood there a wooden shell, discoloured by the weather, disjointed by the frost, and with the wind fluttering the rags of tar-paper which had been intended as a protection against the cold, but which now hung in patches and ribbons. But despite this dilapidation it had a sort of martial air about it, and seemed to watch over its embowered companion, warding off tempests and gradually falling to pieces on guard, like a faithful soldier who suffers at his post. In the road, just between the two, stood a beautiful Lombardy poplar. Its shadow fell upon the little cottage in the morning, and travelled across the garden, and in the evening touched the corner of the tall house, and faded out with the sun, only to float there again in the moonlight, or to commence the journey next morning with the dawn. This shadow seemed, with its constant movement, to figure the connection that existed between the two houses.

The garden of the cottage was a marvel; there the finest roses in the parish grew, roses which people came miles to see, and parterres of old-fashioned flowers, the seed of which came from France, and which in consequence seemed to blow with a rarer colour and more delicate perfume. This garden was a striking contrast to the stony ground about the neighbouring house, where only the commonest weeds grew unregarded; but its master had been born a gardener, just as another man is born a musician or a poet. There was a superstition in the village that all he had to do was to put anything, even a dry stick, into the ground, and it would grow. He was the village schoolmaster, and Madame Laroque would remark spitefully enough that if Monsieur Paul Farlotte had been as successful in planting knowledge in the heads of his scholars as he was in planting roses in his garden Viger would have been celebrated the world over. But he was born a gardener, not a teacher; and he made the best of the fate which compelled him to depend for his living on something he disliked. He looked almost as dry as one of his own hyacinth bulbs; but like it he had life at his heart. He was a very small man, and frail, and looked older than he was. It was strange, but you rarely seemed to see his face; for he was bent with weeding and digging, and it seemed an effort for him to raise his head and look at you with the full glance of his eye. But when he did, you saw the eye was honest and full of light. He was not careful of his personal appearance, clinging to his old garments with a fondness which often laid him open to ridicule, which he was willing to bear for the sake of the comfort of an old pair of shoes, or a hat which had accommodated itself to the irregularities of his head. On the street he wore a curious skirt-coat that seemed to be made of some indestructible material, for he had worn it for years, and might be buried in it. It received an extra brush for Sundays and holidays, and always looked as good as new. He made a quaint picture, as he came down the road from the school. He had a hesitating walk, and constantly stopped and looked behind him; for he always fancied he heard a voice calling him by his name. He would be working in his flower-beds when he would hear it over his shoulder, 'Paul'; or when he went to draw water from his well, 'Paul'; or when he was reading by his fire, someone calling him softly, 'Paul, Paul'; or in the dead of night, when nothing moved in his cottage he would hear it out of the dark, 'Paul.' So it came to be a sort of companionship for him, this haunting voice; and sometimes one could have seen him in his garden stretch out his hand and smile, as if he were welcoming an invisible guest. Sometimes the guest was not invisible, but took body and shape, and was a real presence; and often Paul was greeted with visions of things that had been, or that would be, and saw figures where, for other eyes, hung only the impalpable air.

He had one other passion besides his garden, and that was Montaigne. He delved in one in the summer, in the other in the winter. With his feet on his stove he would become so absorbed with his author that he would burn his slippers and come to himself disturbed by the smell of the singed leather. He had only one great ambition, that was to return to France to see his mother before she died; and he had for years been trying to save enough money to take the journey. People who did not know him called him stingy, and said the saving for his journey was only a pretext to cover his miserly habits. It was strange, he had been saving for years, and yet he had not saved enough. Whenever anyone would ask him, 'Well, Monsieur Farlotte, when do you go to France?' he would answer, 'Next year—next year.' So when he announced one spring that he was actually going, and when people saw that he was not making his garden with his accustomed care, it became the talk of the village: 'Monsieur Farlotte is going to France'; 'Monsieur Farlotte has saved enough money, true, true, he is going to France.'

His proposed visit gave no one so much pleasure as it gave his neighbours in the gaunt, unkempt house which seemed to watch over his own; and no one would have imagined what a joy it was to Marie St Denis, the tall girl who was mother to her orphan brothers and sisters, to hear Monsieur Farlotte say, 'When I am in France'; for she knew what none of the villagers knew, that, if it had not been for her and her troubles, Monsieur Farlotte would have seen France many years before. How often she would recall the time when her father, who was in the employ of the great match factory near Viger, used to drive about collecting the little paper match-boxes which were made by hundreds of women in the village and the country around; how he had conceived the idea of making a machine in which a strip of paper would go in at one end, and the completed match-boxes would fall out at the other; how he had given up his situation and devoted his whole time and energy to the invention of this machine; how he had failed time and again, but continued with a perseverance which at last became a frantic passion; and how, to keep the family together, her mother, herself, and the children joined that army of workers which was making the match-boxes by hand. She would think of what would have happened to them then if Monsieur Farlotte had not been there with his help, or what would have happened when her mother died, worn out, and her father, overcome with disappointment, gave up his life and his task together, in despair. But whenever she would try to speak of these things Monsieur Farlotte would prevent her with a gesture, 'Well, but what would you have me do—besides, I will go some day—now who knows, next year, perhaps.' So here was the 'next year,' which she had so longed to see, and Monsieur Farlotte was giving her a daily lecture on how to treat the tulips after they had done flowering, preluding everything he had to say with, 'When I am in France,' for his heart was already there.

He had two places to visit, one was his old home, the other was the birthplace of his beloved Montaigne. He had often described to Marie the little cottage where he was born, with the vine arbours and the long garden walks, the lilac-bushes, with their cool dark-green leaves, the white eaves where the swallows nested, and the poplar, sentinel over all. 'You see,' he would say, 'I have tried to make this little place like it; and my memory may have played me a trick, but I often fancy myself at home. That poplar and this long walk and the vines on the arbour—sometimes when I see the tulips by the border I fancy it is all in France.'

Marie was going over his scant wardrobe, mending with her skilful fingers, putting a stitch in the trusty old coat, and securing its buttons. She was anxious that Monsieur Farlotte should get a new suit before he went on his journey; but he would not hear of it. 'Not a bit of it,' he would say, 'if I made my appearance in a new suit, they would think I had been making money; and when they would find out that I had not enough to buy cabbage for the soup there would be a disappointment.' She could not get him to write that he was coming. 'No, no,' he would say, 'if I do that they will expect me.' 'Well, and why not—why not?' 'Well, they would think about it—in ten days Paul comes home, then in five days Paul comes home, and then when I came they would set the dogs on me. No, I will just walk in—so—and when they are staring at my old coat I will just sit down in a corner, and my old mother will commence to cry. Oh, I have it all arranged.'

So Marie let him have his own way; but she was fixed on having her way in some things. To save Monsieur Farlotte the heavier work, and allow him to keep his strength for the journey, she would make her brother Guy do the spading in the garden, much to his disgust, and that of Monsieur Farlotte, who would stand by and interfere, taking the spade into his own hands with infinite satisfaction. 'See,' he would say, 'go deeper and turn it over so.' And when Guy would dig in his own clumsy way, he would go off in despair, with the words, 'God help us, nothing will grow there.'

When Monsieur Farlotte insisted on taking his clothes in an old box covered with raw-hide, with his initials in brass tacks on the cover, Marie would not consent to it, and made Guy carry off the box without his knowledge and hide it. She had a good tin trunk which had belonged to her mother, which she knew where to find in the attic, and which would contain everything Monsieur Farlotte had to carry. Poor Marie never went into this attic without a shudder, for occupying most of the space was her father's work bench, and that complicated wheel, the model of his invention, which he had tried so hard to perfect, and which stood there like a monument of his failure. She had made Guy promise never to move it, fearing lest he might be tempted to finish what his father had begun—a fear that was almost an apprehension, so like him was he growing. He was tall and large-boned, with a dark restless eye, set under an overhanging forehead. He had long arms, out of proportion to his height, and he hung his head when he walked. His likeness to his father made him seem a man before his time. He felt himself a man; for he had a good position in the match factory, and was like a father to his little brothers and sisters.

Although the model had always had a strange fascination for him, the lad had kept his promise to his sister, and had never touched the mechanism which had literally taken his father's life. Often when he went into the attic he would stand and gaze at the model and wonder why it had not succeeded, and recall his father bending over his work, with his compass and pencil. But he had a dread of it, too, and sometimes would hurry away, afraid lest its fascination would conquer him.

Monsieur Farlotte was to leave as soon as his school closed, but weeks before that he had everything ready, and could enjoy his roses in peace. After school hours he would walk in his garden, to and fro, to and fro, with his hands behind his back, and his eyes upon the ground, meditating; and once in a while he would pause and smile, or look over his shoulder when the haunting voice would call his name. His scholars had commenced to view him with additional interest, now that he was going to take such a prodigious journey; and two or three of them could always be seen peering through the palings, watching him as he walked up and down the path; and Marie would watch him, too, and wonder what he would say when he found that his trunk had disappeared. He missed it fully a month before he could expect to start; but he had resolved to pack that very evening.

'But there is plenty of time,' remonstrated Marie.

'That's always the way,' he answered. 'Would you expect me to leave everything until the last moment?'

'But, Monsieur Farlotte, in ten minutes everything goes into the trunk.'

'So, and in the same ten minutes something is left out of the trunk, and I am in France, and my shoes are in Viger, that will be the end of it.'

So, to pacify him, she had to ask Guy to bring down the trunk from the attic. It was not yet dark there; the sunset threw a great colour into the room, touching all the familiar objects with transfiguring light, and giving the shadows a rich depth. Guy saw the model glowing like some magic golden wheel, the metal points upon it gleaming like jewels in the light. As he passed he touched it, and with a musical click something dropped from it. He picked it up: it was one of the little paper match-boxes, but the defect that he remembered to have heard talked of was there. He held it in his hand and examined it; then he pulled it apart and spread it out. 'Ah,' he said to himself, 'the fault was in the cutting.' Then he turned the wheel, and one by one the imperfect boxes dropped out, until the strip of paper was exhausted. 'But why,'—the question rose in his mind—'why could not that little difficulty be overcome?'

He took the trunk down to Marie, who at last persuaded Monsieur Farlotte to let her pack his clothes in it. He did so with a protestation, 'Well, I know how it will be with a fine box like that, some fellow will whip it off when I am looking the other way, and that will be the end of it.'

As soon as he could do so without attracting Marie's attention Guy returned to the attic with a lamp. When Marie had finished packing Monsieur Farlotte's wardrobe, she went home to put her children to bed; but when she saw that light in the attic window she nearly fainted from apprehension. When she pushed open the door of that room which she had entered so often with the scant meals she used to bring her father, she saw Guy bending over the model, examining every part of it. 'Guy,' she said, trying to command her voice, 'you have broken your promise.' He looked up quickly. 'Marie, I am going to find it out—I can understand it—there is just one thing, if I can get that we will make a fortune out of it.'

'Guy, don't delude yourself; those were father's words, and day after day I brought him his meals here, when he was too busy even to come downstairs; but nothing came of it, and while he was trying to make a machine for the boxes, we were making them with our fingers. O Guy,' she cried, with her voice rising into a sob, 'remember those days, remember what Monsieur Farlotte did for us, and what he would have to do again if you lost your place!'

'That's all nonsense, Marie. Two weeks will do it, and after that I could send Monsieur Farlotte home with a pocket full of gold.'

'Guy, you are making a terrible mistake. That wheel was our curse, and it will follow us if you don't leave it alone. And think of Monsieur Farlotte; if he finds out what you are working at he will not go to France—I know him; he will believe it his duty to stay here and help us, as he did when father was alive. Guy, Guy, listen to me!'

But Guy was bending over the model, absorbed in its labyrinths. In vain did Marie argue with him, try to persuade him, and threaten him; she attempted to lock the attic door and keep him out, but he twisted the lock off, and after that the door was always open. Then she resolved to break the wheel into a thousand pieces; but when she went upstairs, when Guy was away, she could not strike it with the axe she held. It seemed like a human thing that cried out with a hundred tongues against the murder she would do; and she could only sink down sobbing, and pray. Then failing everything else she simulated an interest in the thing, and tried to lead Guy to work at it moderately, and not to give up his whole time to it.

But he seemed to take up his father's passion where he had laid it down. Marie could do nothing with him; and the younger children, at first hanging around the attic door, as if he were their father come back again, gradually ventured into the room, and whispered together as they watched their rapt and unobservant brother working at his task. Marie's one thought was to devise a means of keeping the fact from Monsieur Farlotte; and she told him blankly that Guy had been sent away on business, and would not be back for six weeks. She hoped that by that time Monsieur Farlotte would be safely started on his journey. But night after night he saw a light in the attic window. In the past years it had been constant there, and he could only connect it with one cause. But he could get no answer from Marie when he asked her the reason; and the next night the distracted girl draped the window so that no ray of light could find its way out into the night. But Monsieur Farlotte was not satisfied; and a few evenings afterwards, as it was growing dusk, he went quietly into the house and upstairs into the attic. There he saw Guy stretched along the work bench, his head in his hands, using the last light to ponder over a sketch he was making, and beside him, figured very clearly in the thick gold air of the sunset, the form of his father, bending over him, with the old eager, haggard look in his eyes. Monsieur Farlotte watched the two figures for a moment as they glowed in their rich atmosphere; then the apparition turned his head slowly, and warned him away with a motion of his hand.

All night long Monsieur Farlotte walked in his garden, patient and undisturbed, fixing his duty so that nothing could root it out. He found the comfort that comes to those who give up some exceeding deep desire of the heart, and when next morning the market-gardener from St Valérie, driving by as the matin bell was clanging from St Joseph's, and seeing the old teacher as if he were taking an early look at his growing roses, asked him, 'Well, Monsieur Farlotte, when do you go to France?' he was able to answer cheerfully, 'Next year—next year.'

Marie could not unfix his determination. 'No,' he said, 'they do not expect me. No one will be disappointed. I am too old to travel. I might be lost in the sea. Until Guy makes his invention we must not be apart.'

At first the villagers thought that he was only joking, and that they would some morning wake up and find him gone; but when the holidays came, and when enough time had elapsed for him to make his journey twice over, they began to think he was in earnest. When they knew that Guy St Denis was chained to his father's invention, and when they saw that Marie and the children had commenced to make match-boxes again, they shook their heads. Some of them at least seemed to understand why Monsieur Farlotte had not gone to France.

But he never repined. He took up his garden again, was as

contented as ever, and comforted himself with the wisdom of Montaigne. The people dropped the old question, 'When are you going to France?' Only his companion voice called him more loudly, and more often he saw figures in the air that no one else could see.

Early one morning, as he was working in his garden around a growing pear-tree, he fell into a sort of stupor, and sinking down quietly on his knees he leaned against the slender stem for support. He saw a garden much like his own, flooded with the clear sun-light, in the shade of an arbour an old woman in a white cap was leaning back in a wheeled chair, her eyes were closed, she seemed asleep. A young woman was seated beside her holding her hand. Suddenly the old woman smiled, a childish smile, as if she were well pleased. 'Paul,' she murmured, 'Paul, Paul.' A moment later her companion started up with a cry; but she did not move, she was silent and tranquil. Then the young woman fell on her knees and wept, hiding her face. But the aged face was inexpressibly calm in the shadow, with the smile lingering upon it, fixed by the deeper sleep into which she had fallen.

Gradually the vision faded away, and Paul Farlotte found himself leaning against his pear-tree, which was almost too young as yet to support his weight. The bell was ringing from St Joseph's, and had shaken the swallows from their nests in the steeple into the clear air. He heard their cries as they flew into his garden, and he heard the voices of his neighbour children as they played around the house.

Later in the day he told Marie that his mother had died that morning, and she wondered how he knew.

# Stephen Leacock

STEPHEN BUTLER Leacock was born in Swanmore, Hampshire, England, on December 30, 1869. When he was six the family moved to a hundred-acre farm (later described by Leacock as 'the damndest place I ever saw') near Sutton, Ontario. From 1882-87 he attended Upper Canada College, then entered University College, University of Toronto, on a scholarship. That year his father abandoned the family, and Leacock left school and took up teaching, first at Uxbridge High School and then, from 1890-99, at Upper Canada College. He then enrolled at the University of Chicago to study economics under Thorstein Veblen, received his Ph.D. in 1903, and became a professor of economics at McGill University in Montreal. He headed McGill's Department of Political Economy from 1908 (the year he bought his celebrated property on Old Brewery Bay, near Orillia, Ontario) until his forced retirement in 1936. He died in Toronto on March 28, 1944, of throat cancer.

Although he was a professor of economics for thirty-three years, and although his first and most profitable book was his *Elements of Political Science* (1906), Leacock is best known throughout the world as a humorist, the natural heir of Mark Twain and O. Henry (and, therefore, of Thomas Chandler Haliburton). In 1912 Sir Hugh Graham (later Lord Atholstan), founder and publisher of the Montreal *Star*, commissioned Leacock to write a series of sketches, 'to be typically Canadian.' These appeared in the *Star* from February 17 to June 22, 1912, and were published in book form that year as *Sunshine Sketches of a Little Town*, his best known and arguably best book. As Robertson Davies notes in his short study, *Stephen Leacock* (1970), if *Sunshine Sketches* 'may not be called a novel, it has a strong appearance of being the work of a man who will write a novel very soon. The twelve chapters have a single setting and a group of characters who are developed by means of description from a variety of viewpoints.' Leacock is thus being more typically Canadian than perhaps even he realized: the revival of the book of 'linked stories' that can be read as a novel is a distinctly Canadian contribution to the genre.

# THE MARINE EXCURSION OF THE KNIGHTS OF PYTHIAS

HALF-PAST six on a July morning! The Mariposa Belle is at the wharf, decked in flags, with steam up ready to start.

Excursion day!

Half-past six on a July morning, and Lake Wissanotti lying in the sun as calm as glass. The opal colours of the morning light are shot from the surface of the water.

Out on the lake the last thin threads of the mist are clearing away like flecks of cotton wool.

The long call of the loon echoes over the lake. The air is cool and fresh. There is in it all the new life of the land of the silent pine and the moving waters. Lake Wissanotti in the morning sunlight! Don't talk to me of the Italian lakes, or the Tyrol or the Swiss Alps. Take them away. Move them somewhere else. I don't want them.

Excursion Day, at half-past six of a summer morning! With the boat all decked in flags and all the people in Mariposa on the wharf, and the band in peaked caps with big cornets tied to their bodies ready to play at any minute! I say! Don't tell me about the Carnival of Venice and the Delhi Durbar. Don't! I wouldn't look at them. I'd shut my eyes! For light and colour give me every time an excursion out of Mariposa down the lake to the Indian's Island out of sight in the morning mist. Talk of your Papal Zouaves and your Buckingham Palace Guard! I want to see the Mariposa band in uniform and the Mariposa Knights of Pythias with their aprons and their insignia and their picnic baskets and their five-cent cigars!

Half-past six in the morning, and all the crowd on the wharf and the boat due to leave in half an hour. Notice it!—in half an hour. Already she's whistled twice (at six, and at six fifteen), and at any minute now, Christie Johnson will step into the pilot house and pull the string for hour. So keep ready. Don't think of running back to Smith's Hotel for the sandwiches. Don't be fool enough to try to go up to the Greek Store, next to Netley's, and buy fruit. You'll be left behind for sure if you do. Never mind the sandwiches and the fruit! Anyway, here comes Mr Smith himself with a huge basket of provender that would feed a factory. There must be sandwiches in that. I think I can hear them clinking. And behind Mr Smith is the German waiter from the caff with another basket—indubitably lager beer; and behind him, the bar-tender of the hotel, carrying nothing, as far as one can see. But of course if you know Mariposa you will understand that why he looks so nonchalant and empty-handed is because he has two bottles of rye whisky under his linen duster. You know, I think, the peculiar walk of a man with two bottles of whisky in the inside pockets of a linen coat. In Mariposa, you see, to bring beer to an excursion is quite in keeping with public opinion. But whisky—well, one has to be a little careful.

Do I say that Mr Smith is here? Why, everybody's here. There's Hussell, the editor of the *Newspacket*, wearing a blue ribbon on his coat, for the Mariposa Knights of Pythias are, by their constitution, dedicated to temperance and there's Henry Mullins, the manager of the Exchange Bank, also a Knight of Pythias, with a small flask of Pogram's Special in his hip pocket as a sort of amendment to the constitution. And there's Dean Drone, the Chaplain of the Order, with a fishing-rod (you never saw such green bass as lie among the rocks at Indian's Island), and with a trolling line in case of maskinonge, and a landing net in case of pickerel, and with his eldest daughter, Lilian Drone, in case of young men. There never was such a fisherman as the Rev Rupert Drone.

Perhaps I ought to explain that when I speak of the excursion as being of the Knights of Pythias, the thing must not be understood in any narrow sense. In Mariposa practically everybody belongs to the Knights of Pythias just as they do to everything else. That's the great thing about the town and that's what makes it so different from the city. Everybody is in everything.

You should see them on the seventeenth of March, for example, when everybody wears a green ribbon and they're all laughing and glad—you know what the Celtic nature is—and talking about Home Rule.

On St Andrew's Day every man in town wears a thistle and shakes hands with everybody else, and you see the fine old Scotch honesty beaming out of their eyes.

And on St George's Day!—well, there's no heartiness like the good old English spirit, after all; why shouldn't a man feel glad that he's an Englishman?

Then on the Fourth of July there are stars and stripes flying over half the stores in town, and suddenly all the men are seen to smoke cigars, and to know all about Roosevelt and Bryan and the Philippine Islands. Then you learn for the first time that Jeff Thorpe's people came from Massachusetts and that his uncle fought at Bunker Hill (anyway Jefferson will swear it was in Dakota all right enough); and you find that George Duff has a married sister in Rochester and that her husband is all right; in fact, George was down there as recently as eight years ago. Oh, it's the most American town imaginable in Mariposa—on the Fourth of July.

But wait, just wait, if you feel anxious about the solidity of the British connection, till the twelfth of the month, when everybody is wearing an orange streamer in his coat and the Orangemen (every man in town) walk in the big procession. Allegiance! Well, perhaps you remember the address they gave to the Prince of Wales on the platform of the Mariposa station as he went through on his tour to the west. I think that pretty well settled that question.

So you will easily understand that of course everybody belongs to the Knights of Pythias and the Masons and Oddfellows, just as they all belong to the Snow Shoe Club and the Girls' Friendly Society.

And meanwhile the whistle of the steamer has blown again for a quarter to seven—loud and long this time, for anyone not here now is late for certain, unless he should happen to come down in the last fifteen minutes.

What a crowd upon the wharf and how they pile on to the steamer! It's a wonder that the boat can hold them all. But that's just the marvellous thing about the Mariposa Belle.

I don't know—I have never known—where the steamers like the Mariposa Belle come from. Whether they are built by Harland and Wolff of Belfast, or whether, on the other hand, they are not built by Harland and Wolff of Belfast, is more than one would like to say offhand.

The Mariposa Belle always seems to me to have some of those strange properties that distinguish Mariposa itself. I mean, her size seems to vary so. If you see her there in the winter, frozen in the ice beside the wharf with snowdrift against the windows of the pilot house, she looks a pathetic little thing the size of a butternut. But in the summer time, especially after you've been in Mariposa for a month or two, and have paddled alongside of her in a canoe, she gets larger and taller, and with a great sweep of black sides, till you see no difference between the Mariposa Belle and the Lusitania. Each one is a big steamer and that's all you can say.

Nor do her measurements help you much. She draws about eighteen inches forward, and more than that—at least half an inch more, astern, and when she's loaded down with an excursion crowd she draws a good two inches more. And above the water— why, look at all the decks on her! There's the deck you walk on to, from the wharf, all shut in, with windows along it, and the after cabin with the long table, and above that the deck with all the chairs piled upon it, and the deck in front where the band stand round in a circle, and the pilot house is higher than that, and above the pilot house is the board with the gold name and the flag pole and the steel ropes and the flags; and fixed in somewhere on the different levels is the lunch counter where they sell the sandwiches, and the engine room, and down below the deck level, beneath the water line, is the place where the crew sleep. What with steps and stairs and passages and piles of cord-wood for the engine—oh, no, I guess Harland and Wolff didn't build her. They couldn't have.

Yet even with a huge boat like the Mariposa Belle, it would be impossible for her to carry all of the crowd that you see in the boat and on the wharf. In reality, the crowd is made up of two classes—all of the people in Mariposa who are going on the excursion and all those who are not. Some come for the one reason and some for the other.

The two tellers of the Exchange Bank are both there standing side by side. But one of them—the one with the cameo pin and the long face like a horse—is going, and the other—with the other cameo pin and the face like another horse—is not. In the same way, Hussell of the *Newspacket* is going, but his brother, beside him, isn't. Lilian Drone is going, but her sister can't; and so on all through the crowd.

And to think that things should look like that on the morning of a steamboat accident.

How strange life is!

To think of all these people so eager and anxious to catch the steamer, and some of them running to catch it, and so fearful that they might miss it—the morning of a steamboat accident. And the captain blowing his whistle, and warning them so severely that he would leave them behind—leave them out of the accident! And everybody crowding so eagerly to be in the accident.

Perhaps life is like that all through.

Strangest of all to think, in a case like this, of the people who were left behind, or in some way or other prevented from going, and always afterwards told of how they had escaped being on board the Mariposa Belle that day!

Some of the instances were certainly extraordinary.

Nivens, the lawyer, escaped from being there merely by the fact that he was away in the city.

Towers, the tailor, only escaped owing to the fact that, not intending to go on the excursion, he had stayed in bed till eight o'clock and so had not gone. He narrated afterwards that waking up that morning at half-past five, he had thought of the excursion and for some unaccountable reason had felt glad that he was not going.

The case of Yodel, the auctioneer, was even more inscrutable. He had been to the Oddfellows' excursion on the train the week before and to the the Conservative picnic the week before that, and had decided not to go on this trip. In fact, he had not the least intention of going. He narrated afterwards how the night before someone had stopped him on the corner of Nippewa and Tecumseh Streets (he indicated the very spot) and asked: 'Are you going to take in the excursion tomorrow?' and he had said, just as simply as he was talking when narrating it: 'No.' And ten minutes after that, at the corner of Dalhousie and Brock Streets (he offered to lead a party of verification to the precise place) somebody else had stopped him and asked: 'Well, are you going on the steamer trip tomorrow?' Again he had answered: 'No,' apparently almost in the same tone as before.

He said afterwards that when he heard the rumour of the accident it seemed like the finger of Providence, and he fell on his knees in thankfulness.

There was the similar case of Morison (I mean the one in Glover's hardware store that married one of the Thompsons). He said afterwards that he had read so much in the papers about accidents lately—mining accidents, and aeroplanes and gasoline— that he had grown nervous. The night before his wife had asked him at supper: 'Are you going on the excursion?' He had answered: 'No, I don't think I feel like it,' and had added: 'Perhaps your mother might like to go.' And the next evening just at dusk, when the news ran through the town, he said the first thought that flashed through his head was: 'Mrs Thompson's on that boat.'

He told this right as I say it—without the least doubt or confusion. He never for a moment imagined she was on the Lusitania or the Olympic or any other boat. He knew she was on this one. He said you could have knocked him down where he stood. But no one had. Not even when he got halfway down—on his knees, and it would have been easier still to knock him down or kick him. People do miss a lot of chances.

Still, as I say, neither Yodel nor Morison nor anyone thought about there being an accident until just after sundown when they—

Well, have you ever heard the long booming whistle of a steamboat two miles out on the lake in the dusk, and while you listen and count and wonder, seen the crimson rockets going up against the sky and then heard the fire bell ringing right there beside you in the town, and seen the people running to the town wharf?

That's what the people of Mariposa saw and felt that summer evening as they watched the Mackinaw lifeboat go plunging out into the lake with seven sweeps to a side and the foam clear to the gunwale with the lifting stroke of fourteen men!

But, dear me, I am afraid that this is no way to tell a story. I suppose the true art would have been to have said nothing about the accident till it happened. But when you write about Mariposa, or hear of it, if you know the place, it's all so vivid and real, that a thing like the contrast between the excursion crowd in the morning and the scene at night leaps into your mind and you must think of it.

But never mind about the accident—let us turn back to the morning.

The boat was due to leave at seven. There was no doubt about the hour—not only seven, but seven sharp. The notice in the *Newspacket* said: 'The boat will leave sharp at seven'; and the advertising posters on the telegraph poles on Missinaba Street that began, 'Ho, for Indian's Island!' ended up with the words:

'Boat leaves at seven sharp.' There was a big notice on the wharf that said: 'Boat leaves sharp on time.'

So at seven, right on the hour, the whistle blew loud and long, and then at seven fifteen three short peremptory blasts, and at seven thirty one quick angry call—just one—and very soon after that they cast off the last of the ropes and the Mariposa Belle sailed off in her cloud of flags, and the band of the Knights of Pythias, timing it to a nicety, broke into the 'Maple Leaf for Ever!'

I suppose that all excursions when they start are much the same. Anyway, on the Mariposa Belle everybody went running up and down all over the boat with deck chairs and camp stools and baskets, and found places, splendid places to sit, and then got scared that there might be better ones and chased off again. People hunted for places out of the sun and when they got them swore that they weren't going to freeze to please anybody; and the people in the sun said that they hadn't paid fifty cents to be roasted. Others said that they hadn't paid fifty cents to get covered with cinders, and there were still others who hadn't paid fifty cents to get shaken to death with the propeller.

Still, it was all right presently. The people seemed to get sorted out into the places on the boat where they belonged. The women, the older ones, all gravitated into the cabin on the lower deck and by getting round the table with needlework, and with all the windows shut, they soon had it, as they said themselves, just like being at home.

All the young boys and the toughs and the men in the band got down on the lower deck forward, where the boat was dirtiest and where the anchor was and the coils of rope.

And upstairs on the after deck there were Lilian Drone and Miss Lawson, the high-school teacher, with a book of German peotry—Gothey I think it was—and the bank teller and the young men.

In the centre, standing beside the rail, were Dean Drone and Dr Gallagher, looking through binocular glasses at the shore.

Up in front on the little deck forward of the pilot house was a group of the older men, Mullins and Duff and Mr Smith in a deck chair, and beside him Mr Golgotha Gingham, the undertaker of Mariposa, on a stool. It was part of Mr Gingham's principles to take in an outing of this sort, a business matter, more or less—for you never know what may happen at these water parties. At any rate, he was there in a neat suit of black, not, of course, his heavier or professional suit, but a soft clinging effect as of burnt paper that combined gaiety and decorum to a nicety.

'Yes,' said Mr Gingham, waving his black glove in a general way towards the shore, 'I know the lake well, very well. I've been pretty much all over it in my time.'

'Canoeing?' asked somebody.

'No,' said Mr Gingham, 'not in a canoe.' There seemed a peculiar and quiet meaning in his tone.

'Sailing, I suppose,' said somebody else.

'No,' said Mr Gingham. 'I don't understand it.'

'I never knowed that you went on to the water at all, Gol,' said Mr Smith, breaking in.

'Ah, not now,' explained Mr Gingham; 'it was years ago, the first summer I came to Mariposa. I was on the water practically all day. Nothing like it to give a man an appetite and keep him in shape.'

'Was you camping?' asked Mr Smith.

'We camped at night,' assented the undertaker, 'but we put in practically the whole day on the water. You see, we were after a party that had come up here from the city on his vacation and gone out in a sailing canoe. We were dragging. We were up every morning at sunrise, lit a fire on the beach and cooked breakfast, and then we'd light our pipes and be off with the net for a whole day. It's a great life,' concluded Mr Gingham wistfully.

'Did you get him?' asked two or three together.

There was a pause before Mr Gingham answered.

'We did,' he said, '—down in the reeds past Horseshoe Point. But it was no use. He turned blue on me right away.'

After which Mr Gingham fell into such a deep reverie that the boat had steamed another half-mile down the lake before anybody broke the silence again. Talk of this sort—and after all what more suitable for a day on the water?—beguiled the way.

Down the lake, mile by mile over the calm water, steamed the Mariposa Belle. They passed Poplar Point where the high sandbanks are with all the swallows' nests in them, and Dean Drone and Dr Gallagher looked at them alternately through the binocular glasses, and it was wonderful how plainly one could see the swallows and the banks and the shrubs—just as plainly as with the naked eye.

As a little further down they passed the Shingle Beach, and Dr Gallagher, who knew Canadian history, said to Dean Drone that it was strange to think that Champlain had landed there with his French explorers three hundred years ago: and Dean Drone, who didn't know Canadian history, said it was stranger still to think that the hand of the Almighty had piled up the hills and rocks long before that; and Dr Gallagher said it was wonderful how the French had found their way through such a pathless wilderness; and Dean Drone said that it was wonderful also to think that the Almighty had placed even the smallest shrub in its appointed place. Dr Gallagher said it filled him with admiration. Dean Drone said it filled him with awe. Dr Gallagher said he'd been full of it since he was a boy and Dean Drone said so had he.

Then a little further, as the Mariposa Belle steamed on down the lake, they passed the Old Indian Portage where the great grey rocks are; and Dr Gallagher drew Dean Drone's attention to the place where the narrow canoe track wound up from the shore to the woods, and Dean Drone said he could see it perfectly well without the glasses.

Dr Gallagher said that it was just here that a party of five hundred French had made their way with all their baggage and accoutrements across the rocks of the divide and down to the Great Bay. And Dean Drone said that it reminded him of Xenophon leading his ten thousand Greeks over the hill passes of Armenia down to the sea. Dr Gallagher said that he had often wished he could have seen and spoken to Champlain, and Dean Drone said how much he regretted to have never known Xenophon.

And then after that they fell to talking of relics and traces of the past, and Dr Gallagher said that if Dean Drone would come round to his house some night he would show him some Indian arrow heads that he had dug up in his garden. And Dean Drone said that if Dr Gallagher would come round to the rectory any afternoon he would show him a map of Xerxes' invasion of Greece. Only he must come some time between the Infant Class and the Mothers' Auxiliary.

So presently they both knew that they were blocked out of one another's houses for some time to come, and Dr Gallagher walked forward and told Mr Smith, who had never studied Greek, about Champlain crossing the rock divide.

Mr Smith turned his head and looked at the divide for half a second and then said he had crossed a worse one up north back of the Wahnipitae and that the flies were Hades—and then went on playing freezeout poker with the two juniors in Duff's bank.

So Dr Gallagher realized that that's always the way when you try to tell people things, and that as far as gratitude and appreciation goes one might as well never read books or travel anywhere or do anything.

In fact, it was at this very moment that he made up his mind to give the arrows to the Mariposa Mechanics' Institute—they afterwards became, as you know, the Gallagher Collection. But, for the time being, the doctor was sick of them and wandered off round the boat and watched Henry Mullins showing George Duff how to make a John Collins without lemons, and finally went and sat down among the Mariposa band and wished that he hadn't come.

So the boat steamed on and the sun rose higher and higher, and the freshness of the morning changed into the full glare of noon, and they went on to where the lake began to narrow in at its foot, just where the Indian's Island is—all grass and trees and with a log wharf running into the water. Below it the Lower Ossawippi runs out of the lake, and quite near are the rapids, and you can see down among the trees the red brick of the power house and hear the roar of the leaping water.

The Indian's Island itself is all covered with trees and tangled vines, and the water about it is so still that it's all reflected double and looks the same either way up. Then when the steamer's whistle blows as it comes into the wharf, you hear it echo among the trees of the island, and reverberate back from the shores of the lake.

The scene is all so quiet and still and unbroken, that Miss Cleghorn—the sallow girl in the telephone exchange that I spoke of —said she'd like to be buried there. But all the people were so busy getting their baskets and gathering up their things that no one had time to attend to it.

I mustn't even try to describe the landing and the boat crunching against the wooden wharf and all the people running to the same side of the deck and Christie Johnson calling out to the crowd to keep to the starboard and nobody being able to find it. Everyone who has been on a Mariposa excursion knows all about that.

Nor can I describe the day itself and the picnic under the trees. There were speeches afterwards, and Judge Pepperleigh gave such offence by bringing in Conservative politics that a man called Patriotus Canadiensis wrote and asked for some of the invaluable space of the Mariposa *Times-Herald* and exposed it.

I should say that there were races too, on the grass on the open side of the island, graded mostly according to ages—races for boys under thirteen and girls over nineteen and all that sort of thing. Sports are generally conducted on that plan in Mariposa. It is realized that a woman of sixty has an unfair advantage over a mere child.

Dean Drone managed the races and decided the ages and gave out the prizes; the Wesleyan minister helped, and he and the young student, who was relieving in the Presbyterian Church, held the string at the winning point.

They had to get mostly clergymen for the races because all the men had wandered off, somehow, to where they were drinking lager beer out of two kegs stuck on pine logs among the trees.

But if you've ever been on a Mariposa excursion you know all about these details anyway.

So the day wore on and presently the sun came through the trees on a slant and the steamer whistle blew with a great puff of white steam and all the people came straggling down to the wharf and pretty soon the Mariposa Belle had floated out on to the lake again and headed for the town.

I suppose you have often noticed the contrast there is between an excursion on its way out in the morning and what it looks like on the way home.

In the morning everybody is so restless and animated and moves to and from all over the boat and asks questions. But coming home, as the afternoon gets later and later and the sun sinks beyond the hills, all the people seem to get so still and quiet and drowsy.

So it was with the people on the Mariposa Belle. They sat there on the benches and the deck chairs in little clusters, and listened to the regular beat of the propeller and almost dozed off asleep as they sat. Then when the sun set and the dusk drew on, it grew almost dark on the deck and so still that you could hardly tell there was anyone on board.

And if you had looked at the steamer from the shore or from one of the islands, you'd have seen the row of lights from the cabin windows shining on the water and the red glare of the burning hemlock from the funnel, and you'd have heard the soft thud of the propeller miles away over the lake.

Now and then, too, you could have heard them singing on the steamer—the voices of the girls and the men blended into unison by the distance, rising and falling in long-drawn melody: 'O—Can-a-da—O—Can-a-da.'

You may talk as you will about the intoning choirs of your European cathedrals, but the sound of 'O Can-a-da,' borne across the waters of a silent lake at evening, is good enough for those of us who know Mariposa.

I think that it was just as they were singing like this: 'O—Can-a-da,' that word went round that the boat was sinking.

If you have ever been in any sudden emergency on the water, you will understand the strange psychology of it—the way in which what is happening seems to become known all in a moment without a word being said. The news is transmitted from one to the other by some mysterious process.

At any rate, on the Mariposa Belle first one and then the other heard that the steamer was sinking. As far as I could ever learn the first of it was that George Duff, the bank manager, came very quietly to Dr Gallagher and asked him if he thought that the boat was sinking. The doctor said no, that he had thought so earlier in the day but that he didn't now think that she was.

After that Duff, according to his own account, had said to Macartney, the lawyer, that the boat was sinking, and Macartney said that he doubted it very much.

Then somebody came to Judge Pepperleigh and woke him up and said that there was six inches of water in the steamer and that she was sinking. And Pepperleigh said it was perfect scandal and passed the news on to his wife and she said that they had no business to allow it and that if the steamer sank that was the last excursion she'd go on.

So the news went all round the boat and everywhere the people gathered in groups and talked about it in the angry and excited way that people have when a steamer is sinking on one of the lakes like Lake Wissanotti.

Dean Drone, of course, and some others were quieter about it, and said that one must make allowances and that naturally there were two sides to everything. But most of them wouldn't listen to reason at all. I think, perhaps, that some of them were frightened.

You see, the last time but one that the steamer had sunk, there had been a man drowned and it made them nervous.

What? Hadn't I explained about the depth of Lake Wissanotti? I had taken it for granted that you knew; and in any case parts of it are deep enough, though I don't suppose in this stretch of it from the big reed beds up to within a mile of the town wharf, you could find six feet of water in it if you tried. Oh, pshaw! I was not talking about a steamer sinking in the ocean and carrying down its screaming crowds of people into the hideous depths of green water. Oh, dear me, no! That kind of thing never happens on Lake Wissanotti.

But what does happen is that the Mariposa Belle sinks every now and then, and sticks there on the bottom till they get things straightened up.

On the lakes around Mariposa, if a person arrives late anywhere and explains that the steamer sank, everybody understands the situation.

You see, when Harland and Wolff built the Mariposa Belle, they left some cracks in between the timbers that you fill up with cotton waste every Sunday. If this is not attended to, the boat sinks. In fact, it is part of the law of the province that all the steamers like the Mariposa Belle must be properly corked—I think that is the word—every season. There are inspectors who visit all the hotels in the province to see that it is done.

So you can imagine, now that I've explained it a little straighter, the indignation of the people when they knew that the boat had come uncorked and that they might be stuck out there on a shoal or a mud-bank half the night.

I don't say either that there wasn't any danger; anyway, it doesn't feel very safe when you realize that the boat is settling down with every hundred yards that she goes, and you look over the side and see only the black water in the gathering night.

Safe! I'm not sure now that I come to think of it that it isn't worse than sinking in the Atlantic. After all, in the Atlantic there is wireless telegraphy, and a lot of trained sailors and stewards. But out on Lake Wissanotti—far out, so that you can only just see the lights of the town away off to the south—when the propeller comes to a stop—and you can hear the hiss of steam as they start to rake out the engine fires to prevent an explosion—and when you turn from the red glare that comes from the furnace doors as they open them, to the black dark that is gathering over the lake—and there's a night wind beginning to run among the rushes—and you see the men going forward to the roof of the pilot house to send up the rockets to rouse the town—safe? Safe yourself, if you like; as for me, let me once get back into Mariposa again, under the night shadow of the maple trees, and this shall be the last, last time I'll go on Lake Wissanotti.

Safe! Oh, yes! Isn't it strange how safe other people's adventures seem after they happen? But you'd have been scared, too, if you'd been there just before the steamer sank, and seen them bringing up all the women on to the top deck.

I don't see how some of the people took it so calmly; how Mr Smith, for instance, could have gone on smoking and telling how he'd had a steamer 'sink on him' on Lake Nipissing and a still bigger one, a side-wheeler, sink on him in Lake Abbitibbi.

Then, quite suddenly, with a quiver, down she went. You could feel the boat sink, sink—down, down—would it never get to the bottom? The water came flush up to the lower deck, and then— thank heaven—the sinking stopped and there was the Mariposa Belle safe and tight on a reed bank.

Really, it made one positively laugh! It seemed so queer and, anyway, if a man has a sort of natural courage, danger makes him laugh. Danger? pshaw! fiddlesticks! everybody scouted the idea. Why, it is just the little things like this that give zest to a day on the water.

Within half a minute they were all running round looking for sandwiches and cracking jokes and talking of making coffee over the remains on the engine fires.

I don't need to tell at length how it all happened after that.

I suppose the people on the Mariposa Belle would have had to settle down there all night or till help came from the town, but some of the men who had gone forward and were peering out into the dark said that it couldn't be more than a mile across the water to Miller's Point. You could almost see it over there to the left— some of them, I think, said 'off on the port bow,' because you know when you get mixed up in these marine disasters, you soon catch the atmosphere of the thing.

So pretty soon they had the davits swung out over the side and were lowering the old lifeboat from the top deck into the water.

There were men leaning out over the rail of the Mariposa Belle with lanterns that threw the light as they let her down, and the glare fell on the water and the reeds. But when they got the boat lowered, it looked such a frail, clumsy thing as one saw it from the rail above, that the cry was raised: 'Women and children first!' For what was the sense, if it should turn out that the boat wouldn't even hold women and children, of trying to jam a lot of heavy men into it?

So they put in mostly women and children and the boat pushed out into the darkness so freighted down it would hardly float.

In the bow of it was the Presbyterian student who was relieving the minister, and he called out that they were in the hands of Providence. But he was crouched and ready to spring out of them at the first moment.

So the boat went and was lost in the darkness except for the lantern in the bow that you could see bobbing on the water. Then presently it came back and they sent another load, till pretty soon the decks began to thin out and everybody got impatient to be gone.

It was about the time that the third boat-load put off that Mr Smith took a bet with Mullins for twenty-five dollars, that he'd be home in Mariposa before the people in the boats had walked round the shore.

No one knew just what he meant, but pretty soon they saw Smith disappear down below into the lowest part of the steamer with a mallet in one hand and a big bundle of marline in the other.

They might have wondered more about it, but it was just at this time that they heard the shouts from the rescue boat—the big Mackinaw lifeboat—that had put out from the town with fourteen men at the sweeps when they saw the first rockets go up.

I suppose there is always something inspiring about a rescue at sea, or on the water.

After all, the bravery of the lifeboat man is the true bravery— expended to save life, not to destroy it.

Certainly they told for months after of how the rescue boat came out to the Mariposa Belle.

I suppose that when they put her in the water the lifeboat touched it for the first time since the old Macdonald Government placed her on Lake Wissanotti.

Anyway, the water poured it at every seam. But not for a moment—even with two miles of water between them and the steamer—did the rowers pause for that.

By the time they were half-way there the water was almost up to the thwarts, but they drove her on. Panting and exhausted (for mind you, if you haven't been in a fool boat like that for years, rowing takes it out of you), the rowers stuck to their task. They threw the ballast over and chucked into the water the heavy cork jackets and lifebelts that encumbered their movements. There was no thought of turning back. They were nearer to the steamer than the shore.

'Hang to it, boys,' called the crowd from the steamer's deck, and hang they did.

They were almost exhausted when they got them; men leaning from the steamer threw them ropes and one by one every man was hauled aboard just as the lifeboat sank under their feet.

Saved! by Heaven, saved by one of the smartest pieces of rescue work ever seen on the lake.

There's no use describing it; you need to see rescue work of this kind by lifeboats to understand it.

Nor were the lifeboat crew the only ones that distinguished themselves.

Boat after boat and canoe after canoe had put out from Mariposa to the help of the steamer. They got them all.

Pupkin, the other bank teller with a face like a horse, who hadn't gone on the excursion—as soon as he knew that the boat was signalling for help and that Miss Lawson was sending up rockets—rushed for a row boat, grabbed an oar (two would have hampered him), and paddled madly out into the lake. He struck right out into the dark with the crazy skiff almost sinking beneath his feet. But they got him. They rescued him. They watched him, almost dead with exhaustion, make his way to the steamer, where he was hauled up with ropes. Saved! Saved!

They might have gone on that way half the night, picking up the rescuers, only, at the very moment when the tenth load of people left for the shore—just as suddenly and saucily as you please, up came the Mariposa Bell from the mud bottom and floated.

*Floated?*

Why, of course she did. If you take a hundred and fifty people off a steamer that has sunk, and if you get a man as shrewd as Mr Smith to plug the timber seams with mallet and marline, and if you turn ten bandsmen of the Mariposa band on to your hand pump on the bow of the lower decks—float? why, what else can she do?

Then, if you stuff in hemlock into the embers of the fire that you were raking out, till it hums and crackles under the boiler, it won't be long before you hear the propeller thud—thudding at the stern again, and before long the roar of the steam whistle echoes over to the town.

And so the Mariposa Belle, with all steam up again and with the long train of sparks careering from the funnel, is heading for the town.

But no Christie Johnson at the wheel in the pilot house this time. 'Smith! Get Smith!' is the cry.

Can he take her in? Well, now! Ask a man who has had steamers sink on him in half the lakes from Temiscaming to the Bay, if he can take her in? Ask a man who has run a York boat down the rapids of the Moose when the ice is moving, if he can grip the steering wheel of the Mariposa Belle? So there she steams safe and sound to the town wharf!

Look at the lights and the crowd! If only the federal census taker could count us now! Hear them calling and shouting back and forward from the deck to the shore! Listen! There is the rattle of the shore ropes as they get them ready, and there's the Mariposa band—actually forming in a circle on the upper deck just as she docks, and the leader with his baton—one—two—ready now—

'O CAN-A-DA!'

# Frederick Philip Grove

THOUGH there has been a great deal of controversy over Grove's early life, most of it seems to have been settled by Douglas O. Spettigue's *FPG: The European Years* (1973). According to Spettigue, Frederick Philip Grove's real name was Felix Paul Greve, a German writer, translator, and dandy who was born in Rodomno on February 14, 1879. In 1898 he entered Friedrich-Wilhelm University in Bonn, but left two years later because of debts. In 1902 he published a slim volume of poems, *Wanderungen*, and began translating the works of Oscar Wilde, borrowing against future royalties and getting further into debt. About this time he met Elsa, with whom he lived for several years. In May 1903 Greve was arrested for fraud and sentenced to a year in Bonn Prison, where he continued to do translations and worked on a novel, *Fanny Essler* (1904). After his release he wrote two more novels, the last of which, *Maurermeister Ihles Haus* (1907), was first published in English in 1976 as *The Master Mason's House*.

In 1909 Greve left Elsa a false suicide note and disappeared. He turned up three years later in Winnipeg as Frederick Philip Grove, and worked as a teacher until 1929. In August 1914 he married Katrina Wiens, and in 1919 completed his first book in English, *Over Prairie Trails*, a collection of nature essays. There followed a second collection, *The Turn of the Year* (1923), and a novel, *Settlers of the Marsh* (1925). With *A Search for America* (1927) Grove's fame, if not his fortune, grew quickly, and *Fruits of the Earth* (1933) and *Master of the Mill* (1944) were also well received by critics, but sold poorly. His largely fictional autobiography, *In Search of Myself*, won the Governor-General's award for non-fiction in 1946, and Grove died at his home in Simcoe, Ontario, on August 19, 1948.

In 1926 the Winnipeg *Tribune* commissioned 26 short stories from Grove, and 'The Boat' appeared there on December 24 of that year. A version of this story was incorporated into Chapter I of *In Search of Myself*: a comparison of 'The Boat' with a passage in Wordsworth's 'The Prelude' (Book I, lines 357-400) throws much light on the purpose and method of Grove's 'autobiography.'

# THE BOAT

WHEN I was last in France, I met, at one of the fashionable watering places, a tall, white-haired old man who proved to be a friend of my early childhood.

Often we sat, after our friendship had been renewed, in a deserted corner of the veranda of the huge hotel and exchanged our memories. We never spoke of the present; for we had drifted far apart in life, being separated in our present abodes from each other by the width of an ocean. One night, my friend—who came from the ancient Norman house of Stone—spoke thus.

As you know, Stone House overlooked the bay. And as there was a good sandy beach along the highwater line, it was only natural that, as a child, I should have spent a good deal of my time down there where such strange things as the tides took place, the water rising and falling over broad sand-flats, with long breakers slowly rolling in from the main; with ships passing in the distance, along the horizon; and with an island lying flat upon the waters at low-tide, some ten miles away; sometimes it seemed to be lifted above them by a sort of mirage.

Inland, the beach was bordered by a line of boulders which formed a low, broken cliff: beyond, a ribbon of grotesquely stunted pines which you no doubt remember grew on ever-shifting dunes, so that they were now buried in the sand and now once more emerging. Behind them came the park.

My mother taught me to swim. We often went down there. I on my pony, and she on a beautiful black mare, an English thoroughbred. She rode a great deal and, as a daring horse-woman, fragile though she looked, filled me—who was timid—with admiration.

You know, too, about my father's physique, his frame of a giant, his love for the chase, and the small response he had for my mother's desperate attempts at creating the semblance of a family life and atmosphere.

Often, too, I went down to that beach alone, both on horseback and afoot.

This cliff line of broken rock had a great fascination for me as a child; and so had the dangerous sand-flats. There, at ebb-tide, I could walk out over slightly rolling sand-banks for miles; and when the tide turned, I had to watch out and use all my wits in order not to be cut off; for in many places the water would run in to a greater depth in the hollow channels dug by sharp currents close in-shore, while the sand-banks farther out would still remain dry— to be submerged by a strong tide which came from both sides.

There was an uncertainty about the sea which had something strangely alluring for me. I did not count for much at home, you know, though I was all in all to my mother. But my mother, too, did not count for much. My father was of the type that extinguishes everything about him. He was like a gigantic steam roller that flattens out a landscape. I was used to slipping about in a furtive way.

Down there, at the beach, I seemed to live: at the house I merely existed.

So I used to delight in pitting my mind against what seemed to be the cunning of the element; I asserted myself. Add to that that the whole countryside was imbued with the supersititions of a seafaring race; the sea itself was alive, plotting to catch me, planning to entangle me in its meshes.

There was a half-witted woman employed at Stone House, a woman who had been young in the days of my grandfather, in Napoleon's time, working then in garden and kitchen, but now living more or less as a pensioner though she still peeled potatoes and cleaned vegetables for use at the table. She was a weird creature, well able to send a shudder along my spine when she emerged, clad in rags, where I least expected her.

One day I had delayed on the sand-flats and, in returning to the shore while the tide was running in, filling the channels and runways of the water with gurgling and foaming floods, I had to dash wildly through some of these sand-troughs, running in to my hips and splashing drops high over my head.

As I approached the shore and at last saw the cliff line, above the beach, I saw this woman standing on one of the boulders bent forward to watch my progress and erratically waving her arms and shouting. Her hair which, in spite of her age, was still coal-black and glossy, had come undone and was floating on the wind, under a dismal, grey sky. To reach the gap in the forest of beeches and poplars behind the beach—the gap that led to the park—I had to pass close by her; but she looked so weird and uncanny that I hesitated. She went on, however, waving and calling to me till I approached.

'Young master,' she wailed, 'young master, beware! Beware of the sea, young master! The sea is wicked! Wicked is the sea. It strikes you down!'

And, with the skin of my back creeping, I shot past.

Many and many a story had I heard and read by that time of shipwrecks and disaster along this coast. But the sea held only the stronger fascination for me.

I still loved to slip down to the beach at dark; and though I did not, anymore, dare to go as far as the water's edge, I used to sit in that gap of the forest whence I could see the lighted windows of Stone House, to serve as a guide for my stealthy return.

And another light I could see from there, an intermittent light far out to the north and to sea. I had never been where that light came from; in fact, at the time of which I am speaking, I had never been away from home. But I knew that a lighthouse stood there washed by the waves at high water and guarding the rock-strewn entrance to the sanded bay—waving stray vessels back from the danger line and sweeping its finger of light all around in a huge semi-circle. Just when it reached a certain point in the gap where I used to sit, it went out, thus seeming to wink at me in a sort of giant's mocking humour. A moment later it swept around again, to wink once more just when I looked straight into its very eye.

Often and often I longed to go there and to see this lighthouse from nearby, so as to find out all about it. I mentioned it to my mother and she told me that it was far away; but she promised to take me there one day, on horseback. Yet somehow no opportunity ever came. Many a time, too, I set out by myself to go and get there but I always had to give up at last; for, no matter how far I went along the shore which ran to the northwest, I did not seem to get any nearer to it.

Till at last, and with that I come to my story, one summer morning when it was very hot and sultry—my father, whom I feared, being away for the day—I was, for some reason or other, released from my lessons. I told my old nurse, 'Lene, that I wanted to make a big trip along the beach and begged her to have a little lunch put up for me so that I should not have to come home at noon. I did not say a word of the lighthouse, of course.

I took Troy, my pony, from the stable and started out.

Down, through the park, I rode to the beach and then, it being ebb-tide, along the ribbon of sand which was beaten hard by the thundering breakers at flow-tide, just within the highwater line.

Across the bay, lifted by the mirage, lay the sandy island, glittering and flickering with an uncertain outline in the ascending waves of heated air that rose from the sand-flats.

I cantered along the beach stretching out in a long, flat, seemingly endless curve. I should have felt oppressed with the lonely aspect of this wilderness had I not had Troy, my pony, with me.

Probably I had not yet gone more than an hour or two at the most; but to me it seemed like many, many hours; for time stretches out to children, boundless and without measure.

I had reached the end of the sand beach and had left it behind. That was as far as I had ever been before. I was riding now along a narrow, pebbly slope, steeper and rougher than the sand beach had been; and at last I could plainly see the lighthouse across the water.

This beach was getting to be more and more impassable on horseback, for it was strewn with huge rocks; and yet it stretched away for miles and miles, swinging out to the west now in a sharper curve; and at its very end there was a hook reaching south, like a huge claw; and at the very end of this hook, the lighthouse stood, snow-white, on a black, dome-shaped rock which was now lifted high above the water.

Not a breath of wind stirred, and I was nearly faint with the heat.

Then, suddenly and without warning, I came to a place where beyond a narrow inlet of the bay, riding became quite impossible.

Now, in that inlet, there lay a boat.

It was drawn up on the pebbles, at its very apex, between two high rocks, but the water was only a few feet below it. I believe the tide was still running out. The shore line did not vary much here, not nearly as much as on the sand-flats, for the beach sloped down steeply into deeper water. I stopped and pondered.

Through the boulders of the cliff line and the scrubby pines beyond a rough path led up. Both cliff and pines were here much closer to the water's edge than nearer home. I followed the path and came out on an inland marsh-flat covered with coarse, long, slender grass, such as thrives on salt-drowned land.

I alighted and tied the bridle rein of the pony to the pommel of the saddle; for I had made up my mind to try the boat. I had espied the oars between the rocks of the cliff line.

From where I left the pony I could see, far to the east, some white-painted fishermen's huts which seemed to be swooning in the sultry heat. I had no doubt but that they were the habitations of some dependents of my father's. As I said, I had never been away from home, and I did not even know that there might be people who did not acknowledge my father's authority. He was the master; and I, his son, had so far been 'the young master' to everybody outside of Stone House with whom I had ever come in contact.

Apart from those white huts, far inland, and the lighthouse which, in a straight line across the water, was now no more than two or at most three miles away, there was not a sign of the world of human beings anywhere.

I left the horse to graze and went down to the cove between the rocks. There, I set to work to push the boat back into the water and, when I had succeeded, I went and fetched the oars to row across the bay.

For a while the tide still continued to run out and aided me; but as, in the course of an hour or so, I neared the lighthouse which now stood like a white, warning finger held up by the very rock, I gradually became aware of strange counter-currents.

I was determined to get there: for I did not know that in this labyrinth of giant blocks I was in one of the most dangerous waters of our coast. More than once, when pushing out into a new channel from between two rocks where the water seemed quiet, subdued, and limpid to the very bottom of its rocky bed, I was suddenly and violently swept sideways or whirled about in an unsuspected eddy.

I did not know of any particular peril; and I seemed to be so close inshore that the work in hand seemed to be good sport rather than a dangerous undertaking.

But at last I realized that it would be quite impossible for me to land at the lighthouse: for by now the tide was running in again; and I suddenly saw that the huge rock dome on which the lighthouse stood had become an island, the water rushing, shallow though it was, with great speed over the neck which joined it to the flat slabs of the peninsula to the north.

I still enjoyed the game, however, and I tarried for some time longer.

Then I became aware of the fact that the sun had disappeared. When I looked for it, I still saw it, to be sure; but it stood pale and white above a scudding veil of vaporous mists running high through the sky: and when I scanned the horizon all about, I discerned, far away in the northwest, approaching thunderheads.

Then I was frightened; for, infected as I was by my mother's nervousness in a thunderstorm, I did not like the thought of being out on the water with lightning flashing overhead.

During these few moments, while I got my bearings, the wild and increasing current of the inrushing waters had carried me far out into the bay: and, turning the bow of the boat to the shore whence I had come, I leaned to my oars and applied myself to the task of getting home.

Since the tide helped, I made good progress; but when I approached the shore and tried to find the place where I had taken the boat, I could not find it. Everything looked unfamiliar and alike to me. For a moment I felt worried; but then I espied Troy, my pony, on the shelving beach.

At once I bent all my efforts towards reaching him.

At last, just when the first wild whirl and blast of the approaching storm hit the beach and ruffled the water, I ran aground. In feverish haste I pulled the boat up as far as I could and ran for Troy.

I had no difficulty in catching him, but just as I swung into the saddle a violent downpour began with a vicious flash of lightning. It was next to impossible here, on the rough, pebbly beach, to make any speed on horseback: and, when a second violent flash tore the sky, my courage failed me.

Instinctively I urged the horse to the left, close to the boulder cliff, and jumped to the ground. The cliff was greatly broken here; and in one point a deep niche between the rocks promised some shelter. Of that I availed myself to wait till the storm was over.

The rain lashed the beach: and the wind tore and whirled through the pinnacles of the rocks. I saw nothing any longer of the water; but I heard the breakers rolling in. At the point which I had chosen, the more wildly it blew, the less Troy and I were hit by the slanting torrent. Yet, I believe, I quavered at every flash and thunderclap.

Then, as suddenly as it had begun, the fury of the storm abated; and in half an hour or so the sun broke through the rifts in the clouds overhead. I was wet, it is true; and so was Troy: but it was midsummer and we soon dried as we were cantering along the beach to the south. The sand was pitted as if with pockmarks.

I was thrilled with the sense of having gone through an adventure. When, after another hour's hard riding. I came to the gap in the forest whence Stone House could be seen, I found my mother and 'Lene, the nurse, on an anxious lookout for me.

My mother came running across the wet lawn; and she burst into tears as she folded me into her arms, lifting me out of the saddle as she did so.

I rather liked to be thus made much of and felt like a hero; nor did I belittle the adventure I had gone through in the telling: and, when my mother exclaimed, 'Promise me, Rolphe, that you will never, never go out on the bay alone again!' I did not like to give such a promise and tried to prevaricate. I suppose I felt that it would lop off half of my freedom if for the future I foreswore adventure and danger.

'But mamma,' I said, 'when I am bigger?'—for I felt that I was getting bigger moment by moment.

I was, of course, taken in and feasted like the prodigal son: and 'Lene, not without pride, had to tell every servant she met that I had been to the lighthouse, all by myself, in a boat . . .

I felt almost offended when I heard that the whole adventure had taken only six hours; for it was still early in the afternoon when I returned.

But the incident was to have its sequel.

Later, about the usual supper hour, my mother sent for me to come down into the huge hall which served as the general living-room and meeting place for all who happened to be at Stone House.

There, I found a gruff old man who was blustering about and threatening her, speaking that mixture of pure French, Norman patois, and Flemish which is peculiar to the country of the Pas de Calais.

'Stealing I call it, madame,' I heard him say when I entered. 'Taking property that belongs to other folk!'

'But surely,' my mother pleaded, 'Monsieur Jupe, you will take into consideration that Rolphe is a child. I am sure he did not realize what he was doing.'

'I am going to take into consideration that it is rich folk stealing from poor,' the old man blustered along with a vicious glint of his watery eye at me as I stood there looking at him with my mouth open.

'Rolphe,' said my mother, 'come here, darling. Monsieur Jupe says you took his boat; and now it is lost.'

'Mamma!' I cried indignantly, 'the boat is on the beach.'

The old man laughed a dry, cackling laugh for which I hated him. 'Yes,' he drawled, nodding two or three times, 'that's where you left it belike, sonny; for you didn't even take the trouble to put it back where you took it. Rich folk don't do that. Let the poor man walk after it if he wants his own property back. What does the rich man care? . . . But there's a law in this country yet! Do you know where the boat is, sonny?'

'I know where I left it,' I said.

Again he laughed his sneering cackle; and then he cleared his throat; and to my unforgettable horror he spat on the hearth-rug and then blew his nose between his fingers. 'I'll tell you,' he said at last, taking great satisfaction in giving the information. 'The boat's gone out to sea. You didn't even take the trouble to throw the anchor out, young man.'

At that, my heart sank. But, my mind working all the more feverishly, I tried to revisualize just how the boat had been fastened when I first took it. As a result of this effort I said with conviction, 'The boat was not fastened either where it lay.'

The old man fixed me with a cold stare from under his bushy, white eyebrows. 'I'll charge you fifty dollars for that lie, sonny,' he said drily. 'A hundred and fifty it is by this time, mind you.'

'But, Monsieur Jupe,' my mother interrupted him soothingly, 'surely you do not want anything beyond the actual value of the boat! As I told you, I am willing to give you fifty dollars now. I suppose even that is more than the boat was worth.'

'I am not so sure about that,' the old man said doubtfully. 'The boat was new. But it isn't the money, madame; it's the principle.'

'Well,' my mother pleaded, 'I should like to spare my husband this annoyance when he comes home: we expect him tonight. But fifty dollars happens to be all the cash I have in the house. I can give you an order on my bank in the city . . . '

'I want cash,' the old man interrupted her. 'I'll see the master, I guess.'

With that he rose; but I saw that he still lingered and divined that he was counting on the efficacy of his threat; I knew that my mother trembled, partly on my account, and partly because just recently things had been smoothed over more or less between her and my father; if he inflicted a severe punishment on me, that fact would go far towards invalidating such attempts at a reconciliation between them as had been made. All this angered me: for I felt guilty beyond my years; guilty as only a boy can feel who has been made precocious by the observation of matters which ordinarily remain hidden from children. And, worst, I saw clearly that this old man saw through her pretences and took a fiendish delight in torturing her in order to strike me in his revengeful spite.

My mother, too, was on the point of adding another word; but she refrained; and eventually he took his departure, leaving the matter as it stood.

As soon as he had gone, I flung myself at my mother's neck. 'Mamma!' I cried in a passion. 'That horrid old man lies! I know that the boat was not fastened.'

'Never mind, Rolphe,' she said and stroked my hair. 'But you should not have taken it.'

'I never thought of it, mamma! I took it as if it had been ours.' Then, in a sudden fear, I added, 'Is a hundred and fifty dollars much money, mamma?'

'Yes,' she said, 'for an old boat . . . But it is not the money, my child. I am afraid of the way your father may take it. You can't understand it yet, my boy: but you will one day. And what I hate most about it is that this old man knows it.'

'He is a brute!' I cried, stamping my foot and trying hard to suppress my tears. I could not understand it yet, she had said; but I thought I did; and today I know that essentially I was right. I judged her relation to my father quite accurately from my own; and that was determined by my desire to admire and love him—a desire that was for ever repulsed and frustrated by the fear in which I stood of him and his, to me, incomprehensible ways.

My mother and I had our supper together, an arrangement which was never permitted when my father was at home.

I thought and thought; for I felt that the occasion called for some heroic action on my part; and I formed a plan.

After supper I waited for another hour or so. Then I slipped quietly out and asked John, the groom, to take Troy to the back of the stables for me. In order to secure his co-operation I gave him a five-franc piece, half of the money I had at the time.

From behind the stables I rode through the park, by a round-about path, and down to the beach; for I must not be seen if I was to carry out my plan. The water in the bay was not yet smooth; big breakers were running slowly up on the sandy shelves. But the air was quiet and fresh; and a bright moon was shining even before the day had fully darkened.

Briskly I galloped along the beach from which the tide was receding again; and as I did so, I scanned both bay and shore for the boat. I knew there would be no very sharp currents out to sea till the ebbing waters began to uncover some of the higher sandbanks and, the farther north I went along this shore, the more steeply it fell away and the less would be the distance over which the tides played back and forth.

I went on for an hour or so; and suddenly I saw the boat.

It was quietly dancing about on the smooth waves, a quarter of a mile from shore and far south of the place where I had taken it in the morning.

I pulled Troy in and considered what to do. I felt sure I could swim out to the boat, even though the swell was running in. But, there being no grass anywhere except beyond the cliff and the cliff being, at this point, too steep and continuous to lead Troy across, I was afraid I might not be able to keep track of the horse. But I decided that I must take that risk.

I tied Troy's bridle-rein up and stripped.

Then I dashed through the combing breakers into the quieter reaches beyond. The water seemed cold for a moment and then strangely warm. I struck boldly out and soon gained on the boat which was slowly drifting out to sea.

It was half an hour's fight before I could place my hand on its gunwale and pull myself up.

A problem presented itself. If I rowed back to shore to get my clothes, I might not be able to keep the boat afloat; for the tide, as I have said, was more and more rapidly running out.

I abandoned that plan, put the oars in their locks, and pulled north, along shore, into the deeper water, naked as I was. It was hard work but I was determined to put the boat back where I had found it. It had been a great shock to me that this unmannerly old man could walk straight into Stone House and threaten and torture my mother. I was full of a boiling indignation against him: and I was taking my revenge; at least he would not get the money!

The waves, which were smooth and long, gave me no trouble; and the evening chill drove me to fullest exertion of what powers my slender body possessed. I was rewarded, for I found the inlet and pulled the boat up on the pebbles in its throat. Then I carried the anchor to the full length of the rope and worked it down into the ground behind a rock.

My bare feet soon became sore and I was thoroughly tired when at last I reached the place again where I had left my clothes. But I was tingling with excitement and satisfaction.

Troy was nowhere to be found: and so I had to walk back. But when, in the advancing night, I reached the gap in the forest whence I could see the lighthouse winking, I heard a sudden nicker: and almost simultaneously I felt the horse's soft, moist muzzle on my cheek.

I jumped into the saddle and galloped straight across the lawn, the lights of Stone House beckoning to me home-like and sheltered, at the head of the park.

In the stables there was a commotion going on by lantern-light: and when I reached them, I saw the dim outline of my father's carriage in front of the shed.

He had come home.

It was probably due to the stir his return had made in the house that I reached my quarters without being questioned by anyone: nobody had even noticed my absence.

Next morning I was called long before I felt that I had slept enough. But the moment I realized that no doubt I should soon have to appear before my father, a deep excitement began to pound through my veins; and I dressed in feverish haste.

Yet I was scarcely ready when my father's man appeared in the door of my room and announced that 'Master Rolphe was wanted downstairs in the office.'

I grabbed collar and tie and put them on while descending the backstairs, for the office was in the rear of the huge building.

To my surprise, when I entered, I found M Jupe, the fisherman, there. I had thought that, so far, only my mother had broken the news.

'Sit down,' my father said and pointed to a chair.

While I obeyed, I scanned his face. He was sitting at a desk, huge, impassive, his usual slightly bored and cynical expression in his eyes. I had expected to find a scowl of anger on his brow, and not to see it rather disconcerted me. I should have liked to plunge into speech: but I knew better: for all I could have expected would have been a brief command, delivered in the accent of surprise, to wait till I was spoken to. My father was in the habit of treating me as he treated his servants. Besides, I knew that he was sitting there in the capacity of a judge, impartial but stern. It was this impersonal and slightly contemptuous way of his which had brought things to the pass to which they had come between him and my mother. He was her judge, not her lover.

Monsieur Jupe had a grim, expectant look in his eyes; and his bare lips, framed by the fan-shaped, grey chin beard showed a set expression.

'Well,' my father turned to him, with measured politeness, 'what is your story, sir?' The formal address was ironical.

'He took the boat,' the old man replied, much less at ease than he had been the day before.

'Did you see him take it?'

'No, but I saw him in it.'

'When was that?'

'At noon. I thought we'd have a storm; and I went down to fasten the boat. The boat was gone. I saw the young master in it across the bay.'

'Then the boat was not fastened?'

'That's what I don't know,' the old man replied, not without reluctance, but in honour of the truth. 'Anyway, it would have been fastened had it been there. That is what I went down for.'

'You said to madame the boat had been fastened when the boy took it.' I could see the ghost of a contemptuous smile flittering around my father's lips.

'I didn't.'

I made a motion as if to speak; but a glassy stare from my father's eye arrested me.

'Since you admit that the boat may not have been fastened, the point is irrelevant. I am not going to drag madame into this. But to my mind, I may mention, one of you two was lying yesterday. I am glad it was not the young master. Now for the boat. I happen to know it. It was worth, at the most, thirty dollars. How can you dare to come here and try to bully five times as much out of madame?' He spoke with a perfectly level voice; but it had a cutting edge.

'The young master needed a lesson,' the old man snarled.

'If he did,' my father said smoothly, 'it was not for you to administer it. I do not care whether he took the boat or not. He is a boy. You have probably taken a boat yourself when you were young; and a boat that did not belong to you, either.'

'Yes,' the old man growled, 'and got thrashed for it.'

'Precisely,' my father agreed. 'But that was not what you did, my man. You don't seem to realize what you did. You knew I was not at home. You thought madame might be willing to pay you, not for the boat, but for your silence about the affair. You came here and tried to blackmail her. It was a good thing she did not happen to have the money in the house. You threatened to have the law on us. But the law, my man, cuts both ways. I can assure you that I am not afraid of it. It threatens the man who attempts blackmail with a term behind iron bars. The point just now is, are you going to be satisfied with the exact value of the boat or not? I'll give you a few minutes to consider the case. Meanwhile I shall see whether the young culprit has anything to say for himself.' And he looked at me with a cool, level look, neither friendly nor hostile.

'No, father.' I said. 'I took the boat. But I took it back where I found it and fastened it, too.' I felt my cheeks reddening; for I knew that a moment of triumph had come for me.

Both men looked up.

'That's a lie!' shouted Monsieur Jupe.

I looked at him with a mocking smile. Since my father remained silent I went on and explained.

There was a slight gleam in my father's eye when he laughed. He had always despised me as my mother's son, not his. He rose.

'The whole thing for nothing,' he said. 'Well, Monsieur Jupe, it seems you don't have much of a case after all. You will be good enough to wait here; for I shall send my inspector down with you so he sees that the boat is there.'

With that he beckoned me and went out.

When we entered the hall where my mother was waiting in anguish he put his hand on my shoulder. It was the first time that I remember his having done so.

My mother looked from one to the other.

'I bring you the boy,' my father said. 'He has had his vindication. And if the old man worried you, believe me, my dear, your son has revenged you as well.'

A strange, happy smile lay on the frail woman's face as she looked up into her husband's eyes. That smile held something I had never seen before; and, strange to say, in spite of my pride, a tiny pang plucked at my heart. It was the first time in my life that I knew jealousy, my friend.

# Raymond Knister

JOHN Raymond Knister was born near Ruthven, Ontario, on May 27, 1899. After a few months at Victoria College, University of Toronto, he caught pneumonia and returned to his father's farm, where he began to write. His first story, 'The One Thing,' appeared in *The Midland*, a small literary magazine from Iowa City, in January 1922, and the following story (originally called 'Lapsed Crisis') was also published in that magazine the following August. Knister accepted an offer from *The Midland*'s editor, John T. Frederick, to go to Iowa to become the magazine's assistant editor in October 1923, but a year later Knister returned to Canada. In 1925 he was made Canadian correspondent to *This Quarter*, the expatriot magazine edited in Paris by Ernest Walsh.

In 1927 Knister married Myrtle Gamble, and his third novel, *White Narcissus*, was accepted in Canada by Macmillan. Also that year Knister was commissioned by Macmillan to edit the first anthology of Canadian short stories. After the book's appearance in 1928 the couple moved to a farm on Lake Erie, and Knister began work on *My Star Predominant*, a 240,000-word novel based on the life of John Keats. In 1930, Frederick Philip Grove, then president of Graphic Press in Ottawa, agreed to publish *My Star Predominant* if Knister would cut it down to 100,000 words. Knister did, and in 1931 the novel was awarded Graphic's first prize of $24,000, half of which Knister collected before the firm went into bankruptcy. In 1931 the Knisters moved to Montreal, where Knister wrote more stories and drew up plans for a novel to be called *Via Faust*. On August 10, 1932, Lorne Pierce offered Knister an editor's job at Ryerson Press, and in celebration of this promise of financial security the Knisters rented a cottage for two weeks on Lake St. Clair. On August 30, while swimming off Stoney Point, Knister drowned.

There has been a special Knister edition of the *Journal of Canadian Fiction* (1975), which brought out nearly 30 hitherto unpublished short stories and much biographical information. Knister's best stories, however, are to be found in *The First Day of Spring: stories and other prose* (1976), edited by Peter Stevens.

# MIST GREEN OATS

IT WAS not until after he arrived home from taking his mother to the railway station that he began to realize how tired he had become. 'Now don't work too hard while I'm away, Len,' had been her last words on kissing him, and before he left the train. While he was riding slowly homeward his thoughts had been busy hopping from one detail to another of the morning's activities: of his coming up from the field at eleven o'clock and stabling the horses, of the bustlings of last-minute preparations, carrying the grips out and expostulating with his mother as she stood before the mirror straight and young-looking in her travelling-dress, of the stirring numbers of people about the station and the platform waiting and staring, who made him conscious of his Sunday coat, overalls and heavy shoes. And his mind had leaped on ahead of her to his cousins whom she would see, and what he thought to be their life in the remote city, as he pictured it from the two or three holidays he had passed there in the course of his childhood.

In the lane at the end of the barn when he arrived home his father was hitching his three-horse team together, square-framed and alike in size; and throwing a word now and then to Syd Allrow who was sitting hunched on the handles of his plow which lay on the ground behind his team of blacks. The boy nodded to Syd, and his father, seeing his look of surprise, said hurriedly, 'Syd's helping us a day or two. Thought I'd get an early start. Go right on in now, and have dinner. We'll be back in the apple orchard when you come.'

The boy began to notice as he had not before that his father's face had become a little thin and bitten of apparently new wrinkles. The acute stridor of haste and the spring work, the heavy anxiety, the lack of help—he turned away when his father hastily came around to that side of the team. Walking toward the house he heard Syd make some inertly voiced remark or query.

The victuals were cold, but his dinner was awaiting him on the table in the kitchen. When a few minutes later he began to take the dishes away he left off abruptly, remembering that he should have time for such tasks in the evening, when the work outside was done. Then he recommenced and finished clearing the table, for

Syd would be there, they would be hungry and wish to have supper as soon as possible after coming from the field.

As he moved about he was not oppressed now by a sense of haste, by a fear, almost, of something unknown threatening their determination which yet chivvied and lured the men of farms through those ontreading days of late spring. The season had been retarded by late frosts and heavy rains at seeding time, and the later work, corn-planting and plowing, must be done quickly before the soil became intractable. Such conjunctures, with their own necessity, were at the source of what might in certain types of men evolve as a race against time as much for the sake of the race as for the prefigured prize. He mused.

This released sense must have come from the variation in the plan of the day. At this hour of the afternoon he was used to being in the field, or choring about the barn. Alone in the house Len Brinder's movements became slower as he made the turn from kitchen to pantry and back again. His mind went to the city toward which his mother was now speeding, where the streets and buildings and the spirit of them, which every one of the crowds about him seemed in a way to share, were wonderful from a distance of two years. It was impossible that the spirit and the crowds could mean anything but life rendered into different terms, understandable and entrancing. Everyone appeared to be full of active keenness, a beauty, and, for all it was deceptive, no one appeared to work. Automatically he continued moving the dishes about.

His father and Syd were both finishing a round when he arrived at the end of the apple-orchard. The horses of their teams were already beginning to show wet about their flanks, despite their hardened condition. As they came toward him the heads of his father's three horses, which were pulling a two-furrow plow, bobbed unevenly, and their loud breaths produced a further and audible discord. The noses of Syd's black team were drawn in to their breasts, for they were pulling a walking-plow and the reins passed around their driver's back. There was little wind among the big mushroom-shaped apple trees.

'Well,' said Sam Brinder from his seat, 'Syd's finishing the lands for me. Do you want to strike them out? It will be pretty hard around those old trunks, though.'

The boy did want to—'Not much difference, is there?'—and at

once turned his team into line. The absence of his father's accustomed brusque unconsciousness struck him readily enough as a blandness affected for the benefit of the neighbour.

The hardness of the ground astonished him. He wondered how he could have thought of anything else since leaving his plow in the morning. He was obliged to hold the handle at a wearying angle in going around the trunks of the big trees, and to twist it back to a normal position in the spaces between. White dust like a smoke burst forth from between the ground and the fresh soil falling heavy upon it. All along the orchard the spurting dust preceded him, thin portions rising with a little wisp of breeze about his face. When he reached the end of the long furrow he was almost panting from the wrestle. "This is going to be hard on horses,' he said to himself. 'The hottest day yet.' The ground seemed to have become petrified since the day before. 'I'll have to rest them oftener now, just after dinner. Later on we can go,' he thought, as he turned again for the return on the other side of the trees.

It was necessary to plow two furrows around each row of trees before the big plow could be used. As the end of the orchard was reached each time the ground seemed harder and the boy's arms more stretched and tired. As the time passed the horses began to give signs of the strain. One of them would put his head down and make a forward rush, straightening the doubletree, while his mate seemed to hang back—then the other in turn dashed ahead, leaving his mate behind.

'Straighten 'em up there. Make 'em behave!' his father called from the riding-plow, and banished Len's own vexation with the team. He tried but languidly to bring it under control, while he thought, 'It's the ground. The horses are all right. They're willing enough.' Nothing could be more willing than a horse. He'd go until he dropped if the driver hadn't sense enough to pull him up, to keep him from foundering himself. It was the cursed soil. The plowing shouldn't have been put off so long. It needn't have been. Why couldn't they have left some of the manure-hauling, some of the pruning, and done this first? And other people were able to get men on some terms, why couldn't his father? Then, why must he take such a busy time as last week had been to go to the city to see about the mortgage? These questions were like arrows pointing a centre in his thoughts: the feeling of being ill-used. Bad management was to blame, but he could not, yet, hold his father responsible, whom circumstances seemed to have rendered powerless. The boy's hat was sticking to his brow as though clamped there with some iron band driven down like hoops on a barrel.

Sam Brinder and Syd were talking at the end of the field. What did they have so important to talk about? They had been at the same spot when he started back from the other end. He didn't rest his horses that much. He was too interested in getting the work done to be so determined to take part in a confab. He would show them what he thought. He'd not give his horses half as much rest as they had theirs. That would shame them, maybe, the lazy—'Ned! Dick! Get up here, you old—'

Tight-throated in the dust, wrestling bitterly with the stony soil, he went up and down the rows. These thoughts lasted him a long time and he forgot everything about him except the wrenching heavy plow and the rhythmic swinging single-trees and the creaking harness. Time and the sun seemed to stand still, breathless.

They started on again with a jerk when an hour later he heard his father hailing him through the trees.

'Go up and get us a pail of water,' Sam Brinder called. 'Your horses can stand the rest anyway, I guess.'

'Well, I'm not thirsty, but if you are, of course—'

'We've been back here longer than you have, remember,' his father added.

The boy looked at him, wrapped the lines about the plow-handles, and went up the lane toward the well. Walking was queer alone now; easier, perhaps? It almost seemed to be done automatically, his body leaning slightly forward.

He went to the house, and brought the pail back to the well, drank slowly and gratefully of the cold water....

He was walking down the lane at a moderate, stooped-shouldered pace. The light summer clothes hung about his gaunt form. Well, the afternoon was going. Four o'clock when he had left the house. It might be nearly half-past four by the time he got back to work. Well, no. Five, ten minutes had gone now. Not more than ten more would pass before he should have taken Syd and his father their drinks. Even at that; twenty minutes after four; the afternoon was going pretty well.... Syd would be for supper, of course. Kind of nice, they had been alone so much since his older sister had left them and gone into an office in the city. Could it be as hot as this in the city, where one might go into the ice-cream parlours and the movie theatres? Different it would be, anyway.

In the orchard the sunlight seemed to pack the heat down below the boughs and above the earth. The boughs seemed to hold it there, and to make room in some way for more heat, which the sun still packed down. His feet in the heavy shoes seemed to be broiling; the socks hung loose about his thin ankles and over the hard unbendable uppers. The horses needed a rest, his father had said, eh? It was they who needed the rest! He'd give them rest enough, all right, from now on. At each end of the field. If his father didn't mind, why should he try to do more than his share?

'Well,' said Syd as he reached for the dipper, standing in the furrow and looking up at him, 'how you standing it?' At the unevadable reply, 'Oh, all right,' he added:

'Getting about enough of farming? I was that way myself for a while. Seems kinda hard work after going to high school, I s'pose.'

That was like him! When it was almost a year since Len had left high school. 'Oh, I'm used to it by now,' the boy replied coldly.

Syd mopped his face with a patterned handkerchief, spat, swung a line, and said, 'Well, I guess I'll have to be getting along. Boss'll be makin' the fur fly, if I don't.' He smiled at the joke, as a farmer's son himself, and independent of the whims of bosses. 'So you're keeping batch now? I better not bother you for supper.'

'Yes, you're to stay for supper. There's no trouble about that. Yes, mother thought she'd take a rest before the canning came on. . . . ' He added, 'Gone to the city,' with a smile he suddenly felt was meant to appear brave.

'Tchka! Bill! Sam! Get outa here!'

His father said: 'You'll have to go up a little earlier than us and get supper ready.'

Len made no reply. Assent he felt was too miserably unnecessary, and he stood looking in silence back of the plow.

'Not making much of a job,' said Brinder. 'I got to stand on it most of the time. You got to be quick and keep shifting the levers. You got to have 'er just so. Some job, all right!'

As he walked across the scarred and lumpy headland the boy made an effort to feel at odds with his father, and to conjure an image proper to the aim. He saw him, a clipped-moustached and almost spruce figure, going away from the house to attend perhaps a meeting of school trustees, to raise his voice among the other men. Trying to find in his memory cue for a critical attitude, Len began to wonder how he himself appeared to those about him, going through the gestures of daily living.

What were people made of anyway, he reflected, bitterly deprecatory—but extravagances, ludicrous to everyone but themselves?

The sweat was caked in salt upon the flanks of his horses when he got back to them. One horse's head was held in a natural position; the other's back and head were level, and its weight slouched on a hind leg.

Stiffly the three plodded on again. As one long round after another was made, night almost seemed to be getting farther away, rather than nearing them. To lean back in the lines as he found himself wanting to do and allow the plowtails to pull him along was impossible. The point would shoot up and the plow slide along the ground until he could get the horses stopped. In spite of him sometimes it did this, when it struck a stone or when it came to a packed area of ground, and then the boy had to drag its weight back several feet into its former position; shouting at the horses and pulling them back at the same time.

But at each end of the field he gave the team a long rest, sitting on the plow-handles as the clumsy implement lay on its side. He dangled his legs and moved his feet about in the heavy shoes. The soles were burning. Looking at the wrinkled tough leather, which seemed to form impenetrable bumps, he noticed that the toe of the right shoe was turned up on the outside with a seemingly immanent bend, given it by the slope of the furrow which he had for days been following. Every day the same! With the impressionableness of youth he could not believe that there had ever been a time at which he had not been tired out. Every day the same. The weariness of last night and of the night before, the same. But this day was far from spent yet. Tonight as well as the usual chores there would be work in the house.

He looked for a long time across the wide pasture at the end of the orchard. Several cattle were on its gently raised surface. Their feet seemed to be above the fence on the lower ground beyond them, which could be seen at either side of the rise. The sky was clear and high, and it seemed to give the cattle a lightness which should make possible for them any feat. It looked as though they might with one fabulous jump easily clear the fence in the distance and be free. For what—free? They would break into the green oats or wet alfalfa and kill themselves. The boy sighed and raised the plow-handles again. Over in the midst of the trees sharp sweet notes of birdsong began to come, giving the place in his present mood a chilled look. The grass became pale before his eyes and the sunlight a little milder broke among the branches as among windy streaming snowflakes.

The horses pulled evenly now. They were going with a seemingly terrible swiftness. The boy staggered and strode along behind them, wrenching the plow as it threatened to jump to the surface. They found it easier, charging through so rapidly, or else they wanted to get each stint over as quickly as possible for the rest at the end of it. Stumbling and striding along behind, Len hated them. Boy and horses began to sweat more profusely. 'They always get that way about this time. It must be getting late.' The sun was shining in his eyes.

As he reached the end his father shouted across to him, and he stooped to undo the tugs.

It was when he reached the house that the desire came to him to take off his shoes. He seemed to have walked on lumpy plates of hot greasy iron for innumerable ages. He sat down and untied them slowly, and the mere loosening of the leathern laces made the feet ache relief. He walked about the cool kitchen oilcloth in his socks. Then a fancy struck him. He opened the screen door and went out on the lawn. He shoved his feet along in the short grass and rubbed them against each other. Such immeasurable sweet pain he had never known. At first he could scarcely bear to raise his weary feet from the depth of the grass. Presently he would lift one at a time in a strange and heavy dance, for the pleasure it was of putting it down again among the cool soft blades. The lowering sun variegated the green of the different kinds of evergreen trees back of the house, of which he always confused the names. Something of beauty which, it seemed, must have been left out of it or which he had forgotten, appeared in the closing day. Something was changed, perhaps. He did not know how long he had been there, scrubbing his soles about like brushes in the grass, and regretfully hopping, until he remembered that the men would be coming in for their supper at any minute. Beginning to wonder whether anyone had witnessed his movements, he went into the house and relaced his shoes.

The men were eating their supper. After they had washed their hands and faces outside of the back door, throwing each dirty basinful away with a dripping hiss into the light breeze, they entered the house. Syd sat very straight on a chair by the wall, with his arms folded, and looked at nothing in particular. His black shirt was still open at the neck. Sam Brinder bustled about helping Len to complete the preparations. 'Now, the eggs. How'll ye have the eggs—Syd?'

'Doesn't make any difference to me,' Syd gravely replied.

'Come now, you've got to say.'

'No, sir. Have 'em how you like. You're the doctor.'

'Well, suppose we have them fried.'

Now, as they ate heartily, they said little, except to urge upon each other and accept or refuse more food. The room became warm and filled with the soft sounds of their eating and the steaming kettle on the stove. There was the humming of one or two flies about and between them recurrently. Presently a prolonged lowing was heard from back of the barn. 'Cows are coming up the lane of themselves,' said Brinder. 'We won't have to go after them. Pretty good, eh, Len?'

Then the two men began to speak of the crops and the comparative state of the work on neighbouring farms.

'We're pretty well forward with our work,' said Syd, 'but there's more of us for the amount of land.' He referred to his two brothers who were at home. 'Still, you fellows are getting along pretty well. You're getting over the ground lately, all right.'

The significance came to Len of 'you fellows,' making him angry and sad. A great partnership it was, he told himself, wherein his share consisted of unrequited work. Then he thought that Syd had meant to be flattering or condoling, and though he imagined that he should be vexed with him for that, he could not. The conversation was sliding on over well-worn topics, with the slight necessary variations. The sun's rays were horizontal now, the raised window blind let them strike on the lower part of Syd's clean-shaven tan face. It was not every night that they had company, even in this fashion. The boy liked Syd, after all. It reminded him how, many years ago as it now seemed, Syd had known of a Hallowe'en prank which he with some of the high-school boys had played on one of the farmers thereabout. And he had never told. . . . The Hallowe'en joke had been to him, as much as anything else in his boy's world, a social due.

The three sat in the room which the flat rays from the window made to seem dusk-filled, and the two elder continued talking. Len moved his fork with the ends of his fingers, tilted his tea-cup, and thought, when he thought, and did not merely fill himself vaguely with a pleasant sense of Syd's identity, of the work to be done yet.

Presently they rose, and the boy remained in the house to do the washing-up while his father did the chores.

Slowly the dishes were assembled and slowly and thoroughly wiped. Unused to the work he took a long time to finish it. Besides, he thought, there is only more work waiting outside. "There's always work waiting outside on a farm,' he reflected. 'There'll be plenty of it right here when we're all dead. Wherever it's all getting us to—' But he saw some of the older farmers about him, and those who were not to that extent in neediness, still working as hard and during longer hours than anyone. They had come to like it. He envied and condemned them for that. There was so much of the world to see, so much of life to discover, to compare with what one might find in oneself! Suddenly Len was confident of this.

He went out into the dusk. Innumerable crickets joined voices to produce a trill. A wind was blowing and he sniffed it gratefully. 'As fresh—as fresh, as on the sea,' he muttered, slouching toward the barn. The cattle were in the yard, spotting the gloom. He could hear their windy coughing sigh, which was at once contrasted with the loud drumming snort of a horse as he burrowed about in the hay of his manger. The closed stable was loud with the grinding of jaws on the tough dried stems.

There was no sign of his father about, though he gave a shout. He wished to know which of the chores remained not done. There was no answer. The milk-pails upside down showed that the milking was not yet begun. 'Likely gone home with Syd for a visit,' he grunted at once, without taking any thought of the matter. He fumbled about the harnesses in the dark. 'Thinks he'll lay the chores on me, I s'pose. I'll only unharness the horses and water them. If he doesn't like that he can do the other.'

When he returned to the house he glanced at the alarm clock on the shelf. A quarter past nine. He picked up a magazine and took it with a lamp into the next room. Frequently when the family went to town a magazine was brought home. Before that his reading had been restricted and this began only after Len had quit high school. He for some time found the change grateful from his dry studies. He was drowsing with his elbows on one of the magazines when the screen-door slammed and Brinder entered the house, coming on into the room where his son was sitting. The boy, fully awake, pretended to continue his reading.

'I saw you weren't out at the barn, so I came in. You didn't get the chores all finished, did you?'

'No, I just worked till a little after nine, and then quit and called it a day.'

'Is that so! You could have quit when you liked, if you'd asked me. I didn't order you to do the chores, remember, I asked you how many of them had been done.'

'As many as I had time to do after doing the work in here.'

'Well, you didn't have many hours work in here, did you? How much did you do?'

'I gave the horses water and unharnessed them.'

'Oh!'

'Why, did the time seem so long over at Allrows'?'

'Over at Allrows'?'

'Yes. Didn't you go home with Syd?'

'Well, that's a joke, that is,' said Brinder, turning away. 'I went back to the pasture after old Belle. She wouldn't bring her calf up with the other cattle.'

Len was nonplussed for an instant. His father went on, 'It'll pay not to pay so much attention to the clock when a busy time's on, you'll find.' He entered the kitchen, shutting the door behind him.

The boy did not try to check his anger at this. It was increased by his knowledge that his father's was controlled.

'I'll find, will I?' he shouted at the closed door. 'I'll find where there's an eight-hour day to be had, you can bet on that!'

He heard his father grunting in the next room, and the creak of his lantern as he jerked it shut. Then the outside door slammed behind him.

Len was painfully awake now, but he could not keep his mind on the printing before him. His imagination ran amuck through possibilities. But he did not see them as possibilities. The actuality stood before him of every movement from now until the time he should have reached the city and entered on some transcendentally congenial and remunerative occupation. The vision, with its minutiae, lasted a considerable time; then another came of his going to sea. When he judged that his father would soon be coming into the house again he took up his lamp and retired to his own room.

The next morning he came downstairs bearing the blackened lamp in his hand, to find that his father had gone out, leaving a fire for cooking the breakfast. It was half-past five by the clock on the shelf, and the boy at once began preparations for the morning meal. Before the table was set his father came in with the milk-pail. They greeted each other somewhat shamefacedly and busied themselves with straining the milk and taking the dishes from the shelves.

As they were sitting down to the table Mr Brinder looked at the clock: 'It's later than it seems; that clock's away slow.' He appeared to be in a hurry, and the meal was consumed in silence. When they had finished the father said, 'You clear up here. I'll not water the driver nor your team. If I'm gone to the field when you come out, you water them.' He went away apparently without hearing Len's monosyllabic assent.

The morning was not yet more than faintly warm. White clouds were loitering about the sky, and dew hung in the grass beside the path worn to the barn. The boy slipped the halter from the head of Lass, the driver, pride of the farm, or at any rate very much that of himself. He drove her out into the yard, where she might go for a drink. Meanwhile he began to harness the team with which he intended to plow.

In a moment Lass entered the end of the stable in which he was working, instead of the other, containing her box-stall. For months one of the rollers on the door leading out of that end of the barn had been broken, so that it had been necessary to lead her forth from the part in which the other horses were quartered. Now, as she came in by the old way, long after the door had been repaired, there was something about the whole matter, about the inertia and preoccupation which had so long made them neglect it, more than about this unnecessary use of the old mode of entry, which enraged Len immeasurably. He could not have explained his rage with its sudden choking of his throat. He leaped at the little mare shouting, 'Get out of here, you! Before I—' He reached her side and struck a blow at her muzzle. She jerked her head up, turning around, and slipping and sprawling on the cement went out. He at once became ashamed of himself, and when he had got her into the stall gave her an extra handful of oats. They watched each other while she, ears pricked, ate it. Lass did not object, as most horses did, to the impertinence of being watched while she consumed feed.

Throughout that morning the boy was nearly as tired and even more languidly bitter than the evening before. The soil seemed as hard as ever, the horses plunged, the orchard was still longer.

Wonderful high steep and billowing clouds were in the sky. They were like vast mounds and towers of tarnished well-lit silver. He sat on the side of the plow and looked over toward the part of the orchard at which he would finish his plowing. The green of an oats field beyond was visible under the apple-boughs. It was even now beginning to take on a grey misty tinge. Soon the oats field would seem an unbelievable blue-grey cloud, glimpsed from beneath the apple trees. In those days the granite of oats would call the eye throughout all the country. The heads would seem to dance in the high sunlight, and fields of wheat would bow and surge in amber-lit crests. The rows of young corn would be arching to either side and touching, black-green and healthy. The smell of it, as he cultivated and the horses nipped off pieces of the heavy leaves, would be more sweet than that of flowers, and more bland. The year would pass on, the harvesting of wheat, of barley and oats, fall-plowing again, threshings, the cutting and husking of corn, the picking of apples in this same orchard. Yes, one could see the beauty of it distantly, but when the time came he would be numbed to all with toil.

That is, this round would take place, the years pass on, if he remained on the farm. Would he, or, rather he asked himself, could he do that? Nothing very alluring was to be seen ahead in the lives of anyone about him. What was his father getting out of it?

His plow could scarcely be held in the ground at all now. The point had become worn off and rounded, and he at last went over to his father for a heavy wrench with which to break it off squarely, which would for a time postpone the necessity of replacing it with a new one. Syd was starting back to the other end of the orchard, and waved a heavy arm at him. Len pretended to be busy disengaging the wrench from his father's plow, but looked up an instant later to watch the steady progress down the field of the team of blacks; and Syd held the plow handles with an appearance of firmness and ease.

'You needn't bother going for the water this morning, I'll go after it,' his father was saying.

'Plows nice, finishing the lands up, don't it?' Len asked significantly, ignoring the remark.

'Well, if you wanted to do that, why didn't you say so in the first place?'

'Oh, don't bother changing us around now! I'm getting used to the hard part.' He still looked after Syd.

'No, I won't ask him to change now.'

Len walked on, more uninterruptedly now, but shouting shrilly at the horses as they jerked ahead. Stopping midway of the field he set the clevis to make the plow go deeper. It saved him some of the effort to hold it in the ground. But the horses found it still heavier going. At the hard spots at each end big blocks of cement-like earth were turned up.

He was calculating the length of the orchard and therefrom the distance walked in a day, when his father came with the drink. Pulling his watch out Sam Brinder said, 'It's not as late as it seems. I've set the clock on, by my watch. It's five minutes to eleven, while the right time is twenty-five minutes to eleven. I'll holler when it's time to quit. Your team is doing all right, not sweating.'

Later as he came to the end of the field he heard his father and Syd, who happened to finish at the same time, talking together.

'Yes, and she can go, all right; nice roader,' his father was saying.

'Well, I think this other one would just suit you.'

Were they speaking of Lass? Once or twice Brinder had considered disposing of her, and Len's dread of such a possibility was such that he would never discuss it. But she might be sold now. Anything, it came to him, might happen now. His father would just like to sell her to spite him, he knew. The ache of his anger was redoubled by the memory of what had happened that morning. He recalled now his deep-founded liking for the little horse. One evening he let her out in the field with the others. How she trotted! Proudly, with arched neck and tail streaming behind, she moved about among the other horses with great high free strides. 'She can trot circles around the others,' he thought. Presently she stopped, standing poised and throbbing with life, snorting, ears forward, looking at him in the doorway. And he clapped his hands and she trotted off once more. Then she became still more frolicsome. Her heels shot up again and again, and he could hear the swish of her long heavy tail as she kicked. . . . Yes, it would be just like him to sell her.

Time passed, as if in despite of itself. The boy plodded on, his mind enfolded in these thoughts, and consciously aware of only the flopping aside of the earth before him, of the dust and the hard gravel slope of the furrow-bottom. The fatal impressibility of youth was lapping chains about him. It seemed that he had never known anything else than this dolorous wrestle in the dust. The hard clamping of his hat-brim pained his forehead. He wiped it and the grime came off on his handkerchief. The ache in his legs was not to be forgotten, but his mind swung from the certainty of the loss of one of the few things—the only one it now seemed for which he could care. He began to wonder about the time. His shadow slanted a little to the east as he faced north: surely it was after noon. He could not remember whether the shadow slanted more in the spring or in the autumn: it was surely more than twelve o'clock.

Automatically he continued work after the accustomed respite. What was the meaning of this clock business? The clock had seemed accurate enough yesterday to catch the train by. But it had been slow this morning, and now, his father said, it was fast, and fast so much. There was something strange about all this.

But as it became later there ceased to be anything strange in the matter to Len. It was part of a plan, that couldn't be doubted. To pretend that they had begun later than usual and at the same stroke keep him at work later—it was sharp, all right. Indignation and a respect for his own penetration filled him. This, he reflected in bitterness, was what he must expect from his father henceforth. And the latter would regard it as no more than just discipline, probably. But he'd be shown. 'He'll only try that once,' the boy muttered, his face fixing and his fingers tightening on the plow-handles.

Standing at the end of the field he looked about him. Through the trees he could see his father's three square-boned horses straining onward amid the shouts of their driver. 'Sitting down, having a nap,' he thought, relishing the fact of taking this as a matter of course. Farther over Syd was going in the opposite direction, holding his plow as steadily it appeared as though the ground had been softened by days of rain.

'I'll not make another round,' he reflected. 'Or it will be a good while before I do, anyway. If he thinks he can do that sort of thing he's going to get left.'

Whistling a shred of an old tune he sat down on his plow. 'Have a good rest, Ned,' he addressed the nigh horse. 'You started early enough, anyway.'

He was aware of the long barred stretch of blue-green oats now still nearer. The high sun instead of making it more vivid seemed to give its surface a hazy quality. A dragonfly hung motionless against the mild breeze and seeming to battle with it, wings alight with a sparkle of swift motion.

'About noon when you see them things,' the boy thought.

From three-quarters of a mile away came the sound of the Allrows' dinner-bell. Old-fashioned people. It was dinner-time, then, all right. Sometimes, though, they had dinner earlier, or later. He pictured the Allrow boys and their father, quitting work in various parts of the farm, and Mrs Allrow, plump, easily pleased woman, with her grown-up daughters preparing the meal. How long was it since he had been over to their place? That, he reflected, was the trouble; one didn't see anyone new for weeks at a stretch. The desire for various contacts had made him impatient of the people he might have known better, had he cared. He got through the day's work, but curiosity demanded leisure and energy. People on a farm, like the men on ship-board in the old days, saw too much of each other. That was it. But that could be remedied in his case, Len reflected with a quickening of the pulses. . . . Not an inch would he drive further. His father must learn that his little trick wouldn't work. As he sat, waiting for the call, he decided that if he discovered that the clock really had been advanced, he must leave. He pictured all the details of this, his father's queries and expostulations and his own determined silence. He would pack his suitcase, take his few dollars out of hiding and walk down the road. . . . He kicked at the side of the furrow, gazing downward. . . . How sore his feet had been last night! . . . But he wouldn't walk very far, only to the railway station. For he was going to the city. No, he would ask to be driven there in the buggy, drive Lass himself. If only one could keep himself unbound! But there'd be that one friend he'd always miss! . . . He would ask politely, unemotionally, and his father would not be able to refuse. . . . He'd just step to the house and phone central and enquire the correct time.

His father's call struck a surprise in him, and he rose stiffly and unhitched the horses. He noticed that both the others were unhitching also. They didn't intend to let him go up and prepare the dinner alone. But he'd never let that hinder him. He'd step to the phone in their presence and find out the truth about this matter. Robbing him from both pockets at once!

He hurried toward the barn, determined to arrive there first. He came to the watering trough; and when, after waiting for the horses to drink, he had stabled them, he was so agitated that he was struck with a weak surprise to hear Syd and his father talking quietly outside while they separated their horses. He intended to go out of the building and directly to the house, having fed the team which he had been driving; but he changed his mind and went back and began to put hay in the other mangers, then made for the house and washed before them.

He heard their voices; their heavy feet scrub the grass of the yard. . . . knock against the step.

'It's a seven-foot cut, they tell me,' Brinder was saying. 'Now wouldn't you have thought a six-foot cut would be big enough, on a farm like that?'

'Old Dunc says he may as well get a big one now. Alfred'll be getting a tractor soon as he's gone, he says.'

'Great old joker. He don't mind having big things around, himself.'

'Then I guess he's sure he'll have the job of driving it now he's getting old.' Syd laughed. 'It'll make the boys hump, to shock behind it, though.'

'Yes, they raise pretty good crops, just the same.' Mr Brinder was putting water in the kettle, while Syd combed his hair. 'How'll we have the eggs, boys?' The voice sounded absent from the pantry, whence the regular sweep of the bread-knife could be heard.

'Well, they were pretty fair like they were last night. . . . '

Len moved from shelves to table with clean dishes. Syd sat with his arms folded on a chair tilted against the wall. He intercepted one of the rounds by asking, 'Well, how you coming? Ground soft where you are, I s'pose!'

The boy grunted in reply and managed a half-smile.

Soon the meal was ready, and as they sat down to it he remembered that he had not gone to the phone as he had promised himself. He would do it as soon as the other two were gone, and he would be left alone to wash the dishes.

The two voices went on, with a calm interest, business-like inevitability, and the meal was almost over before Len realized that there was something in his mind being worn down and smoothed away, as old ice is worn away by spring rain. They talked as though they had been travellers in a desert who had become parted by accident and now met to recount all they had been through. But what they told was nothing, they meant simply to demonstrate to themselves that they were together again. Then what he thought of as the unreality of it oppressed him. A change of circumstances, the presence of strangers seemed to compel one to make little changes in one's words, in one's actions. Elements of the frank, humorous, the straight-forward, of eagerness in the gallantries of conversation were there. Perhaps Syd's family would smile to recognize him. His father was different too. But weren't they both after all as much themselves in any guise as they could be?

It occurred to him that his father was seeking something in the commonplace exchange. His father had been young too, once. He tried to imagine that youth, his aims and desires and ways. The thought unaccustomed held him for a moment, but he could not imagine them as different from his own, and the idea came that his father had betrayed them. Then as he looked at the lines in the face, scars of weather, toil and the scarifications of experience, he began to descry the blind unwitting stupor of life, reaching for what it wanted, an ox setting foot on a kitten before its manger.

He wanted to rise and rush from the room. The sound of the two with their talking kept him from his own thoughts.

They continued to discuss the fallibilities and oddities of neighbours until the table began to look emptier, and then he noticed his father say, 'So you think you'll not be able to help us any more, Syd?'

'Well, not just for the present,' replied Syd pleasantly, as though correcting Mr Brinder in an important inexactitude of statement. 'Maybe sometime after a while.' So Syd was going; going too. They were both going, his conscious mind repeated, though something that had been fierce and silently stridulous began to shrink within him, and he began to wonder how much he meant that.

He rose and left the house. He went down the lane and along the road which led toward the corner where, on the main highway, their mailbox stood.

There was nothing but yesterday's paper, and a post-card from his sister. The latter contained only the most banal message, documenting the fact that its sender was alive and, it added, in good spirits; and that the boss said her vacation would come in the next month.

The relationship of the brother and sister was not known to any especial tenderness, and yet, as he thought of the sense of her presence in the first few days after her return, of the feeling while at work of somebody new waiting for him at mealtimes, he couldn't but look forward to it, and he realized and now admitted to himself that his struggle had found an issue. A dull quietude came upon his mind. He tramped back home, his heavy feet upon the hard rounded road.

He found that the men had gone to the barn when he reached the kitchen. Syd would be hitching his horses and going away.

His mother—she would be beginning her holiday among the impossible wonders of the city. He thought of the endless confidential chats she would have with her sister, his aunt Charlotte, as they would rock together in the first afternoons, and the family would be out at work or at play. Already he began to miss her. Nearly two days were gone. But he should have, though only until realization, for expectance the last one of her absence.

Then he was struck by the triviality of what he allowed to pass as excuses for abandoning the determination he had so highly taken.

Once, clearing the table, he looked at the clock, but he did not let the reminder stay with him. As he wiped the dishes slowly, he looked at it again, and said aloud and consciously:

'What's the use? What's the weary use?'

Then, at the coming of an impulse as he was going out, his brow knitted, and he stopped a moment and went back up the stairs to his room. When he returned it was with a laden suitcase in his hand. He set it plainly on the floor before the table, and then thought, 'No, that's too plain. He'll see it anyway—' and put it to one side.

With a beating heart he went out of the house, whistling.

# Morley Callaghan

MORLEY Edward Callaghan, born in Toronto in 1903, was educated at St Michael's College, University of Toronto, and studied
law at Osgoode Hall. He was called to the bar in 1928, the same
year he met Maxwell Perkins of Scribner's Sons, who bought three
short stories for *Scribner's Magazine* and agreed to publish Callaghan's first novel, *Strange Fugitive* (1928), as well as a book of short
stories, *A Native Argosy*, which appeared in 1929. Callaghan married Loretto Dee in April of that year, and the couple travelled to
Paris, where they associated with Scott Fitzgerald, Robert Mac-
Almon, and Ernest Hemingway, whom Callaghan had met in 1923
when both men worked on the Toronto *Daily Star*. Callaghan has
recorded his Paris experience in *That Summer in Paris*, published in
1963 (for an excellent account of the literary and biographical
connections between Callaghan and Hemingway, see Fraser Suth-
erland's 1972 study, *The Style of Innocence*.)

While in Paris, Callaghan completed his second novel, *It's Never
Over*, and a novella, *No Man's Meat*, before returning to Toronto
via London and Dublin. He and his wife have lived in Toronto ever
since, and Callaghan has written hundreds of short stories and more
than a dozen novels, including *Such Is my Beloved* (1934), *They
Shall Inherit the Earth* (1934), *The Loved and the Lost* (which won
the Governor-General's award for fiction in 1951), and *More Joy in
Heaven* (1960). Outside Canada, Callaghan is best known for his
short stories, which have appeared in such magazines as the *New
Yorker*, *Esquire*, and *Scribner's*. In 1960, the late American critic
Edmund Wilson wrote in *O Canada*: 'Mr Callaghan's underplaying
of drama and the unemphatic tone of his style are accompanied by
a certain greyness of atmosphere, but this might also be said of
Chekhov, whose short stories his sometimes resemble.' Callaghan's
stories have helped bring about the transition in Canada from the
stilted colonialism of the nineteenth century to the modern, hard-
edged realism introduced in the States by the lost generation writers.

# A CAP FOR STEVE

DAVE DIAMOND, a poor man, a carpenter's assistant, was a small, wiry, quick-tempered individual who had learned how to make every dollar count in his home. His wife, Anna, had been sick a lot, and his twelve-year-old son, Steve, had to be kept in school. Steve, a big-eyed, shy kid, ought to have known the value of money as well as Dave did. It had been ground into him.

But the boy was crazy about baseball, and after school, when he could have been working as a delivery boy or selling papers, he played ball with the kids. His failure to appreciate that the family needed a few extra dollars disgusted Dave. Around the house he wouldn't let Steve talk about baseball, and he scowled when he saw him hurrying off with his glove after dinner.

When the Phillies came to town to play an exhibition game with the home team and Steve pleaded to be taken to the ball park, Dave, of course, was outraged. Steve knew they couldn't afford it. But he had got his mother on his side. Finally Dave made a bargain with them. He said that if Steve came home after school and worked hard helping to make some kitchen shelves he would take him that night to the ball park.

Steve worked hard, but Dave was still resentful. They had to coax him to put on his good suit. When they started out Steve held aloof, feeling guilty, and they walked down the street like strangers; then Dave glanced at Steve's face and, half-ashamed, took his arm more cheerfully.

As the game went on, Dave had to listen to Steve's recitation of the batting average of every Philly that stepped up to the plate; the time the boy must have wasted learning these averages began to appal him. He showed it so plainly that Steve felt guilty again and was silent.

After the game Dave let Steve drag him onto the field to keep him company while he tried to get some autographs from the Philly players, who were being hemmed in by gangs of kids blocking the way to the club-house. But Steve, who was shy, let the other kids block him off from the players. Steve would push his way in, get blocked out, and come back to stand mournfully beside Dave. And Dave grew impatient. He was wasting valuable time. He wanted to get home; Steve knew it and was worried.

Then the big, blond Philly outfielder, Eddie Condon, who had been held up by a gang of kids tugging at his arm and thrusting their score cards at him, broke loose and made a run for the club-house. He was jostled, and his blue cap with the red peak, tilted far back on his head, fell off. It fell at Steve's feet, and Steve stooped quickly and grabbed it. 'Okay, son,' the outfielder called, turning back. But Steve, holding the hat in both hands, only stared at him.

'Give him his cap, Steve,' Dave said, smiling apologetically at the big outfielder who towered over them. But Steve drew the hat closer to his chest. In an awed trance he looked up at big Eddie Condon. It was an embarrassing movement. All the other kids were watching. Some shouted. 'Give him his cap.'

'My cap, son,' Eddie Condon said, his hand out.

'Hey, Steve,' Dave said, and he gave him a shake. But he had to jerk the cap out of Steve's hands.

'Here you are,' he said.

The outfielder, noticing Steve's white, worshipping face and pleading eyes, grinned and then shrugged. 'Aw, let him keep it,' he said.

'No, Mister Condon, you don't need to do that,' Steve protested.

'It's happened before. Forget it,' Eddie Condon said, and he trotted away to the club-house.

Dave handed the cap to Steve; envious kids circled around them and Steve said, 'He said I could keep it, Dad. You heard him, didn't you?'

'Yeah, I heard him,' Dave admitted. The wonder in Steve's face made him smile. He took the boy by the arm and they hurried off the field.

On the way home Dave couldn't get him to talk about the game; he couldn't get him to take his eyes off the cap. Steve could hardly believe in his own happiness. 'See,' he said suddenly, and he showed Dave that Eddie Condon's name was printed on the sweat-band. Then he went on dreaming. Finally he put the cap on his head and turned to Dave with a slow, proud smile. The cap was away too big for him; it fell down over his ears. 'Never mind,' Dave said. 'You can get your mother to take a tuck in the back.'

When they got home Dave was tired and his wife didn't understand the cap's importance, and they couldn't get Steve to go to bed. He swaggered around wearing the cap and looking in the mirror every ten minutes. He took the cap to bed with him.

Dave and his wife had a cup of coffee in the kitchen, and Dave told her again how they had got the cap. They agreed that their boy must have an attractive quality that showed in his face, and that Eddie Condon must have been drawn to him—why else would he have singled Steve out from all the kids?

But Dave got tired of the fuss Steve made over that cap and of the way he wore it from the time he got up in the morning until the time he went to bed. Some kid was always coming in, wanting to try on the cap. It was childish, Dave said, for Steve to go around assuming that the cap made him important in the neighbourhood, and to keep telling them how he had become a leader in the park a few blocks away where he played ball in the evenings. And Dave wouldn't stand for Steve's keeping the cap on while he was eating. He was always scolding his wife for accepting Steve's explanation that he'd forgotten he had it on. Just the same, it was remarkable what a little thing like a ball cap could do for a kid, Dave admitted to his wife as he smiled to himself.

One night Steve was late coming home from the park. Dave didn't realize how late it was until he put down his newspaper and watched his wife at the window. Her restlessness got on his nerves. 'See what comes from encouraging the boy to hang around with those park loafers,' he said. 'I don't encourage him,' she protested. 'You do,' he insisted irritably, for he was really worried now. A gang hung around the park until midnight. It was a bad park. It was true that on one side there was a good district with fine, expensive apartment houses, but the kids from that neighbourhood left the park to the kids from the poorer homes. When his wife went out and walked down to the corner it was his turn to wait and worry and watch at the open window. Each waiting moment tortured him. At last he heard his wife's voice and Steve's voice, and he relaxed and sighed; then he remembered his duty and rushed angrily to meet them.

'I'll fix you, Steve, once and for all,' he said. 'I'll show you you can't start coming into the house at midnight.'

'Hold your horses, Dave,' his wife said. 'Can't you see the state he's in?' Steve looked utterly exhausted and beaten.

'What's the matter?' Dave asked quickly.

'I lost my cap,' Steve whispered; he walked past his father and threw himself on the couch in the living-room and lay with his face hidden.

'Now, don't scold him, Dave,' his wife said.

'Scold him. Who's scolding him?' Dave asked, indignantly. 'It's his cap, not mine. If it's not worth his while to hang on to it, why should I scold him?' But he was implying resentfully that he alone recognized the cap's value.

'So you are scolding him,' his wife said. 'It's his cap. Not yours. What happened, Steve?'

Steve told them he had been playing ball and he found that when he ran the bases the cap fell off; it was still too big despite the tuck his mother had taken in the band. So the next time he came to bat he tucked the cap in his hip pocket. Someone had lifted it, he was sure.

'And he didn't even know whether it was still in his pocket,' Dave said sarcastically.

'I wasn't careless, Dad,' Steve said. For the last three hours he had been wandering around to the homes of the kids who had been in the park at the time; he wanted to go on, but he was too tired. Dave knew the boy was apologizing to him, but he didn't know why it made him angry.

'If he didn't hang on to it, it's not worth worrying about now,' he said, and he sounded offended.

After that night they knew that Steve didn't go to the park to play ball; he went to look for the cap. It irritated Dave to see him sit around listlessly, or walk in circles, trying to force his memory to find a particular incident which would suddenly recall to him the moment when the cap had been taken. It was no attitude for a growing, healthy boy to take, Dave complained. He told Steve firmly once and for all he didn't want to hear any more about the cap.

One night, two weeks later, Dave was walking home with Steve from the shoemaker's. It was a hot night. When they passed an ice-cream parlour Steve slowed down. 'I guess I couldn't have a soda, could I?' Steve said. 'Nothing doing,' Dave said firmly. 'Come on now,' he added as Steve hung back, looking in the window.

'Dad, look!' Steve cried suddenly, pointing at the window. 'My cap! There's my cap! He's coming out!'

A well-dressed boy was leaving the ice-cream parlour; he had on a blue ball cap with a red peak, just like Steve's cap. 'Hey, you!' Steve cried, and he rushed at the boy, his small face fierce and his eyes wild. Before the boy could back away Steve had snatched the cap from his head. 'That's my cap!' he shouted.

'What's this?' the bigger boy said. 'Hey, give me my cap or I'll give you a poke on the nose.'

Dave was surprised that his own shy boy did not back away. He watched him clutch the cap in his left hand, half crying with excitement as he put his head down and drew back his right fist: he was willing to fight. And Dave was proud of him.

'Wait, now,' Dave said. 'Take it easy, son,' he said to the other boy, who refused to back away.

'My boy says it's his cap,' Dave said.

'Well, he's crazy. It's my cap.'

'I was with him when he got this cap. When the Phillies played here. It's a Philly cap.'

'Eddie Condon gave it to me,' Steve said. 'And you stole it from me, you jerk.'

'Don't call me a jerk, you little squirt. I never saw you before in my life.'

'Look,' Steve said, pointing to the printing on the cap's sweatband. 'It's Eddie Condon's cap. See? See, Dad?'

'Yeah. You're right, Son. Ever see this boy before, Steve?'

'No,' Steve said reluctantly.

The other boy realized he might lose the cap. 'I bought it from a guy,' he said. 'I paid him. My father knows I paid him.' He said he got the cap at the ball park. He groped for some magically impressive words and suddenly found them. 'You'll have to speak to my father,' he said.

'Sure, I'll speak to your father,' Dave said. 'What's your name? Where do you live?'

'My name's Hudson. I live about ten minutes away on the other side of the park.' The boy appraised Dave, who wasn't any bigger than he was and who wore a faded blue windbreaker and no tie. 'My father is a lawyer,' he said boldly. 'He wouldn't let me keep the cap if he didn't think I should.'

'Is that a fact?' Dave asked belligerently. 'Well, we'll see. Come on. Let's go.' And he got between the two boys and they walked along the street. They didn't talk to each other. Dave knew the Hudson boy was waiting to get to the protection of his home, and Steve knew it, too, and he looked up apprehensively at Dave. And Dave, reaching for his hand, squeezed it encouragingly and strode along, cocky and belligerent, knowing that Steve relied on him.

The Hudson boy lived in that row of fine apartment houses on the other side of the park. At the entrance to one of these houses

Dave tried not to hang back and show he was impressed, because he could feel Steve hanging back. When they got into the small elevator Dave didn't know why he took off his hat. In the carpeted hall on the fourth floor the Hudson boy said, 'Just a minute,' and entered his own apartment. Dave and Steve were left alone in the corridor, knowing that the other boy was preparing his father for the encounter. Steve looked anxiously at his father, and Dave said, 'Don't worry, Son,' and he added resolutely, 'No one's putting anything over on us.'

A tall, balding man in a brown velvet smoking-jacket suddenly opened the door. Dave had never seen a man wearing one of these jackets, although he had seen them in department-store windows. 'Good evening,' he said, making a deprecatory gesture at the cap Steve still clutched tightly in his left hand. 'My boy didn't get your name. My name is Hudson.'

'Mine's Diamond.'

'Come on in,' Mr Hudson said, putting out his hand and laughing good-naturedly. He led Dave and Steve into his living-room. 'What's this about that cap?' he asked. 'The way kids can get excited about a cap. Well, it's understandable, isn't it?'

'So it is,' Dave said, moving closer to Steve, who was awed by the broadloom rug and the fine furniture. He wanted to show Steve he was at ease himself, and he wished Mr Hudson wouldn't be so polite. That meant Dave had to be polite and affable, too, and it was hard to manage when he was standing in the middle of the floor in his old windbreaker.

'Sit down, Mr Diamond,' Mr Hudson said. Dave took Steve's arm and sat him down beside him on the chesterfield. The Hudson boy watched his father. And Dave looked at Steve and saw that he wouldn't face Mr Hudson or the other boy; he kept looking up at Dave, putting all his faith in him.

'Well, Mr Diamond, from what I gathered from my boy, you're able to prove this cap belonged to your boy.'

'That's a fact,' Dave said.

'Mr Diamond, you'll have to believe my boy bought that cap from some kid in good faith.'

'I don't doubt it,' Dave said. 'But no kid can sell something that doesn't belong to him. You know that's a fact, Mr Hudson.'

'Yes, that's a fact,' Mr Hudson agreed. 'But that cap means a lot to my boy, Mr Diamond.'

'It means a lot to my boy, too, Mr Hudson.'

'Sure it does. But supposing we called in a policeman. You know what he'd say? He'd ask you if you were willing to pay my boy what he paid for the cap. That's usually the way it works out,' Mr Hudson said, friendly and smiling, as he eyed Dave shrewdly.

'But that's not right. It's not justice,' Dave protested. 'Not when it's my boy's cap.'

'I know it isn't right. But that's what they do.'

'All right. What did you say your boy paid for the cap?' Dave said reluctantly.

'Two dollars.'

'Two dollars!' Dave repeated. Mr Hudson's smile was still kindly, but his eyes were shrewd, and Dave knew that the lawyer was counting on his not having the two dollars; Mr Hudson thought he had Dave sized up; he had looked at him and decided he was broke. Dave's pride was hurt, and he turned to Steve. What he saw in Steve's face was more powerful than the hurt to his pride; it was the memory of how difficult it had been to get an extra nickel, the talk he heard about the cost of food, the worry in his mother's face as she tried to make ends meet, and the bewildered embarrassment that he was here in a rich man's home, forcing his father to confess that he couldn't afford to spend two dollars. Then Dave grew angry and reckless. 'I'll give you the two dollars,' he said.

Steve looked at the Hudson boy and grinned brightly. The Hudson boy watched his father.

'I suppose that's fair enough,' Mr Hudson said. 'A cap like this can be worth a lot to a kid. You know how it is. Your boy might want to sell—I mean be satisfied. Would he take five dollars for it?'

'Five dollars?' Dave repeated. 'Is it worth five dollars, Steve?' he asked uncertainly.

Steve shook his head and looked frightened.

'No, thanks, Mr Hudson,' Dave said firmly.

'I'll tell you what I'll do,' Mr Hudson said. 'I'll give you ten dollars. The cap has a sentimental value for my boy, a Philly cap, a big-leaguer's cap. It's only worth about a buck and a half really,' he added. But Dave shook his head again. Mr Hudson frowned. He looked at his own boy with indulgent concern, but now he was embarrassed. 'I'll tell you what I'll do,' he said. 'This cap—well, it's worth as much as a day at the circus to my boy. Your boy should be recompensed. I want to be fair. Here's twenty dollars,' and he held out two ten-dollar bills to Dave.

That much money for a cap, Dave thought, and his eyes brightened. But he knew what the cap had meant to Steve; to deprive him of it now that it was within his reach would be unbearable. All the things he needed in his life gathered around him; his wife was there, saying he couldn't afford to reject the offer, he had no right to do it; and he turned to Steve to see if Steve thought it wonderful that the cap could bring them twenty dollars.

'What do you say, Steve?' he asked uneasily.

'I don't know,' Steve said. He was in a trance. When Dave smiled, Steve smiled too, and Dave believed that Steve was as impressed as he was, only more bewildered, and maybe even more aware that they could not possibly turn away that much money for a ball cap.

'Well, here you are,' Mr Hudson said, and he put the two bills in Steve's hand. 'It's a lot of money. But I guess you had a right to expect as much.'

With a dazed, fixed smile Steve handed the money slowly to his father, and his face was white.

Laughing jovially, Mr Hudson led them to the door. His own boy followed a few paces behind.

In the elevator Dave took the bills out of his pocket. 'See, Stevie,' he whispered eagerly. 'That windbreaker you wanted! And ten dollars for your bank! Won't Mother be surprised?'

'Yeah,' Steve whispered, the little smile still on his face. But Dave had to turn away quickly so their eyes wouldn't meet, for he saw that it was a scared smile.

Outside, Dave said, 'Here, you carry the money home, Steve. You show it to your mother.'

'No, you keep it,' Steve said, and then there was nothing to say. They walked in silence.

'It's a lot of money,' Dave said finally. When Steve didn't answer him, he added angrily, 'I turned to you, Steve. I asked you, didn't I?'

'That man knew how much his boy wanted that cap,' Steve said.

'Sure. But he recognized how much it was worth to us.'

'No, you let him take it away from us,' Steve blurted.

'That's unfair,' Dave said. 'Don't dare say that to me.'

'I don't want to be like you,' Steve muttered, and he darted across the road and walked along on the other side of the street.

'It's unfair,' Dave said angrily, only now he didn't mean that Steve was unfair, he meant that what had happened in the prosperous Hudson home was unfair, and he didn't know quite why. He had been trapped, not just by Mr Hudson, but by his own life. Across the road Steve was hurrying along with his head down, wanting to be alone. They walked most of the way home on opposite sides of the street, until Dave could stand it no longer. 'Steve,' he called, crossing the street. 'It was very unfair. I mean, for you to say . . . ' but Steve started to run. Dave walked as fast as he could and Steve was getting beyond him, and he felt enraged and suddenly he yelled, 'Steve!' and he started to chase his son. He wanted to get hold of Steve and pound him, and he didn't know why. He gained on him, he gasped for breath and he almost got him by the shoulder. Turning, Steve saw his father's face in the street light and was terrified; he circled away, got to the house, and rushed in, yelling, 'Mother!'

'Son, Son!' she cried, rushing from the kitchen. As soon as she threw her arms around Steve, shielding him, Dave's anger left him and he felt stupid. He walked past them into the kitchen.

'What happened?' she asked anxiously. 'Have you both gone crazy? What did you do, Steve?'

'Nothing,' he said sullenly.

'What did your father do?'

'We found the boy with my ball cap, and he let the boy's father take it from us.'

'No, no,' Dave protested. 'Nobody pushed us around. The man didn't put anything over us.' He felt tired and his face was burning. He told what had happened; then he slowly took the two ten-dollar bills out of his wallet and tossed them on the table and looked up guiltily at his wife.

It hurt him that she didn't pick up the money, and that she didn't rebuke him. 'It is a lot of money, Son,' she said slowly. 'Your father was only trying to do what he knew was right, and it'll work out, and you'll understand.' She was soothing Steve, but Dave knew she felt that she needed to be gentle with him, too, and he was ashamed.

When she went with Steve to his bedroom, Dave sat by himself. His son had contempt for him, he thought. His son, for the first time, had seen how easy it was for another man to handle him, and he had judged him and had wanted to walk alone on the other side of the street. He looked at the money and he hated the sight of it.

His wife returned to the kitchen, made a cup of tea, talked

soothingly, and said it was incredible that he had forced the Hudson man to pay him twenty dollars for the cap, but all Dave could think of was Steve was scared of me.

Finally, he got up and went into Steve's room. The room was in darkness, but he could see the outline of Steve's body on the bed, and he sat down beside him and whispered, 'Look, Son, it was a mistake. I know why. People like us—in circumstances where money can scare us. No, no,' he said, feeling ashamed and shaking his head apologetically; he was taking the wrong way of showing the boy they were together; he was covering up his own failure. For the failure had been his, and it had come out of being so separated from his son that he had been blind to what was beyond the price in a boy's life. He longed now to show Steve he could be with him from day to day. His hand went out hesitantly to Steve's shoulder. 'Steve, look,' he said eagerly. 'The trouble was I didn't realize how much I enjoyed it that night at the ball park. If I had watched you playing for your own team—the kids around here say you could be a great pitcher. We could take that money and buy a new pitcher's glove for you, and a catcher's mitt. Steve, Steve, are you listening? I could catch you, work with you in the lane. Maybe I could be your coach . . . watch you become a great pitcher.' In the half-darkness he could see the boy's pale face turn to him.

Steve, who had never heard his father talk like this, was shy and wondering. All he knew was that his father, for the first time, wanted to be with him in his hopes and adventures. He said, 'I guess you do know how important that cap was.' His hand went out to his father's arm. 'With that man the cap was—well it was just something he could buy, eh Dad?' Dave gripped his son's hand hard. The wonderful generosity of childhood—the price a boy was willing to pay to be able to count on his father's admiration and approval—made him feel humble, then strangely exalted.

# Malcolm Lowry

CLARENCE Malcolm Lowry was born July 28, 1909, in Liscard, Cheshire, England, the son of a well-to-do Methodist cotton broker. At eighteen, Lowry shipped aboard the SS *Pyrrhus* from Liverpool to Asia as a cabin boy, an experience he later recorded in his first novel, *Ultramarine* (1933). Upon his return he entered St Catherine's College, Cambridge, graduated with a third in English in 1933, and once again began travelling. In Paris he met Jan Gabrial, a friend of Conrad Aiken (whom Lowry had visited in Cambridge, Mass., in 1929 and with whom Lowry had a lifelong—though stormy—friendship). In 1934 Lowry and Jan were married; briefly, for the following year Lowry had himself admitted to the Bellevue Hospital in New York for treatment as an alcoholic. In 1936 Jan joined him in Los Angeles, and the two journeyed to Cuernavaca, Mexico, where Lowry began his most famous novel, *Under the Volcano* (1945). Jan finally left him in Mexico City, and Lowry returned to Hollywood, where he met the novelist Margerie Bonner in 1939. The following year, in Vancouver, Lowry and Margerie were married, and they settled in a small cabin near Dollarton, British Columbia, where they spent the next fourteen years. In 1954 the couple left Vancouver and lived for a short time in Italy and London. On June 27, 1957, in Ripe, Sussex, after a heavy bout of drinking, Lowry choked to death in his sleep.

Lowry left a stack of unfinished manuscripts, many of which have been edited and published by his widow. These include the novels *Lunar Caustic, Dark as the Grave Wherein My Friend Is Laid*, and *October Ferry to Gabriola*, which with *Under the Volcano* were to have formed part of a seven-novel sequence to be called *The Voyage That Never Ends*. A volume of short stories, *Hear Us O Lord From Heaven Thy Dwelling Place* ('less a book of short stories,' Lowry wrote to a friend in 1953, 'than—God help us —yet *another* kind of novel'), won the Governor-General's award for fiction in 1961. The following story, originally intended for *Hear Us O Lord*, did not appear until 1973, when it was published in *The American Review* #17.

# GHOSTKEEPER

Alternate titles:

Henrik Ghostkeeper
Lost and Found
I Walk in the Park
But Who Else Walks in the Park?
O.K. But What Does it Mean?
Wheels Within Wheels

'WHAT TIME is it, Tommy?'

'I don't know, sweetheart, have you forgotten I haven't got my watch now?'

'Do you remember the time we took the alarm clock on the picnic?'

'We should have brought the alarm clock along with us on our walk today.'

'I guess it's about three. It was about quarter to when we left the apartment.'

'Anyhow, we'll be able to see the clocktower in town when we get round the other side of the park.'

The two figures, the man and his wife, continued their walk in Stanley Park, in Vancouver, British Columbia. To their right, people were playing tennis, though it was winter; in fact, to be precise, it was February 5, 1952. There was a fine rough wind, steel blue sea, mountains of rough blue serge topped with snow in the distance. The path they followed had the delicious sense of an English public footpath. Beyond the tennis courts there were dark pines and weeping willows, like fountains of gold thread, when the sun struck them, or bronze harp strings when it didn't. Here at sea level the snow had melted from the ground and early snowdrops were showing faintly under the trees. First they descended to a path that followed the seashore almost on shorelevel, just under the high bank of the park. There was much driftwood on the beach, evidence of winter storms. One cedar snag seemed scooped out by the sea, as if some Indians had started to make a war canoe out of it.

A woman, skirt tucked up, was sitting on a rock in the sun and wind. Someone, ahead of them, where the beach was less cluttered with driftwood, was even swimming, then running up and down the beach in the below freezing temperature. (The point of all this is a certain duality of appearance in the picture: which balances the duality within of the theme, and of existence. The picture was wintry, but it is also summery. This is like a nightmare, but it is also extremely pleasant.)

Stepping over winterbournes the man and his wife had to go up on the embankment again. A hoodlum went screeching by in a car: *threat.* The beach reminded the man of his birthplace, New Brighton, England (if this can be done, because one theme is, or should be, rebirth). At frequent intervals steps descended to the beach and a little further on they went down to the beach again. Above the trees were waving: a soft roaring of trees. Motionless gulls hung in a mackerel sky. The sea now was deserted: one barge, and a far cold lighthouse. (Note: somewhere: his grandfather had been named Henrik Goodheart, had gone down with his ship, a kind of Carlsen.)

And down there now, close under the bank, beneath the softly roaring pines, they found the wrecked boat. But what kind of a boat? On closer inspection it scarcely looked like a boat at all. Nearer, it looked like a wrecked paddlebox. Yet clearly, it was some sort of boat: Very narrow in the beam, blunt-nosed and blunt-sterned, about fifteen feet long, no paint left on it, salt-grey, battered, pock-marked, and it seemed about a hundred years old. It must have weighed God knows how much. However would they launch such a thing even to lee? A tremendous bilge keel, or bilge piece on both sides was what made one think of a paddlebox. But this boat was like a solid block, built into the sand, with sand instead of a bottom. A bolted stalwart formidable bottomless hulk, though externally solid and sturdy. On the starboard side at the bow something had been carved: No. 1. For 16 persons. A F 13/2/45, it looked like. And beneath this had been recently written in chalk: H. Ghostkeeper. At this point a wandering Englishman came up, he was wearing dark glasses and was blind, or nearly blind. Some such conversation as this ensues:

'What is it?'
'It's a lifeboat, I think.'
'Is it a clinker boat?'
'What's that?'

'The one with the laps.' He puts his hands on the boat. 'No, it's a carvel. What length is it? Has it got davit hooks?'

'Where would they be?'

'Down in the deadwood at each end. In the forepost and in the stern posts, if it's a lifeboat there'll be some gudgeons. Generally female gudgeons are on the stern post.'

'Why female?'

'Because it's a round hole. The males have a long pintle on them.'

'These numbers—would they be the date?'

'No, that'll be cubic capacity.'

'Queer it doesn't have a name. Or a port of register.'

'Well, it's a lifeboat all right.'

Or it strikes me as an alternative idea that the Englishman, instead of being blind, should recognize him, saying, 'Haven't I seen you somewhere before, seen your picture in the paper?' It would then devolve that Tom Goodheart's column, *I Walk in the Park*, is the Englishman's favourite column and the exposition can be easily handled in this way. But in any event, just as he is leaving, they ask him the time and he says: 'That's funny, I lost my watch yesterday.'

When he has gone Goodheart makes an entry in his notebook:

Coincidence of the Englishman not having a watch either. The wreck: symbol of something, perhaps bad omen. Or worse—presage of some catastrophe, or death of someone. Then he adds: trouble is, I can't describe it. Once I would have longed to, and gone to endless trouble to find out about the wreck. Now I don't want to bother. How shall I describe it?

(Point is, Goodheart is sick to death of the daily grind of five hundred words, wants to get out of the city and live in the country and do some creative writing, but can never manage to save up the money.)

Mem: bottle like a grebe below in the bay: the bottle almost had the iridescence of a bird's plumage: ethereal, sea-green, bobbing, swimming.

Mem: also the little turnstones, turning stones.

Mem: Perhaps begin the whole story with a suggestion of the ghostly ballet going on behind the blurred bon-amied windows on the old pier used by the Civic Repertory Theatre. Windows like store windows on the disused pier, though it has never been turned properly into a theatre and hasn't been used as a pier for twenty years. Packing cases standing about. In the office a notice, a picture of George V and a crown: Keep Calm and Carry On. The hall-echoing sound of an ill-tuned cottage piano. The dimly seen whirling figures and the dismal echoing and trampling of feet.

Now they pass a man reading a Spiritualist newspaper, with a headline saying: Policemen Pursue Poltergeist.

If not use Englishman, then at this point anyhow we must have exposition, perhaps in dialogue between the Goodhearts. Goodheart is a large, bearded man, and is a columnist on a city paper whose column is entitled *I Walk in the Park*. This is full of human interest stories or observations about nature, etc. and is very popular. Goodheart is extremely familiar with this park since he does indeed 'walk in the park,' to get most of his stories. Goodheart is an Englishman who has emigrated to Canada, his wife is an American, who doesn't think much of Canada and reminds Goodheart on every occasion that he is English. His wife, who is sympathetic in every other respect, and perhaps in this too, has no idea how she wounds Goodheart by these remarks, for her romantic teleologies are the reverse of his and directed toward Europe: for her, England and Europe are romantic and exciting, while to him, the European, it is the frontier, the wild country that is exotic and romantic. Goodheart has been trying to interest an American publisher in a book of short stories to be based on his feuilletons and has finally succeeded. But now, contrarily enough, he suddenly finds he can't write anything, his consciousness is at an agonized standstill; he can hardly write his column. This is at the time of Canada's beginning postwar boom and prosperity, when the Canadian dollar has passed the American dollar in foreign exchange and Americans are taking more interest in Canada. But it is partly this very 'boom' which is distressing Goodheart.

Meantime my protagonists have climbed up on the embankment again. Down below the wild ducks are rising and falling on the waves. Mary Goodheart is delighted with the pretty ducks and points them out: 'Oh look, darling, scaups, golden eyes, and there's even a pair of buffleheads! Do look!' But Goodheart is obsessed with a sense of tragedy about the lifeboat. It was a sort of nothing, yet it seemed ominous. A sense of something obsolescent, dead.

On the park embankment they are in the forest, and follow a narrow footpath between the huge trees. A few lone men pass them, walking, each with a cloud of smoke blowing over his shoulder, like little lone steamboats. Vancouver is full of lonely men like this and they all go walking along the beach or through the forest in Stanley Park.

Now Tommy Goodheart makes another note in his notebook:

Not sure he has any emotion at all about the lifeboat. Perhaps all he wanted to do was to describe it. Something like a sort of velleity of meaning is trying to possess him. Perhaps he felt like the lifeboat. Were they like the lifeboat? What was like the lifeboat? Was it a symbol of something, or just a lifeboat? To hell with it anyway. Then he added: It was important not to have any fraudulent sincerity about the lifeboat . . . as that fake Barzun calls it.

Out of the sky came a hushed roaring which was the trees. Now above them the half moon appeared, and Goodheart made another entry:

The afternoon half moon like an abstracted reading nun.

Trying to find an image for this moon gave Goodheart so much trouble that he couldn't bear to look at it, and he walked on looking at his feet.

Another man passes with an easel: smell of paints.

Mem: Flying Saucers must come in here: perhaps they pass a man sitting on a bench reading the newspaper: and read over his shoulder, or Mary does: 'Vincent Vallach, 1266 Harber Street, was on Strawberry Hill at 10:10 p.m. on Friday night. He saw a spot on the moon, but it started moving across the face of it, and then vanished straight up in the sky, with several other small dots following.'

Mrs Goodheart must be placed as a tiny, pretty woman, all but hidden in your sweet spooky grey costume, Margie dear. She is a very sympathetic character if sometimes tactless, the two have a fine relationship, and she is very interested in nature, flowers, and particularly seabirds and wild ducks.

'A penny for them,' Mary said, taking Tom's arm and shaking it gently.

'I'm a Canadian writer, and that's tough.'

'Nonsense. You're not a Canadian.'

An argument now devolves, as another Englishman goes past, coatless, red-faced, wearing a loud checked vest, on Canada's origins. Mrs Goodheart is cynical.

'After they'd conquered it from the Indians, they colonized it to a large extent by emptying the jails in England, and picking up the riffraff from the streets and shipping them out, though no Canadian would admit it now.'

'Admit it!' Goodheart choked, then said, after a pause. 'And what about Virginia?'

'Oh, it's true, to some extent, in America, but not so much. I read that article too, where somebody was very clever debunking the FFVs. But it doesn't mean what he says is entirely true, any more than all Canadians are descended from convicts.'

Goodheart stopped dead for a moment, then said: 'Do you know, you hurt me. I'm English. I'm Canadian. But I'm not descended from a convict.'

'Oh Tom, how could you be when you just emigrated—'

'—And if I were descended from a convict and had been shipped out here—and how could I help it if I were—I would resent it.'

'So far as I can tell, most Canadians resent the English, no matter how sentimental they may be about England.'

Goodheart tried to follow the logic of this, then said: 'I know it doesn't mean anything to you but to me being an Englishman is a serious matter.'

'But you always say you're Canadian now—'

'This is absurd! But for me, it's tragic too.'

'Ah, tragedy. Why must there always be tragedy?'

'What are we talking about? I'm not English. I'm not Canadian. I am a British Columbian. Ever since I was a kid and collected stamps I have been in love with British Columbia. It had its own stamp once. And I made up my mind to come here, and here I am. I do not recognize Confederation. I deplore American influence. But I also deplore Canadian influence. I am unique, the only British Columbian in British Columbia! Keep Calm and Carry on,' he added.

They laughed and kissed. They had very tender feelings toward each other and did not pursue this ridiculous argument. He made another note as they walked along:

Perhaps moon is omen too.

They came to Siwash Rock: a lonely storm beaten pine tree in the rock, beards of grass. He feels an empathy for the lone tree. Gulls are sailing high. Scoters and scaups in the water below. Higher up, on a topped pine, was a kind of tree house, a loggers' contraption or a look out perhaps.

'Shall we sit down?'

'For God's sake let us sit upon the ground—' Goodheart said.

But the seat was wet and they walked on. (Perhaps there is a crash, they look round, and the loggers' tree house has fallen bang on to the bench where they thought of sitting.)

Then they came to Prospect Point.

Latitude: 49° 18′ 51″

Longitude: 123° 08′ 24″

Above Sea Level: 220 ft.

—Crown Mountain: 4,931 ft. 7 miles.

—Goat Mountain: 4,587 ft. 6.75 miles.

—Grouse Mountain: 3,974 ft. 5.08 miles.

—Second Narrows: 5.45 miles.

Far below an oiltanker, seemingly as long as the park, is sailing by endlessly into Vancouver. With the scarlet and white paintwork all tiddley, her flags flying, it was like an entire promenade in summer in, say New Brighton, gliding by silently, bandstands, ham and egg walks, flagstaffs and all.

They walked on, through a neck of forest and out into a cleared space. A sign read: *Bears. Rose Garden. Pavilion. Garden of Remembrance. Children's Zoo.* Nearly all the trees in the park were topped, giving them a queer bisected look. A heron, antediluvian, meditated aloft upon one topped tree. Mandarin ducks, as if constructed out of sheets of tin or metal, that fitted into one another, painted with gold, sat about on the grass. Peacocks drowsed in the trees. Squirrels ran about. Pigeons feeding from people's hands. A tame dove. A sense of something unearthly, heavenly here, like Paradise in a Flemish painting. Pilgrims wandering here and there among the trees.

Mem: Important: Use Margie's note here about the young Frenchman and his watch. (This note follows)

'—Pardon, but would you like to buy my watch?'

He was very young, nineteen or twenty, tall, thin, blond with hazel or yellow eyes and a meticulously shaven fresh bright face; his smile was clear as a child's except for a certain faint humorous wry curl at the corner of his rather wide but beautifully cut mouth, above a chin that was almost feminine but not weak. His gaze was direct, candid and sparkling. One liked this boy at once. He wore a belted tan raincoat, of a silky texture, that didn't look very warm. It was a cold frosty day with a rough cold wind, the already low sun was a freezing blurred orange and here, at the waterfront, the streets and the bay were dim and opalescent with cold evening mist. He pushed up his sleeve and showed us a beautiful and expensive gold Swiss watch. Malc, a bit taken aback between his desire to help, lack of money, and imaginative sensitiveness, gave me a swift, baffled, imploring blank look. I said quickly:

'I wish we could, but we're rather broke ourselves this week.'

'Next week,' said Malc, giving him a beautiful warm smile, which the boy returned, 'we'll have some money, but by then, I—'

'Next week,' the boy shrugged, 'I cannot wait so—'

'Of course, you need it now.'

'It is a good watch. I bought in Paris.'

'You're French—'

'*Oui.*'

'*Le prochain demain*—'

'*Ah! vous parlez français!*'

'*Oui. Un peu.*'

'*Ah*—' His face glowed.

'We were in Paris—how long, Margie?'

'Four years ago. We were there over a year.' An instant's silence, then:

'It is a good country, France.'

'We love it.'

'I am not long in Canada. I am—new.'

'You are an immigrant, you are going to stay here, in Canada?' I said.

'*Pardon?*—Ah, *oui*. I am immigrant. I shall stay. I have been working in a camp, but is closed, when after the New Year I go back.'

'Oh, a logging camp.'

'*Pardon?*—Ah oui. They are logs. But I cannot get your insurance for not employment until I am three weeks not employed.'

'What will you do?'

'Oh, I will sell my watch.' A light Gallic shrug. 'And then I will be O.K.'

'But what a pity!'

Another shrug. Yes it was sad, but then—

We all shook hands warmly. Good luck! Thank you. We admired the watch. One didn't—couldn't—feel any pathos in this, he was obviously too full of adventure and youth and a sort of wry yet open-hearted joyous, light-hearted, casual, Gallic, resigned, active happiness. Off he went, and we the other way.

They walked back to Lost Lagoon through a sort of inside zoo. This on the contrary was a sort of hell. Songbirds in cages. An owl gave a pathetic mew. A hamster, like a minute chipmunk, worked a toy mill furiously in the corner, though he stopped when he thought anyone was watching him. An anteater, with elephant head and long suede nose, in which were shoe-button eyes, walking on the backs of its hands, with a raccoon coat and stuff tail like the backbone of a fish.

'I can't bear to look at that,' said Mary Goodheart; but Tom made a mysterious note:

Could get anteater at home. Why go out? Perhaps while he is doing that he returns an almost blind man's watch. The man had been winding it and it had fallen out of his hands and Goodheart picked it up and returned it almost absently, though perhaps he didn't notice the time. But he was thinking of how different this would all look soon, in spring, and the pathetic love of the anteaters for each other.

Then they emerged on the right side of Lost Lagoon. Ducks against neon lights coming in downmoon to taxi, sunsetwards, in Lost Lagoon. An advertisement for Segovia. An advertisement for *The Town Crier* (Tom's paper). Platinum street lamps bloomed. They walked along the edge of the lagoon, remote from the town, into the sunset behind the gold thread of the weeping willows, beyond which was the shore where they had started out for their walk. They kept trying to avoid pools left by the recently melted snow. A man came up behind them and squelched right through the pools, wearing sea-boots whose white tops were turned down, looking neither left nor right. To their left, as the day deepened, the ducks were preparing to turn in for the night. Some like sailing ships blown too near to coast in a sou-wester already had their beaks nestled in their plumage. Two little buffleheads—spirit ducks—were doing a little last minute hunting. And a harmless muskrat cruised peacefully beneath the bank and when they stooped down begged like a puppy. Sense of love between the Goodhearts. But also sense of loneliness; of Goodheart, his sense of isolation, partly occasioned by his being an Englishman, from other human beings. Their feeling of love for the ducks. The ducks are indeed their only real companions in British Columbia. There is a notice: *Do Not Molest the Ducks*. The coots, ivory-billed, squat, awkward and raucous, make a noise like twanging guitar strings (Segovia tuning his guitar), they jerk along, while the mallards sweep easily to their berths. It was touching to see the ducks here, safe and protected in the lagoon, and they wondered how many had come in from the sea where they'd been feeding this afternoon, or were the ones they'd seen earlier. The wind was dropping now at sunset and became a cool, cold, sweet, wet wind. There would be rain tonight, Mary said, sniffing the wind.

The pear-shaped lagoon now narrowed to a kind of rustic canal or neck that connected with the shipless bay beyond, bridged by little arched rustic bridges, exquisitely beautiful. There were still a few chunks of snow to the right in a gulch. A tossed bicycle, like a freak of crumpled ice, pedals, sprockets, by the edge of the lagoon. In this narrower part of the lagoon a whole fleet of ducks were sailing. A magic tin Mandarin duck in the sunset light. On the opposite bank beneath the willows, against the sunset, three children were standing like a threat. Mary was feeding peanuts to the ducks. It took Goodheart some little time to understand why the children had seemed to him like a threat, which was the word that had instantly come to mind. But then he realized they were doing something inconceivable. They had suddenly started to throw stones at the massed ducks.

There were two boys, one short and rather stout—but on the other side of the water, some twenty feet away—one thin and lanky, and a tall girl with red hair wearing blue jeans rolled up to the ankle, none looking more than fifteen. And they were throwing stones at the ducks, massed as for a regatta. The fat boy was skimming stones, and the tall one was throwing them very high, and as he watched one dropped on a duck's back; the poor things skimmed and flew in every direction. Bloody murder was in Goodheart's heart but he found he could only gulp and it was his wife who spoke.

'You boys!' she was saying. 'How dare you throw stones at the ducks!'

'Aw.'

'Stop it at once!'

'Aw, we just want to see them fly.'

'How would you like it if people threw stones at you, just to see you run?'

'Aw, we've heard that one before.'

Goodheart was so upset that he was tongue-tied. Anguish trees stood about the suicide lake, apprehension bushes were dotted here and there; and a fear wind rushed through him, depriving him of speech. And that all these emotions were vastly in excess of the situation, which merely demanded a few stern fatherly words—but words which he couldn't deliver—made his anguish worse than ever by frustrating him. A car's horn pealed like cathedral bells for a funeral. Then he just stood there feeling himself simply like an old buttoned up overcoat. But meantime, though more aimlessly, the boys went on throwing stones at the ducks. Finally he said:

'Don't you know it's illegal to throw stones at the ducks? Can't you read that sign?'

Flop! For answer the tall boy skied a stone that landed near a mallard and would have killed it had it not missed.

'Aw, we're not hurting them.'

'Then what are you throwing stones at them for?' Goodheart heard his overcoat speaking.

'We just want to see them flyyyyy,' the boys sneered.

'And anyway, what's it to do with you, you old bastard,' the red haired girl asked sotto voce; the question was followed by giggles.

'If you don't stop throwing stones I'll have you run in, you, taller one,' shouted Goodheart, suddenly losing his temper. He did not like being called an old bastard, for he was not old, but perhaps his beard was at fault.

'One more stone and I'll get a policeman,' Mary said, shaking with fury. 'I won't have anyone hurting the ducks!'

'Aw, go wonn . . .'

'And I'm well known in this town . . .' Goodheart hardly knew what he was saying, 'I'm on a newspaper . . .'

'Beaver!' they shouted at him. 'Beaver!'

They really stopped throwing stones at the ducks, though they pretended to go on skimming them for a while. Mr and Mrs Goodheart now deployed to the right slightly in order to cross the Japanese bridge which brought them abreast of the boys on the same side of the water, Goodheart looking through the trees, trying to make his overcoat appear menacing, and himself like a policeman. As the children sidled away Goodheart threw after them:

'God will punish you for this.' (I think there should be an almost Laurentian analysis here, unsentimental, un-SPCA, of what such cruelty *feels* like: it was as if they were throwing stones at them, at their own love, their home, a feeling of 'But they don't *understand*')

Mary Goodheart began to laugh at her husband's portentousness, and so did Tom Goodheart, though a tear had run down his face and in fact they were very upset and hesitant which route to take (for they truly loved the ducks) in case the children should return: whether to continue this path till it crossed the bridle path that came to the stables, or walk through the miniature golf course: either way would bring them back to their apartment. They go by the bridle path and Mrs Goodheart finds the watch.

(Mem: seagull roosting in the crotch of a tree: Tchekov's Seagull —and coincidence and tragic coincidence of this.)

Description of the watch: it seems a very good man's watch, gold, and still running. In fact it said quarter past six. The boys seemed ruled out. There was a boy now walking behind them. Psychological attitude towards watch: Goodheart had no watch (he'd lost his last one and couldn't afford another), also this is a valuable watch, a wristwatch with the clasp broken. The watch had a name on the back though it was difficult to see beneath the trees in the declining day. Goldkipfer, Goalkeeper, it looked like. But it is a man's watch and they do not connect it with the children. As they reach the street:

'Well, we can wait and see if there's an advertisement for it in tomorrow night's paper. Or tomorrow morning. Then, if nobody puts an advertisement in, you've got a watch.'

It was certainly a temptation. Moreover the watch was clearly worth a hundred dollars.

'Oughtn't *we* to put an advertisement in the paper?' Goodheart said.

'We can't afford to. We haven't got five dollars to pitch away on an advertisement. If anybody wants it back enough they'll advertise.'

'And you mean that we should hang on to the watch? Isn't that being a bit unscrupulous? By gad, aren't you a bit of a hypocrite, Mary. Here a while ago you were accusing us Canadians of being criminals and now you're proposing to steal a watch.'

'Steal it! Must you exaggerate everything?'

A minor quarrel ensues, during which Goodheart feels that he's being a bit of a hypocrite because it had been in his mind to keep the watch himself and even perhaps pawn it, which would have temporarily gotten him out of a hole.

Outside their apartment door the Vancouver *Town Crier* is waiting for them on the floor in the hall. And inside there is a dramatic moment when, in the better light, they see the name on the watch is Henrik Ghostkeeper.

Then, though it seems a bit absurd to do so, they leaf through the *Crier* looking at the Lost and Found... Mr Haythornthwaite asked in the legislature what the government intended to do to prevent 'use of the knout by mounted cossacks on peaceful residents of Vancouver and to protect constitutional rights to peaceable assemblage and free speech.' But that was forty years ago. (Now such things were unknown: that is to say free speech was almost unknown, and of course they order twenty strokes of the lash instead of the knout.)

Under a heading What Right? Mother of Two asked:

May a Vancouver-born mother tell 'Irish' just what she thinks of a so-called 'uncivilized Easterner?' We think the majority of complaining, boasting, insulting people we have in Vancouver must be Easterners. How dare he call our children monsters? Perhaps 'Irish' has had the misfortune to run up against one or two badly behaved children. But just what right does that give him to call our children monsters? Mother of Two.

And that was today all right.

Bill Kath and family gone. Am very sick, all alone. Please come and see me, Skinny. And that was today too, but not in the Lost column, or not the right kind of Lost. But here it was: a twelve foot discharge hose with down pipe and coupling, lost, a brindle bulldog with red harness, a female Boxer pup (anyone harbouring after Feb 15 will be prosecuted), a front pillar shaped piece of wardrobe 5 ft long, and a wine bedroom slipper, lost between bus terminal and Richards. And no less than three watches reported lost.

Lady's gold oblong wristwatch, gold expansion bracelet, lost in Woodward's dept. store Friday. Reward. FA 3411R.

Lady's Bulova watch inscribed 'Vida' Saturday night. Reward. TA 2221.

And another watch lost in their neighbourhood cinema theatre, the Bay Theatre. Apart from that the only thing of interest was that Segovia had objected to a publicity story that a guitar he was playing in Coblenz had broken at the exact moment that it's maker had died in Granada.

But the name on the watch, Ghostkeeper, caused Goodheart to recall the name Ghostkeeper carved on the wreck, and also to recall that the Englishman who'd spoken to them by the wreck had also mentioned that he'd lost his watch. A certain terror also was occasioned by the name, Ghostkeeper. Goodheart privately decides if he returned the watch it will take the curse off the name. Goodheart now decides to try and telephone. So he looks in the telephone book for the strange name, meanwhile remarking the names he encounters are anything but English, save for his own, though it is important that the real reason he is phoning is a compassionate one: he has now decided, from the small span of the strap as it is clasped, that the owner must be a child. But Ghostkeeper was an unlikely name: but then so are these other names unlikely. So was Goodheart.

Zsomber, Zingg, Zero, Pe (Ralph G.) Poffenroth, Peckinpaugh, Pennycuick, Stilborn, Soderroos, Overho, Ovens, Snowball, Shelagh, Snodgrass, Smuck, Smout (he has ceased really looking, being fascinated by these names), Smook, Smitten, Stojcic, Shish, Order of Perceptive Praetorians, Orangecrush, Goodheart, Golf, Goggin, Goranko, Gooselaw, Gathercole—but here we were:

Ghostkeeper, Sigrid, Mrs r 4942 Ruby. DExter 1576 R.
Ghostkeeper, B. H. r 3655 W. 2nd. CEdar 7762.

He phones the second Ghostkeeper and this part is dramatized much as it happened, i.e., it is a female voice, who disclaims any ownership of the watch, but says that the Ghostkeepers must all be related, and that she has read in the paper that a Mrs Ghostkeeper has 'arrived from the east with her small boy.' (Mem: this ties in with 'Mother of Two.')

Before he phones the second Ghostkeeper they examine the watch again and Mary agrees that the owner must be a child. Suddenly it is as if Goodheart realizes for the first time that perhaps the owner of the watch really was the child who had been throwing stones at the duck, or one of the children, which is a dramatic moment, and he remembers how he has said portentously God will punish you. But Mary now says no, it is far too expensive a watch to be entrusted to a young child. Then Tom thinks well, damn it, it may be a girl.

Now they look at the watch: lilliputian universe, jewelled orrery, minuscule planetarium, it now said quarter past seven. And Mary remarked how its very compact, very busy, very efficient, in a fussy kind of way: so important, miniscule order, dragging along time with it (memo: work in ambiguous word *escapement* which is also part of a watch). It is a twenty-one jewel watch, comes from the U.S., not Canadian at all. Perhaps it belonged to yet another Ghostkeeper, an American, who'd come across the border . . . But the real point is, as they open it, that the reader feels that is the *thing*, the machine—

So now Goodheart rings up the first Ghostkeeper, Sigrid, who turns out also a woman, but who sounds somewhat older. This conversation is dramatized, as it occurred, punctuated by Mrs Goodheart's interpolations from the kitchen, where she is getting dinner—'Don't tell them what kind of watch it is—' 'Don't tell *them*, you ninny—' 'Make them tell *you*—'

But the scene should be beautifully funny and so unlikely that it has the unerring stamp of truth, viz: the husband is deaf. The woman is obviously not the widow with the small child, but a watch *is* involved here. The woman has to keep leaving the phone to relay the conversation to her husband, whose name is, to confound matters worse still, Henrik Ghostkeeper. This man says that there is yet another Ghostkeeper to whom he has given a watch when he was overseas. He had it overseas, says Mrs Ghostkeeper, but he gives the impression that this other Ghostkeeper is about nineteen.

Goodheart says he feels the owner is a child, which is why he's rung up, for the child must be grieving, or even being punished. Goodheart is now reproaching himself for not having walked back to the children with the watch, he feels now that one of the children is the owner, and had he done so it would have been both more dramatic and more of a lesson, should he have said: 'Is there anyone here by the name of Henrik Ghostkeeper?' 'Yes, that's me.' 'Have you lost anything? I told you not to throw stones at the ducks.' And then to have returned the watch. How salutary that would have been!

But it is relayed via the deaf Ghostkeeper that his nephew's name *is* Henrik Ghostkeeper, so Goodheart is convinced that he has his man, though his picture of him is a pretty weird one, that of an attenuated or hypertrophied unman of nineteen who had apparently been fighting overseas at the age of twelve.

'Does he have a phone?'

'No, I don't think so. But there's a phone in the house.'

'Can you get hold of them then.'

Mrs Ghostkeeper promises to find the nephew and have him call the Goodhearts. Tom leaves his address and phone number and Mrs Ghostkeeper tells them that the nephew lives at 33 E. 7th St.

There now follows a slight description of the scene outside our apartment: the terricular solid house opposite, now an hotel, sense of old order changeth, and—it is snowing lightly again—the chicken croquettes covered with powdered sugar in the blooming lamplight, the antediluvian monkey tree that still kept up its liaison with the prehistoric era. This little realistic beautiful description possibly combined with a description of the scene through the Venetian blinds with the street lamps and the snow is important contrast.

The Goodhearts now decide to try and discover the phone number of 33 E. 7th. They do so, but whoever answers the phone disclaims all knowledge of the Ghostkeepers. In fact they're irritated, and suspect some sort of joke.

The Goodhearts are now slightly fed up by the whole thing so after dinner they seek relaxation at their local cinema, the Bay, where there is an English film playing called *The Magnet*. They greet the box office girl and manager as neighbours and good acquaintances.

But as soon as they enter the cinema Tommy Goodheart thinks he has gone to the next world, is having a dream within a dream, or suffering from some extraordinary hallucination.

For the scene before his eyes seems at first to be the very scene along the beach this afternoon, then he realizes that the scene is taking place in New Brighton, his own birthplace, on the sands where he played as a boy. And the scene that is playing is that which deals with the exchange of the invisible watch!

There follows a short description of the film which is continually interrupted—for Mary Goodheart—by Tommy saying, 'There's the cathedral! That's Seacombe pier! That's New Brighton pier! There used to be a tower only they knocked it down. That's the old prom —called that the Ham and Egg Parade. Birkenhead Ales, my God! That's the place where I saw the Lion-faced Lady. The tunnel had not quite been completed when I left England though it was already in use,' etc. Finally they stand up while the recording of 'God Save the King' plays.

But the kid imagining that he is being chased by the cops about the magnet has given Goodheart a sense of guilt about having pretended to be a cop to the kids this afternoon in the park and he wonders if his harshness has frightened them. He has now more or less ceased to think that the wristwatch actually belongs to one of these children—unless for purposes of a hypothetical short story for his column—because of the second Ghostkeeper's story but he now is possessed by a purely humane feeling and anxiety to return the watch that he feels is valuable to its owner. And there is something pathetic about the watch ticking away in the kitchen. It is like a symbolic band or nexus relating him to humanity.

Mrs Goodheart is tired and goes to bed when they return, but Goodheart finds his consciousness and inspiration seething to the boiling point where he thinks, 'Well, now I really can write! What a marvellous story this is, right under my nose,' etc. etc. So he gets pencil and paper and in a frenzy of inspiration sets down to write. First, out with all subjectivity, and tell the story just as it happened, or rather the story, just as it has not yet completely happened. But what happens to him as he tries to write is peculiar. He had been worrying himself sick over lack of material, but now he finds he had far too much. (Perhaps the earlier part of this in dialogue, excitedly and enthusiastically to Mary.)

Nor was it that exactly. Every journalist works on a basis of a plethora of material and selects from it, and he himself had long disciplined himself to turning out his five hundred words a day. Moreover the short story writers he admired most, the early Flaherty, Tchekhov, Sodeborg, Jensen, Pontoppidan, the Irishman James Stern, Herman Bang, Flaubert in his tales, Maugham, Pyeskov, Kataev, even one or two of Faulkner's, James Thurber, Bunin, Saroyan, Hoffmanstal, the author of Job, God knows who, all these writers, even if they did not always succeed, aimed at economy of words. (Mem: find early poem of Conrad Aiken's about a watch and quote from it.) Even Joseph Conrad, hard though it evidently was for him, leaned over backwards to try and keep things ship shape. But here Goodheart found himself confronted with something different, something wholly unprecedented in his experience of 'plethora of material.' His first instinct was to cut the first part of their walk this afternoon altogether, and start at the pond in the sunset light. Lex Talionis would be, he thought, a good title for the story. Boy stones ducks. Man warns boy, tells him he'll be punished. Man finds watch. Man discovers, roundabout, that watch is property of boy—though this would be swinging the lead for it obviously wouldn't prove so in fact—man returns watch. Boy has lesson. Good moves in a mysterious way, would be the moral and the result a concise heartwarming little story. But in how much more a mysterious way did God, if it was God—oh God!—seem to move in fact? (All this ties in with the kaleidoscope of life, the complexity, flying saucers, the impossibility of writing good short stories.) For where did Ghostkeeper come in? Perhaps he wouldn't be able to use the name Ghostkeeper at all, which was an uncommon name, just as he wouldn't be able to use his own name Goodheart, that was too much like Pilgrim's Progress. But without the name Ghostkeeper, where was the point of the story, even though it was the name Ghostkeeper that seemed to deprive it of all point. But what was the relation between the owner of the watch and the name on the wreck? Why should the Englishman he'd spoken to by the wreck have lost his watch too? And what was the relation between this and the watch he'd restored to the blind man by the anteater's cage? Why had the wreck seemed a bad omen, and then the tree house had to fall on the seat where the two of them, but for sheer luck, might have been sitting at that moment, which suggested a kind of 'on borrowed time' theme. And what was the relation between all these watches in general and the invisible watch in the movie, and why did the movie have to be set in New Brighton which was his birthplace when he had been thinking of his birthplace this afternoon, just prior to having seen the children. And the French boy who wanted to sell *his* watch. And now he thought of a thousand other things. In fact, no sooner did poor Goodheart come to some sort of decision as to what line his story should take than it was as if a voice said to him: 'But you see, you can't do it like that, that's not the meaning at all, or rather it's only one meaning—if you're going to get anywhere near the truth you'll have twenty different plots and a story no one will take.' And as a matter of fact this was sadly true. For how could you write a story in which its main symbol was not even reasonably consistent, did not even have consistent ambiguity? Certainly the watch did not seem to mean the same thing consistently. It had started by being a symbol of one thing, and ended up—or rather had not yet ended up—by being a symbol of something else. And how after all could you expect the story to mean anything without at least using the name Ghostkeeper. But even as he set down the name Ghostkeeper in desperation, it was as if he seemed to see or hear yet another Ghostkeeper, sitting as it were half way up in the air like Ezekiel's wheel, smiling broadly and saying: 'Wheels within wheels, Mr Goodheart,' or again, 'Wheels within wheels within wheels, my dear Mr Goodheart.' Yes, and controlling the escapement. (Perhaps some of this is a little previous and should take place the next day when the story has further developed.)

Finally Goodheart is so confused that he decides there's nothing to do but wait and see how the story develops in real life—for one thing the very material world seems against him, table rattling, etc. —and tired to death but still unable to sleep he goes to bed and tries to read himself into somnolence with an article in the *Town Crier* entitled British Columbia, Province of Mysteries. 'Never,' he read, 'has any place had a tighter tie-up with the supernatural. From the Yukon border to Washington, from the Rockies to the coast, we found them ... tales that would make the stoutest heart beat faster ...' etc. etc. Tales that would make the stoutest watch run faster. There was even a little filler about watches: 'Finely engraved watches were made in the shape of skulls, little books, octagons, crosses, purses, dogs, and sea-shells in olden days.'

The next morning Goodheart, despite good resolutions to get up early etc. is very tired, gets up late, finds his wife cleaning house, finds watch has stopped at ten o'clock, so he winds it up again. Nothing is wrong with the watch and it begins ticking merrily. It is a mild cloudy way, the night's snow already melted and outside the shadow of smoke, as if from a steamer's funnel on deck (actually from their own apartment chimney) was pouring somewhat menacingly over the green lawn before the chicken croquettes, streaming over the lawn and flowing up the monkey tree. Finally he goes out to buy some cigarettes and post a letter for his wife. First thing he sees is that all flags are at half mast. Then buying cigarettes he sees the headlines at the news stand: The King Is Dead. He feels shocked, and after a while something like crying. He does not however buy the paper, since he's waiting for it to be delivered at the apartment. Death of King makes him very melancholy. Then he remembers that last night in the Bay Theatre was a historic occasion, the last time 'God Save the King' was sung. He wanders along the promenade; he glances at the octopus and the piteous horrible wolf eel: people are still rehearsing on the pier, the ghostly ballet behind the bon-amied windows. Somebody swimming. People still playing tennis despite the cold. But all the time he seems to be hearing the ghostly voice saying, 'Do you remember yesterday, when you said, For God's sake let us sit upon the ground and tell—' Strange stories of the death of kings. Wheels within wheels, Mr Goodheart. Deciding against having another look at the octopus in the aquarium he goes back to the apartment where the *Town Crier* has arrived with the news of the death of the King.

Mary is very sympathetic about the death of the King. In the paper however it says that the King has died about ten o'clock. This reminds Goodheart of something else, though he can't remember what it is. (Of course it is that the wristwatch has stopped at ten o'clock, which he remembers later), but all it now suggests is Segovia—perhaps this in dialogue—the story about Segovia in yesterday's paper which he has forgotten and he hunts all through yesterday's paper looking for the bit about Segovia which he feels he should put in his story but can't find it, meantime feeling he's going completely cuckoo. Then they look at tonight's paper again, and feel gloomy with its report of people—the King's neighbours and friends—already in mourning clothes. 'Queen Mother Elizabeth and Princess Margaret remained in seclusion during the day. At dusk, as rain began to fall, lights burned in only one room of the house.' Then he looks out of the window and sees a newsboy passing with the headline: '*Long Live Queen Elizabeth.*'

This suggested to Goodheart that writer or not, he was now an Elizabethan and he thought that this remark: 'Writer or not, nothing could prevent Gooselaw Goggins from being an Elizabethan,' would make a good end to the story, so he made a note to that effect, feeling more cuckoo than ever. Then suddenly he remembered the watch again and looked in the Lost section of Wednesday's paper.

There was no report of flying saucers in today's paper, though there was a guarded editorial warning against guided missiles, something about 'braced for disaster,' and 'well balanced people,' and 'the situation calls for a little pulling up of reason's socks.' And 'almost every age has seen things in the sky it could not explain.'

In the Lost and Found, the same black and white cat, part Persian, was missing; the same wine bedroom slipper remained lost between the bus terminal and Richards Street, the same front pillar shaped piece of wardrobe 5 feet long was missing, nor had the one 12 ft 2 inch discharge hose lost off Harrington Motors tank truck between Boston Bar and Vancouver yet been recovered. The other watches were still missing, and so was the wallet or watch reported missing in the local theatre, the Bay, where he'd seen the film about New Brighton and the invisible watch. But here it was:

Man's Gold Bulova wrist watch
vicinity Riding Academy, Stanley
Park, Fairmost 1869. Reward.

Goodheart now phones this number, and the exchange is dramatized as it happened. The phone is answered by a girl, who laughs excitedly, 'Mummy, I think they've found the watch,' and then by another woman.

Their conversation is important, you must help me, Margie, with it, but I can't see quite how to dramatize it at the moment. Goodheart does not want to speak to the woman, thinks that he should talk to the watch's owner. Her description of the watch with Henrik Ghostkeeper engraved on its is perfectly correct however: on the other hand Mrs Ghostkeeper insists that the owner is a minor, 'I'm his mother and have to handle all this for him,' etc. Goodheart is now convinced that he has found the owner of the watch at last and moreover now feels sure for some reason, though it is a million to one chance, and though it contradicts what the other Ghostkeeper said, that the boy actually is the boy, one of the boys, who had been throwing stones at the ducks, but feeling somewhat exhausted by this time he turns the telephone over to Mary.

'Tell her to bring the boy with her,' he says, 'so he can see who we are.'

'Why?'

'So that he can see we're the people who told him not to throw stones at the ducks.'

It is decided she will come about seven, and try to bring the boy. For some reason the King's death has made Goodheart feel ten times more isolated and lonely than ever. At the same time the solemn stately occasion makes him feel very formal, even prefectorial, and he dresses very carefully, putting on his old school tie. What is worrying him now is how to make plain to the boy the lesson about the ducks. On the other hand this has to be done subtly without letting the mother know, for ethically speaking it would be unsporting to give away the boy in front of his mother. In any case the death of the King seems to have called forth an added obligation to behave in every way like a very chivalrous Englishman indeed. But at the same time Goodheart is furiously making up further endings for his story. One of these was somewhat sinister: They would refuse the reward. 'No, no. You can buy us a drink some time.' 'I will. I'll be seeing you,' said Mrs Ghostkeeper, and as she and her child departed a tree fell on them.

This scene of Goodheart dressing carefully for this interview should be done realistically and is important and should be exciting for the very good reason that although this is simply a short story, Goodheart so far as I can see is in the kind of *philosophical* situation (although on one plane it is absurd) of the highest dramatic order. That this situation must be in some sense a universal one (even though it is not generally recognized) is what I count on to provide the excitement. What we need too—or rather therefore —is not merely imagination, but hard boiled logical thinking. If this logical thinking is as good as the reasoning in one of your detective stories, Margie, it should more than suffice. In any case Goodheart is now standing *within the possibilities* of his own story and of his own life—something like Sigbjorn in relation to the Volcano, though this is both more complex and of course less serious. The point seems to be that all these possibilities, of his story (as of his own life) wish in some way to fulfil themselves, but what makes it terrifying is that the mind or intelligence that controls these things, or perhaps does not control them, is outside Goodheart and not within. Of this intelligence (that which *we* mean when we say 'they're on the job') the *name* Henrik Ghostkeeper is the symbol. In himself (or themselves) of course Ghostkeeper is many things at once, and many persons, including a child, and so is incomprehensible to human thought. Perhaps what happens is something like this. The minute an artist begins to try and shape his material—the more especially if that material is his own life—some sort of magic lever is thrown into gear, setting some celestial machinery in motion producing events or coincidences that show him that this shaping of his is absurd, that nothing is static or can be pinned down, that everything is evolving or developing into other meanings, or cancelations of meanings quite beyond his comprehension. There is something mechanical about this process, symbolized by the watch: on the other hand the human mind or will or consciousness or whatever; of which the owner knows nothing at all yet which has a will of its own; becomes automatically at such moments in touch as it were with the control tower of this machinery.

(This brings me to Ortega—'A man's life is like a work of fiction, that he makes up as he goes along: he becomes an engineer for the sake of giving it form etc.') I don't think any of the above should appear in the story—or do I?—of course and indeed now I've written it I scarcely know what it means. But that I am on the right track I am certain—at least to the extent that the *lies*, literal falsehoods in this story, such as the name Ghostkeeper on the wreck, the falling tree house, seem valid, as produced by my unconscious. They merely parallel other coincidences we haven't space for such as Dylan Thomas etc. In any case the average short story is probably a very bad image of life, and an absurdity, for the reason that no matter how much action there is in it, it is static, a piece of death, fixed, a sort of butterfly on a pin; there are of course some flaws in this argument—it is a pity I have no philo- sophical training for I unquestionably have some of the major equipment of a philosopher of sorts. But the attempt should be—or should be here—at least to give the illusion of things—appearances, possibilities, ideas, even resolutions—in a state of perpetual meta- morphosis. Life is indeed a sort of delirium perhaps that should be contemplated however by a sober 'healthy' mind. By sober and healthy I mean of necessity limited. The mind is not equipped to look at the truth. Perhaps people get inklings of that truth on the lowest plane when they drink too much or go crazy and become delirious but it can't be stomached, certainly not from that sort of upside-down and reversed position. Not that the truth is 'bad' or 'good': it simply *is*, is incomprehensible, and though one is part of it, there is too much of it to grasp at once, or it is ungraspable, being perpetually Protean. Hence a final need probably for an acceptance of one's limitations, and of the absurd in oneself. So finally even this story is absurd which is an important part of the point if any, since that it should have none whatsoever seems part of the point too.

In any case Goodheart dresses carefully, rehearsing: on plane (a) what he is going to say to Mrs and Master Ghostkeeper, (b) the possible endings for his story. Activity (b) begins to make him feel as if he is going cuckoo again, nor is this feeling mitigated when half way through shaving his eye falls on a phrase in an article by Karl Jasper on Nietzsche in an American magazine: 'He himself corrected his ideas in new ideas,' he reads, 'without explicitly saying so. In altered states he forgot conclusions formerly arrived at.' This seems to have some bearing on the situation though

Goodheart can't make out quite what it is. 'For Nietzsche leads us into realms of philosophy which are anterior to clear logical thought, but which strive toward it.' H'm. 'Not long before his madness he declared that for a number of years he wished only to be quiet and forgotten, for the sake of something that is striving to ripen.' 'Shortly before the end he wrote: "I have never gone beyond attempts and ventures, preludes and promises of all sorts."' I'll say I haven't, thinks Goodheart. 'There remains to be sure a residue of insoluble absurdities—' I'll say there is, thinks Goodheart, tying his tie.

Finally he is ready for Mrs and Master Ghostkeeper's arrival and this part should be dramatized with considerable feeling of tension and suspense, though quietly and realistically, as it were *New Yorker* style. On the other hand I think by this time one should be afraid of the onset of the Ghostkeepers, almost as if on one plane Ghostkeeper is a symbol of death. At the same time the numerous channels of the story now narrow for the moment into one main one (or at least not more than three or four!). Mr and Mrs Goodheart now emerge as if integrated, kindly, wise characters very much in love with each other, their attitude toward the boy largely parental in character. Their ethics will not allow them—should the boy prove to be the one that was throwing stones at the ducks—to give him away in front of his mother. However, can Goodheart take the boy aside? Would the boy laugh at him? *Would he see the point?* Or spoil the whole thing. At the same time perhaps Goodheart wonders if the mother is going to prove to be a pretty girl and perhaps he is wishing in advance to impress her. (Absolutely disregarding the novelist's touch, and the usual laws of selection the story is preparing to end therefore in a manner not remotely suggested by its beginning or indeed having very much to do with it.) At the same time fact is so confounded with fiction in Goodheart's mind that he is sometimes not sure that he is experiencing any valid emotion and has the sense—even while we draw him and Mary realistically—that he is now a character in a story of which perhaps another or that other Henrik Ghostkeeper is the author, though perhaps Henrik Ghostkeeper hasn't yet made up his mind either what to do with him. Goodheart feels as though in short—in Aiken's words—'the whole buzzing cosmic telephone exchange' were going on in his head. Every now and then he walks nervously to the door to see if their visitors are arriving and the Goodhearts have a slight dissension about whether to take the reward or not. Finally Tom clairvoyantly opens the door just as Mrs Ghostkeeper is coming down the corridor. She is of course alone, and not pretty. What happened in fact is now dramatized briefly in neutral entertaining fashion. They do not disclaim the reward perhaps but accept half of it. 'We can make a lot of money that way,' Goodheart could say. Nor does he say 'You can buy us a drink sometime,' and Mrs Ghostkeeper replies sinisterly, 'I'll be seeing you.' Of course the child *is* the child who'd been throwing stones at the ducks, this must be firmly established (and of course he could have, and has, written his name on the wrecked boat), and all during the conversation Goodheart is trying to work in his little prefectorial spiel, while remaining chivalrous.

'Just tell him we were the people who spoke to him about the ducks,' he tries to say several times.

'Just tell him that we—'

'Just say we saw him with the ducks—'

But he never manages any real message at all for the boy and a feeling of frustration becomes so strong he is confused and the incident ends in complete absurdity. And Goodheart looks out of the window after she leaves. Secretly he is wondering whether a tree is going to fall on her after all.

Then, feeling completely frustrated and irritated that the boy will *never know*, but on the whole a sense of pleasure and satisfaction that they had managed to do good, he sits down to write his story (in which the boy does find out) sipping away at a glass of milk. Already he has decided that the shorter version is the one he must write. Lex Talionis. But in this he has to miss out the name Ghostkeeper altogether which even if he could use it, would perhaps involve a libel suit, etc. And naturally his own name in real life he couldn't use anyhow. Finally he decides to give his protagonist no name at all. First he is 'I' then he changes it to 'he.' The man and his wife. The name on the watch—the boy—must, he decides, be a perfectly neutral name like Smithers or Miller—but then he wouldn't be able to find them in the phone book. There is no mention of the falling tree house, the other coincidences of the watches, the invisible watch, or the death of the King, or the feeling that the protagonist is now an Elizabethan. Everything was selection, concision, the story writer's touch. The protagonist himself was not a journalist nor any sort of writer in any kind of crisis about writing. In fact you would never realize what he was. Well, at least this story was touching, Goodheart thinks, compassionate, simple, on the side of 'goodness.' And having the advantage of a lowly and unpretentious theme it could scarcely offend the Almighty Spirit. The only trouble was it wasn't 'true,' that is to say that though it seemed true that the stoning of the ducks had brought upon the child the immediate retribution of the losing of the watch, so much other material that seemed mysteriously relevant had to be tailored away for the sake of art (or cash) that the result was the same: it was a touching little conte perhaps, but by trimming the whole down to what seemed its bare essentials, what was left did not seem even a synecdoche of the events of the last two days, as their seemingly almost insane series affected him.

But as he thought these things it was as if he seemed to hear, as if from on high, a certain divine assent, nodding, as if to say: 'Yes, yes, that is very nice, very touching, Mr Goodheart, it is just as you say,' he seemed to hear yet another voice, as from half way up in the air, saying: 'No, no, Mr Goodheart, that is very lousy,' what did I tell you? What about the King? What about Canada? What about the blind man? What about Segovia? What about the invisible watch? And the young Frenchman? What about the wheels within wheels, Mr Goodheart, and not merely the wheels within wheels, but the wheels within wheels within wheels, Mr Goodheart, that are even now still turning and evolving newer, yet more wonderful and more meaningless meanings—'

And yet within himself he knew there was a meaning and that it was not meaningless.

Goodheart laid his pencil aside. He had finished his story but his mind was still sorely troubled. That Ghostkeeper! And *I Walk in the Park*. But who else walks in the park? Who else, up there, was writing? Suddenly before his eyes the tree house crashed down on the bench again. And tell strange stories—Who else was writing, up there, about Kings dying, Elizabethans, invisible watches, flying saucers, blind men, mandarin ducks . . . Henrik Ghostkeeper! If only one could be sure he were playing a game!

What did we know? And into his mind again came a vision of the ghostly ballet, seen through the half cleaned windows on the pier at the entrance to the park. If one could only be sure!

But suddenly his fear was transformed into love, love for his wife, and that meaningless, menacing fear was transformed into a spring wood bearing with it the scent of peach blossoms and wild cherry blossoms.

Pray for them!

# Gabrielle Roy

GABRIELLE Roy was born on rue Deschambault in St Boniface, Manitoba, on March 22, 1909. She entered Winnipeg Normal School in 1927, and taught in and around St. Boniface until 1937, when she entered the Guildhall School of Music and Drama in London, England. She spent the next two years in the galleries and theatres of Europe, and in 1939 decided she would become a writer. After returning to Montreal she worked for five years as a journalist. Her first novel, *Bonheur d'occasion* (1945: *The Tin Flute*, 1947) won a Governor-General's award in Canada and the Prix Fémina in France. While revisiting St Boniface in 1947 she met and married Dr Marcel Carbotte. Her next book, written in Paris, was *La petite poule d'eau* (1950: *Where Nests the Water Hen*, 1951), a novel based on her experiences as a teacher in northern Manitoba. In 1950 she and her husband returned to Canada and settled in Quebec City, where they still live.

Roy's other works include *Alexandre Chenevert* (1954: *The Cashier*, 1955); *Rue Deschambault* (1955: *Street of Riches*, 1957), which won a second Governor-General's award; *La montagne secrète* (1961: *The Hidden Mountain*, 1962); *La route d'Altamount* (1966: *The Road Past Altamont*, 1966); and *Les enfants de ma vie* (1977: *Children of my Heart*, 1979), which won a third Governor-General's award. The following story is taken from *La rivière sans repos* (1970), and is based on an incident observed by Roy in 1961, while in the Ungava district of northern Quebec, described by Joan Hind-Smith in her book, *Three Voices* (1975): 'She saw a sick Eskimo woman being lifted by a stretcher onto a hydroplane to be taken to a hospital farther south. The woman, she thought, must be frightened and bewildered, removed from the only home she had known. ... "The Satellites" challenges not only the assumption that medical advances always mean an advance in the quality of life, but also the notion that so-called civilized ways are superior to native ones.' It is interesting to compare this story with the poem to which it refers, 'The Forsaken' (1905) by Duncan Campbell Scott.

# THE SATELLITES

### *Translated by Joyce Marshall*

### I

IN THE transparent night of the Arctic summer, beside a little lake
far away in the immense naked land, glimmered the fire lit to
guide the seaplane that was expected at any moment. Stocky shadows all around fed the flames with handfuls of reindeer moss torn
from the soil.

Nearby, at the end of a plank fastened to two empty oil-drums
and placed on the water to serve as a gangway, there were a few
cabins, one of them faintly illuminated. A little farther away were
seven or eight other rickety houses, quite enough, in these parts, to
constitute a village. From all sides rose the lament of the always
famished dogs which no one ever heard any more.

Near the fire the men chatted calmly. They spoke in that smooth
and gentle Eskimo voice with its occasional rises, a voice much like
the summer night and punctuated only by brief bursts of laughter
about everything and nothing. With them such laughter was very
often just a way of concluding a sentence, providing a full stop,
perhaps a sort of commentary on fate.

They had begun to make little wagers among themselves. They
wagered that the seaplane was going to come, that it would not
come, that it had set out but would never arrive, and even that it
had not set out at all.

Fort Chimo had spoken, however. The radio had told them to be
in readiness; the seaplane would stop on its way back from Frob-
isher Bay that evening to pick up the patient. The patient was
Deborah, and it was for her that light had been left in the hut.

The men went on wagering for their own entertainment. For
instance, they said that Deborah would have died before the seaplane arrived, as the Eskimos used to die in former times, without
fuss. Or the seaplane would carry her a long way off and no one
would ever see her again, living or dead. They wagered also that
she would return by the road of the sky cured and looking twenty
years younger. At this notion they all laughed heartily, especially
Jonathan, Deborah's husband, as if he were once more the butt of
the joking of his wedding night. They even went so far as to wager
that the white men might soon find a remedy against death. No

one would die any more. They would live forever—multitudes of old people. At this prospect they fell silent, but impressed even so. There were about ten of them around the fire: old men like Isaac, Deborah's father, reared in the old harsh way; middle-aged men like Jonathan, divided between two influences, the ancient and the modern; and finally young men, more erect of body than their elders, slimmer too, and these were definitely inclined towards the life of today.

Old Isaac, standing slightly to one side, perpetually rolling a round pebble between his fingers, said that nothing now was as it had been in the old days.

'In the old days,' he declared with pride, 'no one would have taken all this trouble to prevent a woman from dying when her hour had come. Nor even a man, for that matter. What sense is it,' he asked, 'to prevent at such great expense someone from dying today who in any event is going to die tomorrow? What is the sense of it?'

No one knew what the sense of it was, so they began to search for it together with touching good will.

Isaac, for his part, continued to gaze attentively at the fire. His eyes filled with memories, and what seemed a sort of compassion mingled with hardness. They knew then what he was going to speak of and even the youngest moved closer, for the subject was fascinating.

'That night you know of,' the old man began, 'was not as cold as some have said. It was a seasonal night, that's all. Nor did we abandon the Old One on the pack-ice as they have also said. We spoke to her first. We said good-bye to her. In short, we behaved as good sons should. We wrapped her in caribou skins. We even left her one that was brand new. Find me any white men,' he asked all in general, 'who would do as much for one of their old people, for all their fine words. We didn't abandon her,' he repeated with a curious stubbornness.

'And isn't it true,' asked one of the young men, 'that you left her something to eat?'

'Yes,' said Benjamin, Isaac's younger brother. 'We left her something to eat—a big piece of fresh seal-meat.'

'That's right,' said Isaac with a sort of disdain, head high, 'but to my thinking she didn't eat.'

'How could we know?' said one of the men. 'She might have wished to hold on for a day, perhaps two . . . to watch for. . . .'

'Not to my thinking,' Isaac repeated. 'She could no longer walk alone. She could scarcely swallow. She was almost blind. Why would she want to hold on for a few days more? And why do they all want to hold on now?'

They were silent, looking at the flames. There was in their eyes a sort of beauty about the death of the Old One in the shadow, wind, and silence; they were still not sure how it had come to pass, whether by water, by the cold, or from shock.

'Didn't they at least find something? The new skin, perhaps?' asked one of the young Eskimos.

'No,' said Isaac. 'Not a trace. The Old One had departed as she came into the world. There wouldn't even have been a scrap of her to bury.'

Jonathan rose then and announced that he would go to see whether Deborah needed anything.

He stood for a moment on the doorsill, looking at a human form that lay stretched upon two old automobile seats placed end to end.

'Are you there?'

'I'm here,' she said weakly.

'You're not worse?'

'I'm not worse.'

'Be patient,' said Jonathan then and went at once to rejoin the others around the fire.


What else could she do but be patient? Emaciated and short of breath, she had been lying there for weeks, victim of a swiftly progressing illness. She was only forty-two, and yet she considered this old enough to die. From the moment one was no longer good for anything, one was always old enough for death.

But then their pastor, the Reverend Hugh Paterson, had passed that way last week. Seated on the ground near Deborah's 'bed,' he had begged her not to let herself die.

'Come, Deborah! At least make an effort!'

Feeble as she was, she had managed to draw from herself something like a grieving laugh.

'What, don't want ... but when the body isn't good any more ... '

'But yours *is* still good—strong and sturdy. You're too young to leave life. Come, a little courage!'

Courage? She was willing, but what was the use? How did you manage to stop death once it was on its way? Was there a means?

There was a means, and it was very simple: arrange for the seaplane to come. Deborah would be put on board. She would be taken to a hospital in the South. And there, almost certainly, she would be cured.

Of all this she chiefly retained a word that for her held magic: South. She had dreamed of it, just as the people of the South—if she had known this, her astonishment would have been boundless— dream of the North at times. Simply for the pleasure of the journey, to see at last what this famous South was like, she might have made up her mind. But she was too weary now.

'As long as there is life,' the pastor continued, 'we must hope, we must try to hold on to it.'

Deborah then turned her head towards the pastor to examine him in her turn, at length. She had already observed that the white men cling to their lives more than the Eskimos.

'Why?' she asked. 'Is it because your lives are better than ours?'

This very simple question seemed to plunge into utter perplexity a man who until then had been able to answer some very perplexing questions.

'It is true,' he replied, 'that the white men fear dying more than you Eskimos do, but why this is so I would find it hard to say. It is very strange when you think of it, for we haven't learned to live in peace with one another or, for that matter, with ourselves. We haven't learned what is most essential, yet it's true that we are bent upon living longer and longer.'

The illogic of this drew from Deborah another rather sad little laugh.

Still, the pastor pointed out a short time later, charity and mutual love had made great progress among the Eskimos since they had accepted the Word.

She knew then that he was going to refer once more to that old story of the grandmother abandoned on the pack-ice—a story he had had from them and had later reworked to his own liking and recalled to them on every occasion; he had even made it the theme of his principal sermon, drawing from it the conclusion that the Eskimos of today were more compassionate than those of past times.

It wasn't that there was no truth in the story as he recounted it, for there was. But he omitted certain illuminating details, for instance that the grandmother had asked to be left on the pack-ice because she could not manage to keep up with the others; she had asked it with her eyes, if not in words. At any rate, this is what her sons had believed they read in her gaze, and why should they have been mistaken?

For several minutes Jonathan, who had returned to the cabin, listened to Deborah thinking aloud and repeating the words of encouragement the pastor had addressed to her before he left.

'The plane still isn't here,' said Jonathan. 'It may come any minute. How are you?'

She said she was not too bad.

'Good,' he said then, and added that he would go and wait with the others.

Next it was Deborah's daughter-in-law, who came from the neighbouring cabin and stopped for a moment on the threshold.

'Do you need anything?'

'No, nothing. Thanks just the same, Mary.'

Alone once more, Deborah dragged herself to the door and leaned her weary back against the frame, her face raised towards the sky. Thus she too would see the arrival of this famous seaplane that was coming to save her.

What had eventually decided her was not the love of life as such. Simply to live did not mean at all that much to her. No, what had decided her was the wish to recover the years that were past. To walk for hours after the men, laden with bundles, over the broken soil of the tundra, camp here, hunt there, fish a little farther along, build fires, mend the clothes—it was this good life she wanted to have once more.

'I don't see why you shouldn't recover sufficiently to do what you used to do,' the pastor had somewhat imprudently promised her.

She had believed him. Had he not spoken the truth so many times before? For instance, when he said that he loved his children of Iguvik with all his heart. This was certainly true, for to remain here one must either become rich or love; and the pastor had not become rich.

He said also that times were changing and that there was good in all these changes. Today the government took better care of its Eskimo children. It spent a great deal of money on them. And the Eskimos themselves had greatly changed.

'You wouldn't any longer—admit it, Deborah—abandon the Old One to the cold and the night.'

This, it was true, might never happen again. In a sense this was precisely what was troubling Deborah. For what would they do now with their poor old people? They would look after them, this was understood, but for what purpose?

She had reached the point now of searching her mind to find imaginary solutions to hypothetical or possible evils, without the least idea, as yet, that it is through this door that sorrow enters a life.

'Good,' she had agreed finally. 'Get your plane to come.'

Just when she had reached that stage in her reflections Jonathan came running.

'We can hear a noise behind the clouds. It must be the seaplane.'

Immediately afterwards, the noise swelled and drowned out his voice. The dogs joined in. There was an indescribable din, a huge splash in the water, then almost silence again.

The cabin of the seaplane opened. The nurse descended first, a tiny bit of a woman with a decided air.

'Where is the patient?' she asked.

She was holding an electric lamp with a handle as long as a rifle, directing its powerful rays all around. From the night emerged objects which seemed to amaze even the Eskimos, who had never beheld them before in this unusual light: for example, the old washbasin Jonathan had found a little while ago, which had remained stranded ever since on the mossy ground without the arrival or outflow of any water but rain; sometimes, when enough had gathered, Jonathan took it into his head when he passed to wash his hands. There were also hundreds of discarded rusted oil-drums; scrap-iron of every sort; and, between two posts, some laundry hung up to dry.

Behind the nurse came the Reverend Hugh Paterson and the pilot. They all walked down the gangway, the young woman in the lead. With white men this wasn't surprising, it was quite often the woman who commanded.

They arrived at the shack. They took Deborah from between

skins and old gnawed blankets and thrust aside almost everything that was hers to wrap her in new clean whiteness. They loaded her upon a sort of plank, despite her protests. Only yesterday, after all, she had got up to prepare meals for her household. They ignored everything she said and hoisted her aboard as if she were a parcel. They then climbed in themselves, slammed the doors, and rose into the air. A moment or so later there was no more trace of them.

Below, returned to the fire, the stupefied men did not quite know what to say about all this. At last they went back to wagering among themselves—what else was there to do? She would not return; she would perhaps return.

'Not to my thinking,' cut in Isaac. 'Not with the wind there is this evening.'

## II

With daybreak Deborah began to see her country. They had tried to keep her lying down, but she had resisted and been granted permission finally to sit up, and now she could see her strange and enormous country from one end to the other. What had she ever been able to see of it before today, always more or less on the move across the barren expanse? It is true. But in winter, pricked and blinded by the winds and the snow, in summer by the mosquitoes, burdened in all weather up to the forehead with bundles, and always preoccupied with something that must be done—hunting, fishing, meals? Only today, at last, was she discovering it. She found it beautiful, much better even than she would have believed from the scraps she had had till then in her head.

She herself, now that the nurse had washed, combed and tidied her, was far from plain. She possessed, in any case, the lively and readily sparkling eyes of her race; but hers, as well—perhaps because of some melancholy of spirit—lingered upon everything they encountered with loving insistence. What astonished and even fascinated her was the lakes—their often peculiar shapes, their unbelievable profusion. Yet she must have known these little lakes, almost all of them stoppered with no visible communication between them, from wandering and toiling entire days with Jonathan in their maze, packs on back, seeking a dry path, skirting this one, turning back on their steps, searching elsewhere—but always ahead of them, hollowed in the rock, there would be yet another basin brimming with water. Yet nothing, perhaps, had more appeal for her now than this curious region she had always found so difficult.

The movement and stir of the journey had done her good, had revived her, unless it was the medicine the nurse had given her. Nothing escaped her watchful attention. In the desert of water and rock stretching far into the distance, she recognized the fur-trading post where they used to trade, the people of her village, and of other villages too. How small it was, scarcely bigger than a die laid on the empty land, the post that since their birth had dominated almost all their journeys, on foot, by sleigh, by kayak—the goal, so to speak, of their lives. There was just time to catch sight of it beside an immense river flowing towards the ocean, with nothing else around it but clouds, and then you could see it no longer.

As she passed, she had taken time even so to say good-day in her heart to the factor, a widower whose life there alone, cut off from his own kind, seemed even to the Eskimos most pitiable.

In the distance she could distinguish the meeting, seemingly quite gentle, of earth and sea. Often, however, in Deborah's country, these two forces met as enemies, amidst piled-up ice, with blows and tumult, as in a savage struggle.

On the other side were the mountains. She contemplated them at length and saw finally just what they were like—old, round mountains, worn away by time. She saw their colours and their summits, how they ended and how they stood one beside the other along the horizon, like an endless encampment of tents of almost equal height. Perhaps really to see mountains one must have the good fortune, as she had at this moment, to be seated calmly in the clouds.

At this thought Deborah's sick face brightened with something very like a gentle desire to laugh.

At Fort Chimo she had to change planes and take a much larger one departing for the South.

While she was waiting, wrapped in a blanket on a stretcher, left by herself for a moment in the midst of cans and bales of all sorts, she noticed something fascinating on the edge of the runway a short distance away. This was a species of small creatures that bowed with the wind, quivering almost without cessation. Doubtless these were what she had heard called trees. She had heard that they came from the South, in an incalculable number first, and very tall when they set out. It was also said that, little by little, as they climbed towards the cold, their ranks dwindled; the survivors, like exhausted humans who had undergone too severe a test, stooped and sagged and could scarcely hold themselves erect.

Deborah glanced quickly around to make sure no one was there to prevent her doing as she wished. She was still feeling very well, probably because of her good medicine, and she had an irresistible impulse to take a closer look at those tiny trees in a row along the tarmac. With some difficulty she managed to extricate herself from the blanket and began to walk towards the midget birches. She tried to unroll their fragile leaves, whose very touch told her they were living things that left a little of their moisture in the hollow of her hand. Then stealthily, as if she were committing a robbery, she filled her pockets quickly with little leaves. These would be for the children of Iguvik when she returned, so that they would have some notion of the foliage of a tree.

After several hours' flight, when the aircraft came out of the clouds and dipped close to earth, it was the white men's country that she began to discover. Luckily she had seen those first spindly trees; otherwise would she ever have believed her eyes when tall spruce-trees and the first big maples appeared. Even from high in the air it was clear that these were creatures of surprising vitality, with numerous branches, some of them reaching higher than the roof-tops. Yet all the houses here seemed at least as big as the factor's imposing residence in Deborah's country. In addition, they had windows on all their surfaces, so that they appeared to be looking from every side at once. There must be firewood here in abundance, since there was no fear of losing heat through all those openings.

Deborah began to wonder why, when their pastor was trying to show them the happiness of a future life, he had not simply described this green land unfolding pleasantly in the sun, all ablaze with the lights cast by windows, roofs, and steeples. Handsome animals seemed also to share in life's sweetness here; they could be seen browsing in very green grass or simply lying in the sun with nothing to do but switch their tails.

As companions among the animals, the Eskimos had only their dogs, and their life now seemed to her very cruel. It was perhaps by contrasting their lean-flanked huskies with these pampered beasts, which even from a distance looked plump and placid, that she began to grasp the impassable distance between the North and the South.

For as long as it was visible, she could not take her eyes from a little white horse that was standing at the end of a meadow beside water—probably in the wind too, to refresh himself. Such a pretty little animal—but for what could anything so slender and delicate be used?

The plane lost more altitude and a great many other details appeared. For instance those walls that cut the land into slices of all shapes and dimensions—what were they?

She was told that they were fences, something in the nature of a marker, a boundary used to separate the fields.

Separate! Cut!

Suddenly she was almost eager to be on her way back to her own people so she could share with them such an extraordinary piece of news. Just think, down there they've actually come to the point of cutting up the land into little pieces surrounded by strands of iron or planks.

'Planks!' they would say. 'Planks wasted like that!'

They perhaps wouldn't believe her, the only one of them who had ever gone to the South.

Now the aircraft was searching out a place to touch down, and Deborah's eyes could not capture all the unexpected things offered. At length the nurse came over to find out what so amazed her patient. There was nothing, however, in the least out of the ordinary. It was simply the approaches to a little city like hundreds in the country, with houses surrounded by massed roses and phlox— here a swing where children played at rising and falling, there a swimming pool into which people plunged; finally great beds of multicoloured flowers and also trees, some with fine white bark, others with foliage as pliant as hair. What would Deborah have felt if she could have understood that, to people living farther in the South, the gracious land beneath her was still the North, with its harsh climate and unrewarding soil?

Suddenly she was afraid, however, and overwhelmed by the sense that the earth was coming straight up to meet her. She clung to the seat. Rising into the air had seemed quite natural. Returning to earth was alarming. She closed her eyes. So it had been no use trying to escape from her death in the North. It had come on ahead to wait for her in the South.

At last she opened her eyes and saw to her great astonishment that the plane had landed without her knowledge and was now rolling quietly. Smiling with embarrassment, she glanced quickly at the other passengers, as if to discover whether she had been caught out in her fear.

She felt stiff with emotion and fatigue. The good medicine no longer seemed to be working so well. Once more she was taken in hand, but now she had no strength to resist. And what was the use, anyway? She was beginning to realize that she had been placed in powerful hands and these hands were already so intent upon curing her that now there was no time or thought for anything else.

She was put once more upon a stretcher; then inside a vehicle that set off at great speed. Other vehicles passed or overtook them. Their occupants, as they glanced towards Deborah, seemed to her to look preoccupied and dispirited, and she wondered whether some crushing event had occurred here today.

But when she looked towards the horizon she felt a sudden, very quiet delight. Travelling along the rim of the sky were several small black sleighs on wheels, attached to one another and drawn by a larger sleigh that gave forth smoke, and from time to time brief peculiar cries, as if they were summoning people to leave what they were doing and come on board. Deborah felt a sort of summons from far back in her life, from her first years. All the children in the world are perhaps summoned in this way; in the north by dog sleighs and here, probably, by this other sort of sleigh.

'It's a train,' she was told. 'Nothing but a train.'

She raised her head and let her eyes follow to the curve of the horizon the magic sleigh, which glided without bounds or jolts, as if there was a road for it along the sky that was as smooth as the air. The team seemingly went of its own accord without strokes of the whip on its spine and without any fatigue. Perhaps to Deborah it looked as if the team went only where it wished.

Later, when she was asked whether there were anything that would particularly please her, her eyes would shine and she would invariably answer, 'Train. Deborah very much like to ride in train.'

III

After a week of examination, sometimes in the dark with the aid of a powerful roaring machine and at other times in floods of blinding light, she received a visit from the government in the person of an interpreter, who sat down unceremoniously beside the fine bed Deborah occupied all by herself in the hospital.

'Well now,' said the government, 'you have a tumour, a nasty lump that's eating you up inside. It must be removed. Do you give your consent?'

Deborah scarcely hesitated. Always the knife had seemed to her the best way to eradicate evil when that was indicated.

'Cut,' she decided, and went off, perfectly calm, almost without fear, to the operation.

Soon afterwards she seemed to be recovering. She was to be seen, in a long dressing-gown lent by the hospital but shod in her mukluks, wandering persistently about the corridors, without asking anything of anyone, until she had found the way out to the garden. It was planted with a few handsome trees. From the windows above they could watch her as she moved with her still slightly shuffling steps along the gravel walks. She approached one of the maples warily, rather as one might a living creature, so as not to startle it. She stretched forth her hand and touched it delicately with her fingertips. It was as if she were trying to tame it. Then she looked at it with delight, listening to it rustle. Finally she put her arm around its trunk and, leaning her cheek there, stood motionless, contemplating the great mass of leaves high in the sky as the wind stirred them gently.

She also made friends among humans. First, among her own people. There was a fair number of them in the hospital, several of whom could once have been considered neighbours, since they all lived only three or four hundred miles from each other; at times, no doubt, by some accident of stopping-point or itinerary—small groups of travellers going towards or away from the trading-post— they had passed very close to one another; perhaps engulfed in blizzards, they had missed one another only by a hair. So their meeting at last today seemed to them a miracle. They visited back and forth continually, always with great signs of delight.

Among the whites she also made friends, and of these several died. When she saw that they were no better off than the Eskimos, that they were attacked by the same bodily afflictions, she felt amazement, first, and later almost as much grief for them as for the sick Eskimos. Then the vague hope she had maintained till then, though half hiding it from herself—that the white men would eventually manage to stretch life out forever—was extinguished once for all. Because she had almost come to believe this for a moment, she now found the truth harder to bear.

Happily she still had two excellent distractions to help her pass the time. First the shower. From the moment she first discovered this seemingly inexhaustible fountain of hot water and soap, it became with her a sort of passion. Perhaps this passion always existed in a latent state, frustrated for centuries among all those of her race. For close to a half-hour at a time, without noticing that people came now and then to try to turn the door-knob, Deborah would soap and then rinse the magnificent dark hair that draped her like a shawl to her knees.

When she returned to her bed, she would brush and brush it with the idea, perhaps, of making it shine like the gentle glow of the seal-oil lamp in the little snow-house of old, the memory of which had suddenly returned to her. After this, she would go back and wash her hair again.

'You'll end by rubbing so hard it will fall out,' the Sister reprimanded her gently.

Deborah's little smile was at once timid and a shade mischievous. For it was the poor Sister, actually, who was rather short of hair.

Her second and almost equally unbridled passion was for smoking cigarettes. When she was not busy tending her hair, she was almost always to be found squatting in the middle of her bed as if it were the ground, shrouded in heavy smoke. Her expression would then be a little less melancholy. It was as if all this smoke managed to obscure, at least slightly, the thought that was now trying to present itself at every instant to Deborah's mind. After the manner of her people, she had thus managed to take from civilization two things that seemed almost incompatible: soap for cleanliness and clarity, tobacco to blur the thoughts and soil the fingers.

The Sister reproached her one day. This was a nun who had been delegated for a long time to visit the sick Eskimos. She knew their language.

'Really, Deborah, I don't understand you.'

Deborah's big astonished eyes seemed to say: Well, do I understand you? But no matter, I love you anyway.

'On the one hand,' the Sister continued, 'you are cleanliness itself, forever washing yourself. On the other hand, you scatter cigarette ashes almost everywhere, you dirty everything. You're like an old bush camp all by yourself. What can this do for you, all this smoke?'

It didn't perhaps do very much. Just gave her some little fragments of dream, pictures she had believed lost. But still it brought the great savage and distant North to some extent into this skimpy room. That was what it did.

One day, through the smoke, Deborah managed to recover almost everything she had ever possessed. The camp appeared before her half-closed eyes. It was all there, down to the wash-basin Jonathan had salvaged after the departure of the troops, which might be full of water at this very moment, down to her washing that no one perhaps had thought of bringing in. She saw the narrow walkway joined to the empty oil-drums, rising and falling with the slight movements of the water, like a creature that breathed; she saw her shack, its door wide open, and all around the pure and naked sky. She felt upon her cheeks what might have been drops of lukewarm rain. She put her fingers to her face and gathered a tear, which she examined with amazement and a trace of shame. What was this now? Except for those drawn from her by the extreme cold or, in summer, by the smoke from the fires lit to drive away the mosquitoes, she had no recollection of ever shedding tears.

In her surprise, the tears for a moment stopped flowing. Then they resumed in a storm. So that she would at least not be seen or heard, she hid herself under the sheet.

Quite often after that, she was found in a motionless little round heap in the middle of the bed.

The Sister began almost to plead with her, 'Smoke, Deborah, or go and wash your lovely hair.'

But this did not mean very much to her now. However, they discovered her from time to time eating oranges, with tears streaming down her face. She had thought of saving those she was given in her drawer or under the mattress to take to the children of her country. Until the day when the smell warned the nurse.

'Now look, Deborah. Oranges don't keep indefinitely.'

'Ah!'

Her face showed that this was a very cruel disappointment. So there was no hope of trying to take them back with her. Well in that case, she would do her best to eat them. However, her heart was not in it. She looked as if she were eating the most bitter of fruit. Many of the fine good things of the South lost interest in her eyes as soon as she learned they could not bear the journey. It was as if she were now refusing to become attached to them. Perhaps she even held it obscurely against them.

From then on she grew sadder from day to day. The idea seemed to have come to her that like the oranges, like the tender leaves on the branches of the trees, like the flowers plucked from the garden, she herself would not last long enough to make the journey back to her country.

She stopped washing herself. She no longer sat leafing through magazines while giving the impression that she was reading the text here and there. She gave up everything except the little cloud of blue smoke in which she enclosed herself more often than ever now, as if inside a precarious wall that defined her modest place in the world.

Then one day the government came back to her again and said, 'So you're as lonesome as that! Come, this isn't reasonable, Deborah.'

So that's what it was—lonesomeness. She had needed to be surrounded with attention, showered with oranges and visits, loved as never before and treated like a queen to know lonesomeness. What a curious illness it was!

'Yes, it must be that I'm lonesome,' Deborah admitted.

'You think about your own country all the time, eh?'

'Yes, I do.'

'Well, in that case,' said the government, 'we're going to let you go. Of course it would have been better for you to stay with us a little longer. Your illness may return. We don't know yet whether it's been rooted out completely and for good. But if you're dying of lonesomeness. . . .'

So she could go if she wanted to. She wouldn't be kept against her will. She had permission? She was free?

Tears flowed from the dark eyes, and this was stranger than ever. For now they did not come from the pain of lonesomeness but because this pain had been removed.

IV

Once more she saw the tender aspect of the world with its trees, all laden these days with gold, and its pleasant valleys in which rivers, winding from one island of greenness to another, seemed to be visiting each in turn.

But she loved the earth beneath her more when there were no longer any trees. Most appealing of all to her were the arid knolls and bald hummocks of the naked land, between which gleamed the icy water of solitary lakes. So many, many lakes, and so remote as well that very few of them have been given a name. Her eyes devoured this singular network of water and rock where she had so often roamed in former days with Jonathan, packs on her back, sometimes with a child in her womb, her face so bathed in sweat that she could scarcely see before her, and now this period of her life seemed to have been of moving tenderness. So one had to go very far in order to judge one's life, and it was perhaps on its most arduous days that the best memories were being prepared.

She remained seated this time, too, to make the crossing of the sky, though she could no longer manage to hold her head erect.

For rather a long time the land disappeared from their sight. Even Deborah closed her eyes and dozed a little, while they were in the clouds, and there was nothing to look at but their masses of snow—very soft snow, it was true, but a little too similar to ever-lasting pack-ice.

Suddenly she sat up. Her eyes, so heavy with fatigue, blazed with interest. Below, once again, was the big river flowing towards the sea, with the little fur-trading post beside it, alone in the infinite barren land.

Now she was nearly home. Almost at once, in fact, she recognized the place in the world which belonged to her and to which she belonged; and finding it again, returning from so far away, must have seemed to her a sort of miracle, for the worn face, so long spiritless, was suddenly radiant.

The seaplane was about to touch water. The various objects of the camp grew closer. There was the wash-basin, which was beginning to fill with moss and rust; there were the discarded oil-drums and, where her washing had been, some skins that had been cleaned and stretched to dry in the sun. And there was Jonathan.

He was standing beside the lake, in almost the same spot where he had watched her leave and in almost the same attitude. With the years he had become a heavy little man, almost as broad as he was high. His head thrown up and his neck drawn back between his shoulders, he followed the movement of the seaplane in the bright sun. Deborah could even distinguish the thick fringe of his hair and the handsome dark colour of his skin. She herself had had time in the hospital to become as pale and ugly as a white woman. At one point he raised his hands above his head. Perhaps in greeting. But it looked, quite truthfully, as if he were saying to the aircraft, 'Hi there, be a bit careful.' Then, without waiting any longer, he went into the cabin. This was perhaps to tidy up a little, at least to conceal the worst of the litter that had lain strewn about for weeks. Even though this meant that they had to go and fetch him to help carry Deborah, at least to lend a hand at the reception of his own wife. And not until then did he let it be clear that he knew who was arriving.

After the event, at least for some time, he seemed fairly pleased to see her back. He even went one day to a lake that was very hard to reach, eight knolls away, and caught her a fine fish with delicate flesh. She scarcely touched it; everything disagreed with her nowadays. He spent some time tinkering with the two automobile seats she used as a bed and finally attached them together so they no longer parted at every moment, leaving a space into which she slipped.

But when he saw that despite all this attention Deborah was still without appetite, nauseated by odours, as if she no longer knew what an Eskimo house was like—hadn't she gone as far as to ask him to remove some animal guts that were only a week old?—and that she lay stretched out in her corner just as before, he lost patience and went to complain to the other men.

'She shouldn't have gone,' he said and then, in the same level tone, 'She shouldn't have come back either.'

'That was my thinking, as I told you,' Isaac reminded him. 'When it's time to die, one doesn't make all this fuss. One dies.'

But Jonathan was irritable these days, and although the old man had essentially just supported his own argument, he turned on him suddenly.

'You're a fine one to talk, old man,' he said. 'Here you are, seventy years old, fat and well fed. What do you do to deserve that? Nothing. You live on the government with your pension. You have nothing to do but you have all you need: your lard, your flour, your tobacco, your sugar, your tea. . . . '

'It's not the same thing,' Isaac defended himself. 'I at least still have my strength. I don't need anyone to help me walk or do what I want to do.'

'Even so, you don't do anything either from morning till night but you still have your lard, your flour, your sugar. . . . '

More than anything, perhaps, the tedium of the enumeration wearied Isaac. He departed, grumbling, to seek refuge in the shack. It was impossible to have peace anywhere now. He sat down in a corner on a wooden crate that bore on one side the warning, *This side up*, and on the other, *Haut*. He looked all around him for something with which to busy himself. It was true that for quite some time he had done nothing. But what was there to do? Hunt? There were no more caribou to speak of. Fish then, perhaps? Yes, but from the moment one had the old-age pension and was no longer pressed from behind, what was the use of all that trouble? Something broke in man, perhaps, when he received without giving as much in return. The perplexed old man, sitting on his crate, looked as if he were glimpsing a little of the misfortune that had befallen the population of the North, not long ago so industrious. He shook himself and picked up an old fishing net which he began to examine to see whether it was worth the trouble of mending.

He caught the eye of his daughter, who had been lying in her own little corner watching him think.

To tell the truth, he scarcely recognized her since she had been in the South. This was not only because she had grown thin and pale. Even the expression of her face seemed to him completely changed. One might have said that she no longer thought quite as they did now, or even that they could not quite guess what she was thinking.

'Do you want me to tell you?' he said. 'I should go off of my own accord and put myself on the pack-ice as we put the Old One in the good time.'

He mused a little.

'It was a beautiful cold night. There were spirits in white tunics dancing and circling all around the sky.'

He was becoming more and more fond of remembering that time.

'Since the wind was from the right direction,' he said, 'the ice must have gone very quickly. It certainly didn't take long. The ice broke loose with a little snap. Then off with it! It was far away.'

In contrast to what he had always said until now, that the Old One had totally disappeared, he now maintained that she must have been preserved by the frost.

'The cold is good and compassionate,' he claimed.

And he began to describe the Old One as he now pictured her, intact, seated in the centre of her column of ice—a tiny white island on the raging black sea—turning and turning continually at the end of the world in the last free waters of the earth, just like those satellites of today, those curious objects, he said, that they were going to hang high in the air so that they would never come down again.

'That's what she has become,' he said dreamily. 'I'd stake my life on it. A satellite.'

He lowered his gaze once more to Deborah's emaciated face, which was marked with suffering and anxieties of the spirit that one did not often find in the old days on Eskimo faces. But it was true that in the old days one did not often see Eskimos grown thin and pale. They had died before that.

Isaac grumbled on, 'Ha, that's all nonsense! Eh, my poor Deborah? What do you think? When do we show more kindness to people? When we keep them from dying? Or when we help them just a little?... Eh?'

V

Then, with the first snows, the Reverend Hugh Paterson chanced to pass that way again on his early-winter rounds. The voices of the dogs were heard resounding sharply in air that had been scoured by the already icy winds. A few moments later in came the pastor, a long lean silhouette beside the Eskimos, most of them round and short. He seated himself on the corner of one of the old automobile seats that weather and perhaps ocean-salt had pitted. He had often wondered how they could have reached this place, by what curious journey, who or what could have brought them—the sea, a plane, or perhaps some old trapper on his back?

'So, my poor Deborah,' he said. 'You're no better?'

He met the gaze of soft and sorrowful eyes that seemed to reproach him for preventing death from striking in its hour.

Dying, Deborah appeared to be thinking, is easier the first time than the second. Who knows, it may even become harder the longer it is deferred.

Sad enough to make one weep and yet in their depths still a little mocking, doubtless from force of habit, Deborah's great dark eyes seemed to appeal for understanding across the silence.

And then, as if he understood perfectly, he stretched out his hands to join Deborah's together, and then draw them towards him, keeping them pressed between his own.

'My poor child, all you have learned, loved, and understood in these few more months you've lived is yours forever. Nothing can take any of it from you. Even a single additional step in life and you are enhanced forever.'

The dark eyes reflected. They seemed to grasp these fine words and take them into herself to keep for the day when she might make something from them. Does one ever know with thoughts?

'Still, you ought to have stayed in the hospital where you'd have been better looked after,' he said without logic but with tender affection.

'Why want so much to look after?' she asked and, powerless to understand, sank into a sort of silent misery.

It was this that disconcerted her most among civilized people, this terrible determination, even when death was close and certain, to defy it still. This absurd preference also, when they must finally die, that it should be in a bed.

'Dear Mr Paterson,' she said, 'Deborah much prefers for dying to be here than there.'

'Who's talking about dying?' Once again he tried to deceive her with false lightness.

Then he remembered to give her the little present of drugs that the government had entrusted to him for her. The government was very concerned about her, he said, and would be anxious to hear whether the operation had been a complete success.

'Say thank you,' she said simply.

Finally the pastor went on to point out that death was not an evil. In fact it was death now, and no longer life, that he described as the best friend of human beings. It was the deliverance from all our ills. At last one was free. We departed with shoulders, hands, and hearts finally unburdened.

These were fine things to hear, though seemingly quite the

opposite to what he had said when he had been encouraging Deborah to live. They were none the less convincing in their fashion. Even Deborah knew now that one ought to say those things that best fitted the affair of the moment, otherwise there would be nothing left to say, it would no longer be worth the trouble of opening one's mouth, and no one would ever speak again.

'Deborah would like to be free right away,' she said.

'Deborah will perhaps not have very long to wait,' he replied tenderly, as if this were his wish for her. 'A few steps more, a little patience still, and she will be in complete happiness.'

Happiness. Another incomprehensible expression. If happiness simply lived somewhere on earth, where was that? When she arrived in the South, she had been able to believe it might be here in the midst of favour and wealth. But soon she had come to feel that there was even less happiness here than in her home. Now, she never stopped puzzling about this.

'When all's said and done,' the pastor was forced to admit, 'we can encounter happiness in all its radiance only on the other side of life.'

She agreed wholeheartedly, her eyes eager, as if hungry for the unknown. And for what else could she hunger now?

'On that side,' he said again, 'all that has been obscure to us will be understood. Clarity will reign. No one will lack again for anything.'

VI

The nights are long in that latitude, as winter approaches, even for those who sleep well. For Deborah they were interminable. Her short life, which had been devoured by needs that left little time for thinking, was coming to an end, paradoxically, in an infinity of time in which there was nothing else to do. So it seemed as if her short life were being prolonged for some reason that Deborah was trying to comprehend.

She lay resting on the automobile seats while the others around her, wrapped in whatever old blankets they still possessed, slept directly on the floor.

The air in the hut was fouled, both by the unpleasant odour her diseased body was beginning to give off and by the Eskimos' own odour of oil and fish, which she now found sickening. With the coming of winter they had reached the point, in this rickety shack which the fierce cold obliged them to keep tightly closed, of restricting one another cruelly. One could cough, spit, turn over, and everyone would stir, cough, turn over.

Deborah had taken it into her head to try to picture that place after death, so different from life, where no one would lack again for anything. She needed all her confidence in the pastor to have faith in such words. For at the present time she lacked almost everything. What she most lacked, moreover, was all she had so recently learned to know, those comforts of life in the South: hot water and soap, the clear and abundant light, always ready to flash on, of electricity; a little space all to herself; but especially, perhaps, that sort of friendliness—or show of friendliness—between people in the South. She had thought this uncalled-for, but now, even though still not entirely convinced it was real affection, she would have liked to feel its warmth around her.

As she now saw it, the better life became, the more needs it satisfied and the more new needs arose. So that it seemed to her quite unlikely that there ever could be a life or a place where one would lack for nothing.

The others around her too were, on her account, in want and deprivation, Isaac of the warm blanket he had 'lent' her—just for a time and not for the whole winter—and Jonathan of love, for to Deborah love had become torture.

The nights therefore were increasingly long and uncomfortable for them all.

Outside the complaining of the dogs would diminish for a moment only to swell again. In the old days she had not heard this. It existed, inevitable as the frost that overtakes the water or as the click of the trap on a prey. It existed, that was all. Now she heard it continually and the sound harassed her. Couldn't they give the dogs just once enough to eat? Jonathan looked at her sidelong. Was she crazy? Satisfy the dogs? You might as well try to satisfy the animals of the tundra, the whole of famished creation.

She came close to suffocating one evening in the tightly closed cabin. Who would have believed that in this frigid land, so full of wind, she would find herself wishing, more than anything in the world, for a single breath of fresh air. It was in the South too, with its wide-open windows, that she had acquired this taste for the movement of air in the house. If only, this night again, they could have left the door open just a crack. But the others were freezing. While she was burning.

More and more, also, she was impatient to be on that other side of life where no one would be sad any more. And for what else now could she be impatient?

She threw off her blankets, then took the warmest and spread it over old Isaac, who lay curled up on the floor. He had coughed a good deal latterly, though without yet making up his mind to ask her for his blanket. She put on her mukluks and pulled open the door. The cutting air seemed to strengthen her.

The night was clear and cold. Snow had fallen. In this fresh but shallow snow Deborah left very clean imprints of her steps.

So it was that they were able to follow next day the journey she had made.

She had first struggled painfully to the top of the nearest knoll. To hear the beating of the surf? Or because she remembered climbing up there often with other children to try to glimpse the ocean, which was not very far away? Whatever her reason had been, she went on. To the next hummock, then to yet another. Moving from knoll to knoll, she finally reached the pack-ice.

There before her eyes, probably revealed to her in the pale glimmer from the snow, lay the most broken terrain on earth, an uneven buckling expanse of ice-floes, roughly hinged to one another.

No doubt the wind on that tormented coast had been blowing with utmost fury.

Yet she had entered it. Here and there, on the crust of snow a few more tracks could be picked out. They showed that Deborah had fallen on several occasions and that at last she had crawled more than she had walked. The tracks continued a little farther. They were to be found right to the edge of the open water.

When they examined the contour of the pack-ice from the ocean side, they saw that a portion of it had recently broken loose.

But though they peered long and searchingly through the dark and tumultuous landscape of black water, it was useless; they could distinguish nothing within it that bore any relation to a human shape. Or hear anything but the shrieking of the wind.

# Hugh Garner

HUGH Garner was born in Batley, Yorkshire, England, on February 22, 1913. 'I was descended from a long line of Yorkshire woollen weavers,' he wrote in his autobiography, 'drunkards on the male side and temperance fanatics on the female.' His father, a mill-hand, abandoned the family soon after bringing them to Toronto in 1919, and Garner grew up on the streets of Toronto's Cabbagetown and Riverdale districts. Like many of his contemporaries, he became a socialist during the Depression (he spent most of the '30s as a hobo, ranging from the tomato fields of California to the Bowery, and from Mexico to the railyards of northern Ontario). In 1937 he joined the International Brigade and fought for the Loyalists in Spain, and from 1940 to 1945 he served with the Canadian Navy on the North Atlantic. After the war he settled more or less permanently in Toronto with his wife Alice and their two children. He died on June 30, 1979.

Garner's first story, 'Cabbagetown,' appeared in the *Canadian Forum* in 1936, but he didn't begin to write seriously until after the war when he supported himself solely from writing. 'My actual literary mentors,' he has written, 'were John Dos Passos, who taught me how realistic fiction should be written, and J. B. Priestley, who has written better about young romantic love than any other author I have ever read.' His first novel, *Storm Below*, was published in 1949, and from then until his death he wrote 16 more novels, 439 magazine articles, 100 short stories—collected in such volumes as *The Yellow Sweater* (1952), *Men and Women* (1966), and *Hugh Garner's Best Stories* (which won the Governor-General's award in 1963)—and an autobiography, *One Damn Thing After Another* (1973). The following story first appeared in *The Tamarack Review* in 1974, and is the title story of a collection published in 1976. 'While he has never lost sight of the victims of society,' wrote Norah Story in 1973, 'he has given increasing attention to human failings, the deterioration of character, alcoholism, and the current wave of violence.

# THE LEGS OF THE LAME

IT WAS only a two hour trip, and I was feeling good. The best two meetings, in Kingston and Carleton Place, had gone off well, and Kingston, being semi-big time, had received quite a play from the media, so that our attendance the next week in Toronto was almost an assured success.

Behind us was the preliminary build-up, beginning with small churches and fraternal halls, and then progressing to war memorial auditoriums and centennial centres. Despite Clay's crazy desire to meet all his obligations, and my trying to impress on him the necessity of honouring only the big towns and their consequent bigger audiences, that he insisted on calling 'congregations,' we were still moving up, and so were our bank accounts.

I hadn't been able to talk him out of it, and so the evening before we'd held a 'visit' in a skating rink in Perth. We'd had a fair-sized audience and the handle had been ten times what it used to be three months before. We'd drawn the faithful from Smiths Falls and other towns around, but to me it was like Sinatra or Dylan playing Belleville.

Clay was quiet, sitting there beside me in the front seat as the Caddy glided along at eighty coming west on Ontario No. 7 after midnight.

'Perth was pretty good for its size,' I said to Clay.

'Yes.'

'It sure beat both Cornwall *and* Sherbrooke.'

'They're largely Roman Catholic cities,' he answered, staring straight ahead through the windshield. 'Perth had a lot of born-again Christians.'

Paula Dunwoody and her husband Fred, sitting in the back seat, were quiet now, and I knew one of them must be asleep. Paula played the harmonium we were pulling behind us in the small covered trailer with the JESUS HEALS signs on its sides. The trailer was about the size of a medium U-Haul and carried, along with Paula's harmonium, our bags and a rack holding Clay's new wardrobe.

I slowed the car as we passed through Kaladar, then let it ease up to eighty again on the open highway. Except for a few tractor-

191

trailers there was very little traffic, and through my open window I caught the spring scent of coniferous trees and an occasional whiff of something like buckwheat. The beam of our lights picked out the stretches of bush and abandoned sapling-growth fields as we raced past them.

'This part of Ontario should never have been cleared for farms,' I said. 'Most of them have been abandoned for years.'

'Yes,' Clay said.

Fred Dunwoody asked, 'How much farther to Peterborough, Gordon?'

'Sixty-five, something like that,' I said. 'Is Paula asleep?'

'Like a baby. I think I'll take forty winks myself.'

I glanced over at Clay and saw he was still wide awake, staring straight ahead. Usually a 'visit,' which was what we called our faith-healing meetings like the one in Perth, exhausted Clay, and he would sleep all the way to our next motel stop. Tonight though for some reason he was wrapped up in sleepless thought. I figured he was thinking of his wife Eileen and his two small kids back in Bridgewater, Nova Scotia. They'd been with us for the two days we took off from the tour in Quebec City, and for some reason he hadn't been the same enthusiastic Clay Burridge since we'd left Quebec.

I'd booked us three units in a motel just east of Peterborough, where we were holding a two-night visit beginning that evening. When it was possible I always got us lodgings outside the towns we appeared in. Most people don't know this, but an evangelical celebrity, even a minor one like Clay, is bothered constantly by women fans. It had only taken me the first two weeks I'd been Clay's business manager and advance man to catch on to that fact. The women as a group were older than the ones that used to bug the rock group I'd managed, but there's a mixture of sexuality and religion in a successful evangelist and faith-healer. A person like Billy Graham must have to beat them off with clubs.

I'd been trying to figure out Clay Burridge now for three months, but still couldn't. He didn't smoke, drink, or swear, and he was completely faithful to Eileen Burridge. Not that he couldn't have had plenty of women, as I say, but he turned them all away politely.

The way I got myself tied in with Burridge is a story in itself.

It was by attending a meeting of his during one of his first big visits, in Halifax. I'd just been left as high and dry as it's possible to get down there by a rock group I'd put together we called 'The Flack.' I know it wasn't a catchy name like 'Three Hits and a Miss,' but did you ever stop and think what a lousy name 'The Beatles' is? I know that the first time I heard it I thought of little black bugs crawling across a floor. Anyhow, all I'd got from 'The Flack' was plenty of woe and a little more than my hotel room and bar bills. My girl vocalist took off on a speed trip with my drummer and my car, which ended up as a write-off near Boston. That disbanded the outfit, and I paid the other two members' plane fares back to Toronto. I guess I attended Clay Burridge's meeting as a penance for my stupidity.

First of all let me say that before I took him over Clay's meetings were strictly from hunger. His approach to the whole soul-saving, faith-healing business was an evangelical road to the welfare office. Take the way he dressed, for instance. Not plain folks like Oral Roberts or no-nonsense religio-commercial like most of the successful preachers on the circuit, but in a way that appealed only to the lowest hayseed denominator in his audience.

After the first meeting I attended was finished I went backstage and met Clay and Fred Dunwoody. They were leery of me at first, but I trotted out my tattered credentials, and they invited me to Clay's hotel room, which wasn't in the Nova Scotian or the Lord Nelson. I began right away to criticize his stage appearance, the general downbeat tone of the whole gig, and after some coaxing on my part got them to tell me the unrealistic financial split he'd made with the theatre owners. I was afraid that Clay or Dunwoody would throw me out of the room, but they listened to me politely.

I told them, 'Who's going to believe a preacher who still wears a fancy buckskin jacket and a ten-gallon hat? You're not out to prove that you're a second Nova Scotia cowboy like Hank Snow. You've got to put yourself over as a dedicated, educated preacher, not as a sideshow freak saving the souls of the rural poor. You're a person with a genuine gift from God who is willing to share it and your message with everybody. You've got to make your audience—all right congregation then—believe in you, not only with hope or religious faith but with their intelligence. You've got to get out of the dimes and into the dollars.'

'I didn't have much of a formal education, Mr Beaton,' Clay said, in the soft but unbelievably earnest way he speaks; the way it had actually gripped me in my seat in the half-filled theatre. 'I'm dedicated though. There's nothing phony or showbiz about my

Christianity, and nothing untruthful about my belief in the healing powers of Jesus Christ. I may sometimes find myself doubting my qualifications to act as His healing surrogate, but my attempts to bring His healing grace down to the poor unfortunates who seek it are real. As for a wider audience—not for me but for the Lord—I'd welcome that. It has nothing to do with either dimes or dollars however.'

I believed him as you'd have believed him too if you'd been in that small hotel room that night. There wasn't the slightest doubt in my mind that the man was telling the truth. Hell, he was that rarest of individuals, an incorruptible one!

Anyhow, in a couple of days Clay Burridge and Dunwoody visited me at my motel and we drew up a simple agreement making me Clay's business manager and advance man. Straight percentage of the gate after expenses.

We had to make the changes in his image gradually, for going too fast would have lost him what few followers he had then. First off we had to change his public picture, and so before leaving Halifax I had him trade in his old panel truck for a second-hand '69 Cadillac, that he bought on time. He made the deal himself, in his own name; I wasn't trying to rip him off.

The beginning of our tour took us up Nova Scotia's Eastern Shore, to places like Sheet Harbour, Port Dufferin, Ecum Secum and Liscomb, then inland to Aspen and up to Antigonish. It was a strictly hungry itinerary scheduled by Clay and Fred Dunwoody before I joined them. It allowed me though to make some changes in the performance itself. Man, Clay's act had more kinks in it than a snake fence. Besides leaving Halifax in the Cadillac I'd work as far ahead of the show as I could, spreading the word and arranging meeting places and cut-rate accommodation.

I stole an idea from Billy Graham, and wherever I could I arranged 'participatory partnerships' with local fundamentalist preachers. At times they were deep-dip Baptists, other times evangelicals, and at least once before we kissed Nova Scotia good-bye the minister was a genuine get-down-on-the-floor-and-pray Holy Roller. Their 'partnerships' paid off in attendance for both the local preacher and Clay Burridge, and the amount of the handle we pulled in.

I succeeded too in getting Clay to change his personal appearance. At first it was the substitution of a Sears mail-order dark suit for his Buffalo Bill buckskins, and before we hit Sackville, New Brunswick, we'd got rid of his ten-gallon hat. And if you think it's easy to separate a let's-play-cowboy Maritimer from his Stetson, try it sometime.

In the bigger towns and small cities like New Glasgow, Pictou, and Amherst I received the co-operation of some of the leading Protestant clergymen, not all of them fundamentalists. The word of Clay's coming was spread by what I can only call a Christian underground telegraph. By now we were booking our visits into war memorial auditoriums and centennial sports arenas.

Where Clay had been satisfied at first with small high school gyms and Sunday schools, now I was counting the gate in hundreds, some 'partners' supplying us with a back-up choir and orchestra, meaning we could leave Paula Dunwoody's harmonium in the trailer. Our first trailer had been a rented one, but the second, that served us right up into Ontario, was a gift from an old man who'd hauled hay in it for years from the salt marshes near Tidnish. He presented it to Clay for curing his arthritis. We had it fixed up and painted in Saint John.

From Sackville on I made up the itinerary, having to talk both Clay and Dunwoody out of heading through Moncton and up the New Brunswick North Shore. I pointed out to them that there were ten times as many Protestants up the John River valley and in towns like Sussex and Woodstock, to say nothing of Saint John, than in the Acadian towns on the shore.

We did real good in Saint John, in four services making three times as much as we'd made on the whole tour up to then. Not only was I planning the trip and doing the advance work, but I'd programmed each service carefully with the help of the participating clergymen. If religious meetings can be called boffo successes, we were succeeding by then.

'What place is this?' Clay asked, as we ran through a village at forty. His voice from beside me jarred me out of my thoughts about the trip so far and about the future, which was as enticing to me as the Pearly Gates.

'Marmora,' I told him. 'We've got another thirty-five miles or so.'

'I've been thinking about the couple of days we stayed in Quebec City, Gordon,' he said.

'Yeah, Clay, it was great for you having Eileen and the children with you. Don't forget they're flying up to Toronto next week.'

'I'm looking forward to it,' he said. I could see him shifting on the seat and staring back at the Dunwoodys.

'They're both asleep,' I said.

'Yes.' After a minute he said, 'I've been thinking of Eileen and the children, naturally, but lately I've been thinking of something else.'

I nodded. 'I know, Clay. I could feel it.'

'Remember the day Eileen and I went out to Ste Anne de Beaupré, to the shrine?'

'Yes, I remember.'

'It's a magnificent place, Gordon.'

'Maybe some day you'll have a shrine like it, Protestant of course, down near Bridgewater,' I said, wondering what he was driving at.

'No, Gordon, I wasn't thinking of anything like that.'

'What then, Clay?'

'I told you that I'd had a visit with the vicar there, a middle-aged priest called Father Lanphier.'

'Yeah?'

'He'd never heard of me, of course, but we had quite a talk. Every pillar of the basilica is ringed almost to the ceiling with crutches, leg braces, wheelchairs, every prosthetic device made to help the maimed and crippled.'

'The Catholics go for that kind of show,' I said.

He said nothing, but I knew he was staring at me.

'There was the man in Truro who walked out of your meeting carrying his crutches under his arm, and how about the old lady who pushed her own wheelchair up the aisle at the end of the Fredericton visit?'

As if he hadn't heard me Clay said, 'Father Lanphier told me that out of the many hundreds, thousands, who have visited the shrine and prayed to God through Ste Anne for a miraculous cure, and out of the great many who have claimed to be cured, and have left their crutches behind as a testament, only a very few have been authenticated as genuine cures by their clerical and medical committees.'

I didn't know what to say.

'The vicar told me that most of those claiming miraculous cures had been temporarily relieved of their pain, and had been able to walk without help temporarily because their crippling diseases had been psychological to begin with. Either that or their profound faith in the miracles of Ste Anne had induced a hysteria that made them *believe* they were cured. Unfortunately, Father Lanphier said, in most cases this had not been so.'

I had to say something so I said, 'But, Clay, how about those that were authenticated as cures? And even if they weren't cured, think of all the people whose spirits were raised by praying at the shrine, just as you have raised people's spirits at all your visits. You've given people *hope*.'

'Yes, Gordon, hope that may last a few hours or until I've left them behind, then what? And what of those who substitute a laying on of hands for the real medical attention they should be getting? What must they think of a preacher who promises them miracles but only gives them a few hours respite from their pain and fears instead?'

'But you're offering them Christian service, Clay. You're leading them to the Lord, and—'

'Nobody needs a preacher to lead them to the Lord,' he said. 'I can only point out the way; only show them the efficacy of prayer. Only give them hope that the Lord Jesus Christ will hear them.'

I remembered one of his biblical homilies and I said, 'Clay, since I met you I've never heard you claim to heal anyone, but only intercede between your penitents and God. I remember you saying, "And I was strengthened as the hand of the Lord my God was upon me."'

'Yes, Ezra 7:28. Haven't you ever thought, Gordon, that I must be the most conceited man in the country to think that this hand—' he stuck it in front of my face so that I swerved the car to see the road ahead '—represents the hand of God?'

I didn't answer him, but drove on. It was the only time since meeting him and working with him that I'd discussed his healing powers with him. What can you do when a preacher, or a performer for that matter, loses his egotistical faith in himself. It's the end of the road. I saw not only the hopes and faith of thousands destroyed but a fortune going up in smoke. It wasn't that we were stealing from the people who were beginning to flock to our visits; they *wanted* to come, and made their often painful way many miles to have Clay Burridge lay his hand on them and intercede between them and God. Watching him over the months had even converted *me*.

I drove on through the small deserted towns of Havelock and Norwood, wondering what I could do to bring Clay back to his senses. I thought at one stage that an appeal to his wife and children might do it, but realized it would be like asking a movie star to give up the glamour and glitter of Hollywood because he felt his acting was ripping off the movie patrons.

The next morning, late, I woke up in my motel room and answered a knock at the door. It was Fred Dunwoody.

'Morning, Fred, what time is it?'

'Nearly eleven, Gord.'

I remembered my conversation in the car with Clay. Panic-stricken for a moment I asked, 'Anything the matter, Fred?'

'No. Not really.'

'Where's Clay?'

'In his room. He's eating breakfast.'

'What's up then?'

'Nothing, Gord, I just thought you might have quite a lot to do in the city this afternoon. You told me yesterday you had to see the arena people and the minister who's supplying the orchestra and choir. I didn't want you to sleep in.'

'No. Thanks, Fred, for waking me. How's Clay acting this morning?'

Dunwoody gave me a bewildered look. 'Acting? He's fine, as well as *I* can make out.'

In utter relief I said, 'Good, Fred. I'll get shaved and dressed and drive into town.'

The minister who was supplying the choir and orchestra was a young man with a beard who wore a huge Christian medallion around his neck over his denims. When I met him he was smoking a long filter-tip cigarette and there was a bottle of Australian sherry on his desk. I don't cotton much to hippie or would-be hippie preachers, and I certainly don't like people who are unsophisticated enough to flaunt bottles of *Australian* sherry instead of the real thing.

After a long give and take about the splitting of the gate, which he tried to up in his favour despite the telephone agreement we'd reached days before, he said, 'I don't hold with nineteenth-century

Methodist hymns. I think the orchestra and choir should open with a medley of modern songs.'

'You mean rock-'n-roll?'

He looked at me, and I realized that modern rock was the only kind of music he knew had ever existed.

It was too late to slough him off now. 'Okay, Rev,' I said. 'But don't forget we insist on "Put Your Hand in the Hand" when Clay Burridge begins his healing.'

'Sure.'

'How big is your choir?'

'Forty. Thirty girls, ten young men.'

'Great. What kind of an orchestra have you, Reverend Smoker?'

'The usual. Six pieces, piano, drums, base, and three guitars.'

'No brass or woodwinds though?'

'As I said, the usual.'

'You've got a copy of the order of the service. Remember you have no more than ten minutes on stage yourself.'

'I've read it carefully. We conduct services all over the holiday country during the summer, and our musical group has performed as far away as Charleston, West Virginia.'

'Okay.'

'Can I offer you a tot of sherry, Mr Beaton?' he asked. I'm only a minor league hustler, but I know the difference between 'can' and 'may,' and I hate non-sailors using words like 'tot' or 'good-o.'

'No thanks,' I said, shaking his hand and getting out of his poster-decorated parsonage.

The arena people were much easier to deal with, and before I left the arena-manager's office we had things laid out just fine.

There was the usual handful of people waiting at the stage door of the arena when we arrived. Clay autographed several Bibles and New Testaments, gave a couple of private benedictions, and then repeated the biblical verse he always did on such occasions. 'Heal me, O Lord, and I shall be healed; save me, and I shall be saved: for Thou are my praise.'

Fred Dunwoody went off to find the arena manager and to station the ushers, while Clay and I went to his dressing room, I carrying his fresh-laundered white shirt, blue suit, and subdued dark blue necktie. Paula Dunwoody remained outside the dressing room, warding off callers by telling them that the Reverend Clay

Burridge was meditating before the service began. Later on she'd apply Clay's light make-up.

Clay changed his clothes and sat at the makeshift dressing table reading his Bible, while I looked through the papers checking the advertising and making sure they had the time of the visit correct. I not only had the Peterborough *Examiner* but papers from Lindsay, Cobourg, and Port Hope. From the tiers of seats ringing the arena and the rows of temporary chairs placed on the arena floor itself I could hear the arrival of the crowd that promised to be the biggest one we'd ever had.

'This is going to be a big one, Clay,' I said as I got up to leave the dressing room.

'Yes. I can hear the crowds coming in,' he said.

I could detect no difference in his attitude from all the times before. 'Good luck, Clay.'

'Thanks, Gordon. The Lord be with us.'

I took my place in an empty seat at the side of the built-up stage next to the wide entrance from backstage. Already the arena was almost jammed to capacity, the tiered seats and those temporarily placed on the floor. The ushers were those regularly employed by the arena management. On stage the choir, the girls and women wearing white blouses and skirts and red blazers, the young men white shirts and trousers and red blazers, were already in place, forming an eye-catching red-and-white background to the stage itself. The small orchestra, mikes wired to the sound system, were in position at the other end of the stage. The sight of the choir surprised me; after meeting with the Reverend Smoker I'd expected something—well, something not as professional looking.

A middle-aged fat man in a dinner jacket came along the entranceway from backstage and after a brief glance at the audience climbed the steps, walked to a spot behind the green-fronted lectern, and raised a baton. The audience hushed momentarily, then the orchestra and choir broke into their opening medley. It wasn't what I'd expected, but was much better. A sort of mixture of Mantovani and the Mormon Tabernacle Choir playing and singing a softened version of Broadway standards. The kind of happy, expectant music I'd been hoping to hear since the early days in Sheet Harbour and Pictou.

When the music finished it seemed a little strange not to hear a burst of applause, and it took me a second or two to realize that the audience was really a religious congregation and that applause, to them, would have been like clapping in church.

The introductory music was followed by an old man in clerical clothes who thanked the crowd for its attendance and gave a short talk about the resurgence of religion among the youth, sweeping his arm behind him at the members of the choir.

The old minister, who I gathered from my notes must have been an Anglican canon named Dumphrey, one of the participating partners, finished his talk on time and left the stage. With superb timing the choirmaster raised his baton, the congregation rose to its feet with a shuffling of clothes and chairs, and all broke into a beautiful modern hymn, unknown to me until then. To say that it shook me up would be an understatement.

There were several verses to the hymn, and the congregation seemed to know them all, and continued to its end.

The choir then furnished a vocal counterpoint to a girl soloist who sang 'Abide With Me' in a beautiful soprano voice. She was no sooner finished than I noticed that the Reverend Smoker had taken his place unobtrusively at the lectern. He was a much different young man than the one I had met that morning at his church. Dressed now in a light grey business suit with a clerical collar, he spoke softly and reverently into the microphone.

I can still remember some of his sermon. 'There is no such thing as new life . . . life was and always will be, and it is not known what life is. There is only one life. The everything is life, the universe, the whole, the all is one life. We give that life a name and that name is God. . . .'

When he finished I glanced at my watch, and he'd ended in precisely ten minutes. For one mad moment I wished I'd given him more time.

The Reverend Smoker was followed by the whole congregation singing another hymn, but by now I was so excited by the wonderful way things were going that I don't remember which one it was. I went backstage to Clay's dressing room, where Paula was applying the finishing touches with the make-up. 'It's going great, Clay!' I exclaimed. 'Come on out to the entrance way and see for yourself. It's sensational!'

Both of us walked to the arena entrance and listened to the final verse of the hymn. I saw Clay's face light up as I'd never seen it light up before. It was a new Clay Burridge who stood beside me that night, and for the first time I thought I knew—me!—what was meant by being possessed of the spirit of the Lord.

When the hymn ended the ushers began passing the offertory bags along the rows of seats. I'd expected the small orchestra to play some soft music but instead one of the guitarists picked up a violin and walked with it to centre stage. With soft orchestral accompaniment he began to play 'Saving Grace,' and so help me I was never so—so touched by anything in my life. If anyone had told me, three months before when I was managing 'The Flack,' that I'd ever be stirred by the sound of a hymn played on a fiddle I'd have known they were crazy.

When the violinist finished, the ushers brought the offertory bags to the stage, coming down the centre aisle in pairs. They handed the wooden-handled leather bags to either me or a gentleman in a business suit who whispered to me that he was Jim Stark, representing the arena. When the offertory was over Stark and I carried the bags, which were heavier than I'd ever expected them to be, back behind the stage to a small office where Fred Dunwoody, the Rev Smoker, and the arena manager were waiting. I usually stayed there, or in offices like it, until the take had been counted and the final split had been made. That night however I just had to go into the meeting and watch Clay Burridge.

Clay had made his subdued entrance and was standing behind the lectern. He had already spoken his introduction, emphasizing that the healing of the sick and the lame was not a mysterious gift given only to him, but one that could be authenticated back through history to the biblical prophets. 'My hand cannot even heal itself, brethren,' he repeated for the fiftieth time at least since we'd been together. He quoted from memory many biblical passages from both the Old and New Testaments dealing with God's divine healing. He ended his peroration with his usual finish from the Book of Acts.

'They brought forth the sick into the streets, and laid them on beds and couches, that at least the shadow of Peter passing by might overshadow some of them. There came also a multitude out of the cities round about unto Jerusalem, bringing sick folks, and them which were vexed with unclean spirits: and they were healed every one. And the people with one accord gave heed unto those things which Philip spake . . . and many taken with palsies, and that were lame, were healed. Paul entered in, and prayed, and laid his hands on him, and healed him. So when this was done, others also, which had diseases in the island, came, and were healed.'

Clay then bowed his head momentarily, and raising it said, 'Will those of you who seek the healing power of the Lord Jesus Christ come forward and receive His healing grace?'

There were the usual shufflings and moving of chairs as the halt, the blind, the deaf, those on crutches and in wheelchairs, and one old lady carried on a stretcher, were brought forward by their friends or relatives down the centre aisle. Clay vaulted from the platform down to the arena floor, never looking so good since I'd met him as he did that evening, his youthful good looks and immaculate clothes, his smile that was both shy but filled with dedicated surety, his politeness and yes, tenderness, won everyone in the audience. I could *feel* it, and I felt at that moment that Clay Burridge, if he'd wanted, could have become prime minister.

The orchestra went into 'Put Your Hand in the Hand,' and Clay took the hand of a little girl, then a palsied old man, followed by a woman with no outward signs of disability, murmuring a prayer over each in turn, asking them each their name, smiling down at them following his prayer on their behalf, turning them away with a word of encouragement, as Paula Dunwoody turned them back to their seats. There were a great many, filling the aisle from the platform back to the rear of the arena, but unhurriedly, as if each person was the only one, Clay spoke to them, prayed over them, and gave them an encouraging word.

The orchestra stopped playing 'Put Your Hand,' and the chior took over and hummed the tune of the song. Then the orchestra again. It was almost an hour before Clay finished his laying on of hands, and with a deep bow to the audience walked slowly between the platform and the first row of seats and, joined by me, left the arena.

In the dressing room he shucked his suit coat, and the back of his shirt was wringing wet with sweat. I handed him a paper cup of Coca-Cola that Fred Dunwoody brought, and he sat there at the dressing table sipping it, not looking at either Fred or me.

The next day was taken over with press and radio interviews, and one of the networks phoned me from Toronto asking me to set up a TV taping of one of Clay's healing visits. I made arrangements with a motel outside of Sutton for accommodation for that night, and set up a stay in Newmarket for the two following nights. They would be much smaller meetings than the two in Peterborough, but they would give us a rest before hitting Toronto. I was to drive down to Toronto the next day to sign the contracts for the auditorium and do my advance press work.

The second night's meeting was an even greater success than the first, and dozens of people had to be turned back at the doors. After Toronto we would all be on easy street. Late that evening before leaving Peterborough we shared the money with Smoker and the other minister, and I could hardly believe the amount we'd taken in. I thanked Smoker for the great show he and his orchestra and choir had put on, and felt him out for repeat performances in the big city. That night before turning in I took a good hooker of scotch, the first drink I'd had since Quebec City.

It was almost eight o'clock when I woke up, dressed and shaved, and had breakfast in the motel dining room. When I was crossing the lobby later, on the way to my room, the motel manager called to me from the desk. He was standing there with the girl desk clerk.

'Mr Beaton, I have something for you,' the manager said. He handed me an envelope and one of the motel's post cards. I shoved them in my pocket, figuring they were probably notes for Clay from a couple of admirers.

'Mr Burridge has checked out,' the manager said.

'Already!' Though it surprised me I thought maybe Clay had gone out for an early morning drive before we left for Sutton. He sometimes did this; to think things out, he'd tell me.

The desk clerk said, 'He drove out of here with the car and trailer after seven. Mr and Mrs Dunwoody were with him.'

Panic hit me then, 'Did he say where he was going?'

The manager said, 'I think he mentioned he was going home.'

'Home! Back to Nova Scotia?'

'He just said "home," wherever that is, Mr Beaton. He paid the bill, including your breakfast. He said you'd understand. I've given you the receipt; it's in the envelope.'

There was nothing for me to say. My agreement with Clay had just covered the percentage of the take and there was nothing in it preventing either one of us from giving up the faith-healing tour whenever we wanted to. Looking back, even before he'd mentioned it to me on the way from Perth, I realized he'd been giving a lot of thought to what he was doing, and not liking it much. As I've said, he was incorruptible, by himself or anyone else.

The desk clerk said, 'He was wearing a buckskin jacket, Levis, and a cowboy hat. He looked real cute.'

I turned away and crossed the lobby in the direction of the inside corridor to the rooms. How could he do such a thing to me, to us? He'd just blown a fortune!

I thought of Clay Burridge driving east on the 401 freeway in his Cadillac, wearing his cowboy get-up, on his way back to Bridgewater, Nova Scotia, and oblivion. A young man who'd had a million dollars in his grasp and had thrown it away.

Though I'd quit smoking a couple of months before at Clay's request, I reached into my pocket for a cigarette. My hand closed over the motel post card, which had a small piece of paper attached to it with a staple. The paper was a small newspaper clipping telling of a little girl who though suffering from diabetes had been taken off insulin by her screwball parents on the word of a faith-healer. The child had died. I guess this had been the last straw that convinced Clay he was doing wrong, though he'd never have been guilty of a thing like that. Hell, he used to *advise* some patients to seek medical help.

The post card bore some words printed in Clay's careful grade-school style. They read: 'Dear Gordon. The following verse from the book of Proverbs will explain everything, I hope: "The legs of the lame are not straight; so is a parable in the mouth of fools." Yours in Christ. Clay.'

I phoned the front desk and asked the girl to get me a taxi to take me to the bus depot.

She said, 'The next bus to Toronto, if that's where you're going, Mr Beaton, isn't until two-twenty.'

I said, 'Good. It'll give me time to get drunk.'

# Mavis Gallant

MAVIS Gallant was born Mavis Young in Montreal, Quebec, in 1922. She was an only child, and her parents died when she was young. After attending seventeen schools in Canada and the U.S. she began working for the Montreal *Standard*, which later became *Weekend Magazine*. But she quit her job in 1950 to live and write in Paris. Her stories almost always appear first in the *New Yorker* (where this story was published in 1957), although one will occasionally appear in Canada (most recently in *The Tamarack Review* #76). She has six collections of short stories: *The Other Paris* (1956); *My Heart Is Broken* (1964); *The Pegnitz Junction* (1973); *The End of the World* (1974); *From the Fifteenth District* (1979), and *Home Truths* (1981). She has also written two novels: *Green Water, Green Sky* (1959); and *A Fairly Good Time* (1970). She still lives in Paris, and has retained her Canadian citizenship.

There has been a special Mavis Gallant issue of *Canadian Fiction Magazine* (#28, 1978), which contains a short story, a bibliography, a long interview by *CFM* editor Geoff Hancock, and critical essays by Robertson Davies, George Woodcock, and Ronald Hatch, who sees Gallant's characters as representing 'the problems besetting the individual conscience, alone in a public world.' In 'Bernadette,' for example, about a young French Canadian servant girl in an anglophone Westmount household, we see how these individual consciences construct prisons around themselves as shields against what may be termed 'the other Montreal.' 'All those small worlds of race and language and religion and class,' Gallant tells Geoff Hancock, 'all shut away from one another. A series of airtight compartments.' She adds today, however, that conditions in Montreal have changed so greatly since 1955, when 'Bernadette' was written, that it was only with the greatest reluctance that she has allowed the story to be reprinted here.

# BERNADETTE

ON THE hundred and twenty-sixth day, Bernadette could no longer pretend not to be sure. She got the calendar out from her bureau drawer—a kitchen calendar, with the Sundays and saints' days in fat red figures, under a brilliant view of Alps. Across the Alps was the name of a hardware store and its address on the other side of Montreal. From the beginning of October the calendar was smudged and grubby, so often had Bernadette with moistened forefinger counted off the days: thirty-four, thirty-five, thirty-six.... That had been October, the beginning of fear, with the trees in the garden and on the suburban street a blaze of red and yellow. Bernadette had scrubbed floors and washed walls in a frenzy of bending and stretching that alarmed her employers, the kindly, liberal Knights.

'She's used to hard work—you can see that, of course,' Robbie Knight had remarked one Sunday, almost apologizing for the fact that they employed anyone in the house at all. Bernadette had chosen to wash the stairs and woodwork that day, instead of resting. It disturbed the atmosphere of the house, but neither of the Knights knew how to deal with a servant who wanted to work too much. He sat by the window, enjoying the warm October sunlight, trying to get on with the Sunday papers but feeling guilty because his wife was worried about Bernadette.

'She *will* keep on working,' Nora said. 'I've told her to leave that hard work for the char, but she insists. I suppose it's her way of showing gratitude, because we've treated her like a human being instead of a slave. Don't you agree?'

'I suppose so.'

'I'm so tired,' Nora said. She lay back in her chair with her eyes closed, the picture of total exhaustion. She had broken one of her nails clean across, that morning, helping Bernadette with something Bernadette might easily have done alone. 'You're right about her being used to hard work. She's probably been working all her life.' Robbie tried not answering this one. 'It's so much the sort of thing I've battled,' Nora said.

He gave up. He let his paper slide to the floor. Compelled to think about his wife's battles, he found it impossible to concentrate on anything else. Nora's weapons were kept sharp for two dragons: crooked politics and the Roman Catholic Church. She had battled for birth control, clean milk, vaccination, homes for mothers, homes for old people, homes for cats and dogs. She fought against censorship, and for votes for cloistered nuns, and for the provincial income tax.

'Good old Nora,' said Robbie absently. Nora accepted this tribute without opening her eyes. Robbie looked at her, at the thin, nervous hand with the broken nail.

'She's not exciting, exactly,' he had once told one of his mistresses. 'But she's an awfully good sort, if you know what I mean. I mean, she's really a good sort. I honestly couldn't imagine not living with Nora.' The girl to whom this was addressed had instantly burst into tears, but Robbie was used to that. Unreasonable emotional behaviour on the part of other women only reinforced his respect for his wife.

The Knights had been married nearly sixteen years. They considered themselves solidly united. Like many people no longer in love, they cemented their relationship with opinions, pet prejudices, secret meanings, a private vocabulary that enabled them to exchange amused glances over a dinner table and made them feel a shade superior to the world outside the house. Their home held them, and their two daughters, now in boarding school. Private schools were out of line with the Knights' social beliefs, but in the case of their own children they had judged a private school essential.

'Selfish, they were,' Robbie liked to explain. 'Selfish, like their father.' Here he would laugh a little, and so would his listeners. He was fond of assuming a boyish air of self-deprecation—a manner which, like his boyish nickname, had clung to him since school. 'Nora slapped them both in St Margaret's, and it cleared up in a year.'

On three occasions, Nora had discovered Robbie in an affair. Each time, she had faced him bravely and made him discuss it, a process she called 'working things out.' Their talks would be formal, at first—a frigid question-and-answer period, with Robbie frightened and almost sick and Nora depressingly unreproachful. For a few nights, she would sleep in another room. She said that this enabled her to think. Thinking all night, she was fresh and ready for talk the next day. She would analyze their marriage, their lives, their childhoods, and their uncommon characters. She would tell Robbie what a Don Juan complex was, and tell him what he was trying to prove. Finally, reconciled, they were able to talk all night, usually in the kitchen, the most neutral room of the house, slowly and congenially sharing a bottle of scotch. Robbie would begin avoiding his mistress's telephone calls and at last would write her a letter saying that his marriage had been rocked from top to bottom and that but for the great tolerance shown by his wife they would all of them have been involved in something disagreeable. He and his wife had now arrived at a newer, fuller, truer, richer, deeper understanding. The long affection they held for each other would enable them to start life again on a different basis, the letter would conclude.

The basic notion of the letter was true. After such upheavals his marriage went swimmingly. He would feel flattened, but not unpleasantly, and it was Nora's practice to treat him with tolerance and good humour, like an ailing child.

He looked at the paper lying at his feet and tried to read the review of a film. It was hopeless. Nora's silence demanded his attention. He got up, kissed her lightly, and started out.

'Off to work?' said Nora, without opening her eyes.

'Well, yes,' he said.

'I'll keep the house quiet. Would you like your lunch on a tray?'

'No, I'll come down.'

'Just as you like, darling. It's no trouble.'

He escaped.

Robbie was a partner in a firm of consulting engineers. He had, at one time, wanted to be a playwright. It was this interest that had, with other things, attracted Nora when they had been at university together. Robbie had been taking a course in writing for the stage—a sideline to his main degree. His family had insisted on engineering; he spoke of defying them, and going to London or New York. Nora had known, even then, that she was a born struggler and fighter. She often wished she had been a man. She believed that to balance this overassertive side of her nature she should marry someone essentially feminine, an artist of some description. At the same time, a burning fear of poverty pushed her in the direction of someone with stability, background, and a profession outside the arts. Both she and Robbie were campus liberals;

they met at a gathering that had something to do with the Spanish war—the sort of party where, as Nora later described it, you all sat on the floor and drank beer out of old pickle jars. There had been a homogeneous quality about the group that was quite deceptive; political feeling was a great leveler. For Nora, who came from a poor and an ugly lower-middle-class home, political action was a leg up. It brought her in contact with people she would not otherwise have known. Her snobbishness moved to a different level; she spoke of herself as working-class, which was not strictly true. Robbie, in revolt against his family, who were well-to-do, conservative, and had no idea of the injurious things he said about them behind their backs, was, for want of a gentler expression, slumming around. He drifted into a beer-drinking Left Wing movement, where he was welcomed for his money, his good looks, and the respectable tone he lent the group. His favourite phrase at that time was 'of the people.' He mistook Nora for someone of the people, and married her almost before he had discovered his mistake. Nora then did an extraordinary about-face. She reconciled Robbie with his family. She encouraged him to go into his father's firm. She dampened, ever so gently, the idea of London and New York.

Still, she continued to encourage his interest in theatre. More, she managed to create such a positive atmosphere of playwriting in the house that many of their casual acquaintances thought he *was* a playwright, and were astonished to learn he was the Knight of Turnbull, Knight & Beardsley. Robbie had begun and abandoned many plays since college. He had not consciously studied since the creative-writing course, but he read, and criticized, and had reached the point where he condemned everything that had to do with the English-language stage.

Nora agreed with everything he believed. She doggedly shared his passion for the theatre—which had long since ceased to be real, except when she insisted—and she talked to him about his work, sharing his problems and trying to help. She knew that his trouble arose from the fact that he had to spend his daytime hours in the offices of the firm. She agreed that his real life was the theatre, with the firm a practical adjunct. She was sensible: she did not ask that he sell his partnership and hurl himself into uncertainty and insecurity—a prospect that would have frightened him very much indeed. She understood that it was the firm that kept them going, that paid for the girls at St Margaret's and the trip to Europe every second summer. It was the firm that gave Nora leisure and scope for her tireless battles with the political and ecclesiastical authorities of Quebec. She encouraged Robbie to write in his spare time. Every day, or nearly, during his 'good' periods, she mentioned his work. She rarely accepted an invitation without calling Robbie at his office and asking if he wanted to shut himself up and work that particular night. She could talk about his work, without boredom or exhaustion, just as she could discuss his love affairs. The only difference was that when they were mutually explaining Robbie's infidelity, they drank whisky. When they talked about his play and his inability to get on with it, Nora would go to the refrigerator and bring out a bottle of milk. She was honest and painstaking; she had at the tip of her tongue the vocabulary needed to turn their relationship and marriage inside out. After listening to Nora for a whole evening, agreeing all the way, Robbie would go to bed subdued with truth and totally empty. He felt that they had drained everything they would ever have to say. After too much talk, he would think, a couple should part; just part, without another word, full of kind thoughts and mutual understanding. He was afraid of words. That was why, that Sunday morning toward the end of October, the simple act of leaving the living room took on the dramatic feeling of escape.

He started up the stairs, free. Bernadette was on her knees, washing the painted baseboard. Her hair, matted with a cheap permanent, had been flattened into curls that looked like snails, each snail held with two crossed bobby pins. She was young, with a touching attractiveness that owed everything to youth.

'Bonjour, Bernadette.'

' 'Jour.'

Bending, she plunged her hands into the bucket of soapy water. A moment earlier, she had thought of throwing herself down the stairs and making it seem an accident. Robbie's sudden appearance had frightened her into stillness. She wiped her forehead, waiting until he had closed the door behind him. Then she flung herself at the baseboard, cloth in hand. Did she feel something—a tugging, a pain? 'Merci, mon Dieu,' she whispered. But there was nothing to be thankful for, in spite of the walls and the buckets of water and the bending and the stretching.

Now it was late December, the hundred and twenty-sixth day, and Bernadette could no longer pretend not to be certain. The Knights were giving a party. Bernadette put the calendar back in the drawer, under her folded slips. She had counted on it so much that she felt it bore witness to her fears; anyone seeing it would know at once.

For weeks she had lived in a black sea of nausea and fear. The Knights had offered to send her home to Abitibi for Christmas, had even wanted to pay her fare. But she knew that her father would know the instant he saw her, and would kill her. She preferred going on among familiar things, as if the normality, the repeated routine of getting up in the morning and putting on Mr Knight's coffee and Mrs Knight's tea would, by force of pattern, cause things to be the way they had been before October. So far, the Knights had noticed nothing, although the girls, home for Christmas, teased her about getting fat. Thanks to St Joseph, the girls had now been sent north to ski with friends, and there was no longer any danger of their drawing attention to Bernadette's waist.

Because of the party, Bernadette was to wear a uniform, which she had not done for some time. She pressed it and put it back on its hanger without trying it on, numb with apprehension, frightened beyond all thought. She had spent the morning cleaning the living room. Now it was neat, unreal, like a room prepared for a colour photo in a magazine. There were flowers and plenty of ashtrays. It was a room waiting for disorder to set in.

'Thank you, Bernadette,' Nora had said, taking, as always, the attitude that Bernadette had done her an unexpected service. 'It looks lovely.'

Nora liked the room; it was comfortable and fitted in with her horror of ostentation. Early in her marriage she had decided that her taste was uncertain; confusing elegance with luxury, she had avoided both. Later, she had discovered French-Canadian furniture, which enabled her to refer to her rooms in terms of the simple, the charming, even the amusing. The bar, for example, was a *prie-dieu* Nora had discovered during one of her forays into rural Quebec just after the war, before American tourists with a nose for a bargain had (as she said) cleaned out the province of its greatest heritage. She had found the *prie-dieu* in a barn and had bought it for three dollars. Sandpapered, waxed, its interior recess deepened to hold bottles, it was considered one of Nora's best *trouvailles*. The party that evening was being given in honour of a priest—a liberal priest from Belgium, a champion of modern ecclesiastical art, and another of Nora's finds. (Who but Nora would have dreamed of throwing a party for a priest?)

Robbie wondered if the *prie-dieu* might not offend him. 'Maybe you ought to keep the lid up, so he won't see the cross,' he said.

But Nora felt that would be cheating. If the priest accepted her hospitality, he must also accept her views.

'He doesn't know your views,' Robbie said. 'If he did, he probably wouldn't come.' He had a cold, and was spending the day at home, in order to be well for the party. The cold made him interfering and quarrelsome.

'Go to bed, Robbie,' said Nora kindly. 'Haven't you anything to read? What about all the books you got for Christmas?'

Considering him dismissed, she coached Bernadette for the evening. They rehearsed the handing around of the tray, the unobtrusive clearing of ashtrays. Nora noticed that Bernadette seemed less shy. She kept a blank, hypnotized stare, concentrating hard. After a whole year in the household, she was just beginning to grasp what was expected. She understood work, she had worked all her life, but she did not always understand what these terrifying, well-meaning people wanted. If, dusting a bookcase, she slowed her arm, lingering, thinking of nothing in particular, one of them would be there, like a phantom, frightening her out of her wits.

'Would you like to borrow one of these books, Bernadette?'

Gentle, tolerant, infinitely baffling, Mr or Mrs Knight would offer her a book in French.

'For me?'

'Yes. You can read in the afternoon, while you are resting.'

Read while resting? How could you do both? During her afternoon rest-periods, Bernadette would lie on the bed, looking out the window. When she had a whole day to herself, she went downtown in a bus and looked in the windows of stores. Often, by the end of the afternoon, she had met someone, a stranger, a man who would take her for a drive in a car or up to his room. She accepted these adventures as inevitable; she had been so overwarned before leaving home. Cunning prevented her giving her address or name, and if one of her partners wanted to see her

again, and named a time and a street number, she was likely to
forget or to meet someone else on the way. She was just as happy
in the cinema, alone, or looking at displays of eau de cologne in
shops.

Reduced to perplexity, she would glance again at the book.
Read?

'I might get it dirty.'

'But books are to be read, Bernadette.'

She would hang her head, wondering what they wanted, wishing they would go away. At last she had given in. It was in the
autumn, the start of her period of fear. She had been dusting in
Robbie's room. Unexpectedly, in that ghostly way they had, he
was beside her at the bookcase. Blindly shy, she remembered
what Mrs Knight, all tact and kindness and firm common sense,
had said that morning: that Bernadette sometimes smelled of per-
spiration, and that this was unpleasant. Probably Mr Knight was
thinking this now. In a panicky motion her hand flew to *L'Amant
de Lady Chatterley*,' which Nora had brought from Paris so that
she could test the blundering ways of censorship. (The English
version had been held at customs, the French let through, which
gave Nora ammunition for a whole winter.)

'You won't like that,' Robbie had said. 'Still . . . ' He pulled it
out of the bookcase. She took the book to her room, wrapped it
carefully in newspaper, and placed it in a drawer. A few days
later she knocked on the door of Robbie's room and returned
*L'Amant de Lady Chatterley*.

'You enjoyed it?'

'*Oui. Merci.*'

He gave her *La Porte étroite*. She wrapped it in newspaper and
placed it in a drawer for five days. When she gave it back, he
chose for her one of the Claudine series, and then, rather doubtfully, *Le Rouge et le noir*.

'Did you like the book by Stendhal, Bernadette?'

'*Oui. Merci.*'

To dinner guests, Nora now said, 'Oh, our Bernadette! Not a
year out of Abitibi, and she was reading Gide and Colette. She
knows more about French literature than we do. She goes
through Stendhal like a breeze. She adores Giraudoux.' When
Bernadette, grim with the effort of remembering what to do next,
entered the room, everyone would look at her and she would
wonder what she had done wrong.

During the party rehearsal, Robbie, snubbed, went up to bed. He knew that Nora would never forgive him if he hadn't recovered by evening. She regarded a cold in the head as something that could be turned off with a little effort; indeed, she considered any symptom of illness in her husband an act of aggression directed against herself. He sat up in bed, bitterly cold in spite of three blankets and a bathrobe. It was the chill of grippe, in the centre of his bones; no external warmth could reach it. He heard Nora go out for some last-minute shopping, and he heard Bernadette's radio in the kitchen.

'*Sans amour, on est rien du tout,*' Edith Piaf sang. The song ended and a commercial came on. He tried not to hear.

On the table by his bed were books Nora had given him for Christmas. He had decided, that winter, to reread some of the writers who had influenced him as a young man. He began this project with the rather large idea of summing himself up as a person, trying to find out what had determined the direction of his life. In college, he remembered, he had promised himself a life of action and freedom and political adventure. Perhaps everyone had then. But surely he, Robbie Knight, should have moved on to something other than a pseudo-Tudor house in a suburb of Montreal. He had been considered promising—an attractive young man with a middling-good brain, a useful background, unexpected opinions, and considerable charm. He did not consider himself unhappy, but he was beginning to wonder what he was doing, and why. He had decided to carry out his reassessment programme in secret. Unfortunately, he could not help telling Nora, who promptly gave him the complete Orwell bound in green.

He read with the conviction of habit. There was Orwell's Spain, the Spain of action and his university days. There was also the Spain he and Nora knew as tourists, a poor and dusty country where tourists became colicky because of the oil. For the moment, he forgot what he had seen, just as he could sometimes forget he had not become a playwright. He regretted the Spain he had missed, but the death of a cause no longer moved him. So far, the only result of his project was a feeling of loss. Leaving Spain, he turned to an essay on England. It was an essay he had not read until now. He skipped about, restless, and suddenly stopped at this: 'I have often been struck by the peculiar easy completeness, the perfect symmetry as it were, of a working-class interior at its best. Especially on winter evenings after tea, when the fire glows in the open range and dances mirrored in the steel fender, when Father, in shirt-sleeves, sits in the rocking chair at one side of the fire reading the racing finals, and Mother sits on the other with her sewing, and the children are happy with a penn'orth of mint humbugs, and the dog lolls roasting himself on the rag mat. . . . '

Because he had a cold and Nora had gone out and left him on a snowy miserable afternoon, he saw in this picture everything missing in his life. He felt frozen and left out. Robbie had never been inside the kitchen of a working-class home; it did not occur to him that the image he had just been given might be idyllic or sentimental. He felt only that he and Nora had missed something, and that he ought to tell her so; but he knew that it would lead to a long bout of analytical talk, and he didn't feel up to that. He blew his nose, pulled the collar of his dressing gown up around his ears, and settled back on the pillows.

Bernadette knocked at the door. Nora had told her to prepare a tray of tea, rum, and aspirin at four o'clock. It was now half past four, and Bernadette wondered if Mr Knight would betray her to Mrs Knight. Bernadette's sleeves were rolled up, and she brought with her an aura of warmth and good food. She had, in fact, been cooking a ham for the party. Her hair was up in the hideous snails again, but it gave her, Robbie thought, the look of a hardworking woman—a look his own wife achieved only by seeming totally exhausted.

'*Y a un* book, too,' said Bernadette, in her coarse, flat little voice. She put the tray down with care. '*Je l'ai mis sur le* tray.' She indicated the new Prix Goncourt, which Robbie had lent her the day it arrived. He saw at once that the pages were still uncut.

'You didn't like it?'

'Oh, *oui*,' she said automatically. '*Merci*.'

Never before had a lie seemed to him more pathetic, or more justfied. Instead of taking the book, or his tea, he gripped Bernadette's plump, strong forearm. The room was full of warmth and comfort. Bernadette had brought this atmosphere with her; it was her native element. She was the world they had missed sixteen years before, and they, stupidly, had been trying to make her read books. He held her arm, gripping it. She stared back at him, and he saw that she was frightened. He let her go, furious with himself, and said, rather coldly, 'Do you ever think about your home in Abitibi?'

'*Oui*,' she said flatly.

'Some of the farms up there are very modern now, I believe,' he said, sounding as if he were angry with her. 'Was yours?'

She shrugged. '*On a pas la television, nous,*' she said.

'I didn't think you had. What about your kitchen. What was your kitchen like at home, Bernadette?'

'*Sais pas*,' said Bernadette, rubbing the released arm on the back of her dress. 'It's big,' she offered, after some thought.

'Thank you,' said Robbie. He went back to his book, still furious, and upset. She stood still, uncertain, a fat dark little creature not much older than this own elder daughter. He turned a page, not reading, and at last she went away.

Deeply bewildered, Bernadette returned to the kitchen and contemplated the cooling ham. She seldom thought about home. Now her memory, set in motion, brought up the image of a large, crowded room. The prevailing smell was the odour of the men's boots as they came in from the outbuildings. The table, masked with oilcloth, was always set between meals, the thick plates turned upside down, the spoons in a glass jar. At the centre of the table, never removed, were the essentials: butter, vinegar, canned jam with the lid of the can half opened and wrenched back, ketchup, a tin of molasses glued to its saucer. In winter, the washing hung over the stove. By the stove, every year but the last two or three, had stood a basket containing a baby—a wailing, swaddled baby, smelling sad and sour. Only a few of Bernadette's mother's children had straggled up past the infant stage. Death and small children were inextricably knotted in Bernadette's consciousness. As a child she had watched an infant brother turn blue and choke to death. She had watched two others die of diphtheria. The innocent dead became angels; there was no reason to grieve. Bernadette's mother did all she could; terrified of injections and vaccines, she barred the door to the district nurse. She bound her infants tightly to prevent excess motion, she kept them by the flaming heat of the stove, she fed them a bouillon of warm water and cornstarch to make them fat. When Bernadette thought of the kitchen at home, she thought of her mother's pregnant figure, and her swollen feet, in unlaced tennis shoes.

Now she herself was pregnant. Perhaps Mr Knight knew, and

that was why he had asked about her mother's kitchen. Sensing a connection between her mother and herself, she believed he had seen it as well. Nothing was too farfetched, no wisdom, no perception, for these people. Their mental leaps and guesses were as mysterious to her as those of saints, or of ghosts.

Nora returned and, soon afterward, Robbie wandered downstairs. His wife had told him to get up (obviously forgetting that it was she who had sent him to bed) so that she could tidy the room. She did not ask how he felt and seemed to take it for granted that he had recovered. He could not help comparing her indifference with the solicitude of Bernadette, who had brought him tea and rum. He began comparing Bernadette with other women he had known well. His mistresses, *faute de mieux*, had been girls with jobs and little apartments. They had in common with Nora a desire to discuss the situation; they were alarmingly likely to burst into tears after lovemaking because Robbie didn't love them enough or because he had to go home for dinner. He had never known a working-class girl, other than the women his wife employed. (Even privately, he no longer used the expression 'of the people.') As far as he could determine now, girls of Bernadette's sort were highly moral, usually lived with their parents until marriage, and then disappeared from sight, like Moslem women. He might have achieved an interesting union, gratifying a laudable social curiosity, during his college days, but he had met Nora straightaway. He had been disappointed to learn that her father did not work in a factory. There was an unbridgeable gap, he had since discovered, between the girl whose father went off to work with a lunch pail and the daughter of a man who ate macaroni-and-cheese in the company cafeteria. In the midst of all her solicitude for the underprivileged, Nora never let him forget it. On the three occasions when she had caught him out in a love affair, among her first questions had been, 'Where does she come from? What does she do?'

  Robbie decided to apologize to Bernadette. He had frightened her, which he had no right to do. He no longer liked the classic role he had set for himself, the kindly educator of young servant girls. It had taken only a glimpse of his thin, busy wife to put the picture into perspective. He allowed himself one last, uncharitable thought, savouring it: compared with Bernadette, Nora looked exactly like a furled umbrella.

Bernadette was sitting at the kitchen table. The ham had been put away, the room aired. She was polishing silver for the party, using a smelly antiseptic pink paste. He no longer felt the atmosphere of warmth and food and comfort Bernadette had brought up to his room. She did not look up. She regarded her own upside-down image in the bowl of a spoon. Her hands moved slowly, then stopped. What did he want now?

Before coming to Montreal, Bernadette had been warned about the licentious English—reserved on the surface, hypocritical, infinitely wicked underneath—and she had, in a sense, accepted it as inevitable that Mr Knight would try to seduce her. When it was over, she would have another sin to account for. Mr Knight, a Protestant, would not have sinned at all. Unique in her sin, she felt already lonely. His apology sent her off into the strange swamp world again, a world in which there was no footing; she had the same feeling as when they tried to make her read books. What was he sorry about? She looked dumbly around the kitchen. She could hear Nora upstairs, talking on the telephone.

Robbie also heard her and thought: Bernadette is afraid of Nora. The idea that the girl might say something to his wife crossed his mind, and he was annoyed to realize that Nora's first concern would be for Bernadette's feelings. His motives and his behaviour they would discuss later, over a drink. He no longer knew what he wanted to say to Bernadette. He made a great show of drinking a glass of water and went out.

By evening, Robbie's temperature was over ninety-nine. Nora did not consider it serious. She felt that he was deliberately trying to ruin the party, and said so. 'Take one good stiff drink,' she said. 'That's all you need.'

He saw the party through a feverish haze. Nora was on top of the world, controlling the room, clergy-baiting, but in the most charming manner. No priest could possibly have taken offence, particularly a nice young priest from Belgium, interested in modern art and preceded by a liberal reputation. He could not reply; his English was limited. Besides, as Nora kept pointing out, he didn't know the situation in Quebec. He could only make little grimaces, acknowledging her thrusts, comically chewing the stem of a cold pipe.

'Until you know this part of the world, you don't know your own Church,' Nora told him, smiling, not aggressive.

The English Canadians in the room agreed, glancing nervously at the French. French Canada was represented by three journalists huddled on a couch. (Nora had promised the priest, as if offering hors d'oeuvres, representatives of what she called 'our chief ethnic groups.') The three journalists supported Nora, once it was made plain that clergy-baiting and French-baiting were not going to be combined. Had their wives been there, they might not have concurred so brightly; but Nora could seldom persuade her French-Canadian finds to bring their wives along. The drinking of Anglo-Saxon women rather alarmed them, and they felt that their wives, genteel, fluffy-haired, in good little dresses and strings of pearls, would disappoint and be disappointed. Nora never insisted. She believed in emancipation, but no one was more vocal in deploring the French Canadian who spoke hard, flat English and had become Anglicized out of all recognition. Robbie, feverish and disloyal, almost expected her to sweep the room with her hand and, pointing to the trio of journalists, announce, 'I found them in an old barn and bought them for five dollars each. I've sandpapered and waxed them, and there they are.'

From the Church she went on to Bernadette. She followed the familiar pattern, explaining how environment had in a few months overcome generations of intellectual poverty.

'Bernadette reads Gide and Lawrence,' she said, choosing writers the young priest was bound to disapprove of. 'She adores Colette.'

'Excellent,' he said, tepid.

Bernadette came in, walking with care, as if on a tightrope. She had had difficulty with her party uniform and she wondered if it showed.

'Bernadette,' Nora said, 'how many children did your mother have?'

'Thirteen, Madame,' said the girl. Accustomed to this interrogation, she continued to move around the room, remembering Nora's instructions during the rehearsal.

'In how many years?' Nora said.

'Fifteen.'

'And how many are living?'

'Six, Madame.'

The young priest stopped chewing his pipe and said quietly, in French, 'Are you sorry that your seven brothers and sisters died, Bernadette?'

Jolted out of her routine, Bernadette replied at once, as if she had often thought about it, 'Oh, no. If they had lived, they would have had to grow up and work hard, and the boys would have to go to war, when there is war, to fight—' About to say, 'fight for the English,' she halted. 'Now they are little angels, praying for their mother,' she said.

'Where?' said the priest.

'In Heaven.'

'What does an angel look like, Bernadette?' he said.

She gave him her hypnotized gaze and said, 'They are very small. They have small golden heads and little wings. Some are tall and wear pink and blue dresses. You don't see them because of the clouds.'

'I see. Thank you,' said Nora, cutting in, and the student of Gide and Colette moved off to the kitchen with her tray.

It ruined the evening. The party got out of hand. People stopped talking about the things Nora wanted them to talk about, and the ethnic groups got drunk and began to shout. Nora heard someone talking about the fluctuating dollar, and someone else said to her, of television, 'Well, Nora, still holding out?'—when only a few months ago anyone buying a set had been sheepish and embarrassed and had said it was really for the maid.

When it was all over and Nora was running the vacuum so that there would be less for Bernadette to do the next day, she frowned and looked tired and rather old. The party had gone wrong. The guest of honour had slipped away early. Robbie had gone to bed before midnight without a word to anybody. Nora had felt outside the party, bored and disappointed, wishing to God they would all clear out. She had stood alone by the fireplace, wondering at the access of generosity that had led her to invite these ill-matched and noisy people to her home. Her parties in the past had been so different: everyone had praised her hospitality, applauded her leadership, exclaimed at her good sense. Indignant with her over some new piece of political or religious chicanery, they had been grateful for her combativeness, and had said so—more and more as the evening wore on. Tonight, they seemed to have come just as they went everywhere else, for the liquor and good food. A rot, a feeling of complacency, had set in. She had looked around the room and thought, with an odd little shock: How old they all seem! Just then

one of her ethnic treasures—a recently immigrated German doctor—
had come up to her and said, 'That the little girl is pregnant.'

'What?'

'The little servant girl. One has only to look.'

Afterward, she wondered how she could have failed to notice.
Everything gave Bernadette away: her eyes, her skin, the characteristic thickening of her waist. There were the intangible signs,
too, the signs that were not quite physical. In spite of her own
motherhood, Nora detested, with a sort of fastidious horror, any of
the common references to pregnancy. But even to herself, now, she
could think of Bernadette only in terms of the most vulgar expressions, the terminology her own family (long discarded, never invited here) had employed. Owing to a 'mistake,' Bernadette was
probably 'caught.' She was beginning to 'show.' She was at least
four months 'gone.' It seemed to Nora that she had better go
straight to the point with Bernadette. The girl was under twenty-
one. It was quite possible that the Knights would be considered
responsible. If the doctor had been mistaken, then Bernadette
could correct her. If Bernadette were to tell Nora to mind her own
business, so much the better, because it would mean that Bernadette had more character than she seemed to have. Nora had no
objection to apologizing in either instance.

Because of the party and the extra work involved, Bernadette had
been given the next afternoon off. She spent the morning cleaning.
Nora kept out of the way. Robbie stayed in bed, mulishly maintaining that he wasn't feeling well. It was after lunch, and Bernadette
was dressed and ready to go downtown to a movie, when Nora
decided not to wait any longer. She cornered Bernadette in the
kitchen and, facing her, suddenly remembered how, as a child, she
had cornered field mice with a flashlight and then drowned them.
Bernadette seemed to know what was coming; she exuded fear. She
faced her tormentor with a beating, animal heart.

Nora sat down at the kitchen table and began, as she frequently
had done with Robbie, with the words 'I think we ought to talk
about a certain situation.' Bernadette stared. 'Is there anything
you'd like to tell me?' Nora said.

'No,' said Bernadette, shaking her head.

'But you're worried about something. Something is wrong. Isn't
that true?'

'No.'

'Bernadette, I want to help you. Sit down. Tell me, are you pregnant?'

'I don't understand.'

'Yes, you do. *Un enfant. Un bébé.* Am I right?'

'*Sais pas,*' said Bernadette. She looked at the clock over Nora's head.

'*Bernadette.*'

It was getting late. Bernadette said, 'Yes. I think so. Yes.'

'You poor little mutt,' said Nora. 'Don't keep standing there like that. Sit down here, by the table. Take off your coat. We must talk about it. This is much more important than a movie.' Bernadette remained standing, in hat and coat. 'Who is it?' said Nora. 'I didn't know you had ... I mean, I didn't know you knew anyone here. Tell me. It's most important. I'm not angry.' Bernadette continued to look up at the clock, as if there were no other point in the room on which she dared fix her eyes. '*Bernadette!*' Nora said. 'I've just asked you a question. Who is the boy?'

'*Un monsieur,*' said Bernadette.

Did she mean by that an older man, or was Bernadette, in using the word '*monsieur,*' implying a social category? '*Quel monsieur?*' said Nora.

Bernadette shrugged. She stole a glance at Nora, and something about the oblique look suggested more than fear or evasiveness. A word came into Nora's mind: sly.

'Can you ... I mean, is it someone you're going to marry?' But no. In that case, he would have been a nice young boy, someone of Bernadette's own background. Nora would have met him. He would have been caught in the kitchen drinking Robbie's beer. He would have come every Sunday and every Thursday afternoon to call for Bernadette. 'It is someone you *can* marry?' Nora said. Silence. 'Don't be afraid,' said Nora, deliberately making her voice kind. She longed to shake the girl, even slap her face. It was idiotic; here was Bernadette in a terrible predicament, and all she could do was stand, shuffling from one foot to the other, as if a movie were the most important thing in the world. 'If he isn't already married,' Nora said, 'which I'm beginning to suspect is the case, he'll marry you. You needn't worry about that. I'll deal with it, or Mr Knight will.'

'*Pas possible,*' said Bernadette, low.

'Then I was right. He *is* married.' Bernadette looked up at the clock, desperate. She wanted the conversation to stop. 'A married man,' Nora repeated. '*Un monsieur.*' An unfounded and wholly outrageous idea rushed into her mind. Dismissing it, she said, 'When did it happen?'

'*Sais pas.*'

'Don't be silly. That really is a very silly reply. Of course you know. You've only had certain hours out of this house.'

The truth of it was that Bernadette did not know. She didn't know his name or whether he was married or even where she could find him again, even if she had desired such a thing. He seemed the least essential factor. Lacking words, she gave Nora the sidelong glance that made her seem coarse and deceitful. She is so uninnocent, Nora thought, surprised and a little repelled. It occurred to her that in spite of her long marriage and her two children, she knew less than Bernadette. While she was thinking about Bernadette and her lover, there came into her mind the language of the street. She remembered words that had shocked and fascinated her as a child. That was Bernadette's fault. It was Bernadette's atmosphere, Nora thought, excusing herself to an imaginary censor. She said, 'We must know when your baby will be born. Don't you think so?' Silence. She tried again: 'How long has it been since you ... I mean, since you missed ... '

'One hundred and twenty-seven days,' said Bernadette. She was so relieved to have, at last, a question that she could answer that she brought it out in a kind of shout.

'My God. What are you going to do?'

'*Sais pas.*'

'Oh, Bernadette!' Nora cried. 'But you must think.' The naming of a number of days made the whole situation so much more immediate. Nora felt that they ought to be doing something— telephoning, writing letters, putting some plan into motion. 'We shall have to think for you,' she said. 'I shall speak to Mr Knight.'

'No,' said Bernadette, trembling, suddenly coming to life. 'Not Mr Knight.'

Nora leaned forward on the table. She clasped her hands together, hard. She looked at Bernadette. 'Is there a special reason why I shouldn't speak to Mr Knight?' she said.

'*Oui.*' Bernadette had lived for so many days now in her sea of nausea and fear that it had become a familiar element. There were greater fears and humiliatons, among them that Mr Knight, who was even more baffling and dangerous than his wife, should try to discuss this thing with Bernadette. She remembered what he had said the day before, and how he had held her arm. 'He must know,' said Bernadette. 'I think he must already know.'

'You had better go on,' said Nora, after a moment. 'You'll miss your bus.' She sat quite still and watched Bernadette's progress down the drive. She looked at the second-hand imitation-seal coat that had been Bernadette's first purchase (and Nora's despair) and the black velveteen snow boots trimmed with dyed fur and tied with tasselled cords. Bernadette's purse hung over her arm. She had the walk of a fat girl—the short steps, the ungainly little trot.

It was unreasonable, Nora knew it was unreasonable; but there was so much to reinforce the idea—'*Un monsieur*,' and the fact that he already knew ('He must know,' Bernadette had said)—and then there was Bernadette's terror when she said she was going to discuss it with him. She thought of Robbie's interest in Bernadette's education. She thought of Robbie in the past, his unwillingness to remain faithful, his absence of courage and common sense. Recalling Bernadette's expression, prepared now to call it corrupt rather than sly, she felt that the girl had considered herself deeply involved with Nora; that she knew Nora much better than she should.

Robbie had decided to come downstairs, and was sitting by the living-room fire. He was reading a detective novel. Beside him was a drink.

'Get you a drink?' he said, without lifting his eyes, when Nora came in.

'Don't bother.'

He went on reading. He looked so innocent, so unaware that his life was shattered. Nora remembered how he had been when she had first known him, so pleasant and dependent and good-looking and stupid. She remembered how he had been going to write a play, and how she had wanted to change the world, or at least Quebec. Tears of fatigue and strain came into her eyes. She felt that the failure of last night's party had been a symbol of the end. Robbie had done something cheap and dishonourable, but he reflected their world. The world was ugly, Montreal was ugly, the street outside the window contained houses of surpassing ugliness. There was nothing left to discuss but television and the fluctuating dollar; that was what the world had become. The children were in boarding school because Nora didn't trust herself to bring them up.

The living room was full of amusing peasant furniture because she didn't trust her own taste. Robbie was afraid of her and liked humiliating her by demonstrating again and again that he preferred nearly any other woman in bed. That was the truth of things. Why had she never faced it until now?

She said, 'Robbie, can I talk to you?' Reluctant, he looked away from his book. She said, 'I just wanted to tell you about a dream. Last night I dreamed you died. I dreamed that there was nothing I could do to bring you back, and that I had to adjust all my thoughts to the idea of going on without you. It was a terrible, shattering feeling.' She intended this to be devastating, a prelude to the end. Unfortunately, she had had this dream before, and Robbie was bored with it. They had already discussed what it might mean, and he had no desire to go into it now.

'I wish to God you wouldn't keep on dreaming I died,' he said.

She waited. There was nothing more. She blinked back her tears and said, 'Well, listen to this, then. I want to talk about Bernadette. What do you know, exactly, about Bernadette's difficulties?'

'Has Bernadette got difficulties?' The floor under his feet heaved and settled. He had never been so frightened in his life. Part of his mind told him that nothing had happened. He had been ill, a young girl had brought warmth and comfort into his room, and he wanted to touch her. What was wrong with that? Why should it frighten him so much that Nora knew? He closed his eyes. It was hopeless; Nora was not going to let him get on with the book. Nora looked without any sentiment at all at the twin points where his hairline was moving back. 'Does she seem sort of unsettled?' he asked.

'That's a way of putting it. Sometimes you have a genuine talent for irony.'

'Oh, hell,' said Robbie, suddenly fed up with Nora's cat-and-mouse. 'I don't feel like talking about anything. Let's skip it for now. It's not important.'

'Perhaps you'd better tell me what you consider important,' Nora said. 'Then we'll see what we can skip.' She wondered how he could sit there, concerned with his mild grippe, or his hangover, when the whole structure of their marriage was falling apart. Already, she saw the bare bones of the room they sat in, the rugs rolled, the cracks that would show in the walls when they took the pictures down.

He sighed, giving in. He closed his book and put it beside his drink. 'It was just that yesterday when I was feeling so lousy she brought me—she brought me a book. One of those books we keep lending her. She hadn't even cut the pages. The whole thing's a farce. She doesn't even look at them.'

'Probably not,' said Nora. 'Or else she does and that's the whole trouble. To get straight to the point, which I can see you don't want to do, Bernadette has told me she's having a baby. She takes it for granted that you already know. She's about four months under way, which makes yesterday seem rather pointless.'

Robbie said impatiently, 'We're not talking about the same thing.' He had not really absorbed what Nora was saying; she spoke so quickly, and got so many things in all at once. His first reaction was astonishment, and a curious feeling that Bernadette had deceived him. Then the whole import of Nora's speech entered his mind and became clear. He said, 'Are you crazy? Are you out of your mind? Are you completely crazy?' Anger paralyzed him. He was unable to think of words or form them on his tongue. At last she said, 'It's too bad that when I'm angry I can't do anything except feel sick. Or maybe it's just as well. You're crazy, Nora. You get these—I don't know—you get these ideas.' He said, 'If I'd hit you then, I might have killed you.'

It had so seldom occurred in their life together that Robbie was in the right morally that Nora had no resources. She had always triumphed. Robbie's position had always been indefensible. His last remark was so completely out of character that she scarcely heard it. He had spoken in an ordinary tone of voice. She was frightened, but only because she had made an insane mistake and it was too late to take it back. Bravely, because there was nothing else to do, she went on about Bernadette. 'She doesn't seem to know what to do. She's a minor, so I'm afraid it rather falls on us. There is a place in Vermont, a private place, where they take these girls and treat them well, rather like a boarding school. I can get her in, I think. Having her admitted to the States could be your end of it.'

'I suppose you think that's going to be easy,' Robbie said bitterly. 'I suppose you think they admit pregnant unmarried minors every day of the year.'

'None of it is easy!' Nora cried, losing control. 'Whose fault is it?'

'It's got nothing to do with me!' said Robbie, shouting at her. 'Christ Almighty, get that through your head!'

They let silence settle again. Robbie found that he was trembling. As he had said, it was physically difficult for him to be angry.

Nora said, 'Yes, Vermont,' as if she were making notes. She was determined to behave as if everything were normal. She knew that unless she established the tone quickly, nothing would ever be normal again.

'What will she do with it? Give it out for adoption?' said Robbie, in spite of himself diverted by details.

'She'll send it north, to her family,' said Nora. 'There's always room on a farm. It will make up for the babies that died. They look on those things, on birth and on death, as acts of nature, like the changing of the seasons. They don't think of them as catastrophes.'

Robbie wanted to say, You're talking about something you've read, now. They'll be too ashamed to have Bernadette or the baby around; this is Quebec. But he was too tired to offer a new field of discussion. He was as tired as if they had been talking for hours. He said, 'I suppose this Vermont place, this school or whatever it is, has got to be paid for.'

'It certainly does.' Nora looked tight and cold at this hint of stinginess. It was unnatural for her to be in the wrong, still less to remain on the defensive. She had taken the position now that even if Robbie were not responsible, he had somehow upset Bernadette. In some manner, he could be found guilty and made to admit it. She would find out about it later. Meanwhile, she felt morally bound to make him pay.

'Will it be expensive, do you think?'

She gave him a look, and he said nothing more.

Bernadette sat in the comforting dark of the cinema. It was her favourite kind of film, a musical comedy in full colour. They had reached the final scene. The hero and heroine, separated because of a stupid quarrel for more than thirty years, suddenly found themselves in the same night club, singing the same song. They had grey hair but youthful faces. All the people around them were happy to see them together. They clapped and smiled. Bernadette smiled, too. She did not identify herself with the heroine, but with the people looking on. She would have liked to have gone to a night club in a low-cut dress and applauded such a scene. She believed in love and in uncomplicated stories of love, even though it was something she had never experienced or seen around her. She did not really expect it to happen to her, or to anyone she knew.

For the first time, her child moved. She was so astonished that she looked at the people sitting on either side of her, wondering if they had noticed. They were looking at the screen. For the first time, then, she thought of it as a child, here, alive—not a state of terror but something to be given a name, clothed, fed, and baptized. Where and how and when it would be born she did not question. Mrs Knight would do something. Somebody would. It would be born, and it would die. That it would die she never doubted. She was uncertain of so much else; her own body was a mystery, nothing had ever been explained. At home, in spite of her mother's pregnancies, the birth of the infants was shrouded in secrecy and, like their conception, suspicion of sin. This baby was Bernadette's own; when it died, it would pray for her, and her alone, for all of eternity. No matter what she did with the rest of her life, she would have an angel of her own, praying for her. Oddly secure in the dark, the dark of the cinema, the dark of her personal fear, she felt protected. She thought: *Il prie pour moi.* She saw, as plainly as if it had been laid in her arms, her child, her personal angel, white and swaddled, baptized, innocent, ready for death.

# Norman Levine

NORMAN Levine was born in 1923 in Ottawa's Lower Town, which is to Ottawa what Mordecai Richler's St Urbain Street is to Montreal. His family was orthodox Jewish, a fact that both isolated him from the rest of Ottawa and insulated him from what he calls 'the usual qualities of a lower-class, near-slum neighbourhood.' He served with the RCAF during the war, and afterwards attended McGill University in Montreal, where he wrote his first novel, *The Angled Road* (1952). He moved to England in 1949, and lived in St Ives, Cornwall, for more than 30 years before returning to Canada in February, 1980. He now lives in Toronto.

Levine has written a second novel, *From a Seaside Town* (1970), but is best known for his short stories, which have been broadcast on radio, published in numerous magazines, and collected into four books: *One-Way Ticket* (1961), *I Don't Want to Know Anyone Too Well* (1971), *Selected Stories* (1975), and *Thin Ice* (1979). In 1958 his autobiographical travel book, *Canada Made Me*, appeared in England, and in 1965-66 he was the University of New Brunswick's first writer-in-residence.

Of his writing technique, specifically in 'By a Frozen River,' Levine has said: 'I like to make traps. It usually starts with a feeling I have about people or a situation, and in order to trap it I literally have to construct an armature, like a sculptor, to build the clay up on. . . . What, on the surface, is the connection between a man going into an isolated community, finding the last Jew, and an unhappy marriage he meets in a hotel? I know there *is* a connection, but I don't know what it is, so I build this trap, and I write to try to explain to myself why I feel there is this connection.'

# BY A FROZEN RIVER

IN THE winter of 1965 I decided to go for a few months to a small town in northern Ontario. It didn't have a railway station—just one of those brown railway sidings, on the outskirts, with a small wooden building to send telegrams, buy tickets, and to get on and get off. A taxi was there meeting the train. I asked the driver to take me to a hotel. There was only one he would recommend. The Adanac. I must have looked puzzled. For he said,

'It's Canada spelled backwards.'

He drove slowly through snow-covered streets. The snowbanks by the sidewalk were so high that you couldn't see anyone walking. Just the trees. He drove alongside a frozen river with a green bridge across it. Then we were out for a while in the country. The snow here had drifted so that the tops of the telegraph poles were protruding like fence posts. Then we came to the town—a wide main street with other streets going off it.

The Adanac was a three-storey wooden hotel on the corner of King and Queen. It had seen better times. Its grey-painted wooden verandah, with icicles on the edges, looked old and fragile. But the woodwork had hand-carved designs, and the white windows had rounded tops. Beside it was a new beer parlour.

Fifty years ago it was the height of fashion to stay at the hotel. It was then called the George. The resident manager told me this, in his office, after I paid a month's rent in advance. His name was Savage. A short, overweight man in his sixties, with a slow speaking voice, as if he was thinking what he was going to say. He sat, neatly dressed, behind a desk, his grey hair crew-cut, and looked out of the large window at the snow-covered street. The sun was shining.

'Well,' he said slowly. 'It's an elegant day.'

His wife was a thin, tall woman with delicate features. She also hardly spoke. But would come into the office and sit, very upright, in a rocking chair near Mr Savage and look out of the window. The office connected with their three-room flat. It was filled with their possessions. A small, bronze crucifix was on the wall. Over the piano a large picture of the Pope. There were a few coloured photographs: a boy in uniform, children, and a sunset over a lake.

231

I rented the flat above. I had a room to sleep in, a room to write and read, and a kitchen with an electric stove and fridge. To get to them I would go up worn steps, along a wide, badly lit corridor— large tin pipes carried heat along the ceiling. But inside the rooms it was warm. They had radiators and double windows.

I unpacked. Then went to the supermarket, by the frozen river, and came back with various tins, fruit, and cheap cigars that said they were dipped in wine. I made myself some coffee, lit one of the thin cigars, and relaxed.

I saw a wooden radio on the side-table in the sitting-room. A battered thing. I had to put twenty-five cents in the back. That, according to a metal sign, gave me two hours' playing time. But that was only a formality. For the back was all exposed, and the twenty-five cents kept falling out for me to put through again.

Listening to the radio—I could only get the local station—the town sounded a noisy, busy place, full of people buying and selling and with things going on. But when I walked out, the first thing I noticed was the silence. The frozen, shabby side-streets. Hardly anything moving. It wasn't like what the radio made out at all. There was a feeling of apathy. The place seemed stunned by the snow piled everywhere.

I quickly established a routine. After breakfast I went out and walked. And came back, made some coffee, and wrote down whatever things I happened to notice.

This morning it was the way trees creak in the cold. I had walked by a large elm when I heard it. I thought it was the crunching sound my shoes made on the hard-packed snow. So I stopped. There was no wind, the branches were not moving, yet the tree was creaking.

In the late afternoon, I made another expedition outside. Just before it got dark, I found a small square. It began to snow. The few trees on the perimeter were black. The few bundled-up people walking slowly through the snow were black. And from behind curtained windows a bit of light, a bit of orange. There was no sound. Just the snow falling. I expected horses and sleighs to appear, and felt the isolation.

That evening I had company. A mouse. I saw it just before it saw me. I tried to hit it with a newspaper, but I missed. And as it ran it slipped and slithered on the linoleum. I was laughing. It ran behind the radiator. I looked and saw it between the radiator grooves where the dust had gathered. It had made a nest out of bits of fluff. I left food out for it. And in the evenings it would come out and run around the perimeter of the sitting-room, then go back behind the radiator.

Birds woke me in the morning. It seemed odd to see so much snow and ice and hear birds singing. I opened the wooden slot in the outside window and threw out some bread. Though I could hear the birds, I couldn't see them. Then they came—sparrows. They seemed to fly into their shadows as they landed on the snow. Then three pigeons. I went and got some more bread.

On the fourth day I met my neighbour across the hall. He rented the two rooms opposite. He wore a red lumberjack shirt and black lumberjack boots with the laces going high up. He was medium height, in his forties, with pleasant features. And he had short, red hair.

'Hi,' he said. And asked me what I was doing.

'Writing a book,' I said.

'Are you really writing a book?'

'Yes.'

'That must be very nice,' he said.

And invited me into his flat. It was the same as mine, except he didn't have a sitting-room. The same second-hand furniture, the used electric stove, the large fridge, the wooden radio.

I asked him what he did.

'I work in a small factory. Just my brother and me. We make canoes. Do you like cheese?'

'Yes,' I said.

He opened his fridge. It was filled with large hunks of an orange cheese.

'I get it sent from Toronto. Here, have some.'

I met the new occupants of the three rooms behind me next morning. I was going to the toilet. (There was one toilet, with bath, for all of us on the first floor. It was in the hall at the top of the stairs.) I opened the door and saw a woman sitting on the toilet, smoking a cigarette. She wasn't young. Her legs were close together. She said, 'Oh.' I said sorry and closed the door quickly. 'I'm sorry,' I said again, this time louder, as I walked away.

A couple of days later she knocked on my door and said she was Mrs Labelle and she was Jewish. She heard from Savage that I had a Jewish name. Was I Jewish? I said I was. She invited me back to meet her husband.

The people who rented these rooms usually didn't stay very long. So there was no pride in trying to do anything to change them. But Mrs Labelle had her room spotless. She had put up bright yellow curtains to hide the shabby window blinds. She had plastic flowers in a bowl on the table. And everything looked neat, and washed, even though the furniture was the same as I had.

Her husband, Hubert, was much younger. He looked very dapper. Tall, dark hair brushed back, neatly dressed in a dark suit and tie and a clean white shirt. He had a tripod in his hand and said he was going out to work.

'Savage told us you were a writer. I have started to write my life story—What the photographer saw—I tell all. You wouldn't believe the things that have happened to me.'

His wife said that the mayor was trying to get them out of town. 'He told the police that we need a licence. It's because he owns the only photograph store here. He's afraid of the competition. We're not doing anything illegal. I knock on people's doors and ask them if they want their picture taken at home. He's very good,' she said, 'especially with children.'

After that Mrs Labelle came to the door every day. She knew all the other occupants. And would tell me little things about them. 'He's a very hard worker,' she said about the man who made canoes. 'He doesn't drink at all.' Then she told me about the cleaning woman, Mabel. 'She only gets fifteen dollars a week. Her husband's an alcoholic. She's got a sixteen-year-old daughter—she's pregnant. I'm going to see her this afternoon and see if I can help. Be careful of Savage. He looks quiet, but I saw him using a blackjack on a drunk from the beer parlour who tried to get into the hotel at night. He threw him out in the snow. Dragged him by the feet. And Mrs Savage helped.' She complained of the noise at night. 'There's three young waitresses. Just above me. They have boys at all hours. I don't blame them. But I can't sleep. I can't wash my face. It's nerves,' she said.

Then I began to hear Mr Labelle shouting at her. 'God damn you. Leave me alone. Just leave me alone.' It went on past midnight.

Next day, at noon, she knocked on the door. She was smiling.

'I found a place where you can get Jewish food.'

'Where?'

'Morris Bischofswerder. He's a furrier. Up on the main street.'

I went to the furrier. He had some skins hanging on the walls. And others were piled in a heap on the floor.

'Do you sell food?' I said.

'What kind of food?'

'Jewish food.'

He looked me over.

He was below middle height, stocky, with a protruding belly. A dark moustache, almost bald, but dark hair on the sides. He was neatly dressed in a brown suit with a gold watch chain in his vest pocket. He was quite a handsome man, full lips and dark eyes. And from those eyes I had a feeling that he had a sense of fun.

'Where are you from?' he asked. 'The West?'

'No, from England.'

'All right, come.'

He led me through a doorway into the back and from there into his kitchen. And immediately there was a familiar food smell, something that belonged to my childhood. A lot of dried mushrooms, on a string, like a necklace, hung on several nails. He showed me two whole salamis and some loose hot dogs.

'I can let you have a couple pounds of salami and some hot dogs until the next delivery. I have it flown in once a month from Montreal.' He smiled. 'I also like this food. Where are you staying?'

'At the Adanac.'

His wife came in. She was the same size as Mr Bischofswerder but thinner, with grey hair, a longish thin nose, deep-set very dark eyes, the hollows were in permanent shadow, and prominent top teeth.

'He's from England,' he told her.

'I come from Canada,' I said quickly. 'But I live in England. The place I live in England doesn't have snow in winter. So I've come back for a while.'

'You came all the way from England for the snow?'

'Yes.'

They both looked puzzled.

'I like winters with snow,' I said.

'What have you got in England?'

'Where I live—rain.'

'Have you got a family?' Mr Bischofswerder said, changing the subject. 'Is your mother and father alive?'

'My mother and father lived in Ottawa, but they moved to California eight years ago.'

'I bet they don't miss Canadian winters,' Mrs Bischofswerder said.

'We have a married daughter in Montreal and five grandchildren,' he said proudly, 'four boys and one girl.'

'Sit down,' Mrs Bischofswerder said. 'I was just going to make some tea.'

And she brought in a chocolate cake, some pastry that had poppy seeds on top, and some light egg cookies.

'It's very good, isn't it?' she said.

'I haven't had food like this since I was a boy,' I said.

'Why are you so thin?' she said. '*Eat. Eat.*' And pushed more cookies in my direction.

'I wonder if you would come to *shul* next Friday,' Mr Bischofswerder said.

My immediate reaction was to say no. For I haven't been in a synagogue for over twenty years. But sitting in this warm kitchen with the snow outside. Eating the food. Mrs Bischofswerder making a fuss. It brought back memories of my childhood. And people I once knew.

'I'll come,' I said.

'Fine,' he said. 'If you come here around four o'clock, we'll go together. It gets dark quickly.'


That night the Labelles quarrelled until after two. Next day, at noon, Mrs Labelle knocked on the door. 'He didn't turn up. This woman was holding her children all dressed up. I told her to send them to school.'

'Is this the first time?'

'No. It's only got bad now. He's an alcoholic.'

She began to weep. I asked her inside. She was neatly dressed in dark slacks and a small fur jacket. 'My sisters won't have me. They say I've sown my wild oats.'

'Would you like some coffee?'

'Thanks. We had a house in Toronto. I have in storage lots of furniture—a fur coat—real shoes—not shoes like this. And where would you see a woman of my age going around knocking on doors? I'm sure I'm going to be killed. He calls me a witch. I found a piece of paper with a phone number. And a name—Hattie. I called up and said to leave my husband alone. I found another piece of paper. It said Shirley. They're all over him. He's a good-looking guy. And when he's working—these women are alone with him. You know—'

That afternoon, while I was writing, the phone went. It was Mrs Labelle.

'I'm in someone's house waiting for him to come and take the picture. Can you see if he's in. He hasn't turned up.'

I knocked on their door. Mr Labelle was sitting on the settee with a middle-aged man in a tartan shirt, and they were both drinking beer out of small bottles.

I said she was on the phone.

'Say you haven't seen me,' he said.

'Yes,' the other man said. 'Say you haven't seen him.'

But Labelle came after me and stood by the open door. 'Why don't you just say hello?' I said.

He went in and I could hear him saying, 'I'm not drunk. I'm coming over.' He hung up and closed the door.

'I'll tell you,' he said. 'Man to man. I'll be forty-one next month. And she's fifty-eight. We've been married fifteen years. I didn't know how old she was when we married. Then she was seven months in a mental home. I used to see her every day. At two. I had to get my job all changed around. But I'll tell you what. I knocked up a woman two years ago. And she heard about it. The child died. She can't have children. She won't give me some rein. I've had her for fifteen years. Don't worry,' he said. 'I won't leave her. You may hear us at night. I shout. I'm French Canadian. But I'll look after her.'

He went back and got his camera and tripod. And he and the other man went down the stairs.

Ten minutes later she rang up again.

'Is he gone?'

'Yes,' I said.

That evening around nine there was a gentle knock at the door. It was Mrs Labelle, in a red dressing-gown. 'He's asleep,' she said. 'Thank you very much. He hasn't eaten anything. I make special things. But he won't eat.'

It was quiet until eleven that night. I could hear them talking.

Then he began to raise his voice. 'Shut up. God damn it. Leave me alone. You should have married a Jewish businessman. You would have been happy.'

On Friday afternoon I put on a clean white shirt and tie and a suit. And went to call on Mr Bischofswerder. He was dressed, neatly, in a dark winter coat and a fur hat. We walked about four blocks. Then he led me into what I thought was a private house but turned out to be the synagogue. It was very small. Around twenty-four feet square and twenty feet high. But though it was small, it was exact in the way the synagogues were that I remembered. There was a wooden ark between a pair of tall windows in the east wall. A few steps, with wooden rails, led to the ark. The Ten Commandments, in Hebrew, were above it. A low gallery extended around the two sides. In the centre of the ceiling hung a candelabra with lights over the reading desk. There were wooden bench seats. Mr Bischofswerder raised one, took out a prayer book, and gave the prayer book to me.

'Shall we start?' he said.

'Aren't we going to wait for the others?'

'There are no others,' he said.

And he began to say the prayers to himself. Now and then he would run the words out aloud so I could hear, in a kind of sing-song that I remembered my father doing. I followed with my eyes the words. And now and then I would say something so he would hear.

I had long forgotten the service, the order of the service. So I followed him. I got up when he did. I took the three steps backwards when he did. But most of the time we were both silent. Just reading the prayers.

Then it was over. And he said,

'Good Shabbus.'

'Good Shabbus,' I said.

On the way back, through the snow-covered streets, it was freezing. Mr Bischofswerder was full of enthusiasm.

'Do you realize,' he said, 'this is the first time I've had someone in the *shul* with me at Friday night for over three years.'

For the next seven Friday nights and Saturday mornings I went with Mr Bischofswerder to the synagogue. We said our prayers in silence.

Then I went back with him to his warm house. And to the enormous Sabbath meal that Mrs Bischofswerder had cooked. Of gefilte fish with chrane, chicken soup with mandlen, chicken with tzimmes, compote, tea with cookies. And we talked. They wanted to know about England. I told them about the English climate, about English money, English society, about London, Fleet Street, the parks, the pubs. How I lived by the sea and a beautiful bay but hardly any trees.

And he told me how the trappers brought him skins that he sent on to Montreal. That he was getting a bit old for it now. 'Thank God I can still make a living.' He told me of the small Jewish community that was once here. 'In 1920 when we came there were ten families. By the end of the last war it was down to three. No new recruits came to take the place of those who died or moved away. When we go,' said Mr Bischofswerder, 'all that will be left will be a small cemetery.'

'Have some more cookies,' his wife said, pushing a plateful towards me. 'You have hardly touched them. You won't get fat. They're light. They're called nothings.'

Mrs Labelle knocked on my door. She looked excited. 'I'm selling tickets,' she said. 'The town's running a sweepstake—when will the frozen river start to move? Everyone's talking about it. I've already sold three books. Will you have one? You can win five hundred dollars.'

'How much are they?'

'Fifty cents.'

'I'll have one,' I said.

'Next time you go to the supermarket,' she said, 'you'll see a clock in the window. There's a wire from the clock to the ice in the river. As soon as the ice starts to move—the clock stops. And the nearest ticket wins.'

She gave me my ticket.

'Good luck,' she said. And kissed me lightly on a cheek.

She looked, I thought, the happiest I had seen her. My ticket said: March 26th, 08: 16: 03.

That night I noticed the mouse had gone. No sign of it anywhere. It was raining. The streets were slushy and slippery. But later that night the water froze. And next morning when the sun came out it was slush again. The snow had started to shrink on the roofs;

underneath the edges I could see water moving. I walked down to the river. It was still frozen, but I saw patches of blue where before it was all white. Crows were flapping over the ice with bits of straw in their beaks. The top crust of the river had buckled in places. And large pieces creaked as they rubbed against each other. Things were beginning to break up. It did feel like something was coming to an end here.

Next day, just before noon, Mrs Labelle came to the door. She looked worried. 'Savage told us we have to leave. I went to see him with our week's rent in advance. But he said he didn't want it. He said we were making too much noise at night. The waitresses make noise, but he doesn't mind them. I don't know where we'll go. We've been in Sudbury, in Timmins, in North Bay—'

'It's OK,' Mr Labelle said, coming to the door. 'We'll be all right,' he said to her gently. And started to walk her back toward their door. Then he called out to me. 'If we don't see you, fellah, good luck.'

'Same to you,' I said.

'But where will we go, Hubert?' Mrs Labelle said, looking up to his face.

'There's lot of places,' he answered. 'Now we got some packing to do.'

After the Labelles had gone, it was very quiet. I had got the reminders I wanted of a Canadian winter. I had filled up three notebooks. It was time that I left. I went down to the office and told this to Mr Savage. He suggested that I stay until the ice started to move.

But I left before it did.

I took a light plane, from the snow-covered field with a short runway. From the air, for a while, I could see the small town. But soon it was lost in a wilderness of snow, trees, and frozen lakes.

# Margaret Laurence

MARGARET Laurence (née Wemyss) was born in 1926 in Neepawa, Manitoba. Her parents died when she was a child, and she was raised by her stepmother and grandfather until 1944, when she entered United College in Winnipeg. After graduating (Honours English), she married Jack Laurence in 1948 and moved with him to England. From there they went to Somaliland (now the Somali Republic), and then in 1952 to the Gold Coast (Ghana) until 1957. They returned to Canada to live, then went back to England for a time before returning to live permanently in Canada in 1974.

Laurence's first short stories began appearing in such Canadian magazines as *Queen's Quarterly* in the early 1950s, and were derived almost exclusively from her African experience. In 1954 she published a book of translations from the Somali, *A Tree for Poverty*, and her first novel, *This Side Jordan* (1960), is also about Africa. In 1963 two books—one of travel essays, *The Prophet's Camel Bell*, the other of short stories, *The Tomorrow Tamer*—completed Laurence's African genesis, and since then all her works have been set in Canada. *The Stone Angel* (1964) is the first of these, and is the story of Hagar Shipley and the fictional town of Manawaka. The same year the following story appeared in the *Ladies' Home Journal*: also set in Manawaka, it is part of a series of stories—with Vanessa MacLeod as their central character—that were collected in *A Bird in the House* (1970). Laurence's other Manawaka books include *A Jest of God* (1966) and *The Diviners* (1974), both of which won Governor-General's awards.

'To Set our House in Order,' she wrote in an essay included in *The Narrative Voice* (edited by John Metcalf, 1972), 'is actually a story about the generations, about the pain and bewilderment of one's knowledge of other people, about the reality of other people which is one way of realizing one's own reality, about the fluctuating and accidental quality of life (God really doesn't love Order), and perhaps more than anything, about the strangeness and mystery of the very concepts of *past, present* and *future*.'

# TO SET OUR HOUSE IN ORDER

WHEN THE baby was almost ready to be born, something went wrong and my mother had to go into hospital two weeks before the expected time. I was wakened by her crying in the night, and then I heard my father's footsteps as he went downstairs to phone. I stood in the doorway of my room, shivering and listening, wanting to go to my mother but afraid to go lest there be some sight there more terrifying than I could bear.

'Hello—Paul?' my father said, and I knew he was talking to Dr Cates. 'It's Beth. The waters have broken, and the fetal position doesn't seem quite—well, I'm only thinking of what happened the last time, and another like that would be—I wish she were a little huskier, damn it—she's so—no, don't worry, I'm quite all right. Yes, I think that would be the best thing. Okay, make it as soon as you can, will you?'

He came back upstairs, looking bony and dishevelled in his pyjamas, and running his fingers through his sand-coloured hair. At the top of the stairs, he came face to face with Grandmother MacLeod, who was standing there in her quilted black satin dressing gown, her slight figure held straight and poised, as though she were unaware that her hair was bound grotesquely like white-feathered wings in the snare of her coarse night-time hairnet.

'What is it, Ewen?'

'It's all right, Mother. Beth's having—a little trouble. I'm going to take her into the hospital. You go back to bed.'

'I told you,' Grandmother MacLeod said in her clear voice, never loud, but distinct and ringing like the tap of a sterling teaspoon on a crystal goblet, 'I did tell you, Ewen, did I not, that you should have got a girl in to help her with the housework? She would have rested more.'

'I couldn't afford to get anyone in,' my father said. 'If you thought she should've rested more, why didn't you ever—oh God, I'm out of my mind tonight—just go back to bed, Mother, please. I must get back to Beth.'

When my father went down to the front door to let Dr Cates in, my need overcame my fear and I slipped into my parents' room. My mother's black hair, so neatly pinned up during the day, was startlingly spread across the white pillowcase. I stared at her, not speaking, and then she smiled and I rushed from the doorway and buried my head upon her.

'It's all right, honey,' she said. 'Listen, Vanessa, the baby's just going to come a little early, that's all. You'll be all right. Grandmother MacLeod will be here.'

'How can she get the meals?' I wailed, fixing on the first thing that came to mind. 'She never cooks. She doesn't know how.'

'Yes, she does,' my mother said. 'She can cook as well as anyone when she has to. She's just never had to very much, that's all. Don't worry—she'll keep everything in order, and then some.'

My father and Dr Cates came in, and I had to go, without ever saying anything I had wanted to say. I went back to my own room and lay with the shadows all around me. I listened to the night murmurings that always went on in that house, sounds which never had a source, rafters and beams contracting in the dry air, perhaps, or mice in the walls, or a sparrow that had flown into the attic through the broken skylight there. After a while, although I would not have believed it possible, I slept.

The next morning I questioned my father. I believed him to be not only the best doctor in Manawaka, but also the best doctor in the whole of Manitoba, if not in the entire world, and the fact that he was not the one who was looking after my mother seemed to have something sinister about it.

'But it's always done that way, Vanessa,' he explained. 'Doctors never attend members of their own family. It's because they care so much about them, you see, and—'

'And what?' I insisted, alarmed at the way he had broken off. But my father did not reply. He stood there, and then he put on that difficult smile with which adults seek to conceal pain from children. I felt terrified, and ran to him, and he held me tightly.

'She's going to be fine,' he said. 'Honestly she is. Nessa, don't cry—'

Grandmother MacLeod appeared beside us, steel-spined despite her apparent fragility. She was wearing a purple silk dress and her ivory pendant. She looked as though she were all ready to go out for afternoon tea.

'Ewen, you're only encouraging the child to give way,' she said. 'Vanessa, big girls of ten don't make such a fuss about things. Come and get your breakfast. Now, Ewen, you're not to worry. I'll see to everything.'

Summer holidays were not quite over, but I did not feel like going out to play with any of the kids. I was very superstitious, and I had the feeling that if I left the house, even for a few hours, some disaster would overtake my mother. I did not, of course, mention this feeling to Grandmother MacLeod, for she did not believe in the existence of fear, or if she did, she never let on. I spent the morning morbidly, in seeking hidden places in the house. There were many of these—odd-shaped nooks under the stairs, small and loosely nailed-up doors at the back of clothes closets, leading to dusty tunnels and forgotten recesses in the heart of the house where the only things actually to be seen were drab oil paintings stacked upon the rafters, and trunks full of outmoded clothing and old photograph albums. But the unseen presences in these secret places I knew to be those of every person, young or old, who had ever belonged to the house and had died, including Uncle Roderick who got killed on the Somme, and the baby who would have been my sister if only she had managed to come to life. Grandfather MacLeod, who had died a year after I was born, was present in the house in more tangible form. At the top of the main stairs hung the mammoth picture of a darkly uniformed man riding upon a horse whose prancing stance and dilated nostrils suggested that the battle was not yet over, that it might indeed continue until Judgment Day. The stern man was actually the Duke of Wellington, but at the time I believed him to be my Grandfather MacLeod, still keeping an eye on things.

We had moved in with Grandmother MacLeod when the Depression got bad and she could no longer afford a housekeeper, but the MacLeod house never seemed like home to me. Its dark red brick was grown over at the front with Virginia creeper that turned crimson in the fall, until you could hardly tell brick from leaves. It boasted a small tower in which Grandmother MacLeod kept a weedy collection of anaemic ferns. The verandah was embellished with a profusion of wrought-iron scrolls, and the circular rose-window upstairs contained glass of many colours which permitted an outlooking eye to see the world as a place of absolute sapphire or emerald, or if one wished to look with a jaundiced eye, a hateful yellow. In Grandmother MacLeod's opinion, these features gave the house style.

Inside, a multitude of doors led to rooms where my presence, if not actually forbidden, was not encouraged. One was Grandmother MacLeod's bedroom, with its stale and old-smelling air, the dim

reek of medicines and lavender sachets. Here resided her mono-
grammed dresser silver, brush and mirror, nail-buffer and button
hook and scissors, none of which must even be fingered by me now,
for she meant to leave them to me in her will and intended to hand
them over in the same flawless and unused condition in which they
had always been kept. Here, too, were the silver-framed photographs of Uncle Roderick—as a child, as a boy, as a man in his
Army uniform. The massive walnut spool bed had obviously been
designed for queens or giants, and my tiny grandmother used to lie
within it all day when she had migraine, contriving somehow to
look like a giant queen.

The living room was another alien territory where I had to tread
warily, for many valuable objects sat just-so on tables and mantelpiece, and dirt must not be tracked in upon the blue Chinese
carpet with its birds in eternal motionless flight and its water-lily
buds caught forever just before the point of opening. My mother was
always nervous when I was in this room.

'Vanessa, honey,' she would say, half apologetically, 'why don't
you go and play in the den, or upstairs?'

'Can't you leave her, Beth?' my father would say. 'She's not
doing any harm.'

'I'm only thinking of the rug,' my mother would say, glancing at
Grandmother MacLeod, 'and yesterday she nearly knocked the
Dresden shepherdess off the mantel. I mean, she can't help it,
Ewen, she has to run around—'

'Goddamn it, I know she can't help it,' my father would growl,
glaring at the smirking face of the Dresden shepherdess.

'I see no need to blaspheme, Ewen,' Grandmother MacLeod
would say quietly, and then my father would say he was sorry, and
I would leave.

The day my mother went to the hospital, Grandmother Mac-
Leod called me at lunch-time, and when I appeared, smudged with
dust from the attic, she looked at me distastefully as though I had
been a cockroach that had just crawled impertinently out of the
woodwork.

'For mercy's sake, Vanessa, what have you been doing with
yourself? Run and get washed this minute. Here, not that way—you
use the back stairs, young lady. Get along now. Oh—your father
phoned.'

I swung around. 'What did he say? How is she? Is the baby
born?'

'Curiosity killed a cat,' Grandmother MacLeod said, frowning. 'I cannot understand Beth and Ewen telling you all these things, at your age. What sort of vulgar person you'll grow up to be, I dare not think. No, it's not born yet. Your mother's just the same. No change.'

I looked at my grandmother, not wanting to appeal to her, but unable to stop myself. 'Will she—will she be all right?'

Grandmother MacLeod straightened her already-straight back. 'If I said definitely yes, Vanessa, that would be a lie, and the MacLeods do not tell lies, as I have tried to impress upon you before. What happens is God's will. The Lord giveth, and the Lord taketh away.'

Appalled, I turned away so she would not see my face and my eyes. Surprisingly I heard her sigh and felt her papery white and perfectly manicured hand upon my shoulder.

'When your Uncle Roderick got killed,' she said, 'I thought I would die. But I didn't die, Vanessa.'

At lunch, she chatted animatedly, and I realized she was trying to cheer me in the only way she knew.

'When I married your Grandfather MacLeod,' she related, 'he said to me, "Eleanor, don't think because we're going to the prairies that I expect you to live roughly. You're used to a proper house, and you shall have one." He was as good as his word. Before we'd been in Manawaka three years, he'd had this place built. He earned a good deal of money in his time, your grandfather. He soon had more patients than either of the other doctors. We ordered our dinner service and all our silver from Birks' in Toronto. We had resident help in those days, of course, and never had less than twelve guests for dinner parties. When I had a tea, it would always be twenty or thirty. Never any less than half a dozen different kinds of cake were ever served in this house. Well, no one seems to bother much these days. Too lazy, I suppose.'

'Too broke,' I suggested. 'That's what Dad says.'

'I can't bear slang,' Grandmother MacLeod said. 'If you mean hard up, why don't you say so? It's mainly a question of management, anyway. My accounts were always in good order, and so was my house. No unexpected expenses that couldn't be met, no fruit cellar running out of preserves before the winter was over. Do you know what my father used to say to me when I was a girl?'

'No,' I said. 'What?'

'God loves Order,' Grandmother MacLeod replied with emphasis. 'You remember that, Vanessa. God loves Order—he wants each one of us to set our house in order. I've never forgotten those words of my father's. I was a MacInnes before I got married. The MacInnes is a very ancient clan, the lairds of Morven and the constables of the Castle of Kinlochaline. Did you finish that book I gave you?'

'Yes,' I said. Then, feeling some additional comment to be called for, 'It was a swell book, Grandmother.'

This was somewhat short of the truth. I had been hoping for her cairngorm brooch on my tenth birthday, and had received instead the plaid-bound volume entitled *The Clans and Tartans of Scotland*. Most of it was too boring to read, but I had looked up the motto of my own family and those of some of my friends' families. *Be then a wall of brass. Learn to suffer. Consider the end. Go carefully.* I had not found any of these slogans reassuring. What with Mavis Duncan learning to suffer, and Laura Kennedy considering the end, and Patsy Drummond going carefully, and I spending my time in being a wall of brass, it did not seem to me that any of us were going to lead very interesting lives. I did not say this to Grandmother MacLeod.

'The MacInnes motto is *Pleasure Arises from Work*,' I said.

'Yes,' she agreed proudly. 'And an excellent motto it is, too. One to bear in mind.'

She rose from the table, rearranging on her bosom the looped ivory beads that held the pendant on which a fullblown ivory rose was stiffly carved.

'I hope Ewen will be pleased,' she said.

'What at?'

'Didn't I tell you?' Grandmother MacLeod said. 'I hired a girl this morning, for the housework. She's to start tomorrow.'

When my father got home that evening, Grandmother MacLeod told him her good news. He ran one hand distractedly across his forehead.

'I'm sorry, Mother, but you'll just have to unhire her. I can't possibly pay anyone.'

'It seems distinctly odd,' Grandmother MacLeod snapped, 'that you can afford to eat chicken four times a week.'

'Those chickens,' my father said in an exasperated voice, 'are how people are paying their bills. The same with the eggs and the milk. That scrawny turkey that arrived yesterday was for Logan

MacCardney's appendix, if you must know. We probably eat better than any family in Manawaka, except Niall Cameron's. People can't entirely dispense with doctors or undertakers. That doesn't mean to say I've got any cash. Look, Mother, I don't know what's happening with Beth. Paul thinks he may have to do a Caesarean. Can't we leave all this? Just leave the house alone. Don't touch it. What does it matter?'

'I have never lived in a messy house, Ewen,' Grandmother MacLeod said, 'and I don't intend to begin now.'

'Oh Lord,' my father said. 'Well, I'll phone Edna, I guess, and see if she can give us a hand, although God knows she's got enough, with the Connor house and her parents to look after.'

'I don't fancy having Edna Connor in to help,' Grandmother MacLeod objected.

'Why not?' my father shouted. 'She's Beth's sister, isn't she?'

'She speaks in such a slangy way,' Grandmother MacLeod said. 'I have never believed she was a good influence on Vanessa. And there is no need for you to raise your voice to me, Ewen, if you please.'

I could barely control my rage, I thought my father would surely rise to Aunt Edna's defence. But he did not.

'It'll be all right,' he soothed her. 'She'd only be here for part of the day, Mother. You could stay in your room.'

Aunt Edna strode in the next morning. The sight of her bobbed black hair and her grin made me feel better at once. She hauled out the carpet sweeper and the weighted polisher and got to work. I dusted while she polished and swept, and we got through the living room and front hall in next to no time.

'Where's her royal highness, kiddo?' she enquired.

'In her room,' I said. 'She's reading the catalogue from Robinson & Cleaver.'

'Good Glory, not again?' Aunt Edna cried. 'The last time she ordered three linen tea-cloths and two dozen serviettes. It came to fourteen dollars. Your mother was absolutely frantic. I guess I shouldn't be saying this.'

'I knew anyway,' I assured her. 'She was at the lace handker-chiefs section when I took up her coffee.'

'Let's hope she stays there. Heaven forbid she should get onto the banqueting cloths. Well, at least she believes the Irish are good for two things—manual labour and linen-making. She's never forgotten Father used to be a blacksmith, before he got the hardware store. Can you beat it? I wish it didn't bother Beth.'

'Does it?' I asked, and immediately realized this was a wrong move, for Aunt Edna was suddenly scrutinizing me.

'We're making you grow up before your time,' she said. 'Don't pay any attention to me, Nessa. I must've got up on the wrong side of the bed this morning.'

But I was unwilling to leave the subject.

'All the same,' I said thoughtfully, 'Grandmother MacLeod's family were the lairds of Morven and the constables of the Castle of Kinlochaline. I bet you didn't know that.'

Aunt Edna snorted. 'Castle, my foot. She was born in Ontario, just like your Grandfather Connor, and her father was a horse doctor. Come on, kiddo, we'd better shut up and get down to business here.'

We worked in silence for a while.

'Aunt Edna—' I said at last, 'what about Mother? Why won't they let me go and see her?'

'Kids aren't allowed to visit maternity patients. It's tough for you, I know that. Look, Nessa, don't worry. If it doesn't start tonight, they're going to do the operation. She's getting the best of care.'

I stood there, holding the feather duster like a dead bird in my hands. I was not aware that I was going to speak until the words came out.

'I'm scared,' I said.

Aunt Edna put her arms around me, and her face looked all at once stricken and empty of defences.

'Oh, honey, I'm scared, too,' she said.

It was this way that Grandmother MacLeod found us when she came stepping lightly down into the front hall with the order in her hand for two dozen lace-bordered handkerchiefs of pure Irish linen.

I could not sleep that night, and when I went downstairs, I found my father in the den. I sat down on the hassock beside his chair, and he told me about the operation my mother was to have the next morning. He kept on saying it was not serious nowadays.

'But you're worried,' I put in, as though seeking to explain why I was.

'I should at least have been able to keep from burdening you with it,' he said in a distant voice, as though to himself. 'If only the baby hadn't got itself twisted around—'

'Will it be born dead, like the little girl?'

'I don't know,' my father said. 'I hope not.'

'She'd be disappointed, wouldn't she, if it was?' I said bleakly, wondering why I was not enough for her.

'Yes, she would,' my father replied. 'She won't be able to have any more, after this. It's partly on your account that she wants this one, Nessa. She doesn't want you to grow up without a brother or sister.'

'As far as I'm concerned, she didn't need to bother,' I retorted angrily.

My father laughed. 'Well, let's talk about something else, and then maybe you'll be able to sleep. How did you and Grandmother make out today?'

'Oh, fine, I guess. What was Grandfather MacLeod like, Dad?'

'What did she tell you about him?'

'She said he made a lot of money in his time.'

'Well, he wasn't any millionaire,' my father said, 'but I suppose he did quite well. That's not what I associate with him, though.'

He reached across to the bookshelf, took out a small leather-bound volume and opened it. On the pages were mysterious marks, like doodling, only much neater and more patterned.

'What is it?' I asked.

'Greek,' my father explained. 'This is a play called *Antigone*. See, here's the title in English. There's a whole stack of them on the shelves there. *Oedipus Rex. Electra. Medea.* They belonged to your Grandfather MacLeod. He used to read them often.'

'Why?' I enquired, unable to understand why anyone would pore over those undecipherable signs.

'He was interested in them,' my father said. 'He must have been a lonely man, although it never struck me that way at the time. Sometimes a thing only hits you a long time afterwards.'

'Why would he be lonely?' I wanted to know.

'He was the only person in Manawaka who could read these plays in the original Greek,' my father said. 'I don't suppose many people, if anyone, had even read them in English translations. Maybe he would have liked to be a classical scholar—I don't know. But his father was a doctor, so that's what he was. Maybe he would have liked to talk to somebody about these plays. They must have meant a lot to him.'

It seemed to me that my father was talking oddly. There was a sadness in his voice that I had never heard before, and I longed to say something that would make him feel better, but I could not, because I did not know what was the matter.

'Can you read this kind of writing?' I asked hesitantly.

My father shook his head. 'Nope. I was never very intellectual, I guess. Rod was always brighter than I, in school, but even he wasn't interested in learning Greek. Perhaps he would've been later, if he'd lived. As a kid, all I ever wanted to do was go into the merchant marine.'

'Why didn't you, then?'

'Oh, well,' my father said offhandedly, 'a kid who'd never seen the sea wouldn't have made much of a sailor. I might have turned out to be the seasick type.'

I had lost interest now that he was speaking once more like himself.

'Grandmother MacLeod was pretty cross today about the girl,' I remarked.

'I know,' my father nodded. 'Well, we must be as nice as we can to her, Nessa, and after a while she'll be all right.'

Suddenly I did not care what I said.

'Why can't she be nice to us for a change?' I burst out. 'We're always the ones who have to be nice to her.'

My father put his hand down and slowly tilted my head until I was forced to look at him.

'Vanessa,' he said, 'she's had troubles in her life which you really don't know much about. That's why she gets migraine sometimes and has to go to bed. It's not easy for her these days, either—the house is still the same, so she thinks other things should be, too. It hurts her when she finds they aren't.'

'I don't see—' I began.

'Listen,' my father said, 'you know we were talking about what people are interested in, like Grandfather MacLeod being interested in Greek plays? Well, your grandmother was interested in being a lady, Nessa, and for a long time it seemed to her that she was one.'

I thought of the Castle of Kinlochaline, and of horse doctors in Ontario.

'I didn't know—' I stammered.

'That's usually the trouble with most of us,' my father said. 'You go on up to bed now. I'll phone tomorrow from the hospital as soon as the operation's over.'

I did sleep at last, and in my dreams I could hear the caught sparrow fluttering in the attic, and the sound of my mother crying, and the voices of the dead children.

My father did not phone until afternoon. Grandmother MacLeod said I was being silly, for you could hear the phone ringing all over the house, but nevertheless I refused to move out of the den. I had never before examined my father's books, but now, at a loss for something to do, I took them out one by one and read snatches here and there. After I had been doing this for several hours, it dawned on me that most of the books were of the same kind. I looked again at the titles.

*Seven-League Boots. Arabia Deserta. The Seven Pillars of Wisdom. Travels in Tibet. Count Lucknor the Sea Devil.* And a hundred more. On a shelf by themselves were copies of the *National Geographic* magazine, which I looked at often enough, but never before with the puzzling compulsion which I felt now, as though I were on the verge of some discovery, something which I had to find out and yet did not want to know. I riffled through the picture-filled pages. Hibiscus and wild orchids grew in a soft-petalled confusion. The Himalayas stood lofty as gods, with the morning sun on their peaks of snow. Leopards snarled from the vined depths of a thousand jungles. Schooners buffetted their white sails like the wings of giant angels against the great sea winds.

'What on earth are you doing?' Grandmother MacLeod enquired waspishly, from the doorway. 'You've got everything scattered all over the place. Pick it all up this minute, Vanessa, do you hear?'

So I picked up the books and magazines, and put them all neatly away, as I had been told to do.

When the telephone finally rang, I was afraid to answer it. At last I picked it up. My father sounded faraway, and the relief in his voice made it unsteady.

'It's okay, honey. Everything's fine. The boy was born alive and kicking after all. Your mother's pretty weak, but she's going to be all right.'

I could hardly believe it. I did not want to talk to anyone. I wanted to be by myself, to assimilate the presence of my brother, towards whom, without ever having seen him yet, I felt such tenderness and such resentment.

That evening, Grandmother MacLeod approached my father, who, still dazed with the unexpected gift of neither life now being threatened, at first did not take her seriously when she asked what they planned to call the child.

'Oh, I don't know. Hank, maybe, or Joe. Fauntleroy, perhaps.'

She ignored this levity.

'Ewen,' she said, 'I wish you would call him Roderick.'

My father's face changed. 'I'd rather not.'

'I think you should,' Grandmother MacLeod insisted, very quietly, but in a voice as pointed and precise as her silver nail-scissors.

'Don't you think Beth ought to decide?' my father asked.

'Beth will agree if you do.'

My father did not bother to deny something that even I knew to be true. He did not say anything. Then Grandmother MacLeod's voice, astonishingly, faltered a little.

'It would mean a great deal to me,' she said.

I remembered what she had told me—*When your Uncle Roderick got killed, I thought I would die. But I didn't die.* All at once, her feeling for that unknown dead man became a reality for me. And yet I held it against her, as well, for I could see that it had enabled her to win now.

'All right,' my father said tiredly. 'We'll call him Roderick.'

Then, alarmingly, he threw back his head and laughed.

'Roderick Dhu!' he cried. 'That's what you'll call him, isn't it? Black Roderick. Like before. Don't you remember? As though he were a character out of Sir Walter Scott, instead of an ordinary kid who—'

He broke off, and looked at her with a kind of desolation in his face.

'God, I'm sorry, Mother,' he said. 'I had no right to say that.'

Grandmother MacLeod did not flinch, or tremble, or indicate that she felt anything at all.

'I accept your apology, Ewen,' she said.

My mother had to stay in bed for several weeks after she arrived home. The baby's cot was kept in my parents' room, and I could go in and look at the small creature who lay there with his tightly closed fists and his feathery black hair. Aunt Edna came in to help each morning, and when she had finished the housework, she would have coffee with my mother. They kept the door closed, but this did not prevent me from eavesdropping, for there was an air register in the floor of the spare room, which was linked somehow with the register in my parents' room. If you put your ear to the iron grille, it was almost like a radio.

'Did you mind very much, Beth?' Aunt Edna was saying.

'Oh, it's not the name I mind,' my mother replied. 'It's just the fact that Ewen felt he had to. You know that Rod had only had the sight of one eye, didn't you?'

'Sure, I knew. So what?'

'There was only a year and a half between Ewen and Rod,' my mother said, 'so they often went around together when they were youngsters. It was Ewen's air-rifle that did it.'

'Oh Lord,' Aunt Edna said heavily. 'I suppose she always blamed him?'

'No, I don't think it was so much that, really. It was how he felt himself. I think he even used to wonder sometimes if—but people shouldn't let themselves think like that, or they'd go crazy. Accidents do happen, after all. When the war came, Ewen joined up first. Rod should never have been in the Army at all, but he couldn't wait to get in. He must have lied about his eyesight. It wasn't so very noticeable unless you looked at him closely, and I don't suppose the medicals were very thorough in those days. He got in as a gunner, and Ewen applied to have him in the same company. He thought he might be able to watch out for him, I guess, Rod being—at a disadvantage. They were both only kids. Ewen was nineteen and Rod was eighteen when they went to France. And then the Somme. I don't know, Edna, I think Ewen felt that if Rod had had proper sight, or if he hadn't been in the same outfit and had been sent somewhere else—you know how people always think these things afterwards, not that it's ever a bit of use. Ewen wasn't there when Rod got hit. They'd lost each other somehow, and Ewen was looking for him, not bothering about anything else, you know, just frantically looking. Then he stumbled across him quite by chance. Rod was still alive, but—'

'Stop it, Beth,' Aunt Edna said. 'You're only upsetting yourself.'

'Ewen never spoke of it to me,' my mother went on, 'until once his mother showed me the letter he'd written to her at the time. It was a peculiar letter, almost formal, saying how gallantly Rod had died, and all that. I guess I shouldn't have, but I told him she'd shown it to me. He was very angry that she had. And then, as though for some reason he were terribly ashamed, he said—*I had to write something to her, but men don't really die like that, Beth. It wasn't that way at all.* It was only after the war that he decided to come back and study medicine and go into practice with his father.'

'Had Rod meant to?' Aunt Edna asked.

'I don't know,' my mother said slowly. 'I never felt I should ask Ewen that.'

Aunt Edna was gathering up the coffee things, for I could hear the clash of cups and saucers being stacked on the tray.

'You know what I heard her say to Vanessa once, Beth? *The MacLeods never tell lies.* Those were her exact words. Even then, I didn't know whether to laugh or cry.'

'Please, Edna—' my mother sounded worn out now. 'Don't.'

'Oh Glory,' Aunt Edna said remorsefully, 'I've got all the delicacy of a two-ton truck. I didn't mean Ewen, for heaven's sake. That wasn't what I meant at all. Here, let me plump up your pillows for you.'

Then the baby began to cry, so I could not hear anything more of interest. I took my bike and went out beyond Manawaka, riding aimlessly along the gravel highway. It was late summer, and the wheat had changed colour, but instead of being high and bronzed in the fields, it was stunted and desiccated, for there had been no rain again this year. But in the bluff where I stopped and crawled under the barbed wire fence and lay stretched out on the grass, the plentiful poplar leaves were turning to a luminous yellow and shone like church windows in the sun. I put my head down very close to the earth and looked at what was going on there. Grasshoppers with enormous eyes ticked and twitched around me, as though the dry air were perfect for their purposes. A ladybird laboured mightily to climb a blade of grass, fell off, and started all over again, seeming to be unaware that she possessed wings and could have flown up.

I thought of the accidents that might easily happen to a person—or, of course, might not happen, might happen to somebody else. I thought of the dead baby, my sister who might as easily have been I. Would she, then, have been lying here in my place, the sharp grass making its small toothmarks on her brown arms, the sun warming her to the heart? I thought of the leather-bound volumes of Greek, and the six different kinds of iced cakes that used to be offered always in the MacLeod house, and the pictures of leopards and green seas. I thought of my brother, who had been born alive after all, and now had been given his life's name.

I could not really comprehend these things, but I sensed their strangeness, their disarray. I felt that whatever God might love in this world, it was certainly not order.

# Hugh Hood

HUGH John Blagdon Hood was born in Toronto on April 30, 1928. After graduating from St Michael's, the Catholic college of the University of Toronto (Morley Callaghan's former college: Hood received his Ph.D. in English with a dissertation on the theory of the imagination), he taught briefly at St Joseph College in West Hartford, Connecticut. He began writing short stories and an unpublished novel in 1956 (the story reprinted here was written in October 1960), and in 1961 he moved to Montreal, where he still lives, writes, and teaches English Literature at the Université de Montréal. He has published four books of short stories—*Flying a Red Kite* (1962), *Around the Mountain* (1967), *The Fruit Man, the Meat Man & the Manager* (1971), and *Dark Glasses* (1976)—and eight novels, the last three of which—*The Swing in the Garden* (1975), *A New Athens* (1977), and *Reservoir Ravine* (1979)—are part of a projected twelve-novel series to be called *The New Age*.

Hood has referred to himself as a 'moral realist,' by which he means, in part, that he deals with credible characters in credible situations, and that he uses this credibility to conduct personal investigations into the moral fabric of society. 'It's the seeing-into-things,' he wrote in an essay called 'Sober Colouring: The Ontology of Super-Realism' in 1971 (*Canadian Literature* #49), 'the capacity for meditative abstraction, that interests me about philosophy, the arts or religious practice. I love most in painting an art that exhibits the transcendental element dwelling in living things. I think of this as super-realism.'

Two magazine issues—*The Tamarack Review* #66 and *Essays on Canadian Writing* #13/14—have been devoted to Hood's work. In the latter, John Orange writes that Hood 'is closer to MacLennan, Garner, Grove, and, particularly, Callaghan than he is to the next generation of writers.' And yet Hood is also a transitional figure; he was in at the very beginning of the Canadian short story's most recent renaissance.

# THREE HALVES OF A HOUSE

EAST OF Kingston the islands—more than eleven hundred of them—begin to sprout in and all around the ship channel, choking and diverting the immense river for forty amazing miles, eastwards past Gananoque, almost down to Stoverville. But a third of the continent leans pushing behind the lakes and the river, the pulse, circulation, artery, and heart, all in one flowing geographical fact, of half the North Americans, the flow we live by all that long way from Minnesota to the Gulf.

Saint Lawrence's Gulf, martyr roasted on a gridiron, Breton saint, legend imported by the French to name the life's current of a hundred million industrious shoredwellers, drinking the water, lighting their houses by it, floating on it in numberless craft. 'Seas of Sweet Water,' the Indians called the lakes, and to the east the marvellous Saint Lawrence with the weight of the American Northeast inclining to the Gulf.

So the channel must be cut, though the islands press against the current in resistance, cut sometimes through needles' eyes and wearing deep, deep, through solid pressed ancient rock a hundred and fifty feet down, two hundred, icy cold ten feet below the surface. A holidaying swimmer floats up half-frozen in the narrow channel from a shallow dive, swept forty feet downstream in three seconds by the drive of the current, lucky to catch an exposed tree-root at the edge of a corroded island and haul himself ashore, the water sliding and driving beneath him two hundred feet down to the anonymous rock.

Try to swim upstream, brother, at Flowerlea! And feel yourself carried backwards through your best stroke, feel yourself whipped out of yourself as the river pulls at your thighs, hauling you down away eastwards as though you were falling helpless down a chute. Then grab at the skeletal roots, hang on, swing in the water and ride an eddy ashore! Fight the weight of eleven states and half of Canada, something to think about swinging on your sodden shredded branching root while fifty feet away—not an inch more—a ship seven hundred and fifty feet long glides ghostly past, soundless, what a thing to meet on a holiday beach! Not a thing to swim too close to, glistening black walls rising out of the water above you like an apartment building—SCOTT MISENER on the bows and the name of the line reading backwards to the stern in letters twice your height, swimmer, and not a sound from the ship, the current moving the ship as easily as it moves you. A deckhand leans incuriously at the rail, lifting a friendly hand, and is gone, whirled away eastwards while he lowers his arm.

SCOTT MISENER, ERIKA HAMBURG, TOSUI MARU, BRISTOL CITY, MOOREMACGLEN—they hail from everywhere, upper lakers, tankers, the few remaining canallers, ocean-going freighters built by thrifty Danes for the lakes trade, drawing twenty-seven feet precisely, up and down all day and all night with their myriads of sirens sounding the whole range of the tempered scale. The shipmaster confers anxiously with his pilot through the forty perilous miles, threading needle after needle. At Flowerlea the channel is so narrow the summer cottagers can lean over and assess the deck-hands' breakfast bacon. In the fall the last of the cottagers sit around their barbecue pits with a liner in the front yard, the shipmaster pacing about above them, cursing them and their hot-dogs, the handiest things to curse. He is afraid of the Flowerlea channel, so narrow, and of the weight of water astern hurrying him along, the navigation season waning and his insurance rate about to jump skyhigh if he doesn't clear the locks by the appointed day.

Late last autumn a shipmaster drove aground off Stoverville at the end of the season; he lost the closing date at the locks and passed the winter iced into the river with a ruined cargo. Each day the sailors walked to Stoverville over the three feet of ice, but the captain, a ruined man, brooded in solitary humiliation all winter in his cabin. He was never seen in Stoverville, although hysterical cables addressed to him arrived daily from Oslo.

He was unlucky, mistrusted his pilot, didn't know the river, hated it, and the river ruined him. He missed all the signs, the waning of the islands, the widening of the channel, the three trees —tamaracks with fifty feet of bare trunk and perky coronas on top —that stand on the promontory west of Stoverville. Making his move to starboard towards the New York shore minutes too late, he felt the current drive his bows so deep into the river bottom he knew he'd never haul her off. He stared at the three tamaracks all winter, counting them and counting them and there were never more than three. This summer, in Oslo, he killed himself.

The tamaracks mark the end of the islands, the beginning of the river's free run from Stoverville to the Atlantic, nothing in the way but the mammoth new locks, then Montreal, Quebec, wider and wider until you can't see across, at last the sleety Gulf. But at Stoverville the river's freedom is a newborn thing, the mass of water has just begun to run, eroding, finding the fastest way down. At Stoverville it's hardly two miles across.

Over there on the New York shore are the old resort towns, fading now, the gingerbread hotels coming down, their gilt furnishings sold off. Now and then a welterweight contender trains here and sometimes a powerboat regatta invites the curious. But the real tourist money goes to Europe or Montego Bay and the old millionaires, who found their way upstate in the seventies from Saratoga, are dead and gone. Between Watertown and Plattsburg, back a few miles from the river, there's nothing. An Army camp, a NIKE site, trees and woods and dunes and the snow belt. And that's it.

On the Canadian side there's Highway Number Two, the worst main highway in the world, with the small river towns dotted along it—Kingston, Gananoque, Stoverville, Prescott—dreaming their dreams dating from the 1830s of a prosperity which never came. Yet they sleep there along the shore waiting for things to pick up when the hundred and fifty years' slack season shall be over, an occasional coal-boat putting in and water-buses running thrice-daily tours of the islands up to the bridge and back.

Twenty miles north of the riverfront strip the towns begin to shrink in size—Tincap, Newboro, Athens; the farms are scrubbier and smaller and hillier. You still see television aerials but now the rocks begin to stick up through the thin topsoil and you are into the Laurentian Shield with a rocky uninterrupted thousand miles clear to James Bay of round old rock, polished by the last Ice Age. Saint Lawrence again but this time choking off life, not conferring it. And from this hinterland, from the little towns like Athens, people have been moving back down to the shore for sixty years, as soon as they broke their first ploughshares on the intractable rock humping up out of the hillsides. They come back to Stoverville and cherish their disappointments, the growth of their numbers limited by their situation between the river and the rock, the same smooth incredibly ancient rock which beds the river. Life and power flowing beside them and old impregnable rock, out of which nothing can be forced to grow, above them northerly, so they come back one by one into Stoverville from Athens and the other little towns, and here they fashion their lamentations.

'They are painting the house,' says Mrs Boston vengefully, 'green and white, so unoriginal. In the thirty years we lived there they never offered to paint it for us. Your father painted every four years, always green and white. He spent thousands on paint, and always the best white lead—money I might have had, or you, that has been absorbed into the walls of that place, with the Hungarians living in the other side.'

'Hungarians must live somewhere,' offers her daughter mildly.

'But need they live in Stoverville?'

'They make their choices unknowingly, the poor things,' says Maura even more mildly, 'and I suppose once here they must abide by the original choice. I must say, I think it kind of Grover to let them have the other half of the house.'

'Most Stoverville people won't rent to them,' says Mrs Boston, 'but Grover does, in preference to me.'

'You didn't wish to stay in the smaller half. You had the opportunity.'

'Taken a crumb from his table you mean? Accepted the little half, and maintained it as we did the other side for thirty years until they pushed us out? That I should lie awake alone in my bedroom in the smaller half and listen to Grover rattling around on the other side of the wall! I don't know what he proposes to do with all that space, with just the two of them. Ellie, of course, doesn't go out any more, the poor unfortunate. Can you imagine it? Cooped up all day with that man, green and white? The very least he could have done would be to choose new colours. Green and white were your poor father's choice. Heavens, what it cost! It was that dirty grey, you know, but of course you couldn't know. You weren't five years old when we moved in. Your father had to pay for three coats of the finest white lead to cover the grey, the way they'd let it all run down, Ellie's crazy mother!'

'Was she crazy? I remember her.'

'Undeniably, and her husband was worse. I tell you, Maura, there's a warped streak in that family somewhere, and it comes out, it comes out. I'm glad they're not my blood relations.'

'But they were father's.'

'He was a medical doctor, my dear,' says Mrs Boston stiffly, 'and he understood these things.'

'These things?' asks Maura delicately, lighting a cigarette. She does not wish to pass the entire weekend in these debates.

'Tubercular bone,' says her mother, 'congenital physical rot. And other things than physical for they've never been right, none of them. Your father at least went from Stoverville to the city, though in the end he came back. But these clumps of Phillipses— they move from the farm to Athens looking for the easy life, and from Athens to Stoverville believing they've found it because they don't have to rise at four in the morning. My dear girl, they infest the countryside, they're a positive plague.'

'I'm one-eighth Phillips,' says Maura with a faint apprehension.

'But you live in Montreal where medicine and science have penetrated.'

'The weak drive out the strong, Mother,' says Maura, 'like vines driving through rock. You're better off away from either side of that house.'

'But to be driven out! And then those Hungarians.' She smiles maliciously. 'I understand that the ships' sirens terrify the Hungarians, wake them up at night. They think of Russians, I expect.' The sirens give everyone dreams, thinks Maura to herself, everyone in Stoverville. *Paaaaarrrrrrpppp.* I am going to starboard. *Mmeeeuuuhhhhhhhh.* I am going to port. They never collide in the channel, even at Flowerlea; they do not astonish us with freakish mishaps, sinkings, or groundings except for a single dead Norwegian, but they are all around us in the night. *Paaarrrrpppp. Mmeeeuuuhhhhh.* They give us dreams in Stoverville, but in Montreal, though they circumnavigate the city, no one notices them. I forget the river in Montreal or in New York while here it rolls through me, head to thighs. I dreamt as a child in my bed at the dark top of the house, their house, probably Grover's room now; he can't sleep with Ellie, she'd never allow it, so virginal at sixty. Poor Grover Haskell, sleeping in my bed in my room listening first to the sirens and then to the cranky breathing of his good wife who has done everything for him, according to Mother, subjugated herself entirely to him, yielded him up her house, for of course it's her house, not his—she's legitimately Phillips. I'm only one-eighth, thank God, so she has the house that was my father's by temporary arrangement because he was only a quarter Phillips and had the house at a nominal rent while Ellie, disguised as Mrs Grover Haskell, tried to get away to other parts of the world. What is a nominal rent? Daddy never complained of the rent and we knew that one day the Haskells would drift back, allowing Daddy the smaller side while they all four enjoyed a polite Stoverville retirement, except that they didn't. Daddy is dead and Ellie is dying slowly and Grover is not. And my dear mother flourishes.

The year we moved in, the tamarack trees were lonely and beginning to lean over the river, earthfall exposing part of their roots on the promontory's side.

'We'll fix that,' Daddy said, and he poured in cement and fill, so the trees are still there. 'Those tamaracks look lonely,' he said to me, 'and they're important. Did you know, Maura,' he said, talking as if I were an adult, 'that sailors talk about our three trees from here to Duluth?' Then he told me where Duluth was and I remember it still. I think of the sailors at the Lakehead, talking about our three tamaracks, only of course they were never really ours at all but belonged first to her grandfather who was the town saddler and unsuccessful, and then the town magistrate and tubercular. Then they were her mad father's, whom I knew, who moved into the little half of the house to rent us the larger and to resent us—we paid a nominal rent for the privilege of becoming an object of resentment to that frustrated painter.

When I was five he would beckon to me from his side of the porch to show me his new picture, clutching at his brushes with arthritic paws and aiming unsteadily to pat me where he had no business to. 'It's a schooner, Maura, do you see?' he said, pulling at the frill on my sleeve. 'It's a schooner on the river.'

'I like the steamers, Uncle Wallace,' I said, and he changed colour, 'but I can't help it, I like them.'

'This is a schooner, don't you see?'

'But I like the steamers' horns better.'

Then Ellie came onto the porch, calming the morning with her still face. She picked up her father's pencils which were rolling hastily away along the porch towards the shrubbery and, handing them to him, kissed him while he stormed at me.

'The child's difficult, Ellie! She abuses my pictures. Everyone always does, everyone but you.' She patted him and was silent, listening to his vacuities and smiling secretly at me from her still face around her lashes, drawing her father's sting as he went on rebuking me, not directly—he said nothing to me directly, but he let me hear. 'My house, my house. I let them have my house, which I love, and their child must criticize. Let her stay on her side of the porch. Edward Boston is a young fool and his wife is malicious. When I asked him what was the matter with me, he declined to say, the coward—he knows all right but he daren't say. Only he sends his little girl around the corner of my house to make sure that my hands aren't right, that they shake, that my schooners look like steamers because I can't hold my pencil straight, a poor old man; they laugh at me. I'll raise his rent!'

Sitting on the arm of the deep chair in which her father crouches, mouthing his poison, she smiles sweetly along her lashes at me, frightened and trembling, five years old, misunderstanding it all because my father, young and poor as he is, worries about rent, cement and fill and the three trees.

'Look at the new white paint,' I wail, starting to cry. 'Daddy painted your old house for you.' But old Mr Phillips can't hear as he begins to slide into a soothed nearly senile sleep. Ellie tucks his blanket around him, watches him slide away, and takes me by the hand, walking me back around the corner of the porch to our front door.

'I only said I like the steamers. I didn't mean to make him mad.'

'It's all right, darling, he's an old man. It's nothing you've said, he's an old man. He's been disappointed and he's sick.'

'But he'll be all right, won't he?'

She stands with me at the door to our half of the house. We look through the screen into the hall, and at the back of the house my mother bustles, moving kitchen furniture with a cheerful scraping noise.

'He'll be all right soon,' says Ellie full of comfort, placing her hand on her forehead and drawing me down after her on to the porch swing which rocks gently with a creak of chains as we look into each other's eyes, hers the Phillips eyes, rapt, violet, staringly intense, and her face so sweet and still, mine the brown eyes my mother imported into the family, round and direct, eyes I hated as a child, so agate-like and unblinking, my mother's and mine, not glancing and vivid like Ellie's. All at once she hugs me and whispers secretly: 'I wish you were mine.'

I am appalled by the notion. 'I belong to Daddy.'

Ellie kisses me briskly and for a moment we stare together at the tamarack trees on the point. 'We love our fathers,' she says absently, and turning gives me again her ineffable saint's gaze, visionary, violet, preoccupied. 'Find your mother, sweetheart,' she tells me, and I trot into the house vaguely disappointed.

'If you were not such an intractable mule,' says Mrs Boston, fixing her agate eyes in a persuasive stare, 'you might do well in Stoverville. There are four distinct pieces of house property you might inherit if only you'd be nice to people.' She holds up her fingers, beginning to itemize them. 'There's our house, to begin with.'

Maura emerges from her reverie, balking at this projected deathwatch which jerks her suddenly over nearly thirty years to her pallid present prospects. What had been the frill on the arm of a child's frock becomes a table-napkin across which she's thrown a suddenly adult arm, plumper and hairier than a five-year-old's.

'I've stayed away too much.'

'Then come home more often!'

'This is home? Pardon me, Mother, but the only thing that brings me to Stoverville is you. And this isn't your home, any more than Montreal is mine. You weren't born here.'

'It has grown into my home. The thought makes me weep sometimes now that your father is three years dead.'

'You don't go back to your birthplace.' Maura hopes to make a point.

'I do not. Nobody there remembers me or my family. We're obliterated. If I have any home, which is dubious, it's here in this crazy town beside these damned ships.'

'What's the matter with the ships?'

'They're getting bigger and bigger. I don't know where it'll stop. It was never like this before.'

'It's the new locks,' says Maura. 'The big ships used to stop at Montreal.'

'You're past thirty, Maura,' says Mrs Boston. 'Do you imagine that Montreal will provide you with a home?'

The faintest enlivening blush dabbles Maura's cheek as she folds and re-folds a table-napkin in her hands. 'I meet men of my own age at the studios,' she says reluctantly, 'and you never can tell.'

At this indecency her mother recoils, her life's scheme all at once readjusted. 'You do not think of marriage?'

'I think of it all the time,' says Maura, crossing her legs irritably, 'all the blessed time and I wish somebody would ask me.'

'A particular somebody?'

'Since you ask, yes.' And then she grows defensive. 'You were close to thirty when you married.'

'But not past it.'

'Thirty is no immutable barrier. Women past thirty have married before this, and will again.'

'You mean that you will?'

'Given the chance!'

'Then think,' says Mrs Boston, adapting her tactics, 'of the uses of our home as, perhaps, a summer place. Right on the river, a most desirable location.'

'I thought that you disapproved of the location.'

'I should disapprove less,' says Mrs Boston with regal dignity, 'were the house legally mine.'

'Ah!'

'There is no need to be ironic, Maura. I am your mother, after all, and I have your best interests at heart.'

Maura thinks this over solemnly, seeming from her attitude to fancy a world in which fewer people have her interests more personally at heart. Identification with her interests, not cool appraisal of them, is the desideratum.

'I mean to protect you from Grover and his schemes,' her mother pursues. 'It is not a Haskell house but a Phillips house, and should come to you. He has no children.'

'The poor man,' exclaims Maura involuntarily.

'Poor man, bosh!' says her mother with energy. 'He never wanted them and Ellie gave in to him everywhere. Poor woman, rather! You know what Grover Haskell is, a monster of selfishness.'

'Has he the necessary wit and tenacity?'

'All that he requires. You remember how, three years ago, he brutalized me, wouldn't even let me go on clinging to the littler half, but insisted on what he calls "a proper rent, considering." That man had the audacity to ask me to move your father's workbench from one side of the cellar to the other as soon as it was convenient, the tools still warm from your father's palms. I offered him a cord of firewood that your father had stored in the cellar to dry—out of the purest neighbourly feelings—and he told me, as curtly as you please, that he meant to use the fireplaces ornamentally, to fit into their new decor.'

'It is their house.'

'It is her house, and will be yours, I tell you, if you behave properly. She must know by now what he is, even though she's sick. She has sacrificed everything to him, given in to him, followed him through all his failures like a saint, I tell you, like a saint, and now she's sick. She has never been well since her father died.'

'When I was small,' says Maura, remembering it with deep pleasure, 'I really loved Ellie, she was so good.'

'She is a saint. But queer, Maura, queer. She has these visions, you know.' And Mrs Boston begins a rambling account of the phenomenon called 'second sight' by means of which events occurring at a distance in space or time may be observed directly by persons with certain particular spiritual equipment. 'Your father's great-aunt had it,' she concludes, 'and I believe Ellie has it, or something like it. When I go to see her I have the feeling that there are other people in the room.'

'You go to see her?'

'I do.'

'When Grover isn't there?'

'He is always there. He daren't leave her, you know, for fear she'll die while he's out of the house. But I'll grant him one good grace. He usually goes down to the cellar while I'm there. Can't face me, I suppose.'

'How does she act?'

'Well, she wanders. She is sorry for what Grover has done to me; she is ashamed for him. She always asks for you, Maura, and you should go to see her, if only out of kindness.'

'What's the matter with her?'

'She was always a visionary and religious, and of a self-sacrificing temperament, first her mother and father and now Grover. She seems to have gone completely religious, speaking in symbols and so on. She has been reading Revelation, I suspect.'

'I'll go and see her,' concedes Maura, not entirely reluctantly.

Peering through blue spruce and cedar, Grover studies the three tamaracks from the porch, trying to ignore the river below them which he has never loved, and assessing fondly the intervening plantings which have suddenly devolved upon Ellie and himself. When he courted his wife thirty years ago, coming fearfully to the old house because of the uncertainties of her father's temper, pausing on the front walk and studying the movement of dragonflies in the porch light, he had wished that it were warmer near the house, that someone might fill the space between the house and the tamaracks with sod, flowers, and other trees and vines, to take away something of the starkness of the house's situation, perched icily on the promontory unscreened from the winter reflection off the river's ice. He had been lucky. For most of the subsequent thirty years while he and Ellie tried their luck in Kingston, Belleville, and for a few desperate years in Toronto, they had had a caretaker who paid them for the privilege of keeping the property up and even improving it. A nominal rent but one that paid the taxes—and the house was regularly painted, heated, kept immaculate, ventilated, and the memory of Ellie's terrible father gradually expunged.

Grover had liked Dr Boston, though he couldn't abide his widow, and had tried to deal fairly with him. He had accepted forty dollars a month from him for nearly thirty years and had never counted it up to see what it came to. Edward had had inexpensive living accommodation and had been free to improve the property for his own comfort if he wished. That the Bostons had come in time to think of his house as immutably their home was certainly natural enough but scarcely his concern. That Dr Boston had planted and cultivated a perfectly splendid arbour, a lovely jungle of carefully selected trees and shrubs between the house and the tamaracks, that he had installed a darkroom and a new furnace, was his business, done with his eyes wide open. However much the Bostons might have resented their involuntary move into the smaller half of the house, they had been given fair—and more than fair, generous—notice of the event.

Grover knew that the enforced move was not what had killed Dr Boston, although his death had certainly followed hard upon the move, coming three months after it had been accomplished. He didn't see why he shouldn't do over the house the way he and Ellie wanted it; but Dr Boston had inconsiderately died and he was to be blamed for it, he supposed. The doctor's widow didn't seem at all interested to see what he was doing with so much unaffected delight to remodel the place according to his own ideas of comfort, his and Ellie's.

But they had gone ahead the way they'd planned during long years of living in inconvenient apartments, dreaming of the wealth of space they'd one day enjoy. They had saved, made sketches, eyed antique stores and scrabbled around in back-concession attics looking for curly maple antiques, planning at length to reclaim the house and furnish their half with their painfully acquired and stored treasures. And when the time had come, despite Edward's inconvenient death, they had gone ahead with their plans. He had done it all for Ellie, had followed her in all things, had done everything for her because he'd cherished her and had hoped to exorcize the crazy memory of her parents.

'Softening of the brain,' they'd called it when her mother died, the state of medical science being what it was in the Stoverville of thirty years ago. Like mother, like daughter, and like father too. For Ellie was going the same way—he saw it though he tried not to —and here he was in a house, or half of a house, that wasn't really his, had never been and would never be his, that now, watching her sicken prematurely, he hated and didn't want any more. He couldn't get out of the house, not even to go to the grocery store; there were razor-blades lying loose in the medicine cabinets, mirrors that might be broken and wrists to slash. He didn't know what they might come to and couldn't leave the house for fear.

Light, not sunny light but cold white light, slides through the cedars and spruce, giving them a smoothy suave waxy sheen. Standing on the south corner of the porch, catching sharp gleams off the water through the glancing leaves, he wishes now that they'd kept their last mean apartment in Toronto. It is with a sense of felt physical release that he watches Maura push through a hole in the fence, enter the arbour, and make her way automatically, without pausing to place her feet safely on the springy overgrown turf, along winding paths aslant the promontory, coming to pay her call. Now he sees the oddness of their situation: Maura is a native of the place who's fled and felt no ties; he's an outsider who's gotten stuck fast inside. 'Softening of the brain.' They have a hospital of a kind these days in Stoverville and he knows what they'll call it.

Then the shrubbery shakes and parts and Maura stands revealed, mounting the sagging porch steps. Behind her the small green and copper leaves whisper together and, all at once, miles away to the east, a steamer hoots once.

'Hello,' they say together, almost strangers, and again, with embarrassment, 'well, hello!'

'I'm here for the weekend,' she says with constraint, 'and I wanted to see you both.'

'You can see her,' he says, forever an inside outsider. How the girl resembles her father! More and more he feels sixty-five and out of place.

'How is she? You know, Grover, she's the one person in Stover-ville . . . well . . . she was a second mother to me.'

'I wish we'd had children.'

'You do?'

'Certainly I do. But her health was never up to it.'

'Oh! How is she now?'

'Lying down,' he says abruptly, with a shiver. 'Come along, I'll show you what we've done with the house.' He pauses. 'You don't mind our doing it over, do you?'

'Of course not. It's yours, after all. But how *is* she?'

She won't be diverted, it seems. 'When her mother died, you remember, it was the same thing. But they've a new name for it now, which sounds a little better.'

'Most people said that old Mrs Phillips was out of her mind.'

'She wasn't, exactly. They called it "softening of the brain." That's the trouble. It runs in the family, don't you see?'

'But there isn't any such thing.'

'They don't call it that any more. Now they call it,' and he rattles off the foolish phrase, 'premature senility induced by an insufficient supply of oxygen to the brain. Her circulation is poor and the artery which feeds the brain is narrowing—like hardening of the arteries—I don't recollect the medical term.'

'Sclerosis?'

'That's it. Arteriosclerosis affecting the brain, and hypertension too, of course. She's all right sometimes but she wanders. And then she was always religious, you know.'

'Is she still?'

'Worse, if anything. Good heavens, Maura, she sees ghosts. According to her the house is full of people. And I—I can't see anything. I tell you, it's frightening. Come inside, I'll show you around. You see on the floor here in the hall I've installed a parquet, black and white squares. Very cheerful, don't you think?'

He conducts her around the familiar rooms, exhibiting them in their novel guise. Soon they hear a voice calling from upstairs. Ellie's.

'I'm coming down. I've a housecoat here,' she warbles with enthusiasm, 'and I've had a good sleep, Grover.'

She has no footfall. She had been soundless in Maura's memory, never letting the floorboards announce her coming. She had floated around her unfortunate father and mother like a creature from another world, a wraith. Now she floats down the quiet staircase more impalpable than ever, her face bloodless, her hair gone silver, white white white, like someone who lives in the river, Maura thinks, like somebody made of water. She stretches out her arms and floats along, singing that thin melody. What happens in her head, does she hear anything? She doesn't look at you but over your shoulder, seeing things beyond and to one side of you. Poor Grover. No wonder he's afraid that the house is full of people who can't be seen or heard. Her gaze closes around and behind you like water, and you aren't solid.

'My dear child,' says Ellie moving soundlessly over the black and white squares while Maura, entranced, feels but doesn't see Grover melt away out of vision bound for his workbench, to feel the cutting edges of his chisels and wonder about them.

The two women embrace and Ellie is so weightless that Maura can hardly feel her hug. She, poor chunky brown-eyed girl, solidly there, whoever else vanishes, feels as if she's tearing an invisible tissue of air as she follows Ellie into the drawing-room. So she takes good care to sit facing her across the room, not relishing the idea of that disturbing weightlessness at her side.

'You're always the same girl,' says Ellie, plucking at the sleeves of her flowered housecoat with birdlike hands, blue in the veins, crooked fingers locked in an immutable grasp, 'and I thank God you've got your mother's eyes and not ours.'

Her own eyes can't be still but rove desperately around the room.

'I'm embarrassed for myself and Grover,' she says. 'I feel as though we've wronged you, although I'm thankful he feels nothing of it, the dear man, I don't believe he knows what's going on.' All at once a nervous tic starts up in her left cheek and she straightens her spine, sitting up abruptly on the sofa.

'He showed me the river of the water of life, clear as crystal,' she says, blinking.

There is just nothing to be said to this for apparently she has left lucidity behind her, putting Maura in the position of an unwilling witness to a personal collapse. How can she get out, what can she do? There is nothing to do but sit there and make conversation during the rare lucid intervals.

'Seven stars and seven gold crowns, seven tapers, three trees, three thrones,' says Ellie, shivering slightly. Then she shakes herself and tries to fix her eyes on Maura. 'Grover wouldn't understand, would he?' she begs, and launches into the unforgettable.

'The house is full of gods,' she begins, 'all around us, gods and the dead. I saw my father yesterday, staring hatefully at the parquetry, and he told me that he didn't understand or like it, finding it bad taste and confusing to the eye. He told me not to marry and I wouldn't listen. I refused to listen though he told me from my cradle upwards. I couldn't bear children though I wanted them so. I mustn't transmit my milky brains to them and yet I tried and tried because Grover wanted them so. They warned me against Grover, both of them. He'll never understand, they said, he'll never guess and you mustn't tell him. And yet our children might have been saved from it, if the doctors knew all they claimed, instead of letting my father go to his grave in the belief that he'd lost his mind.

'Naturally I meant to marry Edward. We were born in the same month to the same family, and outside the forbidden degrees of kindred by a hairsbreadth. He might have helped me and there'd be no question about the house. Because he was a physician, don't you see, and could have stopped me before I came this far. You'd have been my child and you *are* my child though you won't admit it.' She glares almost directly at Maura, just missing her eyes.

'*There* he is,' she says flatly, 'sitting beside you, your father.' And Maura vainly resists the motion of her head which assures her that the three-years'-dead man is not there at all.

'I see him. The house is full of him, twenty-eight years of him, poor Edward. He lived his soul into this house and *there* he is.'

'He's dead,' says Maura, speaking for the first time in minutes.

'Don't stare at me with those hard brown eyes. They don't belong to you. God knows I wanted children and where am I now? A sick old woman being kept a prisoner by a stranger who won't let me alone. I know. He's afraid, afraid.' She spreads her palms over her cheeks and smoothes the twitches out. 'Do you like the way we've changed the house?'

'I think it's all lovely, Ellie,' says Maura, crossing the room and taking her by the arm, helping her to her feet. 'I've been through it all with Grover. It's all lovely.' She leads the other woman into the hallway.

'Are you leaving?'

'I think so. I told mother I'd be home for lunch. Perhaps I can come over Sunday night.'

'And then you go back to the city? You'll have children, Maura, I know it. You're going to be married, aren't you?'

At this prescience, Maura shudders. 'I hope so,' she admits, kissing a dry cheek, 'and please take good care of yourself.'

As she pushes the yielding shrubbery aside, as it whistles softly around her, she hears Ellie call: 'It comes to Grover or to you, and soon, soon.' And she resolves to herself that it can't possibly come to her.

'Oho!' says Mrs Boston with delight of a kind. 'Oho, oho! I told you, didn't I?'

'You told me something, but not all that,' says Maura, utterly exhausted.

'She must have been having one of her bad days.'

'All her days must be like that,' reasons Maura tiredly. 'She can't have any good days if she's as bad as that.'

'It's partly assumed, you know.'

'Oh, mother, for goodness' sake! She's dying. She can't reason.'

'The poor woman,' says Mrs Boston with real compassion, 'and so she said that it would come to you or Grover.'

'Yes.'

'She must have meant the house.'

'Oh, that and everything else.'

'There's nothing else to inherit.'

'You don't know. You don't know.'

'There could be no two people more hard-hearted, Maura, than you and Grover Haskell!'

'Why do you dislike him so much? You should be grateful to him.'

'For heaven's sake, why?'

'Oh, I don't know,' exclaims Maura, petulantly. 'Perhaps because he got her out of the way. He's not a malicious person at all. I like him. I pity him.'

'And well you may,' says Mrs Boston, 'because he's caught,

there's nothing he can do. He hoped for years to get his hands on our house and now he hasn't got it—it's got him. He caught a shark.'

'I'll make a prediction,' says Maura grimly, 'and I want you to remember it. If Ellie dies and leaves the house to him, as I hope to God she does, you, Mother, will be over there three nights a week playing cards with him within six months.'

Mrs Boston springs to her feet and begins to pace up and down the narrow bed-sitting-room which comprises the bulk of her small apartment. She doesn't resemble her daughter, at this strained point in their relationship, nearly as much as usual. She shows in her walk and in the defiant toss of her head how completely she knows that there can be no estrangement between them; she can trust Maura.

'My God, how right you are,' she confesses with a full agitation, crushing a hand over her neat straw-coloured hair. 'Of course I will be. Out of idle curiosity, you believe, and loneliness.' She turns briskly to Maura. 'I know mine is not a dignified position. I'm quite aware of what people say.'

'People don't say anything, as far as I know.'

'You live in Montreal.'

'But I hear what goes on.'

'Nonsense! You haven't been here in a year.' As Maura protests, her mother puts up a grim hand for silence. 'I'm not reproaching you. In your place I should do exactly the same. Stay away! Hunt some man down! You can do it!' She smiles at her daughter because they love one another. 'I sound like a cheerleader.'

'I've nearly done it,' grins Maura sourly, 'and Ellie knew all about it before I said a word.'

'She has radar,' says Mrs Boston, 'or second sight.'

'You would adore your grandchildren if you had any.'

Mrs Boston winces. 'My God, how right you are,' she exclaims for the second time in three minutes. 'Have some!' she begs. 'Start the whole thing off again. I don't want you to be the last. We never meant you to be the only child.'

'I've borne it,' says Maura.

'So you see me over at Grover's house, playing double solitaire with him, the two of us mourning our barrenness, all alone and exactly like each other. Very well, I've admitted that I don't hate the man. He's not a wicked man, I suppose.'

'It's simply that you're both caught.'

'He's caught worse than I am, Maura. He's planned and worked to possess himself of that place. He used to come to us on vacations, and when we had him in to dinner he'd look around as if it were already his. You could see his mind at work, estimating the cost of new velour drapes for the dining-room. I used to laugh.'

'Not tactful, anyway.'

'No, he's like an infant. He has no notion of tact. And then he asked us to move while your father was sickening with what killed him, though I will admit in justice that he couldn't have suspected it, and then he moved in and Ellie began to collapse, and now she's gone the way her parents did and at the end they were both suicidal.'

'Her mother killed herself.'

'So she did, so she did. He knows it and he can't get out; the house owns him.' It is complete triumph for her. 'When your father and I lived there, we owned the house, we had tenants in the smaller side and we mailed their rent to Ellie. But we had the house, it didn't have us. Now the only people he can find to live in the smaller side are the Hungarians, because everybody in town who can speak English is afraid to go near the place. So the house has him. Oh, I'll go and see him,' she concludes.

But Maura is ahead of her, already at the door. 'You and he can do the gardening together,' she observes. 'You can preserve Daddy's arbour. Grover loves the trees.'

'You don't have to go down there tonight. You're under no obligation and you've got a train to catch.'

'It's been a long weekend,' says Maura, 'but I told him I'd drop in.'

'Well, don't *you* get caught!'

It was a promise fairly made, though one which she repents of as she walks along the shore towards the three tamaracks which guide her into the leafy paths. The river is flat calm, an end-of-autumn calm, with here and there faint smudges on the surface moved by the slight breeze. Maura pauses for a moment before she pushes through the hole in the fence to study the river and wish it altered. What we need here, she decides, are docks and cranes, smoke, drydocks, slipways, a hundred factories; the river has strangled

Stoverville. Straining her eyes she looks across to the desolate New York banks behind which, she remembers from the motor trips of childhood, there is nothing. Daddy promised me bears on the New York side but there weren't any, not a bear. Oh God, she allows herself for one second to reflect, oh God, I want children. I want two children.

She pushes through the hole in the fence, remembering the afternoon she caught her party frock on a nail in this same board, sneaking home late from a birthday party by her secret route. She looks for the hole in her frock and the red splash of the rust but there isn't anything there at all, and up she goes along the path to where Grover stands in the twilight on the sagging steps, anxiously looking out for her, with his hands outstretched to help her through the leaves.

'The husband,' he begins shakily as soon as he can see all of her, 'is not really a blood relation of the wife, is he? That is, he isn't related to her. After all I come from another part of the province and I'm not a Phillips. Am I?' He insists on it. 'I'm not a blood relation to my wife, am I? Because this place should be transmitted according to the blood strain and should naturally come to you, all to you. I tell you, Maura, and I'd tell your father too, if I could, that I never wanted this place for myself. We have no children and you're part Phillips. You should get it, and I'm going to see that you do. Because I don't want it. I never did, not for myself. Never. For two whole days Ellie has been going over and over the matter, threatening to leave the place to me, but I told her that I'm not a blood relation. I'm related to her by marriage only.'

'That's a closer relation.'

'No it isn't,' he shouts, leaping like a trout in a still pool. 'This place belongs to you through your father and I've insisted to Ellie for thirty-six hours that she leave it to you. I've torn up her will. I'll make her write another before she gets worse.' He shudders. 'I'm afraid she's going to die soon.' It has gone from twilight to dark through his speech.

'Where is she now?'

'She made me move her bed. She's lying down in your room at the top of the house. She's exhausted. I tell you, Maura, when she isn't herself she says things you wouldn't believe. I don't mean to complain or bear tales but I've never seen her like this and I can't bear it.' His throat dries up and closes convulsively and then miraculously opens for his final words as they pace up and down hand in hand on the creaking porch.

'You'll take it, won't you? Look at me, Maura, please! It's so dark I can't see you.' He turns to face her and throws his arms stiffly wide apart. 'It's yours. It's yours! I don't want it. You will take it, won't you? Take it, take it, please!'

Her little bedroom is dark like a virginal cell in a cloister and Ellie lies on her bed with arms folded on her chest like an effigy on a tomb, her mind whirling with the effort to concentrate and control her thoughts. At regular intervals of maybe thirty seconds her body arches rigidly, projecting her torso and thighs forward and upward into the air, drawing her lower back up off the sheets, the cramped writhings of a woman in childbirth forcing her thighs apart and racking her abdomen, and all to no purpose. But her consciousness doesn't record these convulsions as the stream of her ideas grows fuller and stronger, swollen by many tributaries, sliding faster and faster. *Ppaaaarrrrpp.* I am going to starboard. *Mmeeeeuuuuuuuuhhhh.* I am going to port. SS *Renvoyle* upbound with package freight for Toronto. MV *Prins Willem Oranje* downbound for the locks and the Atlantic, half-laden, looking for a full hull at Quebec City. The horns grow louder and merge with the full downward current of her thoughts. They were never like this before, never so loud, never right in my room like this. The ships are swimming over me and the river through me and the horns are inside my head muddling my ideas all together with the family downstairs in the living-room with the captain from Oslo, seven stars and seven coronets and the three trees on the point for Christ and the two thieves hanging so straight and dark in the twilight on the darkening water I am going to starboard under the stars on the current down the river down east past the Plains of Abraham, farther, to where the river yawns its mouth eleven miles wide, invisibly wide, bearing me away at last to the darkness, the sleety impassible impassable Gulf.

# Hubert Aquin

HUBERT Aquin was born in Montreal on October 24, 1929. He studied philosophy (Husserl and Sartre) at the Université de Montréal, then spent three years, 1948-51, at the Institut d'Etudes politiques in Paris before returning to Montreal to work as a director for Radio-Canada and the National Film Board. In the early 1960s, a seminal decade for Quebec writers, Aquin helped found the magazine *Liberté* and later contributed to *Parti pris*, the leftist publication set up in opposition to the *Cité libre* group of which Pierre Eliott Trudeau was a member. In 1964, while he was vice-president of the Rassemblement pour l'Indépendence National, Aquin was arrested for carrying an illegal weapon. While under detention in a psychiatric hospital he wrote his first novel, *Prochain épisode* (1965). Two more novels followed: *Trou de mémoire* (1968: *Blackout*, 1974), for which he declined the Governor-General's award; and *L'Antiphonaire* (1969: *The Antiphonary*, 1973) for which he accepted the Prix du gouvernement du Québec. In 1972 he was awarded the Prix David, and his last novel, *Neige noir* (1974: *Hamlet's Twin*, 1979) received the Grande Prix de la ville de Montréal. He was named literary director of Les Editions la Presse in 1975, but resigned in August 1976. Less than a year later—on March 15, 1977—Aquin shot himself on the grounds of the Villa-Maria convent in Montreal.

'De retour, le 11 avril' first appeared in *Liberté* (March, 1969). The story prophesizes Aquin's own death, but it also underlines the self-destructive element he saw in many Quebec intellectuals. His style moves in frenzied, spontaneous bursts that have a kind of mesmeric effect on the reader. As Gilles Dorion has observed in *Etudes français* (October, 1977), Aquin 'solicits (his reader's) complicity, in police or spy adventures that are often dishevelled, or at least senseless and unprecedented. Whether the knot is ever unravelled is unimportant. What *is* important is the unhesitating commitment of the reader to Aquin's mock universe. The author says to his reader, Come play this game with me. And if the acceptance is total, without reservations, then the communication will also be total.'

# BACK ON APRIL ELEVENTH

## *Translated by Alan Brown*

WHEN YOUR letter came I was reading a Mickey Spillane. I'd already been interrupted twice, and was having trouble with the plot. There was this man Gardner, who for some reason always carted around the photo of a certain corpse. It's true I was reading to kill time. Now I'm not so interested in killing time.

It seems you have no idea of what's been going on this winter. Perhaps you're afflicted with a strange intermittent amnesia that wipes out me, my work, our apartment, the brown record-player .... I assure you I can't so easily forget this season I've passed without you, these long, snowy months with you so far away. When you left the first snow had just fallen on Montreal. It blocked the sidewalks, obscured the houses, and laid down great pale counterpanes in the heart of the city.

The evening you left—on my way back from Dorval—I drove aimlessly through the slippery empty streets. Each time the car went into a skid I had the feeling of going on an endless voyage. The Mustang was transformed into a rudderless ship. I drove for a long time without the slightest accident, not even a bump. It was dangerous driving, I know. Punishable by law. But that night even the law had become a mere ghost of itself, as had the city and this damned mountain that we've tramped so often. So much whiteness made a strong impression on me. I remember feeling a kind of anguish.

You, my love, probably think I'm exaggerating as usual and that I get some kind of satisfaction out of establishing these connections between your leaving and my states of mind. You may think I'm putting things together in retrospect in such a way as to explain what happened after that first fall of cerusian white.

But you're wrong: I'm doing nothing of the kind. That night, I tell you, the night you left, I skidded and slipped on that livid snow, fit to break your heart. It was myself I lost control of each time the Mustang slid softly into the abyss of memory. Winter since then has armed our city with many coats of melting mail, and here I am already on the verge of a burnt-ivory spring....

Someone really has to tell you, my love, that I tried twice to take my life in the course of this dark winter.

Yes, it's the truth. I'm telling you this without passion, with no bitterness or depths of melancholy. I'm a little disappointed at having bungled it; I feel like a failure, that's all. But now I'm bored. I've fizzled out under the ice. I'm finished.

Have you, my love, changed since last November? Do you still wear your hair long? Have you aged since I saw you last? How do you feel about all this snow that's fallen on me, drifting me in? I suppose a young woman of twenty-five has other souvenirs of her travels besides these discoloured postcards I've pinned to the walls of our apartment?

You've met women . . . or men; you've met perhaps one man and . . . he seemed more charming, more handsome, more 'liberating' than I could ever be. Of course, as I say that, I know that to liberate oneself from another person one has only to be unfaithful. In this case you were right to fly off to Amsterdam to escape my black moods; you were right to turn our liaison into a more relative thing, the kind that other people have, any old love affair, any shabby business of that kind. . . .

But that's all nonsense. I'm not really exaggerating, I'm just letting myself go, my love, letting myself drift. A little like the way I drove the Mustang that night last November. I'm in distress, swamped by dark thoughts. And it's no use telling myself that my imagination's gone wild, that I'm crazy to tell you these things, for I feel that this wave of sadness is submerging both of us and condemning me to total desolation. I can still see the snowy streets and me driving through them with no rhyme or reason, as if that aimless motion could magically make up for losing you. But you know, I already had a sedimentary confused desire to die, that very evening.

While I was working out the discords of my loneliness at the steering wheel of the Mustang, you were already miles high in a DC-8 above the North Atlantic. And a few hours later your plane would land gently on the icy runway of Schipol—after a few leisurely manoeuvres over the still plains of the Zuider Zee. By then I would be back in our apartment, reading a Simenon—*The Nahour Affair*—set partly in a Paris blanketed in snow (a rare occurrence), but also in that very city of Amsterdam where you had just arrived. I went to sleep in the small hours of the morning, clutching that bit of reality that somehow reconnected me to you.

The next day was the beginning of my irreversible winter. I tried to act as if nothing had changed and went to my office at the Agency (Place Ville Marie) at about eleven. I got through the day's work one way or another. While I was supposed to be at lunch I went instead to the ground-floor pharmacy. I asked for phenobarbital. The druggist told me, with a big stupid grin, that it called for a prescription. I left the building in a huff, realizing, however, that this needed a little thought.

I had to have a prescription, by whatever means, and information about brand-names and doses. And I needed at least some knowledge of the various barbiturate compounds.

With this drug very much on my mind I went next day or the day after to the McGill medical bookstore. Here were the shelves dealing with pharmacology. I was looking for a trickle and found myself confronted by the sea. I was overcome, submerged, astonished. I made a choice and left the store with two books under my arm: the *Shorter Therapeutics and Pharmacology*, and the *International Vade Mecum* (a complete listing of products now on the market).

That night, alone with my ghosts, I got at the books. To hell with Mickey Spillane, I had better things to read: for example, this superbook (the *Vade Mecum*) which has the most delicious recipes going! Your appetite, your tensions, your depressions—they are all at the command of a few grams of drugs sagely administered. And according to this book of magic potions, life itself can be suppressed if only one knows how to go about it. I was passionately engrossed by this flood of pertinent information, but I still had my problem of how to get a prescription. Or rather, how to forge one that wouldn't turn into a passport to prison. A major problem.

His name was in the phone book: Olivier, J. R., internist. I dialled his number. His secretary asked what would be the best time of day for an appointment and specified that it would be about a month as the doctor was very busy. I answered her with a daring that still surprises me.

'It's urgent.'

'What is it you have?' asked the secretary.

'A duodenal ulcer.'

'How do you know?'

'Well, I've consulted several doctors and they strongly advised me to see Doctor O.'

'Tomorrow at eleven,' she suggested, struck by my argument. 'Will that be convenient?'

'Of course,' I replied.

I spent forty-five minutes in the waiting room with the secretary I'd phoned the day before. I flipped through the magazines on the table searching for subjects of conversation to use on this doctor friend I hadn't seen for so long.

He appeared in the doorway and his secretary murmured my name. I raised my gloomy gaze to greet this smiling friend. He ushered me into his overstuffed office.

After the usual halting exchange of memories from college and university days I took a deep breath and, talking directly to Olivier, J. R., I told him straight out that I was having trouble sleeping. He burst into laughter, while I crouched deeper in the armchair he kept for patients.

'You're living it up too much, old boy,' he said, smiling.

Just then his intercom blinked. Olivier lifted the phone.

'What is it?' he asked his secretary.

(I had been hoping for something like this.)

'Just a second. I have something to sign. You know how it is. They're making bureaucrats out of us.'

He got up and went out to the reception room, carefully closing the door. At once I spied on his hand-rest the prescription pad with his letterhead. I quickly tore off a number of sheets and stuck them in the left inside pocket of my jacket. I was trembling, dripping with sweat.

'Well, bring me up to date,' said Olivier, coming back. 'Is she running around on you?'

He obviously found his own humour as irresistible as I found it offensive and our chat didn't get much farther. We fell silent and Olivier took his pen. Before starting to write on his prescription pad he looked up at me.

'What was it, now? You wanted some barbiturates to get you to sleep?'

'Yes,' I said.

'Okay, here's some stuff that'll knock out a horse.' He tore off the sheet and held it out to me.

'Thanks, thank you very much.' I suppose I was a bit emotional.

'I've put *non repetatur* at the bottom for these pills have a tendency to be habit-forming. If you really need more after a couple of weeks come and see me again.'

I folded the prescription without even searching out the *non repetatur*, an expression I had learned only a couple of days before. The intercom blinked again. Olivier, annoyed, picked up his phone but I paid no attention. I was already far away. Afterwards Olivier started telling me how his wife complained—or so he said—that she never got to see him any more.

'I'm working too hard,' he said, hand on brow. 'I probably need a holiday, but there it is. My wife's the one who's off to Europe. And it's only a month or so since she did the Greek Islands.'

In my mind I saw you in the streets of Breda and The Hague. I imagined your walks in Scheveningen, your visits to the Mauri-thuis. I wasn't sure any more just where in Europe you were: at the Hook of Holland, the flying isle of Vlieland, or the seaside suburb of Leiden at Kalwijk aan Zee....

I was out again on the chilly street. The sky was dark and lowering. Black clouds scudded by a rooftop level, presaging an-other snowstorm. Let the snow come to beautify this death-land-scape, where I drove in a Mustang while you moved in the clear celestial spaces of the painters of the Dutch school....

Back in our apartment I analyzed the prescription I had obtained by trickery. Twelve capsules of sodium amobarbital. I had no intention of remaining the possessor of a non-repeatable number of pills and began practising Olivier's handwriting. On ordinary paper. I had stolen ten sheets of his letterhead but that precious paper must not be wasted. In two or three hours I'd managed four good prescriptions. I fell asleep on the strength of my success.

It took me some days to accumulate a *quoad vitam* dose with the help of my forged scribbles. But I wasn't satisfied with the *quoad vitam* dose indicated in the *Vade Mecum*. I went on accumulating the little sky-blue capsules, each with its three-letter stamp—SK&F. There were nights when I slept not at all rather than dip into my stock of precious sodic torpedoes.

Quite a few days passed this way. Strange days. Knowing that I had my stock of death in hand I felt sure of myself and almost in harmony with life. I knew that I was going to die and at that moment it would have been upsetting to receive a letter from you, my love, for I had come too close to the end of living.

When your letter came on November sixteenth it in no way disturbed this harmony, as I had feared it might. After reading it I still wanted to end my life by using, some evening, my surprising accumulation of sodium amobarbital. You'd written in haste (I could tell by your hand) from the Amstel Hotel, but the postmark said Utrecht. So you'd mailed it from there! What were you doing in Utrecht? How had you gone from Amsterdam to that little town where the treaty was signed ratifying the conquest of French Canada? Symbol of the death of a nation, Utrecht became a premonitory symbol of my own death. Had you gone with someone? A European colleague, as you usually describe the men you meet on your travels? Are there many interior decorators in Utrecht? Or perhaps I should ask if they are friendly and charming. I imagined you sitting in the car of a decorator colleague, lunching on the way and perhaps spending the night in Utrecht. I grew weary of calling back so many memories of you, your charm, your beauty, your hot body in my arms. I tore up your letter to put an end to my despair.

By the twenty-eighth of November I'd heard nothing more from you. My days grew shorter and emptier, my nights longer and more sleepless. They finally seemed barely to be interrupted by my days and I was exhausted. Recurrent insomnia had broken my resistance. I was destroyed, hopeless, without the slightest will to organize what was left of my life.

For me an endless night was about to begin, the unique, final, ultimate night. I'd at last decided to put an arbitrary end to my long hesitation, a period to our disordered history; decided, also, no longer to depend on your intermittent grace, which had been cruel only in that I had suffered from it.

That day I made a few phone calls to say I was not available and spent my time tidying the apartment. When it was evening I took a very hot bath copiously perfumed from the bottle of Seaqua. I soaked for a long time in that beneficent water. Then I put on my burnt-orange bathing trunks and piled a few records on our playback: Ray Charles, Feliciano, Nana Mouskouri. I sprawled on our scarlet sofa, a glass of Chivas Regal in my hand, almost naked, fascinated by the total void that was waiting for me. I put Nana Mouskouri on several times. Then I finally made up my mind and swallowed my little sky-blue capsules four at a time, washing them down with great gulps of Chivas Regal. At the end I took more scotch to help me absorb the lot. I put the nearly empty bottle on the rug just beside the couch. Still quite lucid, I turned on the radio (without getting up) so that the neighbours would not be alerted by the heavy breathing which, according to my medical sources, would begin as soon as I dropped into my coma.

To tell you the truth I wasn't sad but rather impressed, like someone about to start a long, very long, voyage. I thought of you, but faintly, oh, so faintly. You were moving around in the distance, in a funereal fog. I could still see the rich colours of your dresses and bathrobes. I saw you enter the apartment like a ghost and leave it in slow-motion, but eternally in mirror perspective leading to infinity. The deeper I slipped into my comatose feast the less you looked my way, or rather the less I was conscious of you. Melancholy had no grip on me, nor fear. In fact I was blanketed in the solemnity of my solitude. Then, afterwards, obliteration became less complex and I became mortuary but not yet dead, left rocking in a total void.

And now, you ask, how are you managing to write this letter from beyond the tomb?

Well, here's the answer. I failed! The only damage I received in this suicide attempt resulted from the coma that lasted several hours. I was not in the best condition. My failure—even if I had no other devastating clues—would be proof enough of my perfect weakness, that diffuse infirmity that cannot be classified by science but which allows me to ruin everything I touch, always, without exception.

I woke up alive, as it were, in a white ward of the Royal Victoria, surrounded by a network of intravenous tubes that pinned me to the bed and ringed by a contingent of nurses. My lips felt frozen and dried and I remember that one of the nurses sponged my lips from time to time with an anti-herpetic solution.

Outside it was snowing, just as it had been on the day you left. The great white flakes fell slowly and I became aware that the very fact of seeing them silently falling was irrefutable proof that I was still, and horridly, alive. My return to a more articulated consciousness was painful, and took (to my relief) an infinity. As soon as I reached that threshold of consciousness I began to imagine you in the Netherlands or somewhere in Europe. Was there snow in Holland? And did you need your high suede boots that we shopped for together a few days before you left?

Suddenly I feel a great fatigue: these thoughts, returning in all their disorder, are taking me back to my stagnant point again. . . .

It was really quite ironic that your telegram from Bruges should have become the means of your tardy (and involuntary) intervention on behalf of my poisoned body. I suppose the message was phoned first. But I didn't hear the ring and Western Union simply delivered the typed message to my address. The caretaker, who has no key to the letter boxes in our building, felt the call of duty and decided to bring me the envelope himself. There is something urgent about telegrams, you can't just leave them lying around. People can't imagine a harmless telegram that might read: HAPPY BIRTHDAY. WEATHER MARVELLOUS. KISSES. And yet that's exactly what was written in that telegram from Bruges.

I suppose the caretaker rapped a few times on our door. He probably couldn't see how I'd be out when the radio was blasting away. Finally, his curiosity must have got the better of him. He opened the door with his pass-key and stepped in to leave the envelope on the Louis XV table under the hall mirror. It's easy to imagine the rest: from the door he saw that I was there, he noted my corpse-like face, etc. Then, in a panic, he phoned the Montreal Police who transported me—no doubt at breakneck speed—to the emergency ward of the Royal Victoria. I spent several days under an oxygen tent. I even underwent a tracheotomy. That, in case the term means nothing to you, involves an incision in the trachea, followed by the insertion of a tracheal drain.

I must tell you everything, my love. I'm alive, therefore I am cured. The only traces are an immense scar on my neck and a general debility. While I was surviving one way or another in Montreal, you were continuing your tour of Europe. You saw other cities, Brussels, Charleroi, Amiens, Lille, Roubaix, Paris. . . . Bruges had been just a stopover where you perhaps had dinner with a stranger, but no one hangs around in Bruges when the continent is waiting. Though God knows Bruges is a privileged place, an amorous sanctuary, a fortress that has given up a little terra firma to the insistent North Sea. I feel a soft spot for that half-dead city which you left with no special feeling. I stayed on in Bruges after you left, immured beneath its old and crumbling quays, for that was where you wished me (by telegram) a happy birthday.

There is no end to this winter. I don't know how many blizzards I watched from my hospital window. Around the fifteenth of December some doctor decided I should go home, that I was—so to speak—cured. Easy to say! Can one be cured of having wanted to die? When the ambulance attendants took me up to the apartment I saw myself in a mirror. I thought I would collapse. As a precaution I lay down on the couch where I had almost ended my days in

November. Nothing had changed since then, but there was a thin film of dust on our furniture and the photos of you. The sky, lowering and dark, looked like more snow. I felt like a ghost. My clothes hung loose on me and my skin had the colour of a corpse. The sleepless nights again took up their death march but I no longer had my reserve of suicide-blue amobarbital pills. And I'd used up all my blank prescription forms. I couldn't sleep. I stared at the ceiling or at the white snowflakes piling up on our balcony. I imagined you at Rome or Civitavecchia or in the outskirts of Verona, completely surrendered to the intense experience of Europe.

From my calendar I knew that you were coming back to Montreal on April eleventh, on board the *Maasdam*. If I went to meet you that day at the docks of the Holland-American Line I would be in an emotional state. Too emotional, unable to tell you about what I did in November or about my disintegration since. Of course you'd give me a great hug and tell me all about those marvels, the fascinating ruins in Bruges, the baths of Caracalla, the Roman arches of triumph: the Arch of Tiberius, of Constantine, of Trajan, and so on. And all through your euphoric monologue I'd feel the knot at my throat.

It's for that reason—and all sorts of others, all somehow related to cowardice—that I'm writing you this letter, my love, I'll soon finish it and address it to Amsterdam, from which the *Maasdam* sails, so that you can read it during the crossing. That way you'll know that I bungled my first suicide attempt in November.

You'll understand that if I say 'first' it means there'll be a second.

Don't you see that my hand is trembling? That my writing is beginning to scrawl? I'm already shaky. The spaces between each word, my love, are merely the symbols of the void that is beginning to accept me. I have ten more lucid minutes, but I've already changed: my mind is slipping, my hand wanders, the apartment, with every light turned on, grows dark where I look. I can barely see the falling snow but what I do see is like blots of ink. My love, I'm shivering with cold. The snow is falling somehow within me, my last snowfall. In a few seconds, I'll no longer exist, I will move no more. And so I'm sorry but I won't be at the dock on April eleventh. After these last words I shall crawl to the bath, which has been standing full for nearly an hour. There, I hope, they will find me, drowned. Before the eleventh of April next.

# Mordecai Richler

MORDECAI Richler was born on St Urbain Street in the Jewish quarter of Montreal (his father was a junk dealer) in 1931. He attended Baron Byng High, which he calls Fletcher's Field in his novels and stories (Fletcher's Field is in fact the name of a nearby park), and Sir George Williams University. He left Sir George without taking a degree ('I became quite frightened,' he told critic Nathan Cohen in 1957, 'that if I got a B.A., I'd get an M.A., and then I might try for a Ph.D., and that would be the end of me') and in 1951 sailed for Paris, where he stayed two years (see his article, 'A Sense of the Ridiculous: Paris; 1951 and After,' in the *New American Review* #4, 1968) before returning to Montreal and working briefly for the CBC. In 1954 Richler left Canada again, this time for England where he lived for the next 18 years. He returned to Montreal for good in 1972.

His first novel, *The Acrobats*, was published in 1954, and in the next five years he wrote three more—*Son of a Smaller Hero* (1955), *A Choice of Enemies* (1957), and *The Apprenticeship of Duddy Kravitz* (1959)—that established him as one of the best novelists of his generation. During this period he also wrote many of the stories gathered in *The Street* (1969), from which the following story is taken. Richler has won two Governor-General's awards—for *Cocksure* and *Hunting Tigers Under Glass* in 1968, and for *St Urbain's Horseman* in 1971—and is one of the country's most prolific contributors to popular and literary magazines. No book-length study has been published of Richler, possibly because his own novels, essays, and short stories are autobiographical almost to the point of confessional, but George Woodcock's 60-page monograph, *Mordecai Richler* (New Canadian Library, 1971), is a valuable introduction to a very rich body of work.

# BENNY, THE WAR IN EUROPE, AND MYERSON'S DAUGHTER BELLA

WHEN BENNY was sent overseas in the autumn of 1941 his father, Garber, decided that if he had to yield one son to the army it might just as well be Benny, who was a dummy and wouldn't push where he shouldn't; Mrs Garber thought, he'll take care, my Benny will watch out; and Benny's brother Abe proclaimed, 'When he comes back, I'll have a garage of my own, you bet, and I'll be able to give him a job.' Benny wrote every week, and every week the Garbers sent him parcels full of good things a St Urbain Street boy should always have, like salami and pickled herring and *shtrudel*. The food parcels never varied and the letters—coming from Camp Borden and Aldershot and Normandy and Holland—were always the same too. They began—'I hope you are all well and good'—and ended—'don't worry, all the best to everybody, thank you for the parcel.'

When Benny came home from the war in Europe, the Garbers didn't make an inordinate fuss, like the Shapiros did when their first-born son returned. They met him at the station, of course, and they had a small dinner for him.

Abe was overjoyed to see Benny again. 'Atta boy,' was what he kept saying all evening, 'Atta boy, Benny.'

'You shouldn't go back to the factory,' Mr Garber said. 'You don't need the old job. You can be a help to your brother Abe in his garage.'

'Yes,' Benny said.

'Let him be, let him rest,' Mrs Garber said. 'What'll happen if he doesn't work for two weeks?'

'Hey, when Artie Segal came back,' Abe said, 'he told me that in Italy there was nothing that a guy couldn't get for a couple of Sweet Caps. Was he shooting me the bull or what?'

Benny had been discharged and sent home not because the war was over, but because of the shrapnel in his leg. He didn't limp too badly and he wouldn't talk about his wound or the war, so at first nobody noticed that he had changed. Nobody, that is, except Myerson's daughter, Bella.

Myerson was the proprietor of Pop's Cigar & Soda, on St Urbain, and any day of the week you could find him there seated on a worn, peeling kitchen chair playing poker with the men of the neighbourhood. He had a glass eye, and when a player hesitated on a bet he would take it out and polish it, a gesture that never failed to intimidate. His daughter, Bella, worked behind the counter. She had a clubfoot and mousey brown hair and some more hair on her face, and although she was only twenty-six it was generally agreed that she would end up an old maid. Anyway she was the one—the first one—to notice that Benny had changed. The very first time he appeared in Pop's Cigar & Soda after his homecoming, she said to him, 'What's wrong, Benny?'

'I'm all right,' he said.

Benny was short and skinny with a long narrow face, a pulpy mouth that was somewhat crooked, and soft black eyes. He had big, conspicuous hands which he preferred to keep out of sight in his pockets. In fact he seemed to want to keep out of sight altogether, and whenever possible he stood behind a chair or in a dim light so that the others wouldn't notice him. When he had failed the ninth grade at FFHS, Benny's class master, a Mr Perkins, had sent him home with a note saying: 'Benjamin is not a student, but he has all the makings of a good citizen. He is honest and attentive in class and a hard worker. I recommend that he learn a trade.'

When Mr Garber had read what his son's teacher had written, he had shaken his head and crumped up the bit of paper and said— 'A trade?'—he had looked at his boy and shaken his head and said— 'A trade?'

Mrs Garber had said stoutly, 'Haven't you got a trade?'

'Shapiro's boy will be a doctor,' Mr Garber had said.

'Shapiro's boy,' Mrs Garber had said.

Afterwards, Benny had retrieved the note and smoothed out the creases and put it in his pocket, where it had remained.

The day after his return to Montreal, Benny showed up at Abe's garage having decided that he didn't want two weeks off. That pleased Abe a lot. 'I can see that you've matured since you've been away,' Abe said. 'That's good. That counts for you in this world.'

Abe worked extremely hard, he worked night and day, and he believed that having Benny with him would give his business an added kick. 'That's my kid brother Benny,' Abe used to tell the taxi drivers. 'Four years in the infantry, two of them up front. A tough *hombre*, let me tell you.'

For the first few weeks Abe was pleased with Benny. 'He's slow,' he reported to their father, 'no genius of a mechanic, but the customers like him and he'll learn.' Then Abe began to notice things. When business was slow, Benny, instead of taking advantage of the lull to clean up the shop, used to sit shivering in a dim corner, with his hands folded tight on his lap. The first time Abe noticed his brother behaving like that, he said, 'What's wrong? You got a chill?'

'No. I'm all right.'

'You want to go home or something?'

'No.'

Whenever it rained, and it rained often that spring, Benny was not to be found around the garage, and that put Abe in a foul temper. Until one day during a thunder shower, Abe tried the toilet door and discovered that it was locked. 'Benny,' he yelled, 'you come out, I know you're in there.'

Benny didn't answer, so Abe fetched the key. He found Benny huddled in a corner with his head buried in his knees, trembling, with sweat running down his face in spite of the cold.

'It's raining,' Benny said.

'Benny, get up. What's wrong?'

'Go away. It's raining.'

'I'll get a doctor, Benny.'

'No. Go away. Please, Abe.'

'But Benny . . .'

Benny began to shake violently, just as if an inner whip had been cracked. Then, after it had passed, he looked up at Abe dumbly, his mouth hanging open. 'It's raining,' he said.

The next morning Abe went to see Mr Garber. 'I don't know what to do with him,' he said.

'The war left him with a bad taste,' Mrs Garber said.

'Other boys went to the war,' Abe said.

'Shapiro's boy,' Mr Garber said, 'was an officer.'

'Shapiro's boy,' Mrs Garber said. 'You give him a vacation, Abe. You insist. He's a good boy. From the best.'

Benny didn't know what to do with his vacation, so he slept in late, and began to hang around Pop's Cigar & Soda.

'I don't like it, Bella,' Myerson said. 'I need him here like I need a cancer.'

'Something's wrong with him psychologically,' one of the card players ventured.

But obviously Bella enjoyed having Benny around and after a

while Myerson stopped complaining. 'Maybe the boy is serious,' he confessed, 'and with her club foot and all that stuff on her face, I can't start picking and choosing. Besides, it's not as if he was a crook. Like Huberman's boy.'

'You take that back. Huberman's boy was a victim of circumstances. He was taking care of the suitcase for a stranger, a complete stranger, when the cops had to mix in.'

Bella and Benny did not talk much when they were together. She used to knit, he used to smoke. He would watch silently as she limped about the store, silently, with longing, and consternation. The letter from Mr Perkins was in his pocket. Occasionally, Bella would look up from her knitting. 'You feel like a cup coffee?'

'I wouldn't say no.'

Around five in the afternoon he would get up, Bella would come round the counter to give him a stack of magazines to take home, and at night he would read them all from cover to cover and the next morning bring them back as clean as new. Then he would sit with her in the store again, looking down at the floor or at his hands.

One day instead of going home around five in the afternoon, Benny went upstairs with Bella. Myerson, who was watching, smiled. He turned to Shub and said: 'If I had a boy of my own, I couldn't wish for a better one than Benny.'

'Look who's counting chickens,' Shub replied.

Benny's vacation dragged on for several weeks and every morning he sat down at the counter in Pop's Cigar & Soda and every evening he went upstairs with Bella, pretending not to hear the wise-cracks made by the card players as they passed. Until one afternoon Bella summoned Myerson upstairs in the middle of a deal. 'We have decided to get married,' she said.

'In that case,' Myerson said, 'you have my permission.'

'Aren't you even going to say luck or something?' Bella asked.

'It's your life,' Myerson said.

They had a very simple wedding without speeches in a small synagogue and after the ceremony was over Abe whacked his younger brother on the back and said, 'Atta boy, Benny. Atta boy.'

'Can I come back to work?'

'Sure you can. You're the old Benny again. I can see that.'

But his father, Benny noticed, was not too pleased with the match. Each time one of Garber's cronies congratulated him, he shrugged his shoulders and said, 'Shapiro's boy married into the Segals.'

'Shapiro's boy,' Mrs Garber said.

Benny went back to the garage, but this time he settled down to work hard and that pleased Abe enormously. 'That's my kid brother Benny,' Abe took to telling the taxi drivers, 'married six weeks and he's already got one in the oven. A quick worker, I'll tell you.'

Benny not only settled down to work hard, but he even laughed a little, and, with Bella's help, began to plan for the future. But every now and then, usually when there was a slack period at the garage, Benny would shut up tight and sit in a chair in a dark corner. He had only been back at work for three, maybe four, months when Bella went to speak to Abe. She returned to their flat on St Urbain her face flushed and triumphant. 'I've got news for you,' she said to Benny. 'Abe is going to open another garage on Mount Royal and you're going to manage it.'

'But I don't want to, I wouldn't know how.'

'We're going to be partners in the new garage.'

'I'd rather stay with Abe.'

Bella explained that they had to plan for their child's future. Their son, she swore, would not be brought up over a cigar & soda, without so much as a shower in the flat. She wanted a fridge. If they saved, they could afford a car. Next year, she said, after the baby was born, she hoped there would be sufficient money saved so that she could go to a clinic in the United States to have an operation on her foot. 'I was to Dr Shapiro yesterday and he assured me there is a clinic in Boston where they perform miracles daily.'

'He examined you?' Benny asked.

'He was very, very nice. Not a snob, if you know what I mean.'

'Did he remember that he was at school with me?'

'No,' Bella said.

Bella woke at three in the morning to find Benny huddled on the floor in a dark corner with his head buried in his knees, trembling. 'It's raining,' he said. 'There's thunder.'

'A man who fought in the war can't be scared of a little rain.'

'Oh, Bella, Bella, Bella.'

She attempted to stroke his head but he drew sharply away from her.

'Should I send for a doctor?'

'Shapiro's boy maybe?' he asked giggling.

'Why not?'

'Bella,' he said. 'Bella, Bella.'

'I'm going next door to the Idelsohns to phone for the doctor. Don't move. Relax.'

But when she returned to the bedroom he had gone.

Myerson came round at eight in the morning. Mr and Mrs Garber were with him.

'Is he dead?' Bella asked.

'Shapiro's boy, the doctor, said it was quick.'

'Shapiro's boy,' Mrs Garber said.

'It wasn't the driver's fault,' Myerson said.

'I know,' Bella said.

# Alice Munro

ALICE Munro (née Laidlaw) was born in 1931 in Wingham, in southeastern Ontario, the eldest of three children. She attended the University of Western Ontario, graduating in Honours English in 1952. With her husband, James Munro, she then moved to British Columbia, living first in Vancouver and then later opening a book store in Victoria. In 1972 Alice Munro returned to southeastern Ontario, where she now lives with her second husband, Gerald Fremlin.

Munro has published four books: two collections of short stories —*Dance of the Happy Shades* (1968), which won a Governor-General's award, and *Something I've Been Meaning to Tell You* (1974)—and two collections of 'linked stories'—*Lives of Girls and Women* (1972), and *Who Do You Think You Are?* (1978), which also won a Governor-General's award. Much of the material for Munro's stories is drawn from her own life—her original title for *Lives of Girls and Women* was *Real Life*—but her stories are not strictly biographical nor regional. In a conversation with John Metcalf published in the *Journal of Canadian Fiction* in 1972, she remarked that 'in terms of vision, the writers who have influenced me are probably the writers of the American South: Eudora Welty, Flannery O'Connor, Carson McCullers, Reynolds Price,' and J. R. Struthers has enlarged on the connection between *Lives of Girls and Women* and Eudora Welty's *The Golden Apples* in his essay, 'Alice Munro and the American South' (*Here and Now*, edited by John Moss, 1978).

*Who Do You Think You Are?*, of which this is the title story, continues and in some ways intensifies the themes and form of Munro's earlier work, so that the four books together make a kind of quartet, not only of linked stories but of linked characters and events. The result is a remarkable organic unity comparable to that achieved by Impressionist painters.

# WHO DO YOU THINK YOU ARE?

THERE WERE some things Rose and her brother Brian could safely talk about, without running aground on principles or statements of position, and one of them was Milton Homer. They both remembered that when they had measles and there was a quarantine notice put up on the door—this was long ago, before their father died and before Brian went to school—Milton Homer came along the street and read it. They heard him coming over the bridge and as usual he was complaining loudly. His progress through town was not silent unless his mouth was full of candy; otherwise he would be yelling at dogs and bullying the trees and telephone poles, mulling over old grievances.

'And I did not and I did not and I did not and I did not!' he yelled, and hit the bridge railing.

Rose and Brian pulled back the quilt that was hung over the window to keep the light out, so they would not go blind.

'Milton Homer,' said Brian appreciatively.

Milton Homer then saw the notice on the door. He turned and mounted the steps and read it. He could read. He would go along the main street reading all the signs out loud.

Rose and Brian remembered this and they agreed that it was the side door, where Flo later stuck on the glassed-in porch; before that there was only a slanting wooden platform, and they remembered Milton Homer standing on it. If the quarantine notice was there and not on the front door, which led into Flo's store, then the store must have been open; that seemed odd, and could only be explained by Flo's having bullied the Health Officer. Rose couldn't remember; she could only remember Milton Homer on the platform with his big head on one side and his fist raised to knock.

'Measles, huh?' said Milton Homer. He didn't knock, after all; he stuck his head close to the door and shouted, 'Can't scare me!' Then he turned around but did not leave the yard. He walked over to the swing, sat down, took hold of the ropes and began moodily, then with mounting and ferocious glee, to give himself a ride.

'Milton Homer's on the swing, Milton Homer's on the swing!' Rose shouted. She had run from the window to the stairwell.

Flo came from wherever she was to look out the side window.

'He won't hurt it,' said Flo surprisingly. Rose had thought she would chase him with the broom. Afterwards she wondered: could Flo have been frightened? Not likely. It would be a matter of Milton Homer's privileges.

'I can't sit on the seat after Milton Homer's sat on it!'

'You! You go on back to bed.'

Rose went back into the dark smelly measles room and began to tell Brian a story she thought he wouldn't like.

'When you were a baby, Milton Homer came and picked you up.'

'He did not.'

'He came and held you and asked what your name was. I remember.'

Brian went out to the stairwell.

'Did Milton Homer come and pick me up and ask what my name was? Did he? When I was a baby?'

'You tell Rose he did the same for her.'

Rose knew that was likely, though she hadn't been going to mention it. She didn't really know if she remembered Milton Homer holding Brian, or had been told about it. Whenever there was a new baby in a house, in that recent past when babies were still being born at home, Milton Homer came as soon as possible and asked to see the baby, then asked its name, and delivered a set speech. The speech was to the effect that if the baby lived, it was to be hoped it would lead a Christian life, and if it died, it was to be hoped it would go straight to Heaven. The same idea as baptism, but Milton did not call on the Father or the Son or do any business with water. He did all this on his own authority. He seemed to be overcome by a stammer he did not have at other times, or else he stammered on purpose in order to give his pronouncements more weight. He opened his mouth wide and rocked back and forth, taking up each phrase with a deep grunt.

'And *if* the Baby—*if* the Baby—*if* the Baby—*lives*—'

Rose would do this years later, in her brother's living room, rocking back and forth, chanting, each *if* coming out like an explosion, leading up to the major explosion of *lives*.

'He will live a—good life—and he will—and he will—and he will —*not* sin. He will lead a *good life*—a *good* life—and he will *not sin*. He will *not sin*!'

'And if the baby—if the baby—if the baby—*dies*—'

'Now that's enough. That's enough, Rose,' said Brian, but he laughed. He could put up with Rose's theatrics when they were about Hanratty.

'How can you remember?' said Brian's wife Phoebe, hoping to stop Rose before she went on too long and roused Brian's impatience. 'Did you see him do it? That often?'

'Oh no,' said Rose, with some surpirse. 'I didn't see him do it. What I saw was Ralph Gillespie *doing* Milton Homer. He was a boy in school. Ralph.'

Milton Homer's other public function, as Rose and Brian remembered it, was to march in parades. There used to be plenty of parades in Hanratty. The Orange Walk, on the Twelfth of July; the High School Cadet Parade, in May; the schoolchildren's Empire Day Parade, the Legion's Church Parade, the Santa Claus Parade, the Lions Club Old-Timers' Parade. One of the most derogatory things that could be said about anyone in Hanratty was that he or she was fond of parading around, but almost every soul in town—in the town proper, not West Hanratty, that goes without saying— would get a chance to march in public in some organized and approved affair. The only thing was that you must never look as if you were enjoying it; you had to give the impression of being called forth out of preferred obscurity, ready to do your duty and gravely preoccupied with whatever notions the parade celebrated.

The Orange Walk was the most splendid of all the parades. King Billy at the head of it rode a horse as near pure white as could be found, and the Black Knights at the rear, the noblest rank of Orangemen—usually thin, and poor, and proud and fanatical old farmers—rode dark horses and wore the ancient father-to-son top hats and swallow-tail coats. The banners were all gorgeous silks and embroideries, blue and gold, orange and white, scenes of Protestant triumph, lilies and open Bibles, mottoes of godliness and honour and flaming bigotry. The ladies came beneath their sunshades, Orangemen's wives and daughters all wearing white for purity. Then the bands, the fifes and drums, and gifted step-dancers performing on a clean hay-wagon as a movable stage.

Also, there came Milton Homer. He could show up anywhere in the parade and he varied his place in it from time to time, stepping out behind King Billy or the Black Knights or the step-dancers or the shy orange-sashed children who carried the banners. Behind the

Black Knights he would pull a dour face, and hold his head as if a top hat was riding on it; behind the ladies he wiggled his hips and diddled an imaginary sunshade. He was a mimic of ferocious gifts and terrible energy. He could take the step-dancers' tidy show and turn it into an idiot's prance, and still keep the beat.

The Orange Walk was his best opportunity, in parades, but he was conspicuous in all of them. Head in the air, arms whipping out, snootily in step, he marched behind the commanding officer of the Legion. On Empire Day he provided himself with a Red Ensign and a Union Jack, and kept them going like whirligigs above his head. In the Santa Claus parade he snatched candy meant for children; he did not do it for a joke.

You would think that somebody in authority in Hanratty would have put an end to this. Milton Homer's contribution to any parade was wholly negative; designed, if Milton Homer could have designed anything, just to make the parade look foolish. Why didn't the organizers and the paraders make an effort to keep him out? They must have decided that was easier said than done. Milton lived with his two old-maid aunts, his parents being dead, and nobody would have liked to ask the two old ladies to keep him home. It must have seemed as if they had enough on their hands already. How could they keep him in, once he had heard the band? They would have to lock him up, tie him down. And nobody wanted to haul him out and drag him away once things began. His protests would have ruined everything. There wasn't any doubt that he would protest. He had a strong, deep voice and he was a strong man, though not very tall. He was about the size of Napoleon. He had kicked through gates and fences when people tried to shut him out of their yards. Once he had smashed a child's wagon on the sidewalk, simply because it was in his way. Letting him participate must have seemed the best choice, under the circumstances.

Not that it was done as the best of bad choices. Nobody looked askance at Milton in a parade; everybody was used to him. Even the Commanding Officer would let himself be mocked, and the Black Knights with their old black grievances took no notice. People just said, 'Oh, there's Milton,' from the sidewalk. There wasn't much laughing at him, though strangers in town, city relatives invited to watch the parade, might point him out and laugh themselves silly, thinking he was there officially and for purposes of comic relief, like the clowns who were actually young businessmen, unsuccessfully turning cartwheels.

'Who is that?' the visitors said, and were answered with nonchalance and a particularly obscure sort of pride.

'That's just Milton Homer. It wouldn't be a parade without Milton Homer.'

'The village idiot,' said Phoebe, trying to comprehend these things, with her inexhaustible unappreciated politeness, and both Rose and Brian said that they had never heard him described that way. They had never thought of Hanratty as a village. A village was a cluster of picturesque houses around a steepled church on a Christmas card. Villagers were the costumed chorus in the high school operetta. If it was necessary to describe Milton Homer to an outsider, people would say that he was 'not all there.' Rose had wondered, even at that time, what was the part that wasn't there? She still wondered. Brains, would be the easiest answer. Milton Homer must surely have had a low IQ. Yes; but so did plenty of people, in Hanratty and out of it, and they did not distinguish themselves as he did. He could read without difficulty, as shown in the case of the quarantine sign; he knew how to count his change, as evidenced in many stories about how people had tried to cheat him. What was missing was a sense of precaution, Rose thought now. Social inhibition, though there was no such name for it at that time. Whatever it is that ordinary people lose when they are drunk, Milton Homer never had, or might have chosen not to have —and this is what interests Rose—at some point early in life. Even his expressions, his everyday looks, were those that drunks wear in theatrical extremity—goggling, leering, drooping looks that seemed boldly calculated, and at the same time helpless, involuntary; is such a thing possible?

The two ladies Milton Homer lived with were his mother's sisters. They were twins; their names were Hattie and Mattie Milton, and they were usually called Miss Hattie and Miss Mattie, perhaps to detract from any silly sound their names might have had otherwise. Milton had been named after his mother's family. That was a common practice, and there was probably no thought of linking together the names of two great poets. That coincidence was never mentioned and was perhaps not noticed. Rose did not notice it until one day in high school when the boy who sat behind her tapped her on the shoulder and showed her what he had written in his English book. He had stroked out the word *Chapman's* in the title of a poem and inked in the word *Milton*, so that the title now read: *On First Looking into Milton Homer*.

Any mention of Milton Homer was a joke, but this changed title was also a joke because it referred, rather weakly, to Milton Homer's more scandalous behaviour. The story was that when he got behind somebody in a line-up at the Post Office or a movie theatre, he would open his coat and present himself, then lunge and commence rubbing. Though of course he wouldn't get that far; the object of his passion would have ducked out of his way. Boys were said to dare each other to get him into position, and stay close ahead of him until the very last moment, then jump aside and reveal him in dire importunity.

It was in honour of this story—whether it was true or not, had happened once, under provocation, or kept happening all the time —that ladies crossed the street when they saw Milton coming, that children were warned to stay clear of him. *Just don't let him monkey around* was what Flo said. He was allowed into houses on those ritual occasions when there was a new baby—with hospital births getting commoner, those occasions diminished—but at other times the doors were locked against him. He would come and knock, and kick the door panels, and go away. But he was let have his way in yards, because he didn't take things, and could do so much damage if offended.

Of course, it was another story altogether when he appeared with one of his aunts. At those times he was hangdog-looking, well-behaved; his powers and his passions, whatever they were, all banked and hidden. He would be eating candy the aunt had bought him, out of a paper bag. He offered it when told to, though nobody but the most greedy person alive would touch what might have been touched by Milton Homer's fingers or blessed by his spittle. The aunts saw that he got his hair cut; they did their best to keep him presentable. They washed and ironed and mended his clothes, sent him out in his raincoat and rubbers, or knitted cap and muffler, as the weather indicated. Did they know how he conducted himself when out of their sight? They must have heard, and if they heard they must have suffered, being people of pride and Methodist morals. It was their grandfather who had started the flax mill in Hanratty and compelled all his employees to spend their

Saturday nights at a Bible Class he himself conducted. The Homers, too, were decent people. Some of the Homers were supposed to be in favour of putting Milton away but the Milton ladies wouldn't do it. Nobody suggested they refused out of tender-heartedness.

'They won't put him in the Asylum, they're too proud.'

Miss Hattie Milton taught at the high school. She had been teaching there longer than all the other teachers combined and was more important than the Principal. She taught English—the alteration in the poem was the more daring and satisfying because it occurred under her nose—and the thing she was famous for was keeping order. She did this without apparent effort, through the force of her large-bosomed, talcumed, spectacled, innocent and powerful presence, and her refusal to see that there was any difference between teen-agers (she did not use the word) and students in Grade Four. She assigned a lot of memory work. One day she wrote a long poem on the board and said that everyone was to copy it out, then learn it off by heart, and the next day recite it. This was when Rose was in her third or fourth year at high school and she did not believe these instructions were to be taken literally. She learned poetry with ease; it seemed reasonable to her to skip the first step. She read the poem and learned it, verse by verse, then said it over a couple of times in her head. While she was doing this Miss Hattie asked her why she wasn't copying.

Rose replied that she knew the poem already, though she was not perfectly sure that this was true.

'Do you really?' said Miss Hattie. 'Stand up and face the back of the room.'

Rose did so, trembling for her boast.

'Now recite the poem to the class.'

Rose's confidence was not mistaken. She recited without a hitch. What did she expect to follow? Astonishment, and complements, and unaccustomed respect?

'Well, you may know the poem,' Miss Hattie said, 'but that is no excuse for not doing what you were told. Sit down and write it in your book. I want you to write every line three times. If you don't get finished you can stay after four.'

Rose did have to stay after four, of course, raging and writing while Miss Hattie got out her crocheting. When Rose took the copy to her desk Miss Hattie said mildly enough but with finality,

'You can't go thinking you are better than other people just because you can learn poems. Who do you think you are?'

This was not the first time in her life Rose had been asked who she thought she was; in fact the question had often struck her like a monotonous gong and she paid no attention to it. But she understood, afterwards, that Miss Hattie was not a sadistic teacher; she had refrained from saying what she now said in front of the class. And she was not vindictive; she was not taking revenge because she had not believed Rose and had been proved wrong. The lesson she was trying to teach here was more important to her than any poem, and one she truly believed Rose needed. It seemed that many other people believed she needed it, too.

The whole class was invited, at the end of the senior year, to a lantern slide show at the Miltons' house. The lantern slides were of China, where Miss Mattie, the stay-at-home twin, had been a missionary in her youth. Miss Mattie was very shy, and she stayed in the background, working the slides, while Miss Hattie commented. The lantern slides showed a yellow country, much as expected. Yellow hills and sky, yellow people, rickshaws, parasols, all dry and papery-looking, fragile, unlikely, with black zig-zags where the paint had cracked, on the temples, the roads and faces. At this very time, the one and only time Rose sat in the Miltons parlour, Mao was in power in China and the Korean War was underway, but Miss Hattie made no concessions to history, any more than she made concessions to the fact that the members of her audience were eighteen and nineteen years old.

'The Chinese are heathens,' Miss Hattie said. 'That is why they have beggars.'

There was a beggar, kneeling in the street, arms outstretched to a rich lady in a rickshaw, who was not paying any attention to him.

'They do eat things we wouldn't touch,' Miss Hattie said. Some Chinese were pictured poking sticks into bowls. 'But they eat a better diet when they become Christians. The first generation of Christians is an inch and a half taller.'

Christians of the first generation were standing in a row with their mouths open, possibly singing. They wore black and white clothes.

After the slides, plates of sandwiches, cookies, tarts were served. All were home-made and very good. A punch of grape juice and ginger-ale was poured into paper cups. Milton sat in a corner in his thick tweed suit, a white shirt and a tie, on which punch and crumbs had already been spilled.

'Some day it will just blow up in their faces,' Flo had said darkly, meaning Milton. Could that be the reason people came, year after year, to see the lantern slides and drink the punch that all the jokes were about? To see Milton with his jowls and stomach swollen as if with bad intentions, ready to blow? All he did was stuff himself at an unbelievable rate. It seemed as if he downed date squares, hermits, Nanaimo bars and fruit drops, butter tarts and brownies, whole, the way a snake will swallow frogs. Milton was similarly distended.

Methodists were people whose power in Hanratty was passing, but slowly. The days of the compulsory Bible Class were over. Perhaps the Miltons didn't know that. Perhaps they knew it but put a heroic face on their decline. They behaved as if the requirements of piety hadn't changed and as if its connection with prosperity was unaltered. Their brick house, with its overstuffed comfort, their coats with collars of snug dull fur, seemed proclaimed as a Methodist house, Methodist clothing, inelegant on purpose, heavy, satisfactory. Everything about them seemed to say that they had applied themselves to the world's work for God's sake, and God had not let them down. For God's sake the hall floor shone with wax around the runner, the lines were drawn perfectly with a straight pen in the account book, the begonias flourished, the money went into the bank.

But mistakes were made, nowadays. The mistake the Milton ladies made was in drawing up a petition to be sent to the Canadian Broadcasting Corporation, asking for the removal from the air of the programmes that interfered with church-going on Sunday nights: Edgar Bergen and Charlie McCarthy; Jack Benny; Fred Allen. They got the minister to speak about their petition in church—this was in the United Church, where Methodists had been outnumbered by Presbyterians and Congregationalists, and it was not a scene Rose witnessed, but had described to her by Flo— and afterwards they waited, Miss Hattie and Miss Mattie, one on each side of the outgoing stream, intending to deflect people and make them sign the petition, which was set up on a little table in the church vestibule. Behind the table Milton Homer was sitting.

He had to be there; they never let him get out of going to church on Sunday. They had given him a job to keep him busy; he was to be in charge of the fountain pens, making sure they were full and handing them to signers.

That was the obvious part of the mistake. Milton had got the idea of drawing whiskers on himself, and had done so, without the help of a mirror. Whiskers curled out over his big sad cheeks, up towards his bloodshot foreboding eyes. He had put the pen in his mouth, too, so that ink had blotched his lips. In short, he had made himself so comical a sight that the petition which nobody really wanted could be treated as a comedy, too, and the power of the Milton sisters, the flax-mill Methodists, could be seen as a leftover dribble. People smiled and slid past; nothing could be done. Of course the Milton ladies didn't scold Milton or put on any show for the public, they just bundled him up with their petition and took him home.

'That was the end of them thinking they could run things,' Flo said. It was hard to tell, as always, what particular defeat—was it that of religion or pretension?—she was so glad to see.

The boy who showed Rose the poem in Miss Hattie's own English class in Hanratty high school was Ralph Gillespie, the same boy who specialized in Milton Homer imitations. As Rose remembered it, he hadn't started on the imitations at the time he showed her the poem. They came later, during the last few months he was in school. In most classes he sat ahead of Rose or behind her, due to the alphabetical closeness of their names. Beyond this alphabetical closeness they did have something like a family similarity, not in looks but in habits or tendencies. Instead of embarrassing them, as it would have done if they had really been brother and sister, this drew them together in helpful conspiracy. Both of them lost or mislaid, or never adequately provided themselves with, all the pencils, rulers, erasers, pen-nibs, ruled paper, graph paper, the compass, dividers, protractor, necessary for a successful school life; both of them were sloppy with ink, subject to spilling and blotting mishaps; both of them were negligent about doing homework but panicky about not having done it. So they did their best to help each other out, sharing whatever supplies they had, begging from their more provident neighbours, finding someone's homework to copy. They developed the comradeship of captives, of soldiers who have no heart for the campaign, wishing only to survive and avoid action.

That wasn't quite all. Their shoes and boots became well acquainted, scuffling and pushing in friendly and private encounter, sometimes resting together a moment in tentative encouragement; this mutual kindness particularly helped them through those moments when people were being selected to do mathematics problems on the blackboard.

Once Ralph came in after noon hour with his hair full of snow. He leaned back and shook the snow over Rose's desk, saying, 'Do you have those dandruff blues?'

'No. Mine's white.'

This seemed to Rose a moment of some intimacy, with its physical frankness, its remembered childhood joke. Another day at noon hour, before the bell rang, she came into the classroom and found him, in a ring of onlookers, doing his Milton Homer imitation. She was surprised and worried; surprised because his shyness in class had always equalled hers and had been one of the things that united them; worried that he might not be able to bring it off, might not make them laugh. But he was very good; his large, pale, good-natured face took on the lumpy desperation of Milton's; his eyes goggled and his jowls shook and his words came out in a hoarse hypnotized singsong. He was so successful that Rose was amazed, and so was everybody else. From that time on Ralph began to do imitations; he had several, but Milton Homer was his trademark. Rose never quite got over a comradely sort of apprehension on his behalf. She had another feeling as well, not envy but a shaky sort of longing. She wanted to do the same. Not Milton Homer; she did not want to do Milton Homer. She wanted to fill up in that magical, releasing way, transform herself; she wanted the courage and the power.

Not long after he started publicly developing these talents he had, Ralph Gillespie dropped out of school. Rose missed his feet and his breathing and his finger tapping her shoulder. She met him sometimes on the street but he did not seem to be quite the same person. They never stopped to talk, just said hello and hurried past. They had been close and conspiring for years, it seemed, maintaining their spurious domesticity, but they had never talked outside of school, never gone beyond the most formal recognition of each other, and it seemed they could not, now. Rose never asked him why he had dropped out; she did not even know if he had found a job. They knew each other's necks and shoulders, heads and feet, but were not able to confront each other as full-length presences.

After a while Rose didn't see him on the street any more. She heard that he had joined the Navy. He must have been just waiting till he was old enough to do that. He had joined the Navy and gone to Halifax. The war was over, it was only the peacetime Navy. Just the same it was odd to think of Ralph Gillespie, in uniform, on the deck of a destroyer, maybe firing off guns. Rose was just beginning to understand that the boys she knew, however incompetent they might seem, were going to turn into men, and be allowed to do things that you would think required a lot more talent and authority than they could have.

There was a time, after she gave up the store and before her arthritis became too crippling, during which Flo went out to Bingo games and sometimes played cards with her neighbours at the Legion Hall. When Rose was home on a visit conversation was difficult, so she would ask Flo about the people she saw at the Legion. She would ask for news of her own contemporaries. Horse Nicholson, Runt Chesterton, whom she could not really imagine as grown men; did Flo ever see them?

'There's one I see and he's around there all the time. Ralph Gillespie.'

Rose said that she had thought Ralph Gillespie was in the Navy.

'He was too but he's back home now. He was in an accident.'

What kind of accident?'

'I don't know. It was in the Navy. He was in a Navy hospital three solid years. They had to rebuild him from scratch. He's all right now except he walks with a limp, he sort of drags the one leg.'

'That's too bad.'

'Well, yes. That's what I say. I don't hold any grudge against him but there's some up there at the Legion that do.'

'Hold a grudge?'

'Because of the pension,' said Flo, surprised and rather contemptuous of Rose for not taking into account so basic a fact of life, and so natural an attitude, in Hanratty. 'They think, well, he's set for life. I say he must've suffered for it. Some people say he gets a lot but I don't believe it. He doesn't need much, he's all on his own. One thing, if he suffers pain he don't let on. Like me. I don't let on. Weep and you weep alone. He's a good darts player. He'll play anything that's going. And he can imitate people to the life.'

'Does he still do Milton Homer? He used to do Milton Homer at school.'

'He does him. Milton Homer. He's comical at that. He does some others too.'

'Is Milton Homer still alive? Is he still marching in parades?'

'Sure he's still alive. He's quietened down a lot, though. He's out there at the County Home and you can see him on a sunny day down by the highway keeping an eye on the traffic and licking up an ice cream cone. Both the old ladies is dead.'

'So he isn't in the parades any more?'

'There isn't the parades to be in. Parades have fallen off a lot. All the Orangemen are dying out and you wouldn't get the turnout, anyway, people'd rather stay home and watch their TV.'

On later visits Rose found that Flo had turned against the Legion.

'I don't want to be one of those old crackpots.' she said.

'What old crackpots?'

'Sit around up there telling the same stupid yarns and drinking beer. They make me sick.'

This was very much in Flo's usual pattern. People, places, amusements, went abruptly in and out of favour. The turnabouts had become more drastic and frequent with age.

'Don't you like any of them any more? Is Ralph Gillespie still going there?'

'He still is. He likes it so well he tried to get himself a job there. He tried to get the part-time bar job. Some people say he got turned down because he already has got the pension but I think it was because of the way he carries on.'

'How? Does he get drunk?'

'You couldn't tell if he was, he carries on just the same, imitating, and half the time he's imitating somebody that the newer people that's come to town, they don't know even who the person was, they just think it's Ralph being idiotic.'

'Like Milton Homer?'

'That's right. How do they know it's supposed to be Milton

Homer and what was Milton Homer like? They don't know. Ralph don't know when to stop. He Milton Homer'd himself right out of a job.'

After Rose had taken Flo to the County Home—she had not seen Milton Homer there, though she had seen other people she had long believed dead—and was staying to clean up the house and get it ready for sale, she herself was taken to the Legion by Flo's neighbours, who thought she must be lonely on a Saturday night. She did not know how to refuse, so she found herself sitting at a long table in the basement of the hall, where the bar was, just at the time the last sunlight was coming across the fields of beans and corn, across the gravel parking lot and through the high windows, staining the plywood walls. All around the walls were photographs, with names lettered by hand and taped to the frames. Rose got up to have a look at them. The Hundred and Sixth, just before embarkation, 1915. Various heroes of that war, whose names were carried on by sons and nephews, but whose existence had not been known to her before. When she came back to the table a card game had started. She wondered if it had been a disruptive thing to do, getting up to look at the pictures. Probably nobody ever looked at them; they were not for looking at; they were just there, like the plywood on the walls. Visitors, outsiders, are always looking at things, always taking an interest, asking who was this, when was that, trying to liven up the conversation. They put too much in; they want too much out. Also, it could have looked as if she was parading around the room, asking for attention.

A woman sat down and introduced herself. She was the wife of one of the men playing cards. 'I've seen you on television,' she said. Rose was always a bit apologetic when somebody said this; that is, she had to control what she recognized in herself as an absurd impulse to apologize. Here in Hanratty the impulse was stronger than usual. She was aware of having done things that must seem high-handed. She remembered her days as a television interviewer, her beguiling confidence and charm; here as nowhere else they must understand how that was a sham. Her acting was another matter. The things she was ashamed of were not what they must think she was ashamed of; not a flopping bare breast, but a failure she couldn't seize upon or explain.

This woman who was talking to her did not belong to Hanratty.

She said she had come from Sarnia when she was married, fifteen years ago.

'I still find it hard to get used to. Frankly I do. After the city. You look better in person than you do in that series.'

'I should hope so,' said Rose, and told about how they made her up. People were interested in things like that and Rose was more comfortable, once the conversation got on to technical details.

'Well, here's old Ralph,' the woman said. She moved over, making room for a thin, grey-haired man holding a mug of beer. This was Ralph Gillespie. If Rose had met him on the street she would not have recognized him, he would have been a stranger to her, but after she had looked at him for a moment he seemed quite unchanged to her, unchanged from himself at seventeen or fifteen, his grey hair which had been light brown still falling over his forehead, his face still pale and calm and rather large for his body, the same diffident, watchful, withholding look. But his body was thinner and his shoulders seemed to have shrunk together. He wore a short-sleeved sweater with a little collar and three ornamental buttons; it was light-blue with beige and yellow stripes. This sweater seemed to Rose to speak of aging jauntiness, a kind of petrified adolescence. She noticed that his arms were old and skinny and that his hands shook so badly that he used both of them to raise the glass of beer to his mouth.

'You're not staying around here long, are you?' said the woman who had come from Sarnia.

Rose said that she was going to Toronto tomorrow, Sunday, night.

'You must have a busy life,' the woman said, with a large sigh, an honest envy that in itself would have declared out-of-town origins.

Rose was thinking that on Monday at noon she was to meet a man for lunch and to go to bed. This man was Tom Shepherd, whom she had known for a long time. At one time he had been in love with her, he had written love letters to her. The last time she had been with him, in Toronto, when they were sitting up in bed afterwards drinking gin and tonic—they always drank a good deal when they were together—Rose suddenly thought, or knew, that there was somebody now, some woman he was in love with and was courting from a distance, probably writing letters to, and that there must have been another woman he was robustly bedding, at the time he was writing letters to her. Also, and all the time, there was his wife. Rose wanted to ask him about this; the necessity, the difficulties, the satisfactions. Her interest was friendly and uncritical but she knew, she had just enough sense to know, that the question would not do.

The conversation in the Legion had turned on lottery tickets, Bingo games, winnings. The men playing cards—Flo's neighbour among them—were talking about a man who was supposed to have won ten thousand dollars, and never publicized the fact, because he had gone bankrupt a few years before and owed so many people money.

One of them said that if he had declared himself bankrupt, he didn't owe the money any more.

'Maybe he didn't owe it then,' another said. 'But he owes it now. The reason is, he's got it now.'

This opinion was generally favoured.

Rose and Ralph Gillespie looked at each other. There was the same silent joke, the same conspiracy, comfort; the same, the same.

'I hear you're quite a mimic,' Rose said.

That was wrong; she shouldn't have said anything. He laughed and shook his head.

'Oh, come on. I hear you do a sensational Milton Homer.'

'I don't know about that.'

'Is he still around?'

'Far as I know he's out at the County Home.'

'Remember Miss Hattie and Miss Mattie? They had the lantern slide show at their house.'

'Sure.'

'My mental picture of China is still pretty well based on those slides.'

Rose went on talking like this, though she wished she could stop. She was talking in what elsewhere might have been considered an amusing, confidential, recognizably and meaninglessly flirtatious style. She did not get much response from Ralph Gillespie, though he seemed attentive, even welcoming. All the time she talked, she was wondering what he wanted her to say. He did want something. But he would not make any move to get it. Her first impression of him, as boyishly shy and ingratiating, had to change. That was his surface. Underneath he was self-sufficient, resigned to living in bafflement, perhaps proud. She wished that he would speak to her from that level, and she thought he wished it, too, but they were prevented.

But when Rose remembered this unsatisfactory conversation she seemed to recall a wave of kindness, of sympathy and forgiveness, though certainly no words of that kind had been spoken. That peculiar shame which she carried around with her seemed to have been eased. The thing she was ashamed of, in acting, was that she might have been paying attention to the wrong things, reporting antics, when there was always something further, a tone, a depth, a light, that she couldn't get and wouldn't get. And it wasn't just about acting she suspected this. Everything she had done could sometimes be seen as a mistake. She had never felt this more strongly than when she was talking to Ralph Gillespie, but when she thought about him afterwards her mistakes appeared unimportant. She was enough a child of her time to wonder if what she felt about him was simply sexual warmth, sexual curiosity; she did not think it was. There seemed to be feelings which could only be spoken of in translation; perhaps they could only be acted on in translation; not speaking of them and not acting on them is the right course to take because translation is dubious. Dangerous, as well.

For those reasons Rose did not explain anything further about Ralph Gillespie to Brian and Phoebe when she recalled Milton Homer's ceremony with babies or his expression of diabolical happiness on the swing. She did not even mention that he was dead. She knew he was dead because she still had a subscription to the Hanratty paper. Flo had given Rose a seven-year subscription on the last Christmas when she felt obliged to give Christmas presents; characteristically, Flo said that the paper was just for people to get their names in and hadn't anything in it worth reading. Usually Rose turned the pages quickly and put the paper in the firebox. But she did see the story about Ralph which was on the front page.

### FORMER NAVY MAN DIES

Mr Ralph Gillespie, Naval Petty Officer, retired, sustained fatal head injuries at the Legion Hall on Saturday night last. No other person was implicated in the fall and unfortunately several hours passed before Mr Gillespie's body was discovered. It is thought that he mistook the basement door for the exit door and lost his balance, which was precarious due to an

old injury suffered in his naval career which left him partly
disabled.

The paper went on to give the names of Ralph's parents, who
were apparently still alive, and of his married sister. The Legion
was taking charge of the funeral services.

Rose didn't tell this to anybody, glad that there was one thing at
least she wouldn't spoil by telling, though she knew it was lack of
material as much as honourable restraint that kept her quiet. What
could she say about herself and Ralph Gillespie, except that she felt
his life, close, closer than the lives of men she'd loved, one slot over
from her own?

# Beth Harvor

BETH Harvor was born in Saint John, New Brunswick, in 1936, of Danish immigrant parents. She grew up in Summerville, a small town in New Brunswick's Kennebecasis River valley, and after high school became a student nurse in Saint John. Like Anna in many of her short stories, however, she quit nursing in her final year without graduating. In 1957 she married, and has since lived in Montreal, Copenhagen, and Ottawa, where she still lives with one of her two sons.

Harvor's stories have appeared in the *New Yorker*, *Saturday Night*, and the *Hudson Review*, and have been included in such anthologies as *Best American Stories of 1971* and three of the Oberon annuals (1972, 1973, and 1977). Her first collection of short stories, *Women and Children* (1973) will soon be followed by two books now nearing completion: *Foreigners* and *A Year at Court*. Reviewing *Women and Children* in the *Canadian Forum*, Phyllis Bruce remarked that 'Harvor's women want more than to love and to be loved, they want to reconcile life's contradictions and injustices. Because they usually fail, the endings of the stories are often disquieting, at times oppressive.' The ending of 'Foreigners' is certainly disquieting, as Anna settles into a relationship with Karl that seems destined to be disastrous.

# FOREIGNERS

THE NIGHT staff in the Operating Room would set up strange banquets in the night—rows of scissors, blades, clamps—sterile surgical cutlery laid out on dull green tablecloths. And when they had finished setting up every table, every room, they would make themselves coffee, using the Pyrex pot in the supervisors' kitchen. If they wanted a glass of milk as well, or a glass of orange juice, they could walk down the hall to Blood Bank. There was always a quart of milk and a bottle of orange juice in the refrigerator there, in with the bottles of blood. But usually they didn't. Coffee was the drink of hospitals and night. They would carry it into the stretcher room and sit on old office swivel chairs, their feet up on the stretchers, and drink cup after cup of it, black. Then the sun would rise and they would hear the kitchen help calling out to each other, far below them in the hospital courtyard, in Estonian and Italian and Portuguese.

At the end of her night duty in the Operating Room, Anna had two days off and so she decided to go home. But in the residence there was a message for her: she was to go over to Male Surgery to see Miss Killeen. She packed her nightgown and jeans in a suitcase and got into a skirt and blouse. I can't have done anything wrong, she thought. And besides, Killeen was her friend. (The year before, when Killeen had still been a student, she'd been the senior on a night duty they'd shared on Male Surgery, and from working with her then Anna liked her a lot.) But of course it wasn't true she hadn't done wrong. She had. They both had. The only two nurses for forty patients, they had faked graphs on temperature charts, skipped dressings, left comatose patients unwashed.

Anna took the elevator up to the fifth floor. When the doors parted she saw Killeen, over at the medicine cupboard, pouring pills into paper cups. In spite of her fondness for Killeen, in spite of the soft summer morning, she felt a surge of terror. Killeen turned around. 'Oh, Annie,' she said, 'did I scare you, calling you over like this? I'm sorry, but they said you were coming off nights and I wanted to catch you before you took off. I've got a little problem here and I wondered if you could help me out.'

'What is it?'

'They brought in this sailor a couple of nights ago,' Killeen said. 'Off a boat docked in the harbour. A Danish boat. He doesn't speak any English. We know what's wrong with him because we've been in contact with the doctor out there. But this morning I suddenly remembered, you come from a Danish family. I wondered if you'd go and talk to him a little.'

'I don't speak much Danish,' Anna said. Really, she didn't know much more than a few songs and jingles and silly things. Her parents had assimilated completely and spoke perfect English. The Danish language was only something her family made jokes about— they said it was not a language at all but a disease of the throat; they said it sounded like the baaing of sick sheep.

'Don't worry,' said Killeen. 'All we need is to have you say a few words to him in his native tongue, to cheer him up. And if you could find out if he has any problems or complaints.'

Anna walked down the hall and into the sailor's room. There were three men in there who were sitting cranked up in their beds, eating their breakfasts in the bright morning light.

'The Danish man?'

'Behind the curtain, Miss.'

She parted the curtains and let herself in. He was about thirty-five, dark and taciturn-looking. She wished him good morning in Danish. The dark face broke into a slight but hopeful smile. You speak Danish, he said to her in Danish. In Danish she answered no. Yes you do, he said. He thought it was some kind of game. So she decided to show him what she knew, to make joke of it, to show him that all she could do was count to ten, wish him a merry Christmas, ask him how he felt (but not understand too elaborate an answer), and thank him a thousand times for the lovely evening. She hoped he would laugh but he did not. Then she remembered that the way to say 'good luck' in Danish was *til lykke*, but after this she didn't dare to say it to him, she just put her hand on his shoulder as a way of saying good-bye. But it wasn't to be so simple as that. He grabbed her hand and brought it down between his blanketed thighs so that through the blankets she could feel what he wanted her to feel; he held her so hard by the wrist that it hurt. She just stood there, like someone doing penance. She didn't look at him so she didn't know if he was looking at her. And after a while he let her go. She walked out into the hall.

Killeen was at her desk. 'Were you able to communicate with each other?'

'I think he's lonely,' Anna said. She could feel herself blushing.

'Oh well, there's nothing much wrong with him anyway. We'll have him back on his boat in a couple of days.'

'I don't really speak Danish at all,' Anna said. 'We never spoke it at home.'

'Well, it seems you did okay, at least you were able to understand he was lonely,' Killeen said. 'So thanks a million for coming over.'

The person Anna sat next to on the New Sharon bus was a woman in her sixties. Her hands were covered with liver spots and freckles and three of her fingers were fitted out with diamond rings. She had a smoker's cough and an American accent. It turned out she was a nurse too and had been born and raised in Canada, not far from the countryside they were at that moment travelling through. She had trained in Halifax. In 1933 she had moved to the States, had married there, and had ended up in Florida, where she was now, in 1957, the owner of a nursing home. She said she was very successful. She said she wasn't telling this to boast but only to show how it pays to stick to your training. Then she turned to Anna and took her by the sleeve as if she could read her mind. 'Oh honey!' she cried. 'I can see that you have doubts!'

'Yes,' Anna said. 'I'm thinking of giving it up.'

'Oh, no,' the old nurse said. 'Oh, don't do that. Don't ever do that. Remember, it's always something to fall back on.'

The strange thing was, a year ago Anna had been even closer to leaving than she was now. She had sat in her parents' car and cried and said that she wanted to give the whole thing up. They had persuaded her to stay until her third year. Then you will have tried everything, they said. You will have been to the Case Room and the Operating Room and Emergency. If you still want to leave then, after you've tried everything, then we won't argue with you.

When Anna got out of the bus at New Sharon, her hoarse and freckled Florida friend touched her arm again and said, 'Now you remember what I told you, honey,' and she told her she would. She made a good connection with the bus to Athens, and had plenty of time to think about her life on the long trip there. She thought of the first death she'd seen, the first birth, the first post-mortem. The first post-mortem had been easy, coming over a year after the first death. Six student nurses walked over to the morgue together and on the way there they met three interns. It was a hot afternoon, and there was the smell of tar in the ocean air. The morgue sat behind the hospital and looked like a garage; it was made of concrete blocks, painted white, and it had a big, garage-like door. The moment they got inside they saw the body, lying on a marble-topped table. It was a woman, past middle-age, with a look of authority about her. Anna imagined that she had once been head of something—the purse section of a department store, say, or maybe a business office. Maybe she had even been a nurse. She was glad she wasn't young.

One of the interns stretched. 'Cooler in here, anyway,' he said, and then the door opened and the chief pathologist came in. He was a Scotsman and small and quick, in a very clean white coat. 'Good day,' he said, and he picked up a scalpel and made a long vertical incision. Anna took a deep breath and made herself recall the definition of anatomy that they'd been given at the beginning of Anatomy and Physiology:

> Anatomy is the science which deals with the structure of the bodies of men and animals. It is studied by the dissection of the bodies of those who die in hospitals and other institutions, unclaimed by relatives.

This woman had no one who cared for her, then.

'Ladies and gentlemen,' said the chief pathologist. 'Look at the lady's lungs.' They all looked. They were very flecked with black. 'A lifetime resident of this city,' the pathologist said, and they all laughed. Then he started asking people to show him things. The Falciform ligament. The seventh costal cartilege. The interns did all the showing; they were good at it. And after a while the pathologist forgot about the nurses and addressed his remarks to the interns entirely. He pointed out a small globe of flesh deep within the abdominal cavity. 'Who knows what this is?' he asked them. And he allowed his eyes to shine. He was sure, this time, he had them stumped. And in fact they seemed to be. But Anna was not. At the time they had studied it she had been infatuated with one of the orderlies on Male Surgery, a dark solid boy named Douglas MacKinnon.

'The Pouch of Douglas?' she said.

The pathologist gave her a quick, sharp look.

'Dead right,' he said.

As for the first birth, when she saw her first birth she had a sense that she'd never had before of the fierce beauty of life, of the logic of the mystery, a sense of the connection between tension and bringing forth, and at the same time the feeling of being in *good hands*; every death she saw after the first birth was easier to take, except for the deaths of a few children. But then she'd hated the children's ward anyway; it had almost done her in. The sunniest place in the whole hospital, walled with glass, everything else about it was desperate: the noise, the smell, the overcrowding—it was as noisy and smelly as a zoo set up in a greenhouse but without the blessing of green plants. But the crazy thing was, the odd silent wards were no better. Here a great many small children were in a state of shock from having been separated from their parents and sat, hardly moving, in pyjamas sporting pink lambs or pink poodles, their eyes as un-seeing as black pools. And in the chronic wards there was a deceptive lightness—here the children smiled and joked and knew all the routines and all the nurses' names; but they were the worst of all—it was as if the bewitched monstrous children of German fables had been given medical verity. Here was what you found in the chronic ward: children whose legs had grown to different lengths; children who had got puffed up into strangers overnight—their eyes turned into slits by the held-in fluid; children with enormous circus heads; there were medical names for all of it. Anna got sick on the children's ward— diarrhea, bronchitis, high child-style fevers—even though normally, like the others, she was immune to everything. The thing was, courage in very young children was a frightening thing—so pure, so absolute, so detached from the very experience that could give it meaning; she knew they would give up life as easily and naturally as they would take their medicine.

And the children's ward wasn't all; there had been other places, places where the students hadn't just been overworked, they'd been humiliated too—some of the older supervisors, especially, had taken pleasure in humiliating them. On certain night duties, where the supervisors coming on duty in the mornings had made them stay late doing things they said they'd left undone or threatened to take their free time away from them until it seemed to them that these supervisors held not only their freedom and self-respect, but even their whole lives in their hands, Anna had given up eating almost entirely, preferring to sleep instead. The new wing of the nurses' residence was under construction then, and every morning before she went off duty she'd fill up her pockets with sleeping pills, to blot out the sound of the drills. She felt she couldn't open her window either. Her best friend, Joan Cosman, would come up to her room around suppertime and let up the blind and open the window to show a part of the hospital wall going pinkly light from the last of the sun. Or was it the sunrise? Rising out of a drugged sleep, it was scary not to know which. 'What time is it?' Anna would say, and she'd scrabble around on her dressing table, looking for her watch. 'Six o'clock,' Joan would say. But the words 'six o'clock' wouldn't have any meaning to Anna; until she could remember where she was working, where she was supposed to be, she couldn't figure them out.

Joan would sit heavily down on the bed, smelling of the day's smells. She was working in the Case Room then; there was the sweet-sick blend of ether, Dettol, coffee. She'd take the food she'd brought Anna out of a paper bag: peanut butter sandwiches that she'd made up herself in the nurses' kitchen; bananas and cookies left over from supper in the cafeteria.

Eat, she would say.

I'm not hungry.

You've got to eat.

Maybe they'll notice how thin I'm getting and give me time off to rest up, Anna said to Joan on one of these evenings.

Do you think they give a good goddamn?

They make us weigh ourselves every month, don't they?

You're a dreamer. Eat.

During the time Anna was in training in Hocksville her cousin Kamille was living with her family in Athens, helping out with the housework. Anna's parents had invited Kamille out from Denmark to live with them for as long as she wanted to, but after she had been in Canada for a year she planned to leave for the States. She was twenty-two and came from Anna's mother's side of the family. She always dressed in black. Black pants, black T-shirts, black aprons, black umbrella. 'Elegant,' people said. 'You can certainly tell she doesn't come from around *here*.' Kamille was the most practical person her Canadian relatives had ever seen—she had sewn all her own black clothes with the exception of the umbrella, she could make men's jackets and coats, she could even upholster chairs and sofas.

When Anna got out of the bus on Victoria Street and started walking up the hill toward her house, she could see Kamille in the distance, up on the front steps in her black clothes, shelling or peeling something. Kamille looked classic, forebodingly right, against the great white backdrop of Anna's parents' Greek Revival house. Anna's parents bought the Athens place after she started her training. When they got it it was a hovel, but a hovel with grandeur—all partitioned and warped and cracked inside, but with a good foundation and a beautifully proportioned shell. They spent several thousand dollars fixing it up. They asked Anna if it would be okay if they took the two thousand dollars they'd kept in a fund for her education and used it for renovations for the house, and she said it would be fine. She liked denial; she believed her capacity for it made her a better person than Arnie and Chess, her brother and sister. It was why she had chosen to be a nurse. Hard work, doing good. She approached the point where the driveway split, sweeping up on either side of a great heart of green grass.

'Hello, Annie!' called Kamille. 'We are having a party tonight! Chess has gone off to the liquor store. She has with her two missionaries.'

Anna sat down on the steps beside Kamille. 'Are there still missionaries in these parts?' she asked her.

'These boys are Mormons,' Kamille said. 'They come from America.' Her voice sounded very tender when she said America.

'You should call it the States, Kamille.'

'The States,' Kamille said, tender again. 'Utah. Wyoming.'

'Wyoming,' Anna said. 'I read a book about Wyoming when I was little. *My Friend Flicka*. About a horse.' And she told herself to be sure to remember to ask the Wyoming Mormon if he knew Cheyenne.

Then Chess came back with the boys and the liquor. She brought the two of them over to the front of the house to introduce them to Anna. Anna hoped Chess would not introduce her as her "little sister" as she sometimes did. The terrible part about this was that whenever Chess did it people always believed her. But she didn't. She just told her their names: Elder Rodale, Elder Cayton.

'Sometimes also known by the names Al and Gary,' Chess said. 'I'm trying to talk them into staying for the party tonight. I've even promised them apple juice instead of punch in their paper cups. And they have to promise not to try to convert people.' She smiled. They both smiled back at her, although the one called Al looked a little uneasy. But Gary gave Chess a serious tender look. 'We know how to behave,' he said. 'Help me take this stuff inside,' she said to him then, and they went into the house together. Al stood on the porch a moment, looking unhappy, then he went inside too.

'God, that Gary guy really seems to like Chess,' Anna said.

'I guess so,' said Kamille. 'The trouble is, Chess has invited an older man to this party. Someone she really likes. A Norwegian. She met him somewhere at someone's house. He's twenty-seven.'

'What's his name?'

'Karl something.'

'Oh him,' Anna said, in the despairing voice people will use about someone they covet. 'I thought that's who it would be.' And she told Kamille everything she knew about this Karl. How he had come to Canada after the war and learned English in no time at all. How he had done so brilliantly in high school and on the junior matriculation exams that the *Hocksville Herald* had written a special editorial about him. How his father was a veterinarian and had once saved the life of their late dog Ted. How the first time Ted was almost dying, she and her mother had driven him all the way to the vet's place and how, while they were there, they saw this Karl (a college boy by now) and how, going back home in the car, she'd said to her mother, 'That's the man I'm going to marry.'

'Chess is very nervous,' said Kamille.

At supper that night Chess flirted with Gary. Al continued to look unhappy. Anna asked him if he was the one who came from Wyoming. He said he was. She asked him if he'd read *My Friend Flicka*, and he said he had. She told him she'd read it when she was young, that she'd thought it was a very beautiful book. Al asked her if she'd read *The Book of Mormon*. She said no. '*The Book of Mormon* is a very beautiful book too,' he said. 'It's an even more beautiful book than *My Friend Flicka*.' Everyone smiled. Except Kamille. She was banging lids on counters and slapping plates on the table. She said to the Mormons, 'These girls! They are not very domestic!' This was true, but it hadn't always been that way. At fourteen, fifteen, sixteen, Anna had worked as a cook in her mother's music camp, cooking meals for the campers. She'd made pails of puddings and basins of macaroni salad, and jugs of custard sauce to pour over Lemon Snow. In her spare time she read *Fanny Farmer's Boston Cooking School Cook Book*. On Sundays she made Maryland Chicken and in the middle of the week she made something the mother of one of the campers had taught her to do: ham and pineapple slices fried together, then simmered in Coca-Cola. But then she went into training in Hocksville and learned what real work was. Real work wasn't anything like cooking for thirty children, real work was running from seven in the morning till seven at night; real work was something that made you too tired to read, or eat. They usually did have some time off in the middle of the day though, but only if they weren't too far behind in their work, and even then it was tied in with a lunch hour or a class they had to go to. These classes were given by the doctors in a classroom in the basement of the nurses' residence. One of these doctors, in a class on obstetrics and gynecology, had distinguished himself by defining menstruation as 'the weeping of the disappointed uterus.' They had a lot of fun with that afterward. They would go around saying to each other, 'Is your uterus disappointed? Has it wept yet?' Or: 'Well, my *uterus* may be disappointed, but *I* sure as hell am not.'

While they were clearing the table Chess was describing Anna to Gary. 'Anna is a sweet person,' she said. 'A gentle person. Always kind to everyone.' There was something about this that made Anna uneasy but she wasn't sure what it was. After they'd done up the dishes she went into Chess's room. 'What are you wearing tonight?' she asked her. Chess took out her red dress and laid it down on her bed.

'Can I wear the green one, then?'

Chess took out the green dress and laid it down on the bed beside the red one. Anna loved the green dress; it was almost exactly the colour of the gowns they used in the OR, but a little softer, embossed with little flowers that were also green but slightly lighter, almost silver. She held it up to herself in front of the mirror. It was a colour that went well with tanned skin.

'On second thought,' said Chess, lifting the dress away from Anna, 'I think I'll wear this one myself.'

'What'll I wear then? I can't wear the red.'

'Borrow something from Mother.'

Anna went into their mother's dressing room. Everything in there was in zippered bags. Rich formal things—for winter and for her mother's piano recitals. She took out a black cocktail dress and put it on. She thought: black goes well with tanned skin. She looked in one of the shoe bags and found a pair of golden sandals. She put them on and went over to the dressing table in them. She unstoppered the perfumes and sniffed them. She put Tigress on her wrists and Fleures de Rocailles between her breasts. She felt uneasy with her mother, but not with her mother's clothes. Her mother never minded lending things; she had more clothes than anyone; not just clothes for concert tours but young clothes—plaid dresses, square dance skirts. Sometimes she would give Chess and Anna clothes too, things she'd simply got tired of wearing. There was a certain innocence about her mother—she was in so many ways innocent of the dull and thankless responsibilities of parenthood; when they were little children and she embraced them her embraces were almost never to pat or celebrate *them*, her children, they were rather entreaties to her children to endorse some fine quality in herself. She used to hug them and say, 'Do you know how lucky you are to have a mother who doesn't smell? I never smell, do you realize that? I always smell sweet.' They would wriggle away from her as soon as seemed decent. Or at least Anna would. She was self-centred herself.

Downstairs, the doorbell rang and Anna ran down to answer it. A lot of people she didn't know were standing there, a shy group, wondering who she was.

'Come in!' she said. 'I'll call Chess.'

Chess came down the stairs then and Kamille and the Mormons came down behind her.

The next time the doorbell rang Anna and Chess both ran to get it. And when they opened the door there were two men there— Karl and someone else. 'I knew right away,' Chess told Anna later. 'Right there at the door I knew he was falling in love with you. He had such a dumb, enthralled look.'

The next morning when Chess and Anna were in their bedroom, combing their hair before breakfast, Chess said to Anna: 'Do you know what Gary said last night, about you?'

'You mean Gary the Mormon?'

'You don't have to keep calling him Gary the Mormon like that.'

'I'm sorry. What did he say?'

'He said, "Do you still think Anna is a sweet person and a gentle person and kind to everyone now?"'

Everyone was at the table when Chess and Anna came out to the kitchen. All the people who'd stayed the night—Karl, Gary and Al, two old friends of the family named Dorie and Kay. Karl fetched a chair for Anna and fitted it in beside his own. A picnic was being planned. They were all supposed to go to White Church River Cove in Dorie's car. Kamille had already made the sandwiches.

But then Gary and Al said they'd have to stay in town, calling on people. And Kay said she had a headache. This was the excuse Anna had planned to use and for a moment she felt confused. Then she said, 'That's funny, I have a headache too,' and everyone laughed. Karl leaned over and whispered, 'But you're coming anyway, aren't you?' and she shook her head no. A few minutes later her mother excused herself from the table and a short time after that she called down to Anna from her room, telling her to come upstairs.

When Anna got up there her mother was in the little bathroom adjoining the bedroom, running a glass of water. She shook two aspirins out of a bottle and handed them and the drink to Anna. 'Chess has had lots of boyfriends,' she said. The terrible corollary to that hung unspoken between them. 'Take these,' she said. Anna took them. Why not? She wanted to go. She wanted to be *ordered to go*. Chess came into the room then and closed the door tightly behind her. 'It's not fair if Anna comes,' she said. 'Chess darling,' their mother said to her, 'Don't take this too hard! You've had lots of boyfriends. And you'll have many more. But facts are facts, darling. Karl seems to care for Anna.' Chess started to cry. And Anna stood and rubbed her thumb the length of the wide white window sill; she felt amazed and uneasy.

Chess talked a great deal on the way there. And after they'd found a place to eat and had finished eating and had taken shelter in an old covered bridge to wait out the rain that they'd feared and predicted all the way there she started to sing. Songs from *South Pacific, Oklahoma, An American in Paris*. She sang well, in a light, sad, chanteusey voice, but it was clear (at least to Anna) that Karl didn't care for that kind of thing. And after Chess had been singing for a while, Anna leaned back against the wall of the bridge and closed her eyes.

In the middle of the following week Anna got a letter from Karl. He was coming to Hocksville two days later and wondered if he could see her. Maybe we could go to a beach, he wrote. He signed the letter love.

On the beach, Karl told Anna about his childhood in Norway, under the Germans, and about coming to Canada in 1945 when he was sixteen and about how people had laughed at him when he went out skating because he wore britches and knee-socks. He told her about going to school in Oslo in '42, '43, and about trying to get in the back end of the soup line so he could get more of the meat that sank to the soup pot's bottom. Anna found she liked him even better for the romance and deprivations of his past. He told her that a Norwegian Nazi had been shot by someone from the Underground in the street right in front of his school. He said that at the end of the war the Americans wanted to make a goodwill gesture to the Norwegians (who had suffered so much). They hit on the idea of sending over a freighter filled with peanut butter. But the Norwegians had never seen peanut butter before, and they found it, when it arrived, to be revolting stuff—*they* thought the goodwill boat was filled with excrement. 'The Norwegians were hungry,' Karl said, 'but they were not *that* hungry.' Anna smiled. 'Speaking of excrement,' she said, 'I should tell you about my life at the hospital.' His turn to smile. But she only told him the funny things, she didn't want him to know she was thinking of leaving there. It was her secret. She would move when she was ready. She saw it happening on a clear, fall day. She saw herself decently, adultly concealing her pleasure at getting free. She saw herself walking out of the nurses' residence carrying a little red overnight case, her coat over her arm; she saw how her eyes would give the impression of being nobly infatuated with a far horizon, like the eyes of a Red Cross nurse in one of the wartime posters from her childhood.

In real life, she was transferred to the Emergency wing. She liked it there. It was the first place she'd worked where they weren't short-staffed. And she liked the people she was working with—Smitty, Jackson, Devine, Becky Agulnick. Her first day off Karl was able to get his father's car to drive down to see her. He could stay overnight so they drove out to the Stone Bay house where Anna was born, now used by her family as a summer house. Anna's mother was out there and was expecting them and seemed overjoyed to see them. She was wearing a pink towel, boxer-style, around her neck; she had just washed her hair. When she gave concerts she always did her hair up into a dignified confection of braids and buns—using her own young braids, kept in a hat box— but now it hung fair and fluffy down to her shoulders. She was barefoot, perfumed. She gave them each a hard, theatrical hug. She had hot drinks already fixed for them and a fire in the fire-place. Anna got the impression that her mother thought she'd dreamed them up, that they were her production. She wanted to say to her: Listen, this would have happened anyway. He's already told me that my coming on that picnic didn't make any difference, we would have seen each other again, he's crazy about me. And he never was interested in Chess, not seriously; he thinks she likes herself too much. Her mother took Karl on a tour of the house and showed him the paintings and the things from Europe and her 'country piano.' She said, 'Later, if you would like, I will play for you.' Karl said that would be marvellous. And when Karl and Anna went out for a walk after they'd done the dishes Anna's mother came with them. By then there were big clouds, thin as smoke, moving fast across the sky. It was the first night that summer seemed conclusively over. Even the river had got more wild and fall-like, they could hear the waves coming in harder against the beach. Karl held hands with Anna's mother. They swung their hands back and forth like two children. Anna's hand he lifted into his pocket with his own. He made love to her between all her fingers with his thumb. 'Isn't this inspiring?' cried Anna's mother, sniffing the wind, inhaling the view of the sky and the river.

The next morning when Anna woke up she smelled coffee and breakfast cooking. She went downstairs in her nightgown. Her mother was standing at the stove, frowning. Her fair hair was brushed, tied back. She was wearing a sky blue sundress. She was frying french toast in one pan and scrambling eggs with chives in another. In the big black skillet bacon was cooking. She had also made muffins, put peach jam in a blue bowl and strawberry jam in a clear glass dish. She had picked fresh flowers for the table, poured orange juice into wine goblets, and made up pots of both coffee and tea.

'My God,' Anna said. 'This is fantastic.'

'I suppose I better put all this in the oven to keep it warm,' her mother said. She seemed to be cross about something.

Anna went up to her room and pulled off her nightgown. She inspected her tan, then washed and dressed. She rubbed cologne on her arms and neck and hand lotion on her hands and legs. She fastened on a pair of high-heeled sandals and put on two rings and a bracelet. Then she went down the hall and knocked on Karl's door. He told her to come in. She went in there and closed the door behind her. The whole house smelled of sleeping breath and sun on rugs and coffee. Karl yawned and stretched and then pulled her down on the bed.

Lying beside him she posed one leg in its sandal. 'My mother's made a big breakfast,' she whispered. And then she whispered, 'Do you know what I think? I think my mother wants to marry you.' And then she felt her face start to glow because she had come so dangerously close to saying, 'I think my mother wants to marry you *herself.*'

But Karl, instead of answering her (and maybe not even having heard her—what she'd said, what she'd stopped herself from saying), started using one of his fingers to trace the outline of her sandaled heel, calf, thigh. It was a phrase he was writing. When he got to her panties he put a period between her legs. She spread them a little.

'Children!' called her mother, in the musical voice she used for company.

Karl took his finger out from under Anna's dress and brought it up over her belly and then up over one breast. At the nipple he pressed in another period. Then he proceeded up her neck and around her chin. He outlined her mouth. She parted her lips. He put a period in her mouth. She bit his finger.

'Everything's going to get cold!' called her mother. Less music in the voice now.

'Coming!' Karl shouted in a cheerful, sing-song voice.

And then the finger started outlining Anna's nose. She hated that. Her nose was too big and had a bump in it. She believed it had ruined her life. 'If we got married . . .' Karl said. The finger came down over her nose again, ' . . . do you think our children would have big noses?'

She sat up. 'We'd better get down there,' she said, 'or she's going to start to get angry.'

At the end of that summer Karl was ready to leave for Toronto where he had a job waiting. He stretched the time out a little longer to coincide with Anna's coming off days in Emergency so that they could spend a last day together in Athens.

His bus came in two hours after Anna's, and when he arrived at the house, pale as a dying prince, they all went into the living room for cakes and tea. Kamille had left for the States by this time, but Anna's brother Arnie was at home and so was Chess. It was a cold, cloudy, fall day, and the house seemed very draughty and polished. Karl talked in a very informed way about the Royal Danish Ballet, and Chess asked him a lot of questions.

After they'd brought the tea things out to the kitchen Arnie took Anna aside and said, 'Hey little sister, are you going to marry this Karl, with his clipped English?' She said maybe I will, I don't know yet. And then she started to help Chess with the dishes.

While Chess and Anna were alone out there, Chess said, 'Everything Karl said about the ballet was very interesting, I thought.'

Anna said she thought so too.

'He got it all out of *Time* magazine,' Chess said. 'All of it. I read the whole review when I came down here on the bus. Those opinions weren't his own.'

'That can't be true.' Anna said. 'He doesn't even read *Time*. He's a socialist.'

'I have it in my suitcase.' Chess said. 'I can show it to you.'

'I've got better things to do,' Anna said. But her heart felt like it was beating ten times faster than usual.

Karl left for Toronto and Anna went back to the hospital. She was transferred to Male Surgery and with the fair-minded Killeen in charge she didn't mind it too much there. A whole month went by. She was now into the third month of her third year. 'What a pity you're leaving,' she imagined people would say, 'when you've only nine months left to go.' And then she imagined the way their eyes would drop, quite understandably, down to her belly.

The first snow came. Karl and Anna wrote to each other every day. His letters made her ache they were so sweet, full of quotes from Andrew Marvell, full of missing her body. More snow came. The supervisors got out boxes of Christmas decorations and for part of one peaceful hospital afternoon they all unrolled bandage-sized rolls of red and green crêpe paper and decorated the nursing stations. People started talking about Christmas and New Year's and on some wards they started making trades. The patients' radios played Christmas carols. Then suddenly (and inexplicably, because she'd already worked a long stretch there before), Anna was transferred to 6E, the worst ward in the whole hospital, run by a supervisor who was considered, even by the other supervisors, to be a sadist. Her name was M. K. Howard. If she had a first name no one seemed to know what it was, although there was a rumour the M stood for Mary. Sometimes, in fact, she was called the Virgin Mary. ('Hear you're spending Christmas with the Virgin Mary, you poor bastard,' a girl named Connors said to Anna one day in the cafeteria.) At the end of a week with Howard, Anna felt she was in hell. And in the middle of hell she got a letter from Karl. He'd been at a party where he'd met a lot of new people. He had dropped ice-cubes down a girl's back. She was an amusing girl, he wrote, very dark and lively. You would like her. He thought it would be a good idea if they occasionally went out with other people.

After this, Anna started having trouble sleeping. Her skin itched; she lay awake parts of every night, scratching, panicked. What if the lack of sleep made her make a mistake with the medicines? What if she gave someone someone else's injection? And during the days she felt herself in the grip of a secret rage. The patients' radios played the same carols over and over—bouncy barbershop renditions of songs about roasting chestnuts and Christmastime in the city. She did not hear from Karl again and she did not write to him; but sometimes, in the middle of passing out pills or giving the needles, her eyes would fill up with tears. Three nights after his letter she didn't sleep at all, but she made up her mind. She would phone home in the morning and tell them that she had broken up with Karl and that she was sick and wanted to come home. She knew her mother would be alarmed enough to come and get her; her mother would not want Karl to escape.

When she came off duty the night of her last day she found her room filled up with people. People from her own class, people from other years, other classes. They were everywhere: on the bed, on the desk, on chairs, on suitcases. It wasn't a popular move, leaving; it inspired envy. And it left yet another ward short-staffed. The traditional way to leave was to tell one or two friends, swear them to secrecy, leave when the night and day staffs were safely at work or at supper in the hospital cafeteria. And pregnancy was the traditional reason.

Someone asked her if she was pregnant. She said no. 'As a matter of fact, I'm menstruating,' she said.

'The weeping of the disappointed uterus,' someone said, and there was a patch of uneasy laughter.

Connors said, 'Let's undress her and see if she's lying,' and Anna felt really scared then because technically, at least, she *was* lying. She had had cramps all day but nothing had happened yet.

'Anna's been wanting to leave here for more than a year,' said Joan Cosman, her friend. And no move was made against her.

She started to pack. She gave away her cape, caps, textbooks, uniforms. Also her late-leave card, to be forged later.

A delegation came with her to the elevator. Smitty and Becky Agulnick kissed her good-bye. Jackson and Devine told her to write. Connors punched her on the shoulder and said, 'No hard feelings, I hope.' She said no. Joan loaded her stuff into the elevator.

Outside it was snowing again and Anna's mother's coat was turned into a fat fur bell by the wind. Anna hurried behind it down the wide concrete steps. She never expected her mother to refuse to speak to her, and yet it often happened; it was happening now. In silence they fitted the suitcases into the back seat and climbed into the front and closed themselves in. In silence they drove down Porter Street and in silence they left Hocksville and the ocean and the lights of Port Charlotte behind. At Black Bay the river had frozen and been snowed on, but a channel had been kept open for the ferry. They drove in silence onto the ferry, bumping over its wooden flap, and in silence watched the snow fall into its road of black water. On the other side of the river they drove up and down hills that seemed a little steeper with the new snow on them. But by then the snow had stopped. East of Bucksfield there was even some fog. Cedar trees stood in fog on white fields. Country schools and country churches appeared, ghostly close to the highway. Anna's mother drove slowly after this, through settlements and small towns named to hold the wilderness at bay—Richmond, Cambridge, Annetteville, New Sharon—and as they came into New Sharon she even spoke.

'I think you should know what Jack Kinkaid said when he heard you were giving up,' Anna's mother said. (Jack Kinkaid, dead now, in those days owned the men's wear store in Athens. When he was trying to persuade someone to buy from his range of fur-lined suede gloves he would say, 'Feel that. Softer than a mouse's titty.')

'What did he say?' Anna asked her mother. For some mad reason she expected good news.

'He said, "What that girl needs is a good whipping."'

Anna laughed a harsh, light laugh. 'Oh, I would not put great stock in anything Jack Kinkaid might say,' she said. 'I would not greatly respect any opinion Jack Kinkaid might have.'

'Someone who's done what you've done is hardly entitled to sit in judgment on other people,' her mother said. 'You turned your back on the sick,' her mother said.

Anna turned and looked out the window and would not answer.

When Karl came down the following Easter (by Christmas already they had patched things up—Karl had written to her; she had answered him in the next mail) they spent a lot of their time together talking about Anna's mother. Anna found she could talk more easily to Karl than she'd ever been able to talk to anyone else. But still she was careful, settled for telling him the little irritations, not the dark things. She said, 'When she comes back from the post office she tells me I didn't get any mail. Then two hours later, when we're all sitting down to supper, she lifts the cover off the casserole dish and there is your letter. I never know what piece of crockery I'm going to find a letter in next.'

He looked startled. 'But what if she decided not to even give you a letter at all?' he asked her. She could have said, 'Oh, I came into her room one night and found her sitting up in bed reading a letter you'd sent to me,' but it didn't seem wise to let him know that. How could he continue to write to her about the sweet weight of her breasts if he knew a thing like that? She could have said, 'She tried to kill herself once, with me in the car.' She could have said, 'Once, when she was having her nap, she called me in to her room to cover her with an extra blanket and later, when she woke up, she came out to kitchen and said, "You made me dream I was dead. You covered me with that heavy, heavy blanket, you made me dream I was dead."' But there were things she didn't want him to know; for instance she didn't want him to know what her mother had shouted out to her the time they were in the car and her mother had threatened to kill herself. Her mother had shouted out to her, 'You turn people on and off like a tap! You don't love anyone! I might as well kill myself if I'm not loved!' And then she had pressed the accelerator down to the floor and driven their decrepit old car as fast as it could go. Which was only about eighty and besides, the road, for the next ten or fifteen miles, was going to be straight. Still, Anna had finally shouted out, 'Of course I love you!' to her mother, and this was somehow the most humiliating thing to remember of all.

One night in early spring when they were lying in front of the fireplace, late, after the others had all gone to bed, Karl said, 'Do you know what really irritates me about her more than anything else?'

'What,' she said dreamily. 'What.' Whatever it was, she was sure she would love to hear it.

'The way she comes up to me and looks up at me with those innocent big blue eyes of hers and says, "Do you love little Annie? Do you love her very much?"'

Anna snorted, appreciative.

'The way she calls you *little Annie*,' he said.

'Yeah,' she said. 'Little Orphan Annie.'

'Do you know what I feel like answering her?' he asked her. 'When she asks me if I love you?'

Anna felt delicious. Her whole belly was jelly, ready to laugh. She felt weakened and lulled by the coming laughter, by that and the uneven heat—half of her face and one thigh were all hot from the fire. 'What?' she said.

'I feel like saying no,' he said. 'I feel like saying no, I don't love her.'

She sat up at once and drew herself a little away from him. 'Why would you want to say that?' she asked him. 'Whatever would you want to say that for?'

'To shut her up,' he said.

# Roch Carrier

ROCH Carrier was born in Ste-Justine-de-Dorchester, Quebec, in 1937. After receiving his M.A. from the Université de Montréal he taught Greek culture for two years at the Collège St-Louis, in Edmunston, New Brunswick, before completing his doctoral thesis (on André Breton) at the Sorbonne. In 1964 he returned to Canada and taught at the Université de Montréal. He is now the resident dramatist at Montreal's Théâtre du Nouveau Monde, and lives with his wife and two children in nearby Longueuil.

Carrier's first appearance in print, *Les jeux incompris* (1956), was as a poet, but since then he has written mainly fiction and drama. He has published seven novels, including a trilogy—*La Guerre, Yes Sir!* (1968); *Floralie, où es tu?* (1969: *Floralie, Where Are You?*, 1970); and *Il est par là, le soleil* (1970: *Is It the Sun, Philibert?*, 1972)—the first two of which have been adapted by Carrier for Le Théâtre du Nouveau Monde and performed at Stratford. Carrier has published three collections of stories: *Jolis deuils* (1967), *Contes pour milles oreilles* (1969), and *Les Enfants du bonhomme dans la lune* (1979: *The Hockey Sweater and other stories*, 1979), the last of which has been translated by Sheila Fischman and includes the following story.

# A SECRET LOST IN THE WATER

## *Translated by Sheila Fischman*

AFTER I started going to school my father scarcely talked any more.
I was very intoxicated by the new game of spelling; my father had
little skill for it (it was my mother who wrote our letters) and was
convinced I was no longer interested in hearing him tell of his
adventures during the long weeks when he was far away from the
house.

One day, however, he said to me:

'The time's come to show you something.'

He asked me to follow him. I walked behind him, not talking, as
we had got in the habit of doing. He stopped in the field before a
clump of leafy bushes.

'Those are called alders,' he said.

'I know.'

'You have to learn how to choose,' my father pointed out.

I didn't understand. He touched each branch of the bush, one at
a time, with religious care.

'You have to choose one that's very fine, a perfect one, like this.'

I looked; it seemed exactly like the others.

My father opened his pocket knife and cut the branch he'd
selected with pious care. He stripped off the leaves and showed me
the branch, which formed a perfect Y.

'You see,' he said, 'the branch has two arms. Now take one in
each hand. And squeeze them.'

I did as he asked and took in each hand one fork of the Y, which
was thinner than a pencil.

'Close your eyes,' my father ordered, 'and squeeze a little harder
... Don't open your eyes! Do you feel anything?'

'The branch is moving!' I exclaimed, astonished.

Beneath my clenched fingers the alder was wriggling like a
small, frightened snake. My father saw that I was about to drop it.

'Hang on to it!'

'The branch is squirming,' I repeated. 'And I hear something that
sounds like a river!'

'Open your eyes,' my father ordered.

I was stunned, as though he'd awakened me while I was dreaming.

'What does it mean?' I asked my father.

'It means that underneath us, right here, there's a little fresh-water spring. If we dig, we could drink from it. I've just taught you how to find a spring. It's something my own father taught me. It isn't something you learn in school. And it isn't useless: a man can get along without writing and arithmetic, but he can never get along without water.'

Much later, I discovered that my father was famous in the region because of what the people called his 'gift': before digging a well they always consulted him; they would watch him prospecting the fields or the hills, eyes closed, hands clenched on the fork of an alder bough. Wherever my father stopped, they marked the ground; there they would dig; and from there water would gush forth.

Years passed; I went to other schools, saw other countries, I had children, I wrote some books and my poor father is lying in the earth where so many times he had found fresh water.

One day someone began to make a film about my village and its inhabitants, from whom I've stolen so many of the stories that I tell. With the film crew we went to see a farmer to capture the image of a sad man: his children didn't want to receive the inheritance he'd spent his whole life preparing for them—the finest farm in the area. While the technicians were getting cameras and microphones ready the farmer put his arm around my shoulders, saying:

'I knew your father well.'

'Ah! I know. Everybody in the village knows each other . . . No one feels like an outsider.'

'You know what's under your feet?'

'Hell?' I asked, laughing.

'Under your feet there's a well. Before I dug I called in specialists from the Department of Agriculture; they did research, they analyzed shovelfuls of dirt; and they made a report where they said there wasn't any water on my land. With the family, the animals, the crops, I need water. When I saw that those specialists hadn't found any I thought of your father and I asked him to come over. He didn't want to; I think he was pretty fed up with me because I'd asked those specialists instead of him. But finally he came; he went and cut off a little branch, then he walked around for a while with his eyes shut; he stopped, he listened to something we couldn't hear and then he said to me: "Dig right here, there's enough water to get your whole flock drunk and drown your specialists besides." We dug and found water. Fine water that's never heard of pollution.'

The film people were ready; they called to me to take my place.

'I'm gonna show you something,' said the farmer, keeping me back. 'You wait right here.'

He disappeared into a shack which he must have used to store things, then came back with a branch which he held out to me.

'I never throw nothing away; I kept the alder branch your father cut to find my water. I don't understand, it hasn't dried out.'

Moved as I touched the branch, kept out of I don't know what sense of piety—and which really wasn't dry—I had the feeling that my father was watching me over my shoulder; I closed my eyes and, standing above the spring my father had discovered, I waited for the branch to writhe. I hoped the sound of gushing water would rise to my ears.

The alder stayed motionless in my hands and the water beneath the earth refused to sing.

Somewhere along the roads I'd taken since the village of my childhood I had forgotten my father's knowledge.

'Don't feel sorry,' said the man, thinking no doubt of his farm and his childhood; 'nowadays fathers can't pass on anything to the next generation.'

And he took the alder branch from my hands.

# Lawrence Garber

LAWRENCE Garber was born in Toronto in 1937. He attended Vaughan Road Collegiate and the University of Toronto, where he received his B.A. in 1960, his M.A. in 1962, and his Ph.D. in 1973. From 1962 to 1966, like many of his generation, Garber wandered about Europe, living in Paris, Barcelona, London, and northern Italy. In 1967 he returned to Canada, married, and began teaching English at the University of Western Ontario in London, where he still lives.

Garber's first work of fiction was the experimental *Tales from the Quarter* (1969), a long, sequential novel set in Paris in the '60s. His second book, *Circuit* (1970), contains three interrelated stories of which 'Visions Before Midnight' is the middle story and bridge. Although Garber began 'Visions' after the suicide of a close friend, the two characters in the story also represent twin aspects of Garber's own identity, the university professor who has been down and out in Paris and London: 'I am possessed of a schizophrenic personality,' Garber has written, 'and am thus able to exist in uneasy amphibious relationship to the worlds of art and academia; since both sides of my personality are exactly the same, this has not yet caused any serious problems.' This unity in diversity helps explain the fact that Garber is one of the few Canadian writers to have successfully combined experimentalism with realism.

# VISIONS BEFORE MIDNIGHT

SUSCEPTIBLE to illusion as I am, I was not at all surprised when Jack (whom we had buried some few weeks previously) announced his presence at my threshold.

'Do Jack,' I said, 'come in.'

He did not look well. A bit of grease about the jowls, a streak of dirt beneath the chin, lips rather bluish (hair damp and strangely lashed to the scalp), a trace of ashes and tar at the temple: he appeared thin, faint: I didn't like it.

'Chrissssssssst, I'm tired,' he said in that familiar coarse voice, dark pebbles in the throat.

'Take the sofa chair, Jack,' and ran to smoothe it for him as he moved incautiously through the room. I was living on Dexter Place at the time. I had brought all my books with me and they lined the walls like a great army. The floor was broadloomed here, a dull green, and bare patches of space had been fed with brilliant canvas prints: a green Rouault, skull teeth of the clown blooming from a mouth in agony, Picasso fingers like loaves of rye, a Modigliani nude stretching in narrow accusation toward my cherished Hi-Fi set, a Manet profile pouting through its cloud of paint. I had as well a small fireplace which I delighted in after six, and the thin logs turned a crisp black in the grate. Jack tripped as always into the sofa and splashed its fabrics with his smells. But it was a strange odour now. Yes, like the melting tip of a candle, the vague stench of bad water, a bus tire trapped in a pool of slush. 'Good to see you, Jack,' and found my nose and ears clogged with it; its gaseous properties assaulted my brain, steamed from my eyes. I wheezed softly so as not to alarm myself and tried to drive it off by gentle manoeuvrings of the hand. This merely channeled its direction and my lungs spat hysterically. 'Oh God,' I called, and then, 'Jack, let me get you a glass of water,' running in panic to my small sink by the wall. I gargled, sponged my forehead, drew a cold glass of water and brought it at a reluctant gallop across the room. 'Who's thirsty?' he croaked, but took the glass. His eyes: dried yolks, completely drained, coated with green everywhere; they closed tight as he sipped, nose honking. His nostrils were glutted, sheltered by small licks of hair, now cheeks sucking at their flesh, now dry mouth sewn in, little teeth labouring through the lip. I leapt to the wall and applauded my prints. ' ... casso, Jack, and the Rouault is quite fine as prints go, brilliant primitive colour, a rather frightening orange, I think, if you ... ' Yet, and this was odd, I felt ashamed, harrassed. If I multiply by four the vague impressions of my mind I can see an obscure rage where he sat: he miserable in my best seat (looking deathly ill), I singing the praises of my room. He was restless, but it was something else. 'Are you cold Jack?' But he wouldn't answer yet, a game he used to play.

'I'll make some toddy.' I replaced Consevère's *History of the Comb* on its third tier to the left of my mauve drapery and walked ponderously to the kitchenette. 'I've got a kitchenette, too,' I called once inside, and heard the inauspicious grunt. 'You remember my place on Yarborough, don't you Jack? I don't know what I'd do without a fireplace now. You know, it's the mild comforts that cool the pain Jack, not the violent ones.' I measured my toddy in the cups. 'I'm afraid I've changed a bit Jack. But of course you've probably noticed it already.' I lifted the kettle, using a soft, wine mitt, and distributed the hot water proportionately. The chocolate powder bloated and bubbled. 'Are you comfortable?' I could hear him moving about through my room, nasty little half steps in the rug, and smiled with a private anxiety. 'Wait and I'll show you some more of the books Jack,' I cried. His fingers were usually smudged, ear wax under his finger nails and so on; I trembled at the thought of his dark orange thumbs. 'Don't touch Veiburh's *Anecdotes of the Napoleonic Era*, Jack!' I screamed softly, ruining my poise and spoiling the cup measures. Then, more at peace, 'I really want to surprise you, all right? All right, Jack?' I heard a book thud to the broadloom. Frantically, spilling hot toddy on either wrist, I plunged through the door. 'Interesting, huh?' I said and swallowed with some bitterness. The worst had happened: he stood facing my central shelf; he had drawn back the glass panel and was rubbing his knuckles against the velvet binding of my Decateur collection. 'Nice, huh?' and ran towards him, scuffing the petalled bow of my oxfords.

'What ss crap is this,' he grunted, cracking open the fifth volume. 'Decateur,' I said. His nose was running; he tried to breathe up, a spiral bead danced on the lip of his nostril. 'Here, let me show you the famous dedication,' and presumed enough to seize it from him. 'Who hell cares?' he said hoarsely. I gave him the hot toddy, replaced the fifth volume, crimson coat of arms top left, and drew the glass panel carefully. I hesitated; was it proper? then resting my toddy on the broadloom, switched the panel lock as casually as I dared. 'Well,' I resumed the evening, 'Jack.' He held the cup unsteadily. He spotted his knees, tried to scratch away the damp itch. I sat in my basket chair, abdomen hung deep in its hollow. 'Balllllllls said the Queen, if I had two I'd be King.' Crossed my legs firmly and placed the toddy saucer almost beyond reach on the bony flat of my knee.

'What was that, Jack?'

'Balls said the Queen, if I had two I'd be King.'

'Yes.' There was a studied pause (an old trick) through which I withstood intimidation. His lips bit at the cup as he swallowed; pant leg inched back to uncover the secret, pale flank. I tried to move beneath the silence. 'Calvin's married,' I began. Jack took the news patiently. 'To Kaye,' I said. Jack put his finger in the toddy and stirred it slowly. 'But of course, you knew ... ' He pulled his finger back and watched the thin brown drops race to his palm. 'He was a pallbearer at your funeral.' 'Caln?' he said vaguely. 'Calvin and Aaron and Mendelvartch and myself and two of your uncles.' It was difficult. How was one to proceed?

'There once was a man from Nantucket ... ' he began, croaking at the rhythms. 'Oh listen,' I said, 'is it eight yet?' I rose hastily and forced a comfortable smile. 'Alfred Arthur Bonds is on tonight; first Film Talks, and then Bonds Reviews Broadway at eight.' He sneered: it was unmistakeable. His upper lip twisted to the gum and disappeared, his lower lip gupping a mock smile at the heel of his cheek. I turned from it; the inverted centre of my belly shivered. His eyes were a dead angry white. I moved without using my legs; I clutched the black top of my cherished Hi-Fi, stared down in a fit of senseless horror and saw the vague, dark shine of my face laughing with its cheeks pressed against the black mahogany and its eyes trying to enter the forehead. I opened my mouth. A thick red oval half-ball slipped out, wrapped in spittle. 'Oh dear,' I said, 'I suppose this means another headache,' but it came out 'STRORT GUP STRORT GUP STRORT GUP UP UP UP,' and then a small scream and I was finished. 'I'm really sorry Jack,' turning around to face him and at the same instant catching a GUP UP at my throat and a STRORT swelling in my chest. 'I really think it's an abscessed tooth.' His face bent in two; but I would not tolerate his disbelief. 'Yes, really really, an abscessed tooth. Yesterday I woke up and my tongue was coated with a thin white base of all things; it's true Jack. So I brushed my teeth and of all things the point of my brush dipped into a nerve hole somewhere back here: look Jack, back here, here. So then I went for the gland under my cheek and true enough it was swollen and hard: touch it Jack, you'll see; see?' His eyes began to close, preparatory to disdain; I seized his fingers to press them to my gland and screamed. His fingers were like buttered eels; they secreted a hot yellow mess to the touch. 'I think I'll just wash up after that toddy,' I gasped, backing to the kitchenette. It must be all over him, I trembled; 'Perhaps you'd like to wash up too, Jack!' but when I came back with the secretion still wet in my palm, he was toying with my Yolande Daghl Rhodesian Mask. His nails were picking at the great sweep of nose and the flat of his thumb brutally smacked the sad ebony eyelid. 'It's a Yolande Daghl Model,' I said, and also, 'expensive as hell.' The word *hell* lay on the floor bleeding and then it turned on its breast and tried to rise. I tried to ease it away, smoothe the rupture, 'Very expensive,' but it kicked up screaming and Jack put the mask back upon its hook and with the gross mutter 'It's all sort of crap,' lit my last cigar. 'I'm really sorry,' I ventured a pace, puzzled, a swollen gob in my chest. 'What for, chrisssst,' wheezing at the cigar violently, smile like a faceless sponge. He wasn't looking at me any more: he was staring at his own eyes. 'Jack it's all very important to me; my books and my . . . ' and as I was about to maintain the argument and build it, construct it part by part until it resembled myself and made me a pertinent hour in time, he belched with the fervour of a nauseous whale. ' . . . my art, Jack, and the things I do and when the . . . ' His nose went BAAAAAAART-PITSSSS, broke the cigar in half; mouth groomed a spittle egg, eyes bloated with red tears, ears popped like the crack of a beetle's spine ' . . . year is over I want to have achieved something, do you see? an hour in time, because consciousness is . . . ' Here, he sank forward into the chair with his eyes closed and rocked forward almost gently, lips pursed in a gaunt chuckle ' . . . after all, what counts. Jack. Do I make sense? If a moment in space can . . . ' and tenderly raised himself with his back arched and emitted a low whining sound YEWOOWOOWOO.

'There once was a man from Siberia/Whose morals was quite inferior . . . ' he sang. 'How are you feeling?' I asked. 'Ooookay,' he

sang, flat, on the same discord. 'I'm sorry I got so panicky,' I said.
He waved his knuckles, gravied, brown. He began to pick at the
hangnails in his fingers. I sweated during a minimal pause. 'What
do the nuns do, Jack?' 'Wah?' 'The nuns, Jack. When they die, you
know. The nuns.' The gob at my chest was shifting its weight from
the heart in an agonizing manoeuvre. I could feel it flexing its
great ugly spikes. 'Sure,' he groaned, 'they around alot.' 'Are they?'
I began to sweat profusely. It was all very real: yes, the nuns were
around a lot, yes that was the way to say it, yes sure of course they
were around a great deal, nobody would dispute that, no. 'Do they
do much reading, Jack?' this time with the gob leaking a bit all
over my clavicles. 'They was readin the vulgate,' he muttered by
rote, picking at a dead skin root, 'or somethin.' The Vulgate, or
something like it: yes yes, or something or other like it; they were
really reading it. My face stopped. Decisions mounted in my guts.
Was I to broach it? now. He sprawled on the chair, eyes far off,
dull, like melted fire, focussed habitually on green broadloom; I,
arms roughly within the range of control, ears reflective, mouth
compressed to a bee lip. 'Look Jack,' I said, aroused by tremors in
my voice, 'did it hurt?' I chinned myself on the head of a chair.
'Hah?' The dark process of despair flushed his face. 'Did it hurt? I
mean, dying and all, Jack.' He scratched his haunch. A yawn: this
was to make me seem tiresome; a nauseous purr terminating with
the horrendous CAWWWWWW-ULL. A dark shadow now suppressed half his frown, skin exuding a fearsome mask. Legs crossed
in fits of intrigue. I found myself upon the threshold of the monumental secret. History seemed no longer insecure. I trembled plea-
surably; gasped coughed hissed. He pulled an elastic band from his
pocket. A red one, already played out and rather dirty. He wound
it about his thumb and pwanged intently. The thumb jerked
against the constant sting of the rubber, a red sore occurred at the
plumb ball of the joint. I could hear an 'ah-ah-ah-ah' as the elastic
gained its mastery of the thumbflesh, biting, biting; a scarlet flush
appeared where the rubber slapped, and rash red flooded from the
stump hinge. An act of intimidation. But I did not desist; I tried to
organize a proper order for my eternal questions. Did death hurt?
Yes, and then, Did you see the funeral? The second question was
consequent to the first. Did you see who was really sorry you had
died? Okay; the third inquiry gave moral licence to the second and
recommended the first on the grounds of premise. Jack removed

the elastic from the scaled thumb and pushed it methodically into
his pocket. He yawned and half-turned away; the thumb was idle
but for a throb or two. Then, in an act of studied impulse, he
groped for the rubber and caught the thumb at rest, easeful,
pwanging it back to submission. I ignored these pleas for uncondi-
tional attention. Is there a Heaven, I added to my list; the next
three questions would form a sub-series of inquiries. The first three
probed the personal aspects of demise; these would be of a more
universal nature. Who owns it (Heaven), was the second macro-
cosmic; spurred by the first, it attracted the third question, Is God
around much, which neatly rounded out the triadic inquisition,
motivating a third substructure as well. A relationship between the
eternal and the temporal would be pursued. Thus, three questions
probing the paradox of time and the finite. First the Angels: Who
gets to be one? Secondly, a subtle corollary of the first subpart,
What about pain there, and, still the same question, Can you see?
And the final inquiry of the subdivision which approaches the
query in its totality, What do they do all day? (Affixed to which, in
footnote, the variable, Yes, and what does everyone talk about?)
STRORT GUP UP UP UP, I began, a little too impatiently; for
Jack, once more removing the red elastic, massaged his bleating
thumb tenderly. 'Strort Jack,' I felt my way, gaining access to my
honed thoughts, then pulled a rhetorician's hush to collect my
order. Jack purred at his thumb, little whimpers broken by threatening movements towards his pocket, caresses punctured by sudden
seizures. 'Dear Jack,' I smiled. He threw back his head as if antici-
pating the burdensome argument, and closed his eyes. This was
meant to convey faint disdain—a contempt not yet worthy of his
wrath. 'Chrisssst,' came the overwhelming hiss. 'Jack . . . did it hurt?
I mean afterwards. When you were gone . . . like.' He shrugged his
shoulders, now raised in nervous exaltation; cheeks held back their
wind in a cutting gesture of fatigue. I held my pace. There had
been a moment, a spontaneous stirring; the face, tarred and grimy,
the nose stuck green, the eyes a dead yolk white, ears a dusty
orange; yes yes, yet in it I had seen the secret motions of the mind,
a husking innocence that damned me to the quick. His finger nails
with their glut of filth . . . and and . . . the croaking voice, yes of
course the voice sounding far off sounding dead sounding . . . and
what else? . . . well, the limericks, songs of experience with their
omniscient vulgarities setting aside the frock of ages . . . the mystic

contortions of the body . . . 'Jack. Were you at the funeral? Did you
see me? I was in the first row at the chapel; wore a black tie with
mauve diamonds connected at their poles. I helped put the coffin
on the rubber supports. Mendelvartch got sick. Did you see it? My
hand slapped his knee with gay despair. But he was tiring, shattering his pose, neck sinking from its exalted commitment. Was it
folly to proceed? He rose, I after him. Both of us in a lean stride
across the broadloom. I grabbed his sleeve as he made a foul
motion to be rid of me. I attempted to steer him, ' . . . because
Heaven, Jack . . . seems different each season. Is it? I mean weather
STRORT . . . ' He walked right past my question, and also failed to
see my singular first edition of Alphonse André-John's *Selected
Confessions of a Theocrat*; for he pushed it as he passed; his elbow
jarred the vellum jacket and it fell nastily and bruised. 'Do you
really see anything up There? Jack, where are you running to, for
God sakes?' I could feel him shudder at the immense enclosure of
my rooms. He put his forefinger on the knob, and tried to turn it
with his thumb. 'Don't be silly, Jack.' I paused, dragging him to the
left of the threshold. His centre was a dead weight. I tried to find
the root of his balance, but he shifted erratically as I nudged him
half across the room and I was weaker than this loss of gravity. 'Sit
over here Jack; the hassock.' A spark of heat soaked through my
shirt. 'Is there really much gradation There? You know the stories
going around Jack, I just GUP UP UP . . . ' Swallowed angrily, but
the thing lodged in my throat and crawled. Up up it danced, I
could feel its little legs tripping through my skull, a noisy flutter
like the retreat of a spider, dark and grasping toward the heart of
its web. He crouched on the hassock impatiently; he cupped his
hand and brought it to his mouth. BRUUUUGHTKKK, and the
thing was out and jelly green. I stooped to his knee in an act of
careful reverence. 'Jack.' He leaned back to rinse his hand on the
broadloom; the glut made a thick foaming yellow among the tufts.
'Jack.' I could see him gathering secret strength for his next manoeuvre. I grabbed his arm and held it sadly at the wrist, then at the
elbow. 'Jack.' I had lost the art of persuasion, my voice was dulled
by his acts of will. Both of us now on the same side of motion.

  'They onct was this son of a bitch/Who had this perpetual
twitch . . . ' My jaw squared to veil the danger. 'Are the Angels
pretty busy usually? I would certainly guess that they needn't all
share the same responsibilities: huh?' I slipped back in a slow faint;

his knee rammed my chest as he moved past me, and I howled in a high, keening pitch. 'Jack!' with my eyes still closed, for I wouldn't open them, soft flaps tight over the pits, lashes clenched against the bulbs. He was out. I could hear the hard air where it entered my rooms, and the jerk of the door swinging back to stab the wall. 'Is there much sensation, would you say Jack!' and I bounded through the room in my own dark; and my eyes so tight I could feel the twigs of blood snap and wink at the pressure.

Once outside, my lids parted like small wounds. At both ends of the street two small stone bridges to connect the hillocks with the main roads. I caught sight of him navigating painfully to my right, emerging from the arch with a bizarre cobblestep. 'Jack!' I groaned, then moved quickly to the darker part of the street. There were things to know. They climbed about in my mind like peppered worms, sifting through the gaps, gnawing at the flaws where the lines were broken and the noises would not stop. I sped through the arch where the bridge entered the hill, and beyond it only the noises of the bush and the soundless vibrations of something far ahead. Running, swaying, I saw his head float in a gulf past the rise of the street, the thing half-cocked and nonsense, saying 'yes-no', saying 'twitch,' saying nothing at all, but striking a dead centre as it lifted half a strain and forgot the rules of motion. 'Jack!' but no. I leapt forward madly, my exhaustion fed me, and when I had overtaken him he was not there. 'Jack,' I said carefully, for who knew, 'Jack: is it possible for a heavenly being to create something; is manual labour possible in terms of infinity and all?' A splut answered me to a point. It was a small rat harbouring in its ditch. I staggered to the gravel and leaned over, not wanting to go on with it lurking there. But it did not move. 'Jack ... for God's sake ...' but the little beast splut again, and I was unable to contact a reply. 'Silly.' The rat was impeding me. I groaned in wonder; its eyes were up where it crept, it cracked a leaf, it made a muffled gurrr, it ... it ... 'Jack don't move for anything, dear boy.' But I couldn't stir. Horror clung to me like little hairs in the throat. The little monster clung to the ditch with its belly on the slope, tiny guts against the gravel. 'AHHHH,' I threatened, pawing the ground, oh such an ugly little creature, 'AHHHH-AHHH!' I stamped with my foot prone in the dirt, it shifted its head like an eagle, eyes steady and the flap of neck spinning the skull sharply. There was a kissing noise, a sound of two beads rolled together; I felt the small fang catch my forefinger, screamed, oh the rotten little toad, a thin nip just below the nail, oh the rabid little vampire, the blood making a smart little rim for itself. 'YEOWWW,' and I was up, raging, terrified, but everything gone, almost unbelievable; still, a throbbing pain where the skin parted in a smile. 'Jack!' at first hysterically; 'Jack: it's gone; a bat I think. But it's all right. Gave it a good slap in the fangs. Hear it flap away? Or maybe it just scampered off? Did you?' I wanted to draw him out. All this cryptic time watching me intimidate the rat, yet not a sound, somewhere beneath my sense of timing, hiding from my noise. I wrapped a thin pink kleenex about the split. I was walking forward, muscles bound in a rigorous slope, dizzy with contrition, air sucking blood; words lined up in sensory order, hell hump help hulk hruck hetc.

But he was only some small distance ahead of me. And not well of course, not being able to hear, no sense of direction, wandering about in the damp with no beam to catch his path. I found that my legs were tiring. My condition (a weariness of the bones, a hesitancy in the blood) was telling now that I had exposed my system to this thoughtless violence. 'Jack.' But there seemed to be only an atrocious calm confronting me. I was alone. He might be yards, miles, fields ahead. I wanted to hear a trumpet, yes, a trumpet there and then; something to excite me and withdraw my despair. A long, gusty tone reaching into my very intestines, stirring my body to push forward, exalting my mind to its discovery, creating in my bowels an unrest, a furious affirmation. My eyes strained; I strutted in mid-street, trying to hunt out some great propulsive music, the sounds of motion, the heroic clip through the dark. Trumptatamumta . . . but it was infected with the very ring of despair I had forbidden. Hoiroir-oir . . . yet merely the fragment of some minor joy I had misplaced weeks before. Catulalulca . . . a quick and fascinating rhythm, my tongue clinging to its subtle and salivating twists, still it was not enough. One great clear ring with perhaps the shudder of a drum to prompt me more: I heard it once, but it was gone before exploited, trapped in my mind, lost, like an apple spike lodged beneath the tongue. 'Jack.' And what if I came upon him suddenly? The threat of surprise made me uneasy. The first moment of terror when the thing climbs at you from the air, when the forgotten returns, and the underleaf reveals its scarred gum-belly as you pause at peace. What if the face reproached me in the dark? 'But Jack; is diversity of opinion actually possible There? if not, what is the purpose of discussion and exaltation? What I'm getting at, of course, is just how Pure are They willing to get?' I paraded through my dark journey, myself almost footless on the path. The dark recess of the road swallowed me slowly; swift shades moved to my right and left: bellowing, treacherous moans, carpets of the dead twisting among the leaves of night, rustling of the shroud where the balm of the anointed jellies in the vault. Little mysteries withdrew their concern; I shrieked at the knowable pawing me from its stoop. The street hooked sharply to its right and the ditches became smaller by the minute until at last all was flat and then in a few more minutes the pavement grew beneath me and under the first lamp post I could see the grass growing through the rocks.

'My good man,' I said to the drunk who was quite unwilling to cross the road at this tribute to my presence, 'you haven't (by any chance) been accosted by a person—male—oh, so tall, etc.' The drunk was supported by a post that seemed to grow through his arms. I made my way across the road to escape the arcs of light. 'He was, ahhhh, wearing very sickly apparel; face very white, nose running, hair damp and strangely lashed to the scalp, a bit of grease about the jowls, a streak of dirt beneath the chin, lips rather bluish, a trace of ashes and tar at the temple; I'm quite concerned.' 'Thash right,' said the drunk clinging to the post with one arm and drawing with the other a complex in the air, 'oh shure: sleak a filth ina shin ana lishps gleen ana whole mesh like you say ats it a plety coshern okay.' 'Oh really,' I fluted, but containing the greater part of my excitement for a confirmation, 'did he pass due west?' The drunk confided his obscene impression of the world and began to climb the pole, twisting his haunch until it was higher than his head and then falling back to stare at me, voiceless; his knees anchored him from the post and he seemed to hang like a series of inner linings. Inverted, his face was a quilt of terror. The forehead seemed like a mouthless cretin, and the eyes gave you back the stare with a steady cold insensation, impregnable, meaningless, yet as alert as the sheets you die in. The nose, breathing for the body now, curled and flexed dumbly at the nostril where it gave up air. But the mouth: it maintained a diabolic silence that is the noise the quiet makes; liplets strung together, secretive little dugs they were, and a pallor blue at the spreading skin; but I did not panic. 'You've got a little piece of something on your nose,' I said, motioning with a tiresome disdain, cutting, unmistakable. The drunk pried his lips apart; tongue wrestled against a wall of foam, teeth like old candy. 'Leech ana whole bishnash wisha grates.' 'Yes,' I said, for I had detected its apologetic tone. He fell from his perch almost soundlessly, but his head made a great deal of noise and seemed to break in the hollow of the curb. His body exuded a distressing odour that clogged my reactions. The acidic smells of fornication, yes. How repulsive the thing was with its head locked in the rut of its armpit. Flank kicked out to reveal a sallow, hairless leg. I ventured a step and kicked it gently in the neck to measure its remaining reflex. It grunted, as if swallowing a razor blade, and its torso wriggled in the ditch. 'If you took more care . . . ' I said, admonishing as I retreated. Still, I strained to catch every nuance of the thing caught, even at a distance, in the dull silo of light. But at last I thought of Jack instead, maturely thought of him instead: out in the offensive air, that damp colourless glut, exposed to useless sounds that never stop, hygienic habits, of this world turning the memory of his blood cold. 'Jack!' I called, 'meet me at the corner of Ferk and Unter, all right? I mean be there, really. We'll talk.' And hurried down narrow streets and through red lights shamming.

Ferk Street seemed a responsive grey, with a ringing green cloud looped above it. Strutting on it, I inhaled the wrong sounds and brain caught on an involuted wheel turning back and in, back and in until there was the moist whelp of the muscle against the metal catch. 'I feel silliest when trapped,' I groaned. But a sliver of light redeemed me from my anguish; it grew slowly in the distant place and I judged it to be at Ferk and Condle Crescent. The lamplights that spotted Ferk were a dying gold, but that breach in the distance, that little eye of light parting, it throbbed like a cracked tooth through the dim. I shifted my pose (from panic to grace) in order to receive the possibilities well. Perhaps something there to direct me, a pausing stranger with a little torch to light his stogie would set me right (and I was apt and willing), perhaps a lamp cap was shattered and the light leaking out all over Ferk and Condle. I adjusted my ascot. The rays, more a plumed marmalade than a fresh yellow, winked and undulated, operating their own balance, now stark bright, now half-veiled. Tiny elbows of light expanded and withdrew. Spears of cool air bridged my discomfort and I felt rather noble, like moving upcountry in the rain. Strut-ut-ut, legs clipping to an heroic jig, I smiling with grey innocence. The light cropped as I approached her, forming a sphere where she hid, and the rays all crust and pattern. I circled about the huge things, it was a monstrous white truck, a miracle of spokes and hatches, and watched the two little men pack garbage into a great cylindrical mouth. They lifted the wicker barrels, offering them quietly to the lip of the grumbling cone which churned and swallowed. The metallic gulp and belch sounding from a hundred slots along the panel released strange sulphuric odours; a vomitus of cans and glass studded the curb. The man with the red wool cap and undershirt worked by the gutter; the other stood with bare arms extended and half-hunched toward the cylinder itself, twisting and heaving like an enterprising ape. He kept rhythm with the great devouring mouth, feeding the thing in tempo, clearing intermittently the dribble of fungus, lice, things that crawled out of paper. 'Are those your lights?' I phrased. Eyes screwed tightly beneath the red wool cap, squat fearsome things, shoulders hinging and unhinging as the arms banded the containers.

'Yah. That's so. They attached to the truck.'

'I saw them about four blocks off, you see.' I advanced cautiously towards the gutter, away from the great gaping mouth. 'And I'm afraid I assumed a rather possessive sensation. These are the only lights like that around here, are they?'

'Holy Christ. Hey Perce!'

'They were expanding and withdrawing like tiny elbows of light.'

'Yah. Just like that. Hey Perce. You wanna see somethin?'

'Cool spears of air, like slivers of light . . . '

'Whatever you say Napoleon . . . '

'Felt like I was actually moving upcountry in the rain; and the light cropped as I approached her, all crust and pattern.'

'Perce! Come on over here!'

'Jack, a friend, is in the district I think; at least I told him to meet me at Ferk and Unter. You'd like him.'

'Sure,' he said, winking and jerking his head to imitate madness (though not well). 'Me an my buddy is harbingers of joy and these is fairy lights. Right Perce?'

The accomplice at the truck slapped a tick at his neck. The great mouth groaned and opened, revealing pastes and slimes of stunning variety.

'Your lights reach all the way to Dexter almost; quite impressive.'

The mouth seemed black and cavernous now, the mouth of a great dark fish, its swallow immense.

'Boy, you're somethin.'

'Naturally, I'm curious; it throbbed like a cracked tooth through the dim.'

'Jesus,' and then suspiciously, 'me and my buddy Perce here evy night we switch on them magic lights Napoleon and gut the motor an fly all over collectin magic garbage. I'm a angel; Perce here . . . '

'Thank you,' I interrupted, controlling my swallow. Then, intimating venom to crush their noise, 'that's all very nice; yessss, a turd in the hand is worth . . . '

'You wanna smash?'

I manoeuvred across Ferk where it was darker. A clot of ice formed beneath my skin, and my mind lumped with fright and disappointment. I didn't especially want a revelation; just a chance to talk things over. For Ferk Street on its west side is a sudden curve, a hook of pavement, spinning me in a dog's leg towards Unter. I saw Unter in its solemn graphic pose. A nasty clang to my left tested the quiet. An echo at my face parted the hush. Small runlets of water everywhere, as if it had been raining privately. 'I don't mind an occasional joke,' I dissented, 'but Jack, for Christ's sake.' There are tiny moments in time, brief inconclusive seconds that tick through the air into memory, where each breath and pause takes on a minor dignity. I felt that then, exhaling my totality like some divine machine. It slipped, as it always will. I tried to hold it; but like a word in space, its meaning died once past the definition. My tongue tried to taste it; somewhat a vanilla extract as I recall, half-lemon with a twist of joy. My ears heard it die again, though dying well, the sound of sweat trapped in a buttock. My nose smelt it manoeuvring past, a frog in a frog's belly where . . . So my body taut, strung from toe-nail to mucus . . . and the beauty of it leaving out the back world . . . 'Human pain,' I called out, 'is a very private matter.'

I saw him again as a matter of course. His face was blue in the shades. 'Jack,' I hailed. He was leaving Ferk, unwittingly. 'Ina whole ik gaz wisha but . . . ' he mumbled, waving his hands tenaciously. He was smaller than I had remembered him in my rooms; less coherent in his strut; entirely reconstructed, an image less to reckon with now. I pursued him up V.T. Epshaw Heights. I lacked the thrill of the chase; for the hunted, alone, knows its edge.

Victim links himself to the earth naturally; dangling with no re-
grets, consummation of the slaughter. But to chase is a lonely
game. Especially when the hunter pursues his fear and the hunted
dangles from his anger. 'Do they converse in Latin, Jack? Jack?' He
was nowhere to be heard. It thundered; the humbling noise was
pursued by a sickly dart of lightning, creamy, jaundiced. It was
nauseating. Violence has its limits, I confirmed as fog lit the dark.
'Mendelvartch hates you,' I screamed, trying to draw him out with
confidences. 'Smirked all during the ceremony; tried to make me
giggle.' He had affected a limp as V.T. Epshaw Heights arranged a
rather steep rise after its second Stop sign. 'Wouldn't carry the
coffin over the grave pit; thought he'd slip in, the imbecile. So I
carried you over, Jack. I did. I put you on the rubber bands. And I
slipped in, Jack. I fell in. They had to lift me out of the hole. It
wasn't a death-wish, understand; I've just got very bad co-ordina-
tion.' I saw him again negotiating the rise. He had affected that
monumental limp as if hip were pinned to navel. 'Jack, you'll suffer
on the rise. I'm warning you.' I had no frantic wish to pursue my
achievement. The titanic gesture of my upper lip confirmed this
disenchantment: a needle in the lip, a fierce cog of fire in the lobe
of sound, I was exquisite in my hell, an ode to dust and things. At
the summit he turned back to watch me. His face was gone. In the
dark I couldn't find it; that was all. 'Graaaatzzzz,' he called, and
shifted forward like a dismembered rump into the dip of the road.
'Isn't this just awful,' I commented, assuming a dyspeptic glare. But
I felt my heart trigger a clot or two; you swallow hard at a time
like that, by god. I groaned to a post for leverage against the
pavement. I could not hear him now, gone a second time and no
direction to pace his limp. My body was orange with sweat. Ascot
shredded, nuances disordered, legs a mass of contrite oil; faith is so
annoying out of place. 'If you knew Jack what I've gone through.
The heartaches, the migraines; do you think it's easy? You're just
an adventurer but I've got to think about the little things that die.
I'm planned.' That out, I resumed the climb, clutching a small
thistle of fat at my throat. When the rise is steep and the legs move
like string along the climb, then a sudden thought occurs, culled
from the mind's rich haft like a quart of dread and some afterthought. If I were to seek him out in his riddle, follow him till he
vanished from his movement. It is when the man is split and
spinning that ambition quickens. 'Jack, don't turn at Keckle's
Drive; it's a dead end, okay? Just a wall.' But I caught his smell at

the cross section, and knew that he was trapped. 'I'm coming down Jack; coming down,' but heard a sound of grating and clawing and stirring about. Something had slipped downhill into the Drive. There were little sounds.

I tell you that excitement had been replaced by a sense of justice. I claimed my due. I possessed knowledge by tearing off its wings; oh the thing was caught like cow turd below the grass. There are no private hells; public utilities are everywhere.

A wide strip of tar began where the roadway ended. I could hear his shadow very low and prowling downhill toward the bushes. He was moaning, that was clear, but I could no longer define him, he had lost his proper form, and there was I squorting in the muck. 'Stop it! Just stop!' A flock of dogs yarped a hillock away and a small herd of mice shifted. Everything possessed a casual panic; life was like a game of checkers where nobody moved their back row. That was very good. 'Hey Jack. Life is like a game of checkers where nobody moves their back row!' I was very satisfied with it. There was an invulnerable terror behind the line. Also, I delivered it with a flippancy that implied vague conditions. 'Isha grotzzz,' came from the stunted undergrowth. I passed a drunk half-legging it up the rise, caught between the hillock and the road, trapped by his own scream. 'This is all very digusting for Jack.' I moved to the end of the green affair, and everywhere in the dull dark the hoarse whispers arranged their net. I was rotten with body oils. Great amber puddles squelped in my palms. My eyes were lurid smoke, my nostrils confused air and thought and kept inhaling information, my legs felt like turquoise tendrils, cold and wiry, epileptic in the wind. And so on. I was neatly disordered. But what was worse: the babel I sang made sense. Each shriek bricked the tower another tier. Cleft of my heel spun up, toes flung me forward. I saw him deep against the bush wall, eyes up and red, nose hawked with fright, blue lips foaming, and little wordlets climbing past the gums and over the soundless hump into the air. Then he was awkward. He fell through the grass and hid. I ran forward cryptically. 'Jack. Just remember about Mendelvartch. He laughed, but I was solemn for weeks.' I came to the spot. A steel coverlet rose from the grass. Eyes pricked skull as they twisted for light. 'I am confident you are down there. Help.' But there was no laughter to give me poise. I fingered the steel. A little rain. A gush of pipe water bubbling through the dirt. I removed the sewer plate and made the necessary preparations to descend.

# Dave Godfrey

WILLIAM David Godfrey was born in Winnipeg, Manitoba, on August 9, 1938, and moved to Toronto when he was seven. He attended the University of Iowa, where he received his B.A., M.F.A., and, in 1967, his Ph.D., and has since taught English and Creative Writing at Aisadel College (in Ghana), the University of Toronto, and York University. From 1973 to 1975 he was writer-in-residence at Toronto's Erindale College, and since 1977 he has been chairman of the Creative Writing Department of the University of Victoria. In 1966 Godfrey co-founded House of Anansi Press; in 1969 he became Senior Editor of New Press; and since 1971 he has been Senior Editor of Press Porcépic.

Godfrey's first book was *Death Goes Better With Coca-Cola* (1967), a collection of short stories, many of which appeared first in *Saturday Night* 'disguised as a hunting column.' *The New Ancestors*, which received the Governor-General's award in 1970, has been called by W. H. New 'a novel that powerfully seizes the imagination and scorches the mind.' The following story was first published in 1964, in *The Tamarack Review* #30, and is included in Godfrey's second short story collection, *Dark Must Yield* (1978). 'I strive for great complexity in my writing,' he has written, 'because that is how I find life; I do not believe the writer has a duty to simplify or interpret life for his readers; his major tasks are to be as intelligent as possible and to take flights of imagination into bodies, minds and situations other than his own.'

# GOSSIP:
## THE BIRDS THAT FLEW,
## THE BIRDS THAT FELL

IN THE EYES of Mrs Wagwood, perhaps, the garage-owner's wife, her north neighbour Mr Courtney was a man of few joys but luckily fewer troubles. His wife—a frail, finely educated woman who had had little to say to Mrs Wagwood or to the other women of the town—had died many years ago, leaving him able to hold his head somewhat higher in town and with two children to raise. With them he had succeeded beyond anyone's expectations. They were both in university, the boy Mark working on an advanced degree, the girl Michelin studying in California on a nearly full scholarship. It was true that Mr Courtney did not belong to any of the town's churches, but he did not drink as his wife Beryl had done so disastrously and he was somewhat aware, if at times sardonically, of his position as a member of one of the early families. He seemed to lead a steady life, with few friends but trusty ones, and in the company of his son and daughter-in-law who lived with him to keep him from being alone and to save on their own expenses. Still, Mrs Wagwood was aware of how he had long loved the bush which lay on the other side of his property, and as soon as she heard of its coming destruction she kept a little closer watch on him.

To her there seemed little change, although she was known for her sharp eyes. In the morning he got up early to drive Mark and Tanya into the university, and then he came home for a cup of tea before he went up to the high school were he had taught history for thirty-nine years. In the evenings, since it was early June, the three of them nearly always ate out on the back lawn and watched the many birds that flew out of the woods to his feeder. She saw nothing, except that at times he would jump up angrily, curse, and shake his fist at the sparrows and starlings which drove the more brightly coloured birds away, and that had always been one of his habits. In worse moods she had heard him threaten loudly to blast starlings and grackles with a shotgun when they frightened the cardinals away. The night before the bulldozer was due Mrs Wagwood tried to engage him in conversation, but he spoke only in generalities and would not mention the woods. He appeared no more distraught than usual, although his trick of shaking his head in regular motion as though to enforce himself into agreement with whatever was being said seemed stronger.

And a most pleasant night to you, Mrs Wagwood. Yes, he hoped the students would do a little better this year on the provincial exams. It was true without a doubt that the suburban student they were getting nowadays didn't seem as industrious as the farm children of thirty years ago. They were indeed building all over; the school too would get an addition within the year. He trusted Mr Wagwood was well and hoped the new budget would bring no increase in gasoline taxes which certainly were high enough already, although yes the new houses and apartments should bring in a lot of people to the garage, everyone seemed to have a car, and a new one at that, yes, today. No, he was staying close to home this summer, taking a course in Arabic folklore at the university. His children were well; her own son was doing very well at the high school so he heard. Very beautiful weather it was, delightful indeed with the swampy parts drained to the back and new houses there instead of mosquitos. They had progress to thank for that. *Very much* too bad about the Reverend Wrager leaving the United Church. That was four new ones in seven years was it not? What sparked it this time? A new stove against his missions, or just a bigger annual picnic versus new curtains for the manse? No, of course he did not expect her to know everything that went on in town. By no means, by no means. And a most pleasant night to you also.

For, incredible as it seemed to her, Mr Courtney did not know what was to happen to the woods until that next morning when he was awakened a little earlier than usual by the sound of loud engines, first a gasoline and then a diesel. And even after he had gone to the dining room window and seen John Heck & Sons unloading the big bulldozer off a flat truck, he did not let himself become too aware of what was about to happen, not so much by ignoring it as by disassociating it in his mind as a gnat not to be compared to his other problems. These bore on him deeply, internally, in the manner which Beryl's false cures and jagged optimism had taught him, as untended splinters lie corrosively under the skin, poisoning the flesh, until they are themselves softened by infection. A. Mark and Tanya, bolstered by drink, dancing, and ennui at their weekly parties, were skittering back and forth with another couple into a relationship which only the later Romans would have considered proper. B. His daughter Michelin had been writing him about how much she was in love with a young Jewish assistant professor of political science whom she had been dating, hinting at marriage in every other sentence. Yet, when he saw the bulldozer clank down the ramp, he went outside at once and into the bush along one of his many paths, and when he returned he backed the car round so that he could leave in the morning by the south driveway. He did not love to watch dissolutions.

By the time Mark and Tanya got up for their quick cup of coffee before the dash into the city, the bulldozer had cut a deep swath into the centre of the bush and was working away there almost secretly, so that he hid it from them for that one morning. When he came home at noon, however, he felt a wave of winter apathy whelm his mind. He stood outside fingering his suit buttons and watched the bulldozer slash through the wild cucumbers growing over the mazes of old raspberry bushes until he was late for school. When he came home again, too, he went outside and peered at the centre of the woods and was dismayed at the increase of bared earth. The raspberries gone wild, which had long since turned under one another to form intricate prickly mounds of interlocked tunnels where pheasants and rabbits hid, were all levelled and burning, or burnt, upon the huge fire which smouldered in one edge of the cleared circle.

The kids will have to see it, he thought, and felt a crinkled shame at his illogical attempt to hide it from them. Still, that young Jotun will go slower when he gets in the trees—those big poplars will slow him down. He went over to complain about the smoke, but the boy on the bulldozer admitted that he couldn't help which way the wind blew. 'Maybe it'll let up tomorrow, or switch into somebody else's face,' he said. 'This baby costs a hundred bucks a day. We can't wait around for four-way stillness.'. The boy turned from him to thrust a huge ball of bush and raspberry mounds as easily as tumbleweed onto the fire. Mr Courtney was intercepted on his way into the house by Mrs Wagwood, still wiping her hands of dishwater on a flowered apron.

'Aw, isn't it a shame,' she said. 'All those beautiful old trees, even if most of them were rotten.'

'They haven't touched any big trees yet,' he replied, not eager to talk to her, but as always hating to see anyone in error. 'Except maybe a few of the old fruit trees from when Rackerson had it that should go anyhow.'

'I almost expected you to do something about it,' she said. 'That's what I thought you were up to now. As soon as I heard of the rezoning, I said, "Mr Courtney won't have it, not with the way his wife used to love to walk and sketch in those old woods."'

He looked at her in surprise. Meaning the way Beryl'd always wander out of there drunk in the summer afternoons is what you're saying isn't it? And you'd watch me go back in to find her sketch-books and paints scattered all over the bush.

'Been there too damn long already,' he said gruffly to her, feeling a deep bitterness growing within him, aimed at whatever spite she had that would drive her to bring up something like that. 'I don't suppose you've heard who's building in there, eh? Some rich city man who wants some privacy hollowing out himself a little nest like that, no doubt. He's in for a surprise.'

She ignored his tone in her eagerness to give him facts he didn't know. 'It's going to be two huge apartment houses, seven stories high, L-shaped, looking at one another, so to speak, with a big swimming pool in the middle—just for tenants. They're leaving a ring of trees around the outside just because the reeve likes his shade up there in that northeast corner, you know, where he lives. But who would have thought that you didn't care if it went, or that you'd imagine something nice coming like one big house.'

'Might as well cut them all down once you start,' he said. 'No need to impede progress. The reeve can buy an air-conditioner like the rest of them. Stupid to have a lot of things around to remind you of what won't ever be again. Level it off and pour concrete, I say.'

He turned his back on her before he had to listen to her say how surprised she was to hear him voice a sentiment like that, went into the house, and stayed there until Tanya called him for dinner. He wanted to suggest to her that they eat outside even though he knew she would take it as an admission of weakness in him. She was herself afraid to have children, yet if he gave smoke as a reason for not eating outdoors, he knew she would laugh and say that half the people in the world fed on smoke. She came of rich

parents in Montreal, but since she had spent a year on an anthro-
pological study in Peru, she liked to consider herself one of the
world's poor and disparaged anything that smacked of luxury. She
wove her long blonde hair simply or else left it hanging loosely to
her waist, never going to a hairdresser. He could not understand
most of the reactions she took to things and ideas except that he
knew what she would consider weak and shilly-shally. With Mark
she had made a strange agreement that she would remain virtuous
until he first found someone, for she often spoke of the proper
dominance of the male. Her favourite dishes were those that the
Department of Health labelled economical and extra nutritious,
although she usually served them with one of the many bottles of
expensive wine her father was continually sending her on one
pretext or another. Tonight she went ahead with the crock containing kidney beans and ham hocks, leaving him to bear the bottle
and Mark to carry the plates and silverwear. She poured the wine
hastily, as always, as if to say—well, we can't waste it I guess, but
let's drink it up quick then.

Fine ash mingled in the air with dust and drifted out of the
woods, swirls from the bared circle and the fire passed above them.

'The city's reaching out to encircle us,' she said.

'And a damn shame too,' said Mark, trying to console his father.

'I can stand the city,' he said. 'As I said to Mrs Wagwood today
—that loose-tongued old bitch—if we're going to have concrete,
let's pour it and get it done with.' He spoke angrily because he felt
he was breaking trust with someone or something—and worse, that
it had been a trust based on some mendacity which he longed to
maintain. 'I see in the paper the CPR's going to build a new hotel
in Vancouver so they break some agreement they made with the
CNR back in '38 and get out of paying renovations on the one they
used to share. And the government as always gets stuck.'

His daughter-in-law looked at him with quick surprise and suspicion, unable to follow the logic of his two comments and certain
that some slight was meant to her.

'City ways *are* sinful,' she said quickly with her little laugh, as if
to forestall with irony any comment he might make.

'I can stand the city,' he repeated. 'It's young pups that think
they know what city ways are and don't that get to me. When your
mother was studying art in the summers we used to go to some of

the biggest cities in the world, and there wasn't any of this stuff you're fooling around with, this swapping.' He turned to Mark while saying it as if to make the appeal only to his own flesh.

'It's our life,' Tanya retorted. Her face was flushed with excitement and disdain, as though she were glad the argument was out in the open, yet disgusted that they had to argue about anything. 'We just want to live without anyone interfering. We never criticize anyone, we don't expect it back.'

'I suppose you're having another little party here this weekend,' he said to her. 'Just the four of you and a few friends for disguise.'

'Come on now, dad,' his son Mark said in conciliation. 'We haven't done anything yet and you know we probably won't. It's a game we play to take the tension off. Besides, Ann doesn't really think I'm sexy enough. We are having a little party, but it's mostly to celebrate my new poem and Bob's assistantship for next year. Somebody got a better offer and he just stepped into it.'

It was not the least of Beryl's bequests that Mark could lie with a quiet good humour that removed the suspicion of falsehood from the many probablys, won'ts, and reallys that marked such sentences. 'Oh, do what you want, do what you want,' his father said, knowing that he himself could act forcefully only when deeply angered. Now he was merely irritated. 'It's my own fault for raising you as I did. I'm just worried about the consequences to you two when you're older; you're playing with more than fire.' He longed to harrow them with his own painfully gained world knowledge, and yet he had to fight a constant gorge and sense of isolation which rose in him when he saw how little respect they had for his views, how they merely wanted to keep him pacified. In the middle of what he was saying, Tanya got up to go in for the dessert, and when she came back they all three noticed the minister Wrager standing expectantly in Wagwood's yard.

'I wonder what that old boy wants,' Tanya said quietly. 'Hasn't set a foot in here for three years.'

'Hullo,' said her father-in-law loudly. 'Come to save the sinners?'

The minister said no, that he just wondered if his wife could cut through their yard to see the bulldozer at work. It was a long way for her to walk around. Her ankles were weak. 'Of course,' they all said politely, and he waved to a woman who came out from behind Wagwood's house with easy embarrassment. The two of them stood and watched the bulldozer for many minutes in silence as it pushed trees across the dry earth.

'Pioneer mentality,' Mr Courtney said, almost loud enough for them to hear. 'Let it sit there for three years without even wondering if there's any beauty in it, but as soon as it's burn and clear time, something in the blood calls them over for the obsequies. Makes one hope his soul comes back to this same life time and time again.'

He turned from them and gathered his dishes. In his mind the workers remained as a long tableau of some obscure pageantry; the two immigrants gathering stray branches for the fire, the bulldozer dominant like a peasant's ox thrusting with sluggish motion ahead of its blade one slender poplar tree, roots and all, decorated with still green and tossing branches, noble, incredibly long and slow in momentum, a lance fallen to the earth, its ribbon gaying the path to the fire.

'Then the puritans cut down the maypole,' quoted his son, 'which as if to mock them yet wreathed its streamers to the high winds as carelessly as before the young maids had flounced their nine petticoats in the parson's face.' And he felt some of his resentment die in him that his son should pick an image so close to his own mood, should be watching the same things as he. They each carried their own dishes and went into the house, past the minister nodding his assent.

There Mark said something to Tanya and they both set assiduously and self-consciously to work. Mr Courtney went out to the screened porch that had been Beryl's studio and was now his study. About it were hung the disproofs of his demand for concrete quickly poured: many of Beryl's old sketches and water-colours, some of them finished by Michelin, most of them unfinished; snowshoes on the roof, smooth with new varnish, that had not been used since their Quebec winter honeymoon; pictures of them outside the Quebec lodge, with red sashes and fur caps, their eyes bright with cold and exuberance; the shotgun his father had taken during the Boer War from a South African who, supposedly, had used it to kill running negroes from his horse, and whom, supposedly, his father had frightened near to death with a similar chase; textbooks long outdated beside the new ones; papers that had been obscurely or never published. And in his mind, proof of the lie he longed to maintain, as he remembered how many times he had falsely threatened to clear all that junk out. He watched the bull-dozer operator and the two immigrants leave for the night, with the fire still throwing a constant whirl of smoke out of the bush and across his lawn. Ash swirled into the sky and seemed to settle everywhere; a fine layer was collecting on the sun roof of the Volks. Again he felt he should complain of it, this time to the reeve if necessary, but he was so worried about how he was to reason his daughter out of the mistake she was making that he told himself he had no time to let petty things goad him. Besides he knew he dare not antagonize the builders. C. His house was built right to the limit of the lot on the north side and nearly so on the south. On the north he owned not an inch of the driveway; on the south he had access only because the Wagwoods winked at the yard or so of drive which ran along their land. He had convinced himself that if he did not trouble these builders they would leave him the drive-way or at least give him an easement; there had to be some squatter's common law which would give him rights after his long usage. He went back and forth from house to study wondering about this and composing phrases of a letter to his daughter in his mind until Mark told him to quit chasing the tiger. Then he sat down in the chair and opened the books he had collected to prove his daughter's foolishness. Again the wind had gotten stronger, ash-laden, and he had to close all the windows so that he lost the breeze himself. It was hot and stuffy yet, and some smoke crept in so that he could not concentrate.

'In the year 1349,' he read, 'there occurred the greatest epidemic that ever happened. Death went from one end of the earth to the other, on that side and this side of the sea, and it was greater among the Saracens than among the Christians.' Ah, the old lie, he thought, we suffer but not as much as you. The bulldozer in the afternoon had taken more trees from the edge of the raspberry patches closest to his lawn, and he watched the few saplings which were left bend now most unnaturally in the breeze and reverse their leaves to the silvery undersides in protest, like flashes of storm. 'In some lands everyone died so that no one was left. Ships were also found on the sea laden with wares; the crews had all died and no one guided the ship. The Bishop of Marseilles and priests and monks and more than half of the people there died with them.' Listen, Michelin, he began again in his thoughts, all this isn't meant to scare you, but if you've got to join a group, why pick the one at the bottom. You've got to realize, dear, that it's not an abstract world you're going to be living in, but a real one, a nasty one. At Bigwin Inn, if you wanted to waste your money, they wouldn't even let you in the door. You've got to decide yourself, of course. If you really want to marry him, marry him. You know I wouldn't stop you any more than I would stop Mark, or try to stop him, in this stupid wife bartering he's being sucked into. But you'll have to make deals with yourself every day, do you realize that? Every day. People will be watching to see you fall, or do the cheap thing, not clapping as at your graduation. 'And from what this epidemic came, all wise teachers and physicians could only say that it was God's will. And as the plague was now here, so was it in other places, and lasted more than a whole year. This epidemic also came to Strasbourg in the summer of the above-mentioned year, and it is estimated that about sixteen thousand people died.'

He went into the kitchen to make some coffee and clear his thoughts. Except for these few medieval cases and the letter of explanation for Michelin which would precede all, he had nearly finished his summary of the major persecutions of Jews in the Christian world. In the accustomed paths of research into primary and secondary sources he had found no obstacles, his desk was littered with books and file cards, but something within him balked at the letter to his daughter. He knew how he possessed all of his nation's conviction that it wasn't nice to show prejudice, as well as much of his own age's belief that sex should be nicer, freer, happier than it obviously was, and he saw that in the same way that the latter fought as a principle against his desire to warn Mark and Tanya to desist from their experimentation, so did the former act as an anchor to the warnings he longed to cast at his daughter.

Michelin, you know for myself there's nothing but your happiness. If I were the world I would say yes with joy, but I am not. A million little daggers lie between not showing and not being; I do not want them to make you bitter. He wandered back to the desk. In the dusk the fire still shot up in brief smoke-tarnished bursts of flame before the green wood dampened them. I know, you know, this is no Strasbourg in 1349; there's going to be no platforms in the cemetery. But in this little town, which is far from the worst place in the world, there's a doctor who has studied in Vienna and everywhere, who's the best surgeon these people will ever see, who gave your mother an extra three years of life no one else could have, and yet who can operate in the county hospital only by trickery of one kind or another, who can never be on the staff. You know the kind of deals he has to make. I did not raise you altogether in a greenhouse. Is that what you want, that kind of unhappiness?

'In the matter of this plague the Jews throughout the world were reviled and accused in all lands of having caused it through the poison which they are said to have put into the water and the wells —that is what they were accused of—and for this reason the Jews were burnt all the way from the Mediterranean into Germany, but not in Avignon, for the pope protected them there.' Phrases from papal bulls in protection of the Jews came into his mind. He would have to include them too, for Michelin loved as much as he the sense of irony in all such desperate strictures: no Christian shall presume to seize, imprison, wound, torture, mutilate, kill, or inflict violence on them; no one shall disturb them in any way during the celebration of their festivals, whether by day or by night, with clubs or stones or anything else; no one shall dare to devastate or to destroy a cemetery of the Jews or to dig up human bodies for the sake of getting money. And I know what you will say, Michelin, that because people are evil is no reason to forego a right act, but let's not kid ourselves; no one's going to say what you want them to say: look at the brave, daring girl.

Along the edges of the clearing, ferns bent low, almost parallel to the earth from the unchecked force of the wind. One flower of the jack-in-the-pulpit which he had transplanted that noon, not yet fully open, snapped of its own weight when the stem would bend no further. There was no way to get down on paper all his conflicting thoughts and emotions, and he would not have this less than perfect, so he gave up in mild despair. He went back into the house for more coffee and said loudly, almost as if to an audience:

'I'm going to do something about this smoke, damn it. They've gone off and left their fire burning and with this wind we'll be lucky if the fire department saves the cellar.'

He saw that Mark and Tanya were too busy to take the bit out of his mouth, making up the list for the next party. Their general plan, performed almost as if they wanted to pretend the whole thing was unconscious, was to invite a goodly number of people and then in the heat of the party to pair off with the other couple,

Bob and Ann, in a repetition of high-schoolish embraces, as though the attraction of having a married elsewhither partner recaptured for them in some jaded manner the thrills of never having known sex. He phoned the reeve, Mr Norman Braithwaite, whose wife said that he was out at a meeting but would phone when he got back or in the morning. Was it anything important?

'Big poker-game meeting,' he said, again loudly, then the apathy which he thought had fled with the winter came over him again. He went outside to try to shake it off and walked through the dark bush, drawn towards the cleared circle and the fire. It smouldered more than burned because of the dense mass of green wood and earth-clinging roots which composed it. He realized that there was no chance of a fire spreading, and stood watching the white patterns which fresh ash formed upon the burning wood. Phrases from his reading came back to him, and he felt the deep aroma of old sadnesses whirl in his mind like laughter from the grave. He saw himself as one of the old deputies of Strasbourg deposed by the mob for his rationalism. 'The deputies of the city of Strasbourg were asked what they were going to do with the Jews. They answered and said that they knew no evil of them. Then they asked the Strasbourgers why they had closed the wells and put away the buckets, and there was a great indignation and clamour against the deputies from Strasbourg. So finally the bishop and the lords and the Imperial Cities agreed to do away with the Jews. The result was that they were burnt in many cities, and wherever they were expelled they were caught by the peasants and stabbed to death or drowned.' But he knew that even if he had that all written down in the proper context and Michelin were made to feel his own intense horror at it, she would still face it as something romantic, would see herself running swiftly through the dark streets of some medieval town fleeing to the walls, fleeing through the countryside with some improbable tale, sweetly taking confession and mass and justifying it to herself on the grounds of survival of the trickiest.

He turned toward the low, milk-weeded area where he thought the pheasants nested. It had once been a creek and then a swamp and he still, as if in the grip of old habit, raised his feet gingerly while walking through it, as though he expected quicksand or mud pools to lie ahead. What must the birds think, he wondered, seeing something like that tearing up all the world they know. He almost stepped on the hen despite his care. She flew up with a squawking flurry into a pine tree twenty yards off, outlined by the SHELL of Mr Wagwood's garage, and he heard the cock go running off at her warning, but there was no sign of the brood. He wanted to warn them to move over onto the small portion of bush which lay at the back of his land; so, as if to lead them, he walked quietly on a dark trail towards those trees, knowing that they did not follow him. When he got back home he made up the couch in the study. He was beginning to feel that the house itself belonged to Mark and Tanya.

Three days later the bush had been stripped to its limits with the single exception of a blue spruce in the northwest corner which was to be moved in time to the front of the municipal buildings. This complete debunking of Mrs Wagwood's faith in the power of the reeve's desire for shade was of little consolation to Mr Courtney. Illogically he had felt bitterly deceived as they expanded the circle day by day and finally stripped the back edges and then opened the whole front expanse to the gaze of those passing on the road. He had become quite irritable with his students and slipped into his old habit of telling them again and again: you can't just memorize the textbook for me, you've got to think; relate things; compare them to the world you live in; find parallels. The more futile he realized it was, the shriller became his tone. The pheasants had moved into his small bush at the back, which brought him some joy, but they were without their brood and often he saw them in the early mornings wandering the edges of the clearing.

On the final afternoon, as the bulldozers, two now, were clearing away the front trees and levelling the soil for the shovel-crane which had already begun excavating, the reeve, Mr Braithwaite, came over to talk about the fire which was still burning, although now the huge bulk of stumps and roots was higher than either bulldozer and twice as long.

'Must be a by-law about that somewhere, eh Newman?' Mr Courtney said as soon as they exchanged pleasantries. 'Can't have a fire that big burning three days and nights so close to the town.'

'I didn't even see it, you know,' Mr Braithwaite said, 'until they cleared away the back part down by my house. Heck, should know better though, being around here all these years.' And Mr Courtney knew that the battle was lost before joined. The reeve never found fault at the first unless he was prepared to apologize at the close.

'Or maybe he just knows them too well.'

'Well, yes. He knows we're in a bit of a transition bind right now, not knowing if the township or Metro's going to take us over. Nobody's sure about whose laws to change to. Still, it would've cost them builders a bundle if we'd made them cut down all those trees and haul them off, and this place can stand those apartments, no matter who takes us over. Of course if it's an out-and-out fire, now, we'd have a truck down here in no time. And charge them for it too.'

'There's no fire anyhow, I should have phoned you back. Just smoke: to disprove an old saying.'

'Too many regulations now anyhow, you know that. People know what's right, where the power is. Take this house, your father couldn't have even laid it out like this today without twelve inspectors cropping his neck. But who would have stopped him back then? Not enough room to spit out of your dining room window, but he didn't have to care.'

'They'll have to give us an easement there for that drive, though, that's common law. We've been using it since after the first war, since old Rackerson let his orchards go to ruin there when his son died. You know those raspberries he put in were still growing wild up till now?'

'Is that right? I didn't notice any easement in their plans, but I suppose you've got a right if anyone has. I'll talk to them about it. Guess this fire's all right, eh?'

'Sure.'

'Mrs Wagwood says you're pretty upset about the bush going.'

'If her husband could pump gas like she pumps words,' he began, and they both broke into laughter: it was one of the reeve's own jokes. 'Hell no. Like I told her, what's the sense in having a lot of things to remind you. When it's done it's done, just like us.' He knew that Newman didn't believe in anything after death, although he had to pretend he did because of his church connections.

When Mark and Tanya came home he told them of his small victory in getting the reeve to look after the easement, and was disappointed in their lack of interest. Their faces were flushed, from more than the heat of the day and the bus trip home, so that it was obvious they had been fighting. Like Tanya he hated to see a fuss made over anything, he liked things to go smoothly, so even though he was angry at them both he suggested he take them shopping for the party. He knew that this would take the tension off them somewhat, both as a mark of his lessening disapproval and because it was something they both enjoyed doing. Tanya enjoyed it because she saw each such trip as a joust with the manufacturers who tried to deceive her with bright empty boxes, with foods deprived of natural vitamins and fortified with false ones. Mark enjoyed it because he hated big stores so much that he considered it an onerous duty, a venture into the mass-cult's temple to be dared only with a quiver full of wisecracks. Mr Courtney was constantly amused by these pretensions and almost enjoyed himself as he walked through the aisles with them, watching the precision with which Tanya read weights on different packages of oatmeal, the disdain with which Mark added a bottle of gooseberry jam to the cart. As the reeve paid lip service to the church, they paid it to schoolboy ideals, the welfare of mankind, the struggle for justice, feeding the starving Incas, but whereas he existed by accepting a set of patterns which time had made obvious to him, they had not bought those yet; they lived in a sheltered estate supposedly, but a waystation towards the general ideal, although of course they knew we'd never get there. It was too far for words. And in the meantime—since it was a law of anthropology that whenever groups, even of general idealists, became too large, then smaller ones formed—they took their pleasure with their small foursome, a group which endured not only the same academic tensions but the same gentle ideals that made all appear eventually fruitful.

In a way they were in a far safer position than Michelin; they would probably never have to hear the real truths that come out of disaster because they have taken their trade, which in his father's culture would have been a great disaster, and made it the rock of their foursome society. Michelin, on the other hand, had always avoided disaster as if knowing that out of it some truth would arise to strike her. In the summers while her mother was still alive she would play in the woods with her merely to see her not alone, strike whatever antic pose she demanded, follow every whim and flight of her frustrated temper, and say, without childish duplicity, exactly the right thing about each of the never-finished watercolours which were the products of the early portions of those days. For a moment he wondered if what Michelin had avoided then she was seeking now, some deliberate disaster with its resultant scramble of malicious truths. He was glad he had the laden aisles to distract his mind.

The thought came back to him during the party, which was loud and noisy and from which he excused himself as soon as possible. He added a final portion of the Strasbourg account, not only because he delighted in the frankness with which it related economic motives, but because he thought it would help the whole thing appear less purely evil to Michelin. He knew that in a few days he would begin to wonder what the young man was like and whether she really wanted him, so for the moment he longed to keep the whole argument on this abstractly historical level. 'The council, however, took the cash that the Jews possessed and divided it among the working-men proportionately. The money was indeed the thing that killed the Jews. If they had been poor and if the feudal lords had not been in debt to them, they would not have been burned. After this wealth was divided among the artisans, some gave their share to the cathedral or to the Church on the advice of their confessors.' Then he slept.

He awoke once, thinking he heard strange noises, then saw the sun's fire beginning low in the east and crouched back to sleep. Deep in the fearful haze of early morning he was aware that he was in a dream, which, as he remembered it, took place in a large courtyard like the early exchanges, the merchants' attempts to build castles. There men dressed like burghers handed him an ornate sphere rich as a king's orb. He could not remember being afraid or hesitating to open it, but when he did so he saw that inside was a second orb, and he knew that to have opened the first he had dared the ridicule and laughter of the townsmen. A jester had given it to him, a wasted man dressed in a motley coat as though some merchant kept him around but was not kingly enough to clothe him duly nor to treat him properly. The jester made it clear that the second orb was, however, to be opened only upon the bearing of great pain, not at all mitigated by the fact that the burghers now seemed somewhat awed or afraid of him for opening the first. Physical torment coupled closely to death hung like hawks about him awaiting his move, although he woke, naturally, at the moment when he had his hand stretched forth to knock the smaller orb on the floor or to unhasp it, to unclasp its jewelled edges.

He would have returned to sleep if he had not heard noises in the kitchen and felt driven to make them cease their partying. When he went inside, however, still fearful from the dream, he saw that it was only the four of them, bustling about in great mirth, with the kitchen laden with food ready to be cooked.

'Bob and Anna spent the night,' said Tanya, 'so we're having a great lumberjack's breakfast in their honour.'

As far as he could see there was no hidden mirth in what she had said, nor did they appear any different than before except for a slight hurrying in all their actions which could well have been his imagination. They had divided responsibility for the feast: Mark was mixing and cooking pancakes; Tanya was broiling bacon and sausages in the bottom of the oven; Ann was squeezing oranges, setting the table, apparently, and keeping an eye on the pies in the oven; Bob was keeping everyone supplied with cigarettes, beers, and inspiration. He would kiss one woman and then the next, stop in front of Mark to regard him quizzically and then soberly shake hands with him. They asked Mr Courtney to do the scrambled eggs, but he said shortly that that seemed to be their business and went outside. From the wall of the study he took down the shotgun which hung between two of Beryl's most nearly finished watercolours, removed it from its case, loaded it with light shot. My father would have blasted them out of the house, he said to himself as he walked down towards the feeder. When he was about thirty yards away he fired both barrels at once into the throng of starlings and grackles which were about it. He reloaded quickly, out of old custom, before he went forward to the mass of dead birds that lay on the ground amidst the husks of many sunflower seeds. Remorse harrowed his soul and he picked up by the feet the few that were still writhing and quickly snapped them in his hand to break their necks. The futile stupidity of his need to play justice on the basis of beauty made gentle mockery of all his actions, and he kicked at the bodies with his feet. Some of the grackles were amazingly beautiful with the gloss of their blackness revealed, and against that the glow of the few green-black feathers edging their bright eyes.

He saw that it was not as early as he had thought. Mrs Wagwood was standing out on her back porch; the movers who had come for the Rev Wrager's furnishings were watching him; workers with boards in their hands for the footings stood on top of the mounds to see what he was up to; the four children in his house had come out into his study to stare at him. Fear of ridicule reminded him of what he had set out to do. He went deeper into his lot until he reached the bush, and when the hen flushed with a cry of danger, he shot evenly and quickly so that she dropped like any well-winged bird and he did not have to check on her death. Nor did he turn around to watch his audience, for he wanted nothing but to get the cock up quick and to kill it even quicker, season or no season. It could not hide because of its bright plumage, but instead of taking flight it began to run; it scurried towards the lowland where its nest had been, where the thick cover had been, running with a slightly wobbly motion like a lady in a hobbled skirt. The flood of reasons that had started Mr Courtney struck him again and drove him after the quickly moving bird: they'd have both died anyhow and there's no place for them to go now within twenty miles without crossing three eight-lane highways, and it's better not to have things around to remind you of what can't be again. The bird ran to the east and was turned by a fence, came back almost towards him, then took fright to the northwest where the men were silently watching. Mr Courtney was afraid he was heading for the spruce tree. 'Get up, damn you,' he said, his breath short. 'Get up, get up for the love of God.' He saw how ridiculous he was, paying court to this one tenet of sportsmanship after having just killed a hen and with both birds long out of season; then the pheasant hit the first of the foundation ditches which outlined the shape of the coming building and took flight into the air as if from a trap. He stood only twenty yards from it and let it escape into smooth flight while he shouldered the gun. With his cheek firm in the cool-feeling wood he pointed and fired, then went to retrieve the dead cock and then the hen. He felt the workmen were regarding him as if he were mad and yet daring in some bizarre way beyond their comprehension. He avoided all eyes. The birds felt limp and bloody in his hand, yet still beautiful. He knew that if he had awakened Beryl she would have come out into the early sunlight to stand by him and talked with delight of what a startling mock-English oil she could make of them and the ornate old shotgun, laid against the sharp contours of the huge orange-and-blue crane perhaps, for satiric contrast.

'My contribution to the breaking of the fast,' he said, conscious for the second time that morning of the senility of his wit. He hung the birds above the stainless steel sink and sat down to eat with them. None of them wanted to talk of their actions, so the conversation drifted into academic shoptalk and gossip about methods for advancement. So-and-so would give anyone a job who had done a thesis on the Huguenots in Canada, or even on the Huguenot-Catholics which was his own term to designate men like Champlain who were Huguenots by birth or at heart. You had only to believe that ten out of the first twelve governors of Quebec were Huguenot-Catholics.

It reminded him of the anecdotes about parish-hunting which had sickened Julien Sorel in the seminary at Besancon. He remembered that quick moment of clarity which came after the flurry of blindness as the bird went up at last and felt as if he had been graced with a second innocence, one that would withstand anything now. He said the conversation was too worldly for him and went out to bury the starlings and the grackles. In the hole he placed the feeder also, as though sending it on a voyage with them. Having committed these irrational acts, he allowed himself to consider that the pheasants should be buried too in honour of their almost sacrificial death, but some deep prejudice of local custom insisted that they be eaten. Dead, the cock seemed less beautiful to him, and as he plucked the long tail-feathers he was reminded only of the hats women had worn in the late '30s and which you still saw occasionally in the streets of the smaller towns.

A little after noon the reeve came around as he had expected. The pheasants were turning slowly on the outdoor grill Tanya's father had sent her in the spring. It had an electric spit which revolved like clockwork at whatever speed you desired. The reeve told Mr Courtney that he had spoken to the builders that morning about the news of a desired easement and they were very upset. They had planned to build a ramp for the underground parking there and it started to descend almost as soon as it left the street. He had assured them that Mr Courtney was not the kind of man to cause any fuss or trouble with a court scene and they had been much relieved. No mention was made of the pheasants or of the illegality of shooting within the town limits except that when Mr Courtney invited the reeve for lunch, he smiled and said that duty called him elsewhere, to a lunch for the new minister. Though he himself would rather eat game than listen to prayer talk any day in the week.

The two moving vans almost met in the driveway, for as soon as one departed the other pulled in and began unloading. Mrs Wagwood was ready for the new man with fresh coffee to ease the strain of moving into a new house whenever he or his wife desired a cup. Of course in the body of the conversation she mentioned the shooting which had disturbed her early that morning. 'A terrible shame,' she said, 'an old man like that killing those two beautiful birds just for malice. Perhaps you'd better have a talk with him when you're settled.' She knew that it would accomplish nothing, but she saw it as a good chance to find out what kind of stuff the new man was made of.

'Oh, is he of our church?' asked the new minister, somewhat dismayed at finding a problem like this right next door to him on his first day.

'Oh no,' she said, 'he doesn't belong to any. That's part of the problem, no doubt. Though of course he knows all the right people in town, so he won't get into any trouble out of his mischief. The reeve was over to see him just before he went to your lunch.'

'Well then, perhaps I'd best not interfere,' he said, glad to have the excuse to beg out. 'It takes a while to get to know a town,' adding, aware that she looked disappointed in him, 'even a small one like this. Although it seems you're growing.' He felt hurt that he could not find the right thing to say to her.

'Oh, I'm sure he'll be all right now,' she said, as if to someone who wasn't old enough to hear all the details of a debilitating disease.

'Of course, but I tell you what, though,' he said, relieved now that he had caught her probable drift. 'Wouldn't you be so kind as to just keep an eye out on him for me? While I'm getting settled, I mean. Then if anything else shows up, I'll pop right on over to him.'

She smiled in agreement, and he knew that he had found the way to her heart. He hoped that the rest of his problems in the new place would be as easy to settle.

# Jack Hodgins

JACK Hodgins was born in the Comox Valley region of Vancouver Island in 1938. He attended the University of British Columbia, where he studied creative writing under Earle Birney, and since 1961 he has alternated writing and teaching English and creative writing at Nanaimo Senior Secondary School. He and his wife and three children live in Lantzville, 'where we watch the Georgia Strait disappearing behind a screen of arbutus trees gone out of control.'

Hodgins' first published short story appeared in the American *Northwest Review* in 1968, and he published widely in the U.S. and Australia before being accepted by Canadian editors. His first story collection, *Spit Delaney's Island* (1976), established one of his central themes, which he has taken from his life on Vancouver Island and his fascination with *The Tempest*: 'I guess I'm arrogant enough,' he told Jack David (*Essays on Canadian Writing* #11, 1978), 'to think that my island can become a sort of mythical island too, and maybe stand for people everywhere.' The following story, which first appeared in *The Story So Far 5* (1978), is part of Hodgins's most recent collection of stories, *The Barclay Family Theatre* (1981). It takes place not on Vancouver Island but in Ireland, a setting that is equally interesting in light of Hodgins's concern for 'the whole island mythology.' Hodgins is also the author of two novels: *The Invention of the World* (1977) and *The Resurrection of Joseph Bourne* (1979). In 1979 he was writer-in-residence at the University of Ottawa.

# THE LEPERS' SQUINT

TODAY, while Mary Brennan may be waiting for him on that tiny island high in the mountain lake called Gougane Barra, Philip Desmond is holed up in the back room of this house at Bantry Bay, trying to write his novel. A perfect stack of white paper, three black nylon-tipped pens, and a battered portable typewriter are set out before him on the wooden table. He knows the first paragraph already, has already set it down, and trusts that the rest of the story will run off the end of it like a fishing line pulled by a salmon. But it is cold, it is so cold in this house, even now in August, that he presses both hands down between his thighs to warm them up. It is so cold in this room that he finds it almost impossible to sit still, so damp that he has put on the same clothes he would wear if he were walking out along the edge of that lagoon, in the spitting rain and the wind. Through the small water-specked panes of the window he can see his children playing on the lumpy slabs of rock at the shore, beyond the bobbing branches of the fuchsia hedge. Three children; three red quilted jackets; three faces flushed up by the steady force of the cold wind; they drag tangled clots of stinking seaweed up the slope and, crouching, watch a family of swans explore the edges of a small weedy island not far out in the lagoon.

A high clear voice in his head all the while insists on singing to him of some girl so fair that the ferns uncurl to look at her. The voice of an old man in a mountain pub, singing without accompaniment, stretched and stiff as a rooster singing to the ceiling and to the crowd at the bar and to the neighbours who sit around him. *The ferns uncurled to look at her, so very fair was she, was her hair as bright as the seaweed that floats in from the sea.* But here at Ballylickey the seaweed is brown as mud and smells so strong your eyes water.

Mrs O'Sullivan is in the next room, Desmond knows, in her own room listening. If he coughs she will hear. If he sings. She will know exactly the moment he sets down his next word on that top sheet of paper. Mrs O'Sullivan is the owner of this house, which Desmond rented from home through the Borde Failte people before he discovered that she would live in it with them, in the centre of the house, in her two rooms, and silently listen to the life of his family going on around her. She is a tall dry-skinned old woman with grey finger-waves caged in blue hair net, whose thick fingers dig into the sides of her face in an agony of desire to sympathize with everything that is said to her. 'Oh I know I know I know,' she groans. Last night when Desmond's wife mentioned how tired she was after the long drive down from Dublin, her fingers plucked at her face, her dull eyes rolled up to search for help along the ceiling: 'Oh I know I know I know.' There is no end to her sympathy, there is nothing she doesn't already know. But she will be quiet as a mouse, she promised, they won't know she is here.

'Maybe she's a writer,' Desmond's wife whispered to him, later in bed. 'Maybe she's making notes on us. Maybe she's writing a book called *North Americans I Have Eaves-Dropped On.*'

'I can't live with someone listening to me breathe,' Desmond said. 'And I can't write with someone sitting waiting.'

'Adjust,' his wife said, and flicked at his nose. She who could adjust to anything, or absorb it.

On this first day of his novel Desmond has been abandoned by his wife, Carrie, who early this morning drove the car in to Cork. There are still, apparently, a few Seamus Murphy Statues she hasn't seen, or touched. 'Keep half an eye on the kids,' she said before she left. Then she came back and kissed him and whispered, 'Though if you get busy it won't matter. I'm sure Mrs O'Sullivan won't miss anything.' To be fair, to be really fair, he knows that his annoyance is unjustified. He didn't tell her he intended to work today, the first day in this house. She probably thinks that after travelling for six weeks through the country he'll rest a few more days before beginning; she may even believe that he is glad to be rid of her for the day, after all those weeks of unavoidable closeness. She certainly knows that with Mrs O'Sullivan in the house no emergency will be overlooked, no crisis ignored.

Desmond now that his hands have warmed a little lifts one of the pens to write, though silently as possible, as if what he is about to do is a secret perversion from which the ears of Mrs O'Sullivan must be protected. But he cannot, now, put down any new words. Because if the novel, which has been roaring around in his head all summer and much longer looking for a chance to get out, should not recognize in the opening words the crack through which it is to spring forth, transformed into a string of words like a whirring fish line, then he will be left with all that paper to stare at, and an unmoving pen, and he is not ready to face that. Of course he knows the story, has seen it all in his mind a hundred times as if someone else had gone to the trouble of writing it and producing it as a movie just for him. But he has never been one for plunging into things, oceans or stories, and prefers to work his way in gently. That opening paragraph, though, is only a paragraph after all and has no magic, only a few black lifeless lines at the top of the paper. So he writes it out again, beneath the first time, and again under that, and again, hoping that the pen will go on by itself to write the next words and surprise him. But it does not happen, not now. Instead, he discovers he is seeing two other words which are not at all, as if perhaps they are embedded, somehow, just beneath the surface of the paper.

Mary Brennan.

Desmond knows he must keep the name from becoming anything more than that, from becoming a face too, or the pale scent of fear. He writes his paragraph again, over and over until he has filled up three or four pages. Then, crumpling the papers in his hand, he wonders if this will be one of those stories that remain forever in their authors' heads, driving them mad, refusing to suffer conversion into words.

It's the cold, he thinks. Blame it on the bloody weather. His children outside on the rocky slope have pulled the hoods of their jackets up over their heads. Leaves torn from the beech tree lie soaked and heavy on the grass. At the far side of the lagoon the family of swans is following the choppy retreating tide out through the gap to the open bay; perhaps they know of a calmer inlet somewhere. The white stone house with red window frames in its nest of bushes across the water has blurred behind the rain, and looks more than ever like the romantic pictures he has seen on postcards. A thin line of smoke rises from the yellowish house with the gate sign *Carrigdhoun*.

But it is easier than writing, far easier, to allow the persistent daydreams in, and memory. That old rooster-stiff man, standing in the cleared-away centre of the bar in Ballyvourney to pump his song out to the ceiling, his hands clasping and unclasping at his sides as if they are responsible for squeezing those words into life. *The ferns uncurled to see her*, he sings, *so very fair was she*.

Neighbours clap rhythm, or stamp their feet. Men six-deep at the bar-counter continue to shout at each other about sheep, and the weather. With hair as bright as the seaweed that floats in from the sea.

'Tis an island of singers sure!' someone yells in Desmond's ear. 'An island of saints and paupers and bloody singers!'

But Desmond thinks of Mary Brennan's hot apple-smelling breath against his face: 'Islands do not exist until you have loved on them.' The words are a Caribbean poet's, she explains, and not her own. But the sentiment is adaptable. The ferns may not uncurl to see the dark brown beauty of her eyes, but Desmond has seen men turn at her flash of hair the reddish-brown of gleaming kelp. Turn, and smile to themselves. This day while he sits behind the wooden table, hunched over his pile of paper, he knows that she is waiting for him on a tiny hermitage island in a mountain lake not far away, beneath the branches of the crowded trees. Islands, she had told him, do not exist until you've loved on them.

Yesterday, driving south from Dublin across the Tipperary farmland, they stopped again at the Rock of Cashel so that Carrie could prowl a second time through that big roofless cathedral high up on the sudden limestone knoll and run her hands over the strange broken form of St Patrick's Cross. The kings of Munster lived there once, she told him, and later turned it over to the church. St Patrick himself came to baptize the king there, and accidentally pierced the poor man's foot with the point of his heavy staff.

'There's all of history here, huddled together,' she said, and catalogued it for him. 'A tenth-century round tower, a twelfth-century chapel, a thirteenth-century cathedral, a fourteenth-century tower, a fifteenth-century castle, and . . . ' she rolled her eyes, 'a twentieth-century tourist shop.'

But it was the cross itself that drew her. Originally a cross within a frame, it was only the central figure of a man now, with one arm of the cross and a thin upright stem that held that arm in place. Rather like a tall narrow pitcher. There was a guide this second time, and a tour, and she pouted when he insisted they stick to the crowd and hear the official truths instead of making guesses or relying on the brief explanations on the backs of postcards. She threw him a black scowl when the guide explained the superstition about the cross: that if you can touch hand to hand around it you'll never have another toothache as long as you live. Ridiculous, she muttered; she'd spent an hour the last time looking at that thing, marvelling at the beautiful piece of sculpture nature or time or perhaps vandals had accidentally made of it, running her hands over the figures on the coronation stone at its base and up the narrow stem that supported the remaining arm of the cross.

He was more curious, though, about the round swell of land which could be seen out across the flat Tipperary farms, a perfect green hill crowned with a circle of leafy trees. The guide told him that after one of the crusades a number of people returned to Ireland with a skin disease which was mistaken for leprosy and were confined to that hill, inside that circle, and forbidden to leave it. They were brought across to Mass here on Sundays, she said, before leading him back inside the cathedral to show a small gap in the stones far up one grey wall of the empty Choir. 'The poor lepers, a miserable lot altogether as you can imagine, were crowded into a little room behind that wall,' she said, 'and were forced to see and hear through that single narrow slit of a window. It's called the Lepers' Squint, for obvious reasons.'

Afterwards, when the crowd of nuns and priests and yellow-slickered tourists had broken up to walk amongst the graves and the celtic crosses or to climb the stone steps to the round tower, Desmond would like to have spoken to one of the priests, perhaps the short red-faced one, to say, 'What do you make of all this?' or 'Is it true what she told us about that fat archbishop with all his wives and children?' But he was intimidated by the black suit, that collar, and by the way the priest seemed always to be surrounded by nuns who giggled like schoolgirls at the silly jokes he told, full of words Desmond couldn't understand. He would go home without ever speaking to a single member of the one aristocracy this country still permitted itself.

But while he stood tempted in the sharp wind that howled across the high hump of rock the guide came over the grass to him. ''Tis certain that you're not American as I thought at first,' she said, 'for you speak too soft for that. Would you be from England then?'

'No,' he said. And without thinking: 'We're from Vancouver Island.'

'Yes?' she said, her eyes blank. 'And where would that be now?'

'A long way from here,' he said. 'An island, too, like this one, with its own brand of ruins.'

'There's a tiny island off our coast,' he said, 'where they used to send the lepers once, but the last of them died a few years ago. It's a bare and empty place they say now, except for the wind. There are even people who believe that ghosts inhabit it.'

But then there were people too who said he was crazy to take the children to this uneasy country. It's smaller than you think, they said. You'll hear the bombs from above the border when you get there. What if war breaks out? What if the IRA decides that foreign hostages might help their cause? What about that bomb in the Dublin department store?

Choose another country, they said. A warmer safer one. Choose an island where you can lie in the sun and be waited on by smiling blacks. Why pick Ireland?

Jealousy, he'd told them. Everyone else he knew seemed to have inherited an 'old country,' an accent, a religion, a set of customs, from parents. His family fled the potato famine in 1849 and had had five generations in which to fade out into Canadians. 'I don't know what I've inherited from them,' he said, 'but whatever it is has gone too deep to be visible.'

They'd spent the summer travelling; he would spend the fall and winter writing.

His search for family roots, however, had ended down a narrow hedged-in lane: a half-tumbled stone cabin, stony fields, a view of misty hills, and distant neighbours who turned their damp hay with a two-tined fork and knew nothing at all of the cabin's past.

'Fled the famine did they?' the old woman said. 'Twas many a man did that and was never heard from since.'

The summer was intended as a literary pilgrimage too, and much of it was a disappointment. Yeats' castle tower near Coole had been turned into a tourist trap as artificial as a wax museum, with cassette recorders to listen to as you walk through from room to room, and a souvenir shop to sell you books and postcards; Oliver Goldsmith's village was not only deserted, it had disappeared, the site of the little schoolhouse nothing more than a potato patch and the parsonage just half a vine-covered wall; the James Joyce museum only made him feel guilty that he'd never been able to finish *Ulysses*, though there'd been a little excitement that day when a group of women's libbers crashed the male nude-bathing beach just behind the tower.

A man in Dublin told him there weren't any live writers in this country. 'You'll find more of our novelists and poets in America than you'll find here,' he said. 'You're wasting your time on that.'

With a sense almost of relief, as though delivered from a responsibility (dead writers, though disappointing, do not confront you with flesh, as living writers could, or with demands), he took the news along with a handful of hot dogs to Carrie and the kids, who had got out of the car to admire a statue. Watching her eat that onion and pork sausage 'hot dog' he realized that she had become invisible to him, or nearly invisible. He hadn't even noticed until now that she'd changed her hair, that she was pinning it back; probably because of the wind. In the weeks of travel, in constant too-close confinement, she had all but disappeared, had faded out of his notice the way his own limbs must have done, oh, thirty years ago.

If someone had asked, 'What does your wife look like?' he would have forgotten to mention short. He might have said dainty but that was no longer entirely true; sitting like that she appeared to have rounded out, like a copper Oriental idol: dark and squat and yet fine, perhaps elegant. He could not have forgotten her loud, almost masculine laugh of course, but he had long ago ceased to notice the quality of her speaking voice. Carrie, his Carrie, was busy having her own separate holiday, almost untouched by his, though they wore each other like old comfortable unnoticed and unchanged clothes.

'A movie would be nice,' he said. 'If we could find a babysitter.'

But she shook her head. 'We can see movies at home. And besides, by the evenings I'm tired out from all we've done, I'd never be able to keep my eyes open.'

After Cashel, on their way to the Bantry house, they stopped a while in the city of Cork. And here, he discovered, here after all the disappointments was a dead literary hero the tourist board hadn't yet got ahold of. He forgot again that she even existed as he tracked down the settings of the stories he loved: butcher shops and smelly quays and dark crowded pubs and parks.

The first house, the little house where the famous writer was born, had been torn down by a sports club which had put a high steel fence around the property, but a neighbour took him across the road and through a building to the back balcony to show him the Good Shepherd Convent where the writer's mother had grown up, and where she returned often with the little boy to visit the nuns. 'If he were still alive,' Desmond said, 'if he still lived here, I suppose I would be scared to come, I'd be afraid to speak to him.' The little man, the neighbour, took off his glasses to shine them on a white handkerchief. 'Ah, he was a shy man himself. He was back here a few years before he died, with a big crew of American fillum people, and he was a friendly man, friendly enough. But you could see he was a shy man too, yes. Tis the shy ones sometimes that take to the book writing.'

Carrie wasn't interested in finding the second house. She had never read the man's books, she never read anything at all except art histories and museum catalogues. She said she would go to the park, where there were statues, if he'd let her off there. She said if the kids didn't get out of the car soon to run off some of their energy they would drive her crazy, or kill each other. You could hardly expect children to be interested in old dead writers they'd never heard of, she said. It was no fun for them.

He knew as well as she did that if they were not soon released from the backseat prison they would do each other damage. 'I'll go alone,' he said.

'But don't be long. We've got a good ways to do yet if we're going to make it to that house today.'

So he went in search of the second house, the house the writer had lived in for most of his childhood and youth and had mentioned in dozens of his stories. He found it high up the sloping streets on the north side of the river. Two rows of identical homes, cement-grey, faced each other across a bare sloping square of dirt, each row like a set of steps down the slope, each home just a gate in a cement waist-high wall, a door, a window. Somewhere in this square was where the barefoot grandmother had lived, and where the lady lived whose daughter refused to sleep lying down because people died that way, and where the toothless woman lived who between her sessions in the insane asylum loved animals and people with a saintly passion.

The house he was after was half-way up the left hand slope and barely distinguishable from the others, except that there was a woman in the tiny front yard, opening the gate to come out.

'There's no one home,' she said when she saw his intentions. 'They weren't expecting me this time, and presumably, they weren't expecting you either.'

'Then it *is* the right house?' Desmond said. Stupidly, he thought. Right house for what?

But she seemed to understand. 'Oh yes. It's the right house. Some day the city will get around to putting a plaque on the wall but for the time being I prefer it the way it is. My name, by the way,' she added, 'is Mary Brennan. I don't live here but I stop by often enough. The old man, you see, was one of my teachers years ago.'

She might have been an official guide, she said it all so smoothly. Almost whispering. And there was barely a trace of the musical tipped-up accent of the southern counties in her voice. Perhaps Dublin, or educated. Her name meant nothing to him at first, coming like that without warning. 'There would be little point in your going inside anyway, even if they were home,' she said. 'There's a lovely young couple living there now but they've redone the whole thing over into a perfectly charming but very modern apartment. There's nothing at all to remind you of him. I stop by for reasons I don't begin to understand, respect perhaps, or inspiration, but certainly not to find anything of him here.'

In a careless, uneven way, she was pretty. Even beautiful. She wore clothes—a yellow skirt, a sweater—as if they'd been pulled on as she'd hurried out the door. Her coat was draped over her arm, for the momentary blessing of sun. But she was tall enough to get away with the sloppiness and had brown eyes which were calm, calming. And hands that tended to behave as if they were helping deliver her words to him, stirring up the pale scent of her perfume. He would guess she was thirty, she was a little younger than he was.

'Philip Desmond,' he said.

She squinted at him, as if she had her doubts. Then she nodded, consenting. 'You're an American,' she said. 'And probably a writer. But I must warn you. I've been to your part of the world and you just can't do for it what he did for this. It isn't the same. You don't have the history, the sense that everything that happens is happening on top of layers of things which have already happened. Now I saw you drive up in a motor car and I arrived on a bus so if you're going back down to the city centre I'll thank you for a ride.'

Mary Brennan, of course. Why hadn't he known? There were two of her books in the trunk of his car. Paperbacks. Desmond felt his throat closing. Before he'd known who she was she hadn't let him say a word, and now that she seemed to be waiting to hear what he had to offer, he was speechless. His mind was a blank. All he could think of was *Mary Brennan* and wish that she'd turned out to be only a colourful eccentric old lady, something he could handle. He was comfortable with young women only until they turned out to be better than he was at something important to him. Then his throat closed. His mind pulled down the shades and hid.

All Desmond could think to say, driving down the hill towards the River Lee, was: 'A man in Dublin told me there was no literature happening in this country.' He could have bitten off his tongue. This woman *was* what was happening. A country that had someone like her needed no one else.

She would not accept that, she said, not even from a man in Dublin. And she insisted that he drive her out to the limestone castle restaurant at the mouth of the river so she could buy him a drink there and convince him Dublin was wrong. Inside the castle, though, while they watched the white ferry to Swansea slide out past their window, she discovered she would rather talk about her divorce, a messy thing which had been a strain on everyone con-cerned and had convinced her if she needed convincing that mar-riage was an absurd arrangement. She touched Desmond, twice, with one hand, for emphasis.

Oh, she was a charming woman, there was no question. She could be famous for those eyes alone, which never missed a detail in that room (a setting she would use, perhaps, in her next novel of Irish infidelity and rebellion?) and at the same time somehow returned to him often enough and long enough to keep him frozen, afraid to sneak his own glances at the items she was cataloguing for herself. 'Some day,' she said, 'they will have converted all our history into restaurants and bars like this one, just as I will have converted it all to fiction. Then what will we have?'

And when, finally, he said he must go, he really must go, the park was pretty but didn't have all that much in it for kids to do, she said, 'Listen, if you want to find out what is happening here, if you really do love that old man's work, then join us tomorrow. There'll be more than a dozen of us, some of the most exciting talent in the country, all meeting up at Gougane Barra... you know the place, the lake in the mountains where this river rises... it was a spot he loved.'

'Tomorrow,' he said. 'We'll have moved in by then, to the house we've rented for the winter.'

'There's a park there now,' she said. 'And of course the tiny hermitage island. It will begin as a picnic but who knows how it will end.' The hand, a white hand with unpainted nails, touched him again.

'Yes,' he said. 'Yes. We've been there. There's a tiny church on the island, he wrote a story about it, the burial of a priest. And it's only an hour or so from the house, I'd guess. Maybe. Maybe I will.'

'Oh you must,' she said, and leaned forward. 'You knew, of course, that they call it Deep-Valleyed Desmond in the songs.' She drew back, biting on a smile.

But when he'd driven her back to the downtown area, to wide St Patrick's Street, she discovered she was not quite ready yet to let him go. 'Walk with me,' she said, 'for just a while,' and found him a parking spot in front of the Munster Arcade where dummies dressed as monks and Vikings and celtic warriors glowered at him from behind the glass.

'This place exists,' she said, 'because he made it real for me. He and others, in their stories. I could never write about a place where I was the first, it would panic me. I couldn't be sure it really existed or if I were inventing it.'

She led him down past the statue of sober Father Matthew and the parked double-decker buses to the bridge across the Lee. A wind, coming down the river, brought a smell like an open sewer with it. He put his head down and tried to hurry across.

'If I were a North American, like you,' she said, 'I'd have to move away or become a shop girl. I couldn't write.'

He was tempted to say something about plastering over someone else's old buildings, but thought better of it. He hadn't even read her books yet, he knew them only by reputation, he had no right to comment. He stopped, instead, to lean over the stone wall and look at the river. It was like sticking his head into a septic tank. The water was dark, nearly black, and low. Along the edges rats moved over humps of dark shiny muck and half-buried cans and bottles. Holes in the stone wall dumped a steady stream of new sewage into the river. The stories, as far as he could remember, had never mentioned this. These quays were romantic places where young people met and teased each other, or church goers gathered to gossip after Mass, or old people strolled. None of them, apparently, had noses.

Wind in the row of trees. Leaves rustling. Desmond looked at her hands. The perfect slim white fingers lay motionless along her skirt, then moved suddenly up to her throat, to touch the neck of her sweater. Then the nearer one moved again, and touched his arm. Those eyes, busy recording the street, paused to look at him; she smiled. Cataloguing me too? he thought. Recording me for future reference? But she didn't know a thing about him, she listened to people, or tried to find out what they felt?

'I've moved here to work on a book,' he said.

Her gaze rested for a moment on the front of his jacket, then flickered away. 'Not about *here*,' she said. 'You're not writing about *this* place?' She looked as if she would protect it from him, if necessary, or whisk it away.

'I have my own place,' he said. 'I don't need to borrow his.'

She stopped, to buy them each an apple from an old black-shawled woman who sat up against the wall by her table of fruit. Ancient, gypsy-faced, with huge earrings hanging from those heavy lobes. Black Spanish eyes. Mary Brennan flashed a smile, counted out some silver pieces, and picked over the apples for two that were red and clear. The hands that offered change were thick and wrinkled, with crescents of black beneath the nails. They disappeared again beneath the shawl. Desmond felt a momentary twinge about biting into the apple; vague memories of parental warnings. You never know whose hands have touched it, they said, in a voice to make you shudder in horror at the possibilities and scrub at the skin of fruit until it was bruised and raw.

Mary Brennan, apparently, had not been subjected to the same warnings. She bit hugely. 'Here,' she said, at the bridge, 'here is where I'm most aware of him. All his favourite streets converge here, from up the hill. Sunday's Well, over there where his wealthy people lived. And of course Blarney Lane. If you had the time we could walk up there, I could show you. Where his first house was, and the pub he dragged his father home from.'

'I've seen it,' Desmond said, and started across the bridge. She would spoil it all for him if he let her.

But she won him again on the way back down the other side with her talk of castles and churches. Did he know, she asked, the reason there was no roof on the cathedral at Cashel? Did he know why Blackrock Castle where they'd been a half hour before was a different style altogether than most of the castles of Ireland? Did he know the origin of the word 'blarney'?

No he did not, but he knew that his wife would be furious if he didn't hurry back to the park. They passed the noise of voices haggling over second-hand clothes and old books at the Coal Market, they passed the opera house, a tiny yellow book store. She could walk, he saw, the way so many women had forgotten how to walk since high-heeled shoes went out, with long legs and long strides, with some spring in her steps as if there were pleasure in it.

'Now you'll not forget,' she said at his car, in his window. 'Tomorrow, in Deep-Valleyed Desmond where the Lee rises.' There was the scent of apple on her breath. Islands, she leaned in to say, do not exist until you've loved on them.

But today, while Mary Brennan waits on that tiny island for him, Philip Desmond is holed up in the back room of this house at Bantry Bay, trying to write his novel. His wife has taken the car to Cork. When she returns, he doesn't know what he will do. Perhaps he'll get into the car and drive up the snaking road past the crumbling O'Sullivan castle into the mountains, and throw himself into the middle of that crowd of writers as if he belongs there. Maybe he will make them think that he is important, that back home he is noticed in the way Mary Brennan is noticed here, that his work matters. And perhaps late at night, when everyone is drunk, he will lead Mary Brennan out onto the hermitage island to visit the oratory, to speak in whispers of the stories which had happened there, and to lie on the grass beneath the trees, by the quiet edge of the lake. It is not, Desmond knows, too unthinkable. At a distance.

The piece of paper in front of him is still blank. Mrs O'Sullivan will advertise the laziness of writers, who only pretend they are working when they are actually dreaming. Or sleeping. She will likely be able to tell exactly how many words he has written, though if he at the end of this day complains of how tired he is, she will undoubtedly go into her practised agony. He wonders if she too, from her window, has noticed that the tide had gone out, that the lagoon is empty of everything except brown shiny mud and seaweed, and that the nostril-burning smell of it is penetrating even to the inside of the house, even in here where the window hasn't been opened, likely, in years. He wonders, too, if she minds that the children, who have tired of their sea-edge exploring, are building a castle of pebbles and fuchsia branches in the middle of her back lawn. The youngest, Michael, dances like an Indian around it; maybe he has to go to the bathroom and can't remember where it is. While his father, who could tell him, who could take him, sits and stares at a piece of paper.

For a moment Desmond wonders how the medieval masses in the cathedral at Cashel must have appeared to the lepers crowded behind that narrow hole. Of course he has never seen a Mass of any kind himself, but still he can imagine the glimpses of fine robes, the bright colours, the voices of a choir singing those high eerie Latin songs, the voice of a chanting priest, the faces of a few worshippers. It was a lean world from behind that stone wall, through that narrow hole. Like looking through the eye of a needle. The Mass, as close as they were permitted to get to the world, would be only timidly glimpsed past other pressed straining heads. For of course, Desmond imagines himself far at the back of the crowd.

('Yes?' the guide said. 'And where would that be now?'

'A long way from here,' he said. 'An island, too, like this one, with its own brand of ruins. You've never heard of it though it's nearly the size of Ireland?'

'I have, yes. And it's a long way you've come from home.'

'There's a tiny island just off our coast where they used to send the lepers, but the last of them died there a few years ago. It's a bare and empty place they say now, except for the wind. There are even people who believe that ghosts inhabit it.')

What does the world look like to a leper, squinting through that narrow hole? What does it feel like to be confined to the interior of a circle of trees, at the top of a hill, from which everything else can be seen but not approached? Desmond likes to think that he would prefer the life of that famous fat archbishop, celebrating Mass in the cathedral and thinking of his hundred children.

Somewhere in the house a telephone rings. Desmond hasn't been here long enough to notice where the telephone is, whether it is in her part of the house or theirs. But he hears, beyond the wall, the sudden rustling of clothes, the snap of bones, the sound of feet walking across the carpet. Why should Mrs O'Sullivan have a phone? There are so few telephones in this country that they are all listed in the one book. But her footsteps return, and he hears behind him the turning of his door handle, the squeal of a hinge. Then her voice whispering: 'Mr Desmond? Is it a bad time to interrupt?'

'Is it my wife?'

No it is not. And of course Desmond knows who it is. Before he

left the castle-restaurant she asked for his address, for Mrs O'Sullivan's name, for the name of this village.

'I'm sorry, Mrs O'Sullivan,' he said. 'Tell her, tell them I'm
working, they'll understand. Tell them I don't want to be disturbed, not just now anyway.'

He doesn't turn to see how high her eyebrows lift. He can
imagine. Working, she's thinking. If that's working. But when she
has closed the door something in him relaxes a little—or at least
suspends its tension for a while—and he writes the paragraph again
at the top of the page and then after it adds word after word
coming slowly until he discovers he has completed a second. It is
not very good; he decides when he reads it over that it is not very
good at all, but at least it is something. A beginning. Perhaps the
dam has been broken.

But there is a commotion, suddenly, in the front yard. A car horn
beeping. The children run up the slope past the house. He can hear
Carrie's voice calling them. There is a flurry of excited voices and
then one of the children is at the door, calling, 'Daddy, Daddy,
come and see what Mommy has!'

What Mommy has, he discovers soon enough, is something that
seems to be taking up the whole back seat, a grey lumpy bulk. And
she, standing at the open door, is beaming at him. 'Come help me
get this thing out!' she says. There is colour in her face, excitement.
She has made another one of her finds.

It is, naturally, a piece of sculpture. There is no way Desmond
can tell what it is supposed to be and he has given up trying to
understand such things long ago. He pulls the figure out, staggers
across to the front door and puts it down in the hall.

'I met the artist who did it,' she says. 'He was in the little shop
delivering something. We talked, it seemed, for hours. This is
inspired by the St Patrick's Cross, he told me, but he abstracted it
even more to represent the way art has taken the place of religion
in the modern world.'

'Whatever it represents,' Desmond says, 'we'll never get it
home.'

Nothing, to Carrie, is a problem. 'We'll enjoy it here, in this
house. Then before we leave we'll crate it up and ship it home.'
She walks around the sculpture, delighted with it, delighted with
herself.

'I could have talked to him for hours,' she says, 'we got along beautifully. But I remembered you asked me to have the car home early.' She kisses him, pushes a finger on his nose. 'See how obedient I am?'

'I said that?'

'Yes,' she says. 'Right after breakfast. Some other place you said you wanted to go prowling around in by yourself. I rushed home down all that long winding bloody road for you. On the wrong side, I'll never get used to it. Watching for radar traps, for heaven's sake. Do you think the gardai have radar traps here?'

But Desmond is watching Mrs O'Sullivan, who has come out into the hall to stare at the piece of sculpture. Why does he have this urge to show her his two paragraphs? Desmond doesn't even show Carrie anything until it is finished. Why, he wonders, should he feel just because she sits there listening though the wall that she's also waiting for him to produce something? She probably doesn't even read. Still, he wants to say, 'Look. Read this, Isn't it good? And I wrote it in your house, only today.'

Mrs O'Sullivan's hand is knotting at her throat. The sculpture has drawn a frown, a heavy sulk. ''Tis a queer lot of objects they've been making for the tourists, and none of them what you could put a name to.'

'But oh,' Carrie says, 'he must be nearly the best in the country! Surely. And this is no tourist souvenir. I got it from an art shop in Cork.'

Mrs O'Sullivan's hand opens and closes, creeps closer to her mouth. 'Oh,' she says. 'Cork.' As if a lot has been explained. 'You can expect anything at all from a city. Anything at all. There was people here staying in this house, twas last year yes, came back from Cork as pleased as the Pope with an old box of turf they had bought. They wanted to smell it burning in my fire if you don't mind. What you spend your money on is your own business I told them, but I left the bogs behind years ago thank you and heat my house with electricity. Keep the turf in your car so.'

Carrie is plainly insulted. Words struggle at her lips. But she dismisses them, apparently, and chooses diversion. 'I'll make a pot of tea. Would you like a cup with us, Mrs O'Sullivan? The long drive's made me thirsty.'

And Mrs O'Sullivan, whose role is apparently varied and will shift for any occasion, lets her fingers pluck at her face. 'Oh I know I know I know!' Her long brown-stockinged legs move slowly across the patterned carpet. 'And Mr Desmond, too, after his work.

I was tempted to take him a cup but he shouldn't be disturbed I know.'

'Work?' Carrie says. 'Working at what?'

'I started the novel,' Desmond says.

'You have? Then that's something we should celebrate. Before you go off wherever it is you think you're going.'

'It's only a page,' Desmond says. 'And it's not very good at all, but it's a start. It's better than the blank paper.'

Like some children, he thinks, he's learned to make a virtue out of anything. Even a page of scribble. When he'd be glad to give a thousand pages of scribble for the gift of honesty. Or change. Or even blindness of a sort. What good is vision after all if it refuses to ignore the dark?

Because hasn't he heard, somewhere, that artists—painters—deliberately create frames for themselves to look through, to sharpen their vision by cutting off all the details which have no importance to their work?

He follows the women into the kitchen, where cups already clatter onto saucers. 'Maybe after tea,' he says, 'I'll get a bit more done.'

Pretending, perhaps, that the rest of the world sits waiting, like Mrs O'Sullivan, for the words he will produce. Because his tongue, his voice, has made the decision for him. Desmond knows that he may only sit in front of that paper for the rest of that day, that he may only play with his pen—frustrated—until enough time has gone by to justify his coming out of the room. To read one of the books he's bought. To talk with Carrie about her shopping in Cork, about her sculptor. To play with the children perhaps, or take them for a walk along the road to look for donkeys, for ruins. Desmond knows that the evening may be passed in front of the television set, where they will see American movies with Irish commercials, and will later try to guess what *an naught* is telling them about the day's events, and that he will try very hard not to think of Mary Brennan or of the dozen Irish writers at Gougane Barra or of the tiny hermitage island which the famous writer loved. Deep-Valleyed Desmond. He knows that he could be there with them, through this day and this night, celebrating something he'd come here to find; but he acknowledges, too, the other. That words, too, were invented perhaps to do the things that stones can do. And he has come here, after all, to build his walls.

# Margaret Atwood

MARGARET Eleanor Atwood was born in Ottawa in 1939. She graduated from Victoria College, University of Toronto, in 1961, and
received her M.A. from Radcliffe College, Harvard, in 1962. She
has taught at the University of British Columbia, Sir George Williams University, York University, and the University of Alberta
(where she wrote the following story and worked on her Ph.D.
thesis on Rider Haggard). She was writer-in-residence at the University of Toronto in 1972–73, and now lives on a farm near
Alliston, Ontario.

Atwood's first book of poems, *Double Persephone*, won the E. J.
Pratt Medal in 1961, and she has since published, among others,
*The Circle Game* (1966), which won the Governor-General's award
for poetry, *The Animals in That Country* (1968), *The Journals of
Susanna Moodie* (1970), and *You Are Happy* (1974). She is perhaps
best known now for her fiction: *The Edible Woman* (1969), *Surfac-
ing* (1972), *Lady Oracle* (1976), and *Life Before Man* (1979). 'Polarities' first appeared in *The Tamarack Review* #58 (1971), and is
included in her short story collection *Dancing Girls* (1977). Atwood
is also the author of a book of criticism, *Survival: A Thematic
Guide to Canadian Literature* (1972).

The thematic thread that runs through Atwood's best work begins with the title poem in *The Circle Game* and continues in *The
Journals of Susanna Moodie*, 'which explores the tensions between
line and curve,' as she wrote in *Survival*. 'I tend to be on the side
of the curve, and I haven't decided whether that stance is Position
Two defeatism (don't build a fence because it will fall down anyway) or Position Four acceptance of life-as-process (don't build a
fence because you'll be keeping out things you should be letting
in).' Louise, in 'Polarities,' builds fences around herself, but as Morrison, her American friend, observes, 'the point of the circle, closed
and self-sufficient, was not what it included but what it shut out,'
and Louise ends up in a mental institution. This takes us back to
*The Journals of Susanna Moodie*, where Atwood notes in her After-
word that 'if the national mental illness of the United States is
megalomania, that of Canada is paranoid schizophrenia.'

# POLARITIES

*Gentle and just pleasure*
*It is, being human, to have won from space*
*This unchill, habitable interior....*
—MARGARET AVISON, 'New Year's Poem'

HE HADN'T seen her around for a week, which was unusual: he asked her if she'd been sick.

'No,' she said, 'working.' She always spoke of what she had been doing with organizational, almost military briskness. She had a little packsack in which she carried around her books and note-books. To Morrison, whose mind shambled from one thing to an-other, picking up, fingering, setting down, she was a small model of the kind of efficiency he ought to be displaying more of. Perhaps that was why he had never wanted to touch her: he liked women who were not necessarily more stupid but lazier than himself. Sloth aroused him: a girl's unwashed dishes were an invitation to laxity and indulgence.

She marched beside him along the corridor and down the stairs, her short clipped steps syncopating with his own lank strides. As they descended, the smell of straw, droppings and formaldehyde grew stronger: a colony of overflow experimental mice from the science building lived in the cellar. When he saw that she was leaving the building too and probably going home, he offered her a lift.

'Only if you're heading that way anyway.' Louise didn't accept favours, she had made that clear from the start. When he'd asked her if she wanted to take in a film with him she said, 'Only if you let me pay for my own ticket.' If she had been taller he might have found this threatening.

It was colder, the weak red sun almost down, the snow purpling and creaky. She jumped up and down beside the car till he got the plug-in engine heater untangled and the door opened, her head coming out of the enormous second-hand fur coat she wore like a gopher's out of its burrow. He had seen a lot of gophers on the drive across, many of them dead; one he had killed himself, an accident, it had dived practically under the car wheels. The car itself hadn't held up either: by the time he'd made it to the outskirts—though later he realized that this was in fact the city—a fender had come off and the ignition was failing. He'd had to junk

397

it, and had decided stoically to do without a car until he found he couldn't.

He swung the car onto the driveway that led from the university. It bumped as though crossing a metal-plated bridge: the tires were angular from the cold, the motor sluggish. He should take the car for long drives more often; it was getting stale. Louise was talking more than she normally did; she was excited about something. Two of her students had been giving her a hassle, but she told them they didn't have to come to class. 'It's your heads, not mine.' She knew she had won, they would shape up, they would contribute. Morrison was not up on the theories of group dynamics. He liked the old way: you taught the subject and forgot about them as people. It disconcerted him when they slouched into his office and mumbled at him, fidgeting and self-conscious, about their fathers or their love lives. He didn't tell them about his father or his love life and he wished they would observe the same reticence, though they seemed to think they had to do it in order to get extensions on their term papers. At the beginning of the year one of his students had wanted the class to sit in a circle but luckily the rest of them preferred straight lines.

'It's right here,' she said; he had been driving past it. He crunched the car to a halt, fender against the rockbank, snowbank. Here they did not take the snow away; they spread sand on it, layer by layer as it fell, confident there would be no thaw.

'It's finished; you can come in and see it,' she said, suggesting but really demanding.

'What's finished?' he asked. He hadn't been paying attention.

'I told you. My place, my apartment, that's what I've been working on.'

The house was one of the featureless two-storey boxes thrown up by the streetful in the years after the war when there was a housing boom and materials were scarce. It was stuccoed with a greyish gravel Morrison found spiritually depleting. There were a few older houses, but they were quickly being torn down by developers; soon the city would have no visible past at all. Everything else was highrises, or worse, low barrack-shaped multiple housing units, cheaply tacked together. Sometimes the rows of flimsy buildings—snow on their roofs, rootless white faces peering suspiciously out through their windows, kids' toys scattered like trash on the walks—reminded him of old photographs he had seen of mining camps. They were the houses of people who did not expect to be living in them for long.

Her apartment was in the basement. As they went around to the back and down the stairs, avoiding on the landing a newspaper spread with the overshoes and boots of the family living upstairs, Morrison remembered vividly and with a recurrence of panic his own search for a place, a roof, a container, his trudges from address to address, his tours of clammy, bin-like cellars hastily done up by the owners in vinyl tile and sheets of cheap panelling to take advantage of the student inflow and the housing squeeze. He'd known he would never survive a winter buried like that or closed in one of the glass-sided cardboard-carton apartment buildings. Were there no real ones, mellowed, interesting, possible? Finally he had come upon an available second storey; the house was pink gravel instead of grey, the filth was daunting and the landlady querulous, but he had taken it immediately just to be able to open a window and look out.

He had not known what to expect of Louise's room. He had never visualized her as living anywhere, even though he had collected her and dropped her off outside the house a number of times.

'I finished the bookshelves yesterday,' she said, waving at a wall-length structure of varnished boards and cement blocks. 'Sit down, I'll make you some cocoa.' She went into the kitchen, still with her fur coat on, and Morrison sat down in the leatherette swivel armchair. He swivelled, surveying, comparing it with the kind of interior he thought of himself as inhabiting but never got around to assembling.

She had obviously put a lot of energy into it, but the result was less like a room than like several rooms, pieces of which had been cut out and pasted onto one another. He could not decide what created this effect: it was the same unity in diversity he had found in the motels on the way across, the modernish furniture, the conventional framed northern landscapes on the walls. But her table was ersatz Victorian and the prints Picasso. The bed was concealed behind a partly drawn dyed burlap curtain at the end of the room, but visible on the bedside rug were two light blue fuzzy slippers that startled, almost shocked him: they were so unlike her.

Louise brought the cocoa and sat down opposite him on the

floor. They talked as usual about the city: they were both still looking for things to do, a quest based on their shared eastern assumption that cities ought to be entertaining. It was this rather than mutual attraction which led them to spend as much time together as they did; most of the others were married or had been here too long and had given up.

The films changed slowly; the one theatre, with its outdated popular comedies, they had sneered at. They had gone to the opera together when it had come, though: local chorus and imported stars—*Lucia*, it had been, and really quite well done, considering. At intermission Morrison had glanced around at the silent, chunky audience in the lobby, some of the women still in early '60s pointed-toe spike heels, and murmured to Louise that it was like tourist brochures from Russia.

One Sunday before the snow came they had gone for an impromptu drive; at her suggestion they had aimed for the zoo twenty miles from the city. After they made it through the oil derricks there had been trees; not the right kind of trees—he had felt, as he had on the way across, that the land was keeping itself apart from him, not letting him in, there had to be more to it than this repetitive, non-committal drabness—but still trees; and the zoo once they reached it was spacious, the animals kept in enclosures large enough for them to run in and even hide in if they wanted to.

Louise had been there before—how, since she had no car, he didn't ask—and showed him around. 'They choose animals that can survive the winter.' she said. 'It's open all year. They don't even know they're in a zoo.' She pointed out the artificial mountain made of cement blocks for the mountain goats to climb on. Morrison didn't as a rule like any animal bigger and wilder than a cat, but these kept far enough away to be tolerable. That day she had told him a little about herself, a departure: mostly she talked about her work. She had travelled in Europe, she told him, and had spent a year studying in England.

'What are you doing here?' he had asked.

She shrugged. 'They gave me money; nobody else would.'

Essentially it was his reason too. It wasn't the draft; he was really over-age, though here they kept wanting to think he was a dodger, it made his presence more acceptable to them. The job market had been tight back in the States and also, when he tried later, in what they called here the East. But in all fairness it hadn't been only the money or the dismalness of the situation back home.

He had wanted something else, some adventure; he felt he might learn something new. He had thought the city would be near the mountains. But except for the raw gully through which the brownish river curved, it was flat.

'I don't want you to think of it as typical,' Louise was saying. 'You ought to see Montreal.'

'Are *you* typical?' he asked.

She laughed. 'None of us is typical, or do we all look alike to you? I'm not typical, I'm all-inclusive.'

She let her fur coat fall down from around her shoulders as she said this, and he wondered again whether he was expected to make a move, to approach her. He ought to approach someone or something; he was beginning to feel isolated inside his clothes and skin. His students were out of the question. Besides, they were so thick, so impermeable; the girls, even the more slender ones, made him think of slabs of substance white and congealed, like lard. And the other single women on staff were much older than he was: in them Louise's briskness had degenerated into a pinpointing, impaling quality.

There must be a place where he could meet someone, some nice loosely structured girl with ungroomed, seedy breasts, more thing than idea, slovenly and gratuitous. They existed, he was familiar with them from what he had begun to think of as his previous life, but he had not kept in touch with any of them. They had all been good at first but even the sloppiest had in time come to require something from him he thought he was not yet ready to give: they wanted him to be in love with them, an exertion of the mind too strenuous for him to undertake. His mind, he felt, was needed for other things, though he wasn't quite sure what they were. He was tasting, exploring: goals would come later.

Louise wasn't at all like them; she would never lend him her body for nothing, even temporarily, though she had the fur spread out around her now like a rug and had raised one corduroy-trousered knee, letting him see in profile the taut bulge of her somewhat muscular thigh. She probably went skiing and ice skating. He imagined his long body locked in that athletic, chilly grip, his eyes darkened by fur. Not yet, he thought, raising his half-full cocoa cup between them. I can do without, I don't need it yet.

It was the weekend and Morrison was painting his apartment as he habitually did on weekends; he had been at it off and on since he moved in.

'You'll have to have it painted, of course,' he'd said smoothly to the landlady when inspecting it, but he had already shown himself too eager and she'd outfoxed him. 'Well, I don't know, there's another boy wants it says he'll paint it himself. . . . ' So of course Morrison had to say he would too. This was the third coat.

Morrison's vision of wall-painting had been drawn from the paint ads—spot-free housewives gliding it on, one-handed and smiling—but it wasn't easy. The paint got on the floor, on the furniture, in his hair. Before he could even begin he had had to cart out the accumulated discards of several generations of previous tenants: baby clothes, old snapshots, an inner tube, heaps of empty liquor bottles, and (intriguingly) a silk parachute. Messiness interested him only in women; he could not live surrounded by it himself.

One wall of the livingroom had been pink, one green, one orange and one black. He was painting them white. The last tenants, a group of Nigerian students, had left weird magic-looking murals on the walls: a sort of swamp, in black on the orange wall, and an upright shape, in pink on the green wall, was either a very poorly done Christ Child or—could it be?—an erect penis with a halo around it. Morrison painted these two walls first, but it made him uneasy to know the pictures were still there underneath the paint. Sometimes as he rollered his way around the room he wondered what the Nigerians had thought the first time it hit forty below.

The landlady seemed to prefer foreign students, probably because they were afraid to complain: she had been aggrieved when Morrison had demanded a real lock for his door. The cellar was a warren of cubbyholes; he was not sure yet exactly who lived in them. Soon after he had moved in a Korean had appeared at his door, hopefully smiling. He wanted to talk about income tax.

'I'm sorry,' Morrison had said, 'some other time, okay? I have a lot of work to do.' He was nice enough, but Morrison didn't want to get involved with someone he didn't know; and he did have work to do. He felt picayune about it later when he discovered the Korean had a wife and child down in his cubbyhole with him; often in the fall they had put fishes out to dry, stringing them on the clotheslines where they twirled in the wind like plastic gas-station decorations.

He was doing the ceiling, craning his neck, with the latex oozing down the handle of the roller onto his arm, when the buzzer went. He almost hoped it was the Korean, he seldom saw anyone on the weekends. But it was Louise.

'Hi,' he said, surprised.

'I just thought I'd drop in,' she said. 'I don't use the phone any more.'

'I'm painting,' he said, partly as an excuse: he wasn't sure he wanted her in the house. What would she demand from him?

'Can I help?' she asked, as though it was a big treat.

'Actually I was about to stop for the day,' he lied. He knew she would be better at it than he was.

He made tea in the kitchen and she sat at the table and watched him.

'I came to talk about Blake,' she said. 'I have to do a paper.' Unlike him she was only a Graduate Assistant, she was taking a course.

'What aspect?' Morrison asked, not interested. Blake wasn't his field. He didn't mind the earlier lyrics but the prophecies bored him and the extravagant letters in which Blake called his friends angels of light and vilified his enemies he found in bad taste.

'We each have to analyze one poem in *Songs of Experience*. I'm supposed to do the "Nurse's Song." But they don't know what's going on in that course, he doesn't know what's going on. I've been trying to get through to them but they're all doing the one-up thing, they don't know what's happening. They sit there and pull each other's papers apart, I mean, they don't know what poetry's supposed to be *for*.' She wasn't drinking her tea.

'When's it due?' he asked, keeping on neutral ground.

'Next week. But I'm not going to do it, not the way *they* want. I'm giving them one of my own poems. That says it all. I mean, if they have to read one right there in the class they'll get what Blake was trying to do with *cadences*. I'm getting it xeroxed.' She hesitated, less sure of herself. 'Do you think that'll be all right?'

Morrison wondered what he would do if one of his own students tried such a ploy. He hadn't thought of Louise as the poetry-writing type. 'Have you checked with the professor about it?'

'I try to talk to him,' she said. 'I try to *help* him but I can't get *through* to him. If they don't get what I mean though I'll know they're all phonies and I can just walk out.' She was twisting her cup on the table top, her lips were trembling.

Morrison felt his loyalties were being divided; also he didn't want her to cry, that would involve dangerous comforting pats, even an arm around her shoulder. He tried to shut out an involuntary quick image of himself on top of her in the middle of the kitchen floor, getting white latex all over her fur. *Not today*, his mind commanded, pleaded.

As if in answer the reverberations of an organ boomed from beneath their feet, accompanied by a high quavering voice: *Rock of a-ges, cleft for me . . . Let me HIIIDE myself. . . .* Louise took it as a signal. 'I have to go,' she said. She got up and went out as abruptly as she had come, thanking him perfunctorily for the tea she hadn't drunk.

The organ was a Hammond, owned by the woman downstairs, a native. When her husband and nubile child were home she shouted at them. The rest of the time she ran the vacuum cleaner or picked out hymn tunes and old favourites on the organ with two fingers, singing to herself. The organ was to Morrison the most annoying. At first he tried to ignore it; then he put on opera records, attempting to drown it out. Finally he recorded it with his tape recorder. When the noise got too aggravating he would aim the speakers down the hot air register and run the tape through as loudly as possible. It gave him a sense of participation, of control.

He did this now, admiring the way the tape clashed with what she was currently playing: 'Whispering Hope' with an overlay of 'Annie Laurie'; 'The Last Rose of Summer' counterpointing 'Come to the Church in the Wildwood.' He was surprised at how much he was able to hate her: he had only seen her once, looking balefully out at him from between her hideous flowered drapes as he wallowed through the snow on his way to the garage. Her husband was supposed to keep the walk shovelled but didn't.

Louise came back the next day before Morrison was up. He was awake but he could tell by the chill in the room—his breath was visible—and by the faint smell of oil that something had gone wrong with the furnace again. It was less trouble to stay in bed, at least till the sun was well risen, than to get up and try the various ways of keeping warm.

When the buzzer went he pulled a blanket around himself and stumbled to the door.

'I thought of something,' Louise said tragically. She was in the door before he could fend her off.

'I'm afraid it's cold in here,' he said.

'I had to come over and tell you. I don't use the phone any more. You should have yours taken out.'

She stomped the snow from her boots while Morrison retreated into the livingroom. There was a thick crust of frost on the insides of the windows; he lit the gas fireplace. Louise stalked impatiently around the uncarpeted floor.

'You aren't listening,' she said. He looked out obediently at her from his blanket. 'What I thought of is this: *The city has no right to be here.* I mean, why is it? No city should be here, this far north: it isn't even on a lake or an important river, even. Why is it here?' She clasped her hands, gazing at him as though everything depended on his answer.

Morrison, standing on one bare foot, reflected that he had often since his arrival asked himself the same question. 'It started as a trading post,' he said, shivering.

'But it doesn't *look* like one. It doesn't look like anything, it doesn't *have* anything, it could be anywhere. Why is it *here?*' She implored; she even clutched a corner of his blanket.

Morrison shied away. 'Look,' he said, 'do you mind if I get some clothes on?'

'Which room are they in?' she asked suspiciously.

'The bedroom,' he said.

'That's all right. That room's all right,' she said.

Contrary to his fear she made no attempt to follow him in. When he was dressed he returned to find her sitting on the floor with a piece of paper. 'We have to complete the circle,' she said. 'We need the others.'

'What others?' He decided she was overtired, she had been working too hard: she had deep red blotches around her eyes and the rest of her face was pale green.

'I'll draw you a diagram of it,' she said. But instead she sat on the floor, jabbing at the paper with the pencil point. 'I wanted to work out my own system,' she said plaintively, 'but they wouldn't let me.' A tear slid down her cheek.

'Maybe you need to talk to someone,' Morrison said, over-casually.

She raised her head. 'But I'm talking to you. Oh,' she said, reverting to her office voice, 'you mean a shrink. I saw one earlier. He said I was very sane and a genius. He took a reading of my head: he said the patterns in my brain are the same as Julius Caesar's, only his were military and mine are creative.' She started jabbing with the pencil again.

'I'll make you a peanut butter sandwich,' Morrison said, offering the only thing he himself wanted right then. It did not occur to him until months later when he was remembering it to ask himself how anyone could have known about the patterns in Julius Caesar's brain. At the moment he was wondering whether Louise might not in fact be a genius. He felt helpless because of his own inability to respond; she would think him as obtuse as the others, whoever they were.

At first she did not want him to go into the kitchen: she knew the telephone was in there. But he promised not to use it. When he came out again with a piece of bread on which he had spread with difficulty the gelid peanut butter, she was curled inside her coat in front of the fire, sleeping. He laid the bread gently beside her as if leaving crumbs on a stump for unseen animals. Then he changed his mind, retrieved it, took it on tiptoe into the kitchen and ate it himself. He turned on the oven, opened the oven door, wrapped himself in a blanket from the bedroom and read Marvell.

She slept for nearly three hours; he didn't hear her get up. She appeared in the kitchen doorway, looking much better, though a greyish-green pallor still lingered around her mouth and eyes.

'That was just what I needed,' she said in her old brisk voice. 'Now I must be off; I have lots of work to do.' Morrison took his feet off the stove and saw her to the door.

'Don't fall,' he called after her cheerfully as she went down the steep wooden steps, her feet hidden under the rim of her coat. The steps were icy, he didn't keep them cleared properly. His landlady was afraid someone would slip on them and sue her.

At the bottom Louise turned and waved at him. The air was thickening with ice fog, frozen water particles held in suspension; if you ran a horse in it, they'd told him, the ice pierced its lungs and it bled to death. But they hadn't told him that till after he'd trotted to the university in it one morning when the car wouldn't start and complained aloud in the coffee room about the sharp pains in his chest.

He watched her out of sight around the corner of the house. Then he went back to the livingroom with a sense of recapturing lost territory. Her pencil and the paper she had used, covered with dots and slashing marks, an undeciphered code, were still by the fireplace. He started to crumple the paper up, but instead folded it carefully and put it on the mantelpiece where he kept his unanswered letters. After that he paced the apartment, conscious of his own work awaiting him but feeling as though he had nothing to do.

Half an hour later she was back again; he discovered he had been expecting her. Her face was mournful, all its lines led downwards as though tiny hands were pulling at the jawline skin.

'Oh, you have to come out,' she said, pleading. 'You have to come out, there's too much fog.'

'Why don't you come in?' Morrison said. That would be easier to handle. Maybe she'd been into something, if that was all it was he could wait it out. He'd been cautious himself; it was a small place and the local pusher was likely to be one of your own students; also he had no desire to reduce his mind to oatmeal mush.

'No,' she said, 'I can't go through this door any more. It's wrong. You have to come out.' Her face became crafty, as though she was planning. 'It will do you good to get out for a walk,' she said reasonably.

She was right, he didn't get enough exercise. He pulled on his heavy boots and went to find his coat.

As they creaked and slid along the street Louise was pleased with herself, triumphant; she walked slightly ahead of him as if determined to keep the lead. The ice fog surrounded them, deadened their voices, it was crystallizing like a growth of spruce needles on the telephone wires and the branches of the few trees which he could not help thinking of as stunted, though to the natives, he supposed, they must represent the normal size for trees. He took care not to breathe too deeply. A flock of grosbeaks whirred and shrilled up ahead, picking the last few red berries from a mountain ash.

'I'm glad it isn't sunny,' Louise said. 'The sun was burning out the cells in my brain, but I feel a lot better now.'

Morrison glanced at the sky. The sun was up there somewhere, marked by a pale spot in the otherwise evenly spread grey. He checked an impulse to shield his eyes and thereby protect his brain cells: he realized it was an attempt to suppress the undesired knowledge that Louise was disturbed or, out with it, she was crazy.

'Living here isn't so bad,' Louise said, skipping girlishly on the hard-packed snow. 'You just have to have inner resources. I'm glad I have them; I think I have more than you, Morrison. I have more than most people. That's what I said to myself when I moved here.'

'Where are we going?' Morrison asked when they had accomplished several blocks. She had taken him west, along a street he was not familiar with, or was it the fog?

'To find the others, of course,' she said, glancing back at him contemptuously. 'We have to complete the circle.'

Morrison followed without protest; he was relieved there would soon be others.

She stopped in front of a medium-tall highrise. 'They're inside,' she said. Morrison went towards the front door, but she tugged at his arm.

'You can't go in that door,' she said. 'It's facing the wrong way. It's the wrong door.'

'What's the matter with it?' Morrison asked. It might be the wrong door (and the longer he looked at it, plate glass and shining evilly, the more he saw what she meant), but it was the only one.

'It faces east,' she said. 'Don't you know? The city is polarized north and south; the river splits it in two; the poles are the gas plant and the power plant. Haven't you ever noticed the bridge joins them together? That's how the current gets across. We have to keep the poles in our brains lined up with the poles of the city, that's what Blake's poetry is all about. You can't break the current.'

'Then how do we get in?' he said. She sat down in the snow; he was afraid again she was going to cry.

'Listen,' he said hastily, 'I'll go in the door sideways and bring them out; that way I won't break the current. You won't have to go through the door at all. Who are they?' he asked as an afterthought.

When he recognized the name he was elated: she wasn't insane after all, the people were real, she had a purpose and a plan. This was probably just an elaborate way of arranging to see her friends.

They were the Jamiesons. Dave was one of those with whom Morrison had exchanged pleasantries in the hallways but nothing further. His wife had a recent baby. Morrison found them in their Saturday shirts and jeans. He tried to explain what he wanted,

which was difficult because he wasn't sure. Finally he said he
needed help. Only Dave could come, the wife had to stay behind
with the baby.

'I hardly know Louise, you know,' Dave volunteered in the
elevator.

'Neither do I,' said Morrison.

Louise was waiting behind a short fir tree on the front lawn. She
came out when she saw them. 'Where's the baby?' she said. 'We
need the baby to complete the circle. We *need* the baby. Don't
you know the country will split apart without it?' She stamped her
foot at them angrily.

'We can come back for it,' Morrison said, which pacified her.
She said there were only two others they had to collect; she
explained that they needed people from both sides of the river.
Dave Jamieson suggested they take his car, but Louise was now off
cars: they were as bad as telephones, they had no fixed directions.
She wanted to walk. At last they persuaded her onto the bus,
pointing out that it ran north and south. She had to make certain
first that it went over the right bridge, the one near the gas plant.

The other couple Louise had named lived in an apartment overlooking the river. She seemed to have picked them not because
they were special friends but because from their livingroom, which
she had been in once, both the gas plant and the power plant were
visible. The apartment door faced south; Louise entered the building with no hesitation.

Morrison was not overjoyed with Louise's choice. This couple
was foremost among the local anti-Americans: he had to endure
Paul's bitter sallies almost daily in the coffee room, while Leota at
staff parties had a way of running on in his presence about the
wicked Americans and then turning to him and saying, mouth but
not eyes gushing, 'Oh, but I forgot—*you're* an American.' He had
found the best defence was to agree. 'You Yanks are coming up and
taking all our jobs,' Paul would say, and Morrison would nod
affably. 'That's right, you shouldn't let it happen. I wonder why
you hired me?' Leota would start in about how the Americans
were buying up all the industry, and Morrison would say, 'Yes, it's
a shame. Why are you selling it to us?' He saw their point, of
course, but he wasn't Procter and Gamble. What did they want
him to do? What were they doing themselves, come to think of it?
But Paul had once broken down after too many beers in the

Faculty Club and confided that Leota had been thin when he married her but now she was fat. Morrison held the memory of that confession as a kind of hostage.

He had to admit though that on this occasion Paul was much more efficient than he himself was capable of being. Paul saw at once what it had taken Morrison hours, perhaps weeks, to see: that something was wrong with Louise. Leota decoyed her into the kitchen with a glass of milk while Paul conspired singlehandedly in the livingroom.

'She's crazy as a coot. We've got to get her to the loony bin. We'll pretend to go along with her, this circle business, and when we get her downstairs we'll grab her and stuff her into my car. How long has this been going on?'

Morrison didn't like the sound of the words 'grab' and 'stuff.' 'She won't go in cars,' he said.

'Hell,' said Paul, 'I'm not walking in this bloody weather. Besides, it's miles. We'll use force if necessary.' He thrust a quick beer at each of them, and when he judged they ought to have finished they all went into the kitchen and Paul carefully told Louise that it was time to go.

'Where?' Louise asked. She scanned their faces: she could tell they were up to something. Morrison felt guilt seeping into his eyes and turned his head away.

'To get the baby,' Paul said. 'Then we can form the circle.'

Louise looked at him strangely. 'What baby? What circle?' she said testing him.

'*You* know,' Paul said persuasively. After a moment she put down her glass of milk, still almost full, and said she was ready.

At the car she balked. 'Not in there,' she said, planting her feet. 'I'm not going in there.' When Paul gripped her arm and said, soothingly and menacingly, 'Now be a good girl,' she broke away from him and ran down the street, stumbling and sliding. Morrison didn't have the heart to run after her; already he felt like a traitor. He watched stupidly while Dave and Paul chased after her, catching her at last and half-carrying her back; they held her wriggling and kicking inside her fur coat as though it was a sack. Their breath came out in white spurts.

'Open the back door, Morrison,' Paul said, sergeant-like, giving him a scornful glance as though he was good for nothing else. Morrison obeyed and Louise was thrust in, Dave holding her more or less by the scruff of the neck and Paul picking up her feet. She did not resist as much as Morrison expected. He got in on one side of her; Dave was on the other. Leota, who had waddled down belatedly, had reached the front seat; once they were in motion she turned around and made false, cheering-up noises at Louise.

'Where are they taking me?' Louise whispered to Morrison. 'It's to the hospital, isn't it?' She was almost hopeful, perhaps she had been depending on them to do this. She snuggled close to Morrison, rubbing her thigh against his; he tried not to move away.

As they reached the outskirts she whispered to him again. 'This is silly, Morrison. They're being silly, aren't they? When we get to the next stoplight, open the door on your side and we'll jump out and run away. We'll go to my place.'

Morrison smiled wanly at her, but he was almost inclined to try it. Although he knew he couldn't do anything to help her and did not want the responsibility anyway, he also didn't want his mind burdened with whatever was going to happen to her next. He felt like someone appointed to a firing squad: it was not his choice, it was his duty, no one could blame him.

There was less ice fog now. The day was turning greyer, bluer: they were moving east, away from the sun. The mental clinic was outside the city, reached by a curving, expressionless driveway. The buildings were the same assemblage of disparate once-recent styles as those at the university: the same jarring fragmentation of space, the same dismal failure at modishness. Government institutions, Morrison thought; they were probably done by the same architect.

Louise was calm as they went to the reception entrance. Inside was a glass-fronted cubicle, decorated with rudimentary Christmas bells cut from red and green construction paper. Louise stood quietly, listening with an amused, tolerant smile, while Paul talked with the receptionist; but when a young intern appeared she said, 'I must apologize for my friends; they've been drinking and they're trying to play a practical joke on me.'

The intern frowned enquiringly. Paul blustered, relating Louise's theories of the circle and the poles. She denied everything and told the intern he should call the police; a joke was a joke but this was a misuse of public property.

Paul appealed to Morrison: he was her closest friend. 'Well,' Morrison hedged, 'she *was* acting a little strange, but maybe not enough to . . . ' His eyes trailed off to the imitation-modern interior, the corridors leading off into god knew where. Along one of the corridors a listless figure shuffled.

Louise was carrying it off so well, she was so cool, she had the intern almost convinced; but when she saw she was winning she lost her grip. Giving Paul a playful shove on the chest, she said, 'We don't need *your* kind here. *You* won't get into the circle.' She turned to the intern and said gravely, 'Now I have to go. My work is very important, you know. I'm preventing the civil war.'

After she had been registered, her few valuables taken from her and locked in the safe ('So they won't be stolen by the patients,' the receptionist said), her house keys delivered to Morrison at her request, she disappeared down one of the corridors between two interns. She was not crying, nor did she say good-bye to any of them, though she gave Morrison a dignified, freezing nod. 'I expect you to bring my notebook to me,' she said with a pronounced English accent. 'The black one, I need it. You'll find it on my desk. And I'll need some underwear. Leota can bring that.'

Morrison, shamed and remorseful, promised he would visit.

When they got back to the city they dropped Dave Jamieson off at his place; then the three of them had pizza and cokes together. Paul and Leota were friendlier than usual: they wanted to find out more. They leaned across the table, questioning, avid, prying; they were enjoying it. This, he realized, was for them the kind of entertainment the city could best afford.

Afterwards they all went to Louise's cellar to gather up for her those shreds of her life she had asked them to allow her. Leota found the underwear (surprisingly frilly, most of it purple and black) after an indecently long search through Louise's bureau drawers; he and Paul tried to decide which of the black notebooks on her desk she would want. There were eight or nine of them; Paul opened a few and read excerpts at random, though Morrison protested weakly. References to the poles and the circle dated back several months; before he had known her, Morrison thought.

In her notebooks Louise had been working out her private system, in aphorisms and short poems which were thoroughly sane in themselves but which taken together were not; though, Morrison reflected, the only difference is that she's taken as real what the rest of us pretend is only metaphorical. Between the aphorisms were little sketches like wiring diagrams, quotations from the English poets, and long detailed analyses of her acquaintances at the university.

'Here's you, Morrison,' Paul said with a relishing chuckle. '"Morrison is not a complete person. He needs to be completed, he refuses to admit his body is part of his mind. He can be in the circle possibly, but only if he will surrender his role as a fragment and show himself willing to merge with the greater whole." Boy, she must've been nutty for months.'

They were violating her, entering her privacy against her will. 'Put that away,' Morrison said, more sharply than he ordinarily dared speak to Paul. 'We'll take the half-empty notebook, that must be the one she meant.'

There were a dozen or so library books scattered around the room, some overdue: geology and history for the most part, and one volume of Blake. Leota volunteered to take them back.

As he was about to slip the catch on the inside lock Morrison glanced once more around the room. He could see now where it got its air of pastiche: the bookcase was a copy of the one in Paul's livingroom, the prints and the table were almost identical with those at the Jamiesons'. Other details stirred dim images of objects half-noted in the various houses, at the various but nearly identical get-acquainted parties. Poor Louise had been trying to construct herself out of the other people she had met. Only from himself had she taken nothing; thinking of his chill interior, embryonic and blighted, he realized it had nothing for her to take.

He kept his promise and went to see her. His first visit was made with Paul and Leota, but he sensed their resentment: they seemed to think their country-woman should be permitted to go mad without witness or participation by any Yanks. After that he drove out by himself in his own car.

On the second visit Louise initially seemed better. They met in a cramped cubicle furnished with two chairs; Louise sat on the edge of hers, her hands folded in her lap, her face polite, withholding. Her English accent was still noticable, though hard r's surfaced in it from time to time. She was having a good rest, she said; the food was all right and she had met some nice people but she was eager to get back to her work; she worried about who was looking after her students.

'I guess I said some pretty crazy things to you,' she smiled.

'Well . . . ' Morrison stalled. He was pleased by this sign of her recovery.

'I had it all wrong. I thought I could put the country together by joining the two halves of the city into a circle, using the magnetic currents.' She gave a small disparaging laugh, then dropped her voice. 'What I hadn't figured out though was that the currents don't flow north and south, like the bridge. They flow east and west, like the river. And I didn't *need* to form the circle out of a bunch of incomplete segments. I didn't even need the baby. I mean,' she said in a serious whisper, dropping her accent completely, 'I *am* the circle. I have the poles within myself. What I have to do is keep myself in one piece, it *depends* on me.'

At the desk he tried to find out what was officially wrong with Louise but they would not tell him anything; it wasn't the policy.

On his next visit she spoke to him almost the whole time in what to his untrained ear sounded like perfectly fluent French. Her mother was a French Protestant, she told him, her father an English Catholic. '*Je peux vous dire tout ceci*,' she said, '*parce que vous êtes américain.* You are outside it.' To Morrison this explained a lot; but the next time she claimed to be the daughter of an Italian opera singer and a Nazi general. 'Though I also have some Jewish blood,' she added hastily. She was tense and kept standing up and sitting down again, crossing and recrossing her legs; she would not look at Morrison directly but addressed her staccato remarks to the centre of his chest.

After this Morrison stayed away for a couple of weeks. He did not think his visits were doing either of them any good, and he had papers to mark. He occupied himself once more with the painting of his apartment and the organ music of the woman downstairs; he shovelled his steps and put salt on them to melt the ice. His landlady, uneasy because she had still not supplied him with a lock, unexpectedly had him to tea, and the tacky plastic grotesqueries of her interior decoration fueled his reveries for a while. The one good thing in her bogus ranch-style bungalow had been an egg, blown and painted in the Ukrainian manner, but she had dismissed it as ordinary, asking him to admire instead a cake of soap stuck with artificial flowers to resemble a flowerpot; she had got the idea out of a magazine. The Korean came up one evening to ask him about life insurance.

But the thought of Louise out there in the windswept institution grounds with nothing and no one she knew bothered him in twinges, like a mental neuralgia, goading him finally into the section of the city that passed for downtown: he would buy her a gift. He selected a small box of water-colour paints: she ought to have something to do. He was intending to mail it, but sooner than he expected he found himself again on the wide deserted entrance driveway.

They met once more in the visitors' cubicle. He was alarmed by the change in her: she had put on weight, her muscles had slackened, her breasts drooped. Instead of sitting rigidly as she had done before, she sprawled in the chair, legs apart, arms hanging; her hair was dull and practically uncombed. She was wearing a short skirt and purple stockings, in one of which there was a run. Trying not to stare at this run and at the white, loose thigh flesh it revealed, Morrison had the first unmistakably physical stirrings of response he had ever felt towards her.

'They have me on a different drug,' she said. 'The other one was having the wrong effect. I was allergic to it.' She mentioned that someone had stolen her hairbrush, but when he offered to bring her another one she said it didn't matter. She had lost interest in the circle and her elaborate system and did not seem to want to talk much. What little she said was about the hospital itself: she was trying to help the doctors, they didn't know how to treat the patients but they wouldn't listen to her. Most of those inside were getting worse rather than better; many had to stay there because no one would take the responsibility of looking after them, even if they were drugged into manageability. They were poor, without relations; the hospital would not let them go away by themselves. She told him about one girl from further north who thought she was a caribou.

She hardly glanced at the water-colour paints, though she thanked him sluggishly. Her eyes, normally wide and vivacious, were puffed shut nearly to slits and her skin appeared to have darkened. She reminded him of someone, though it took him several minutes to remember: it was an Indian woman he had seen early in the fall while he was still searching for a place to have a civilized drink. She had been sitting outside a cheap hotel with her legs apart, taking off her clothes and chanting, 'Come on boys, what're you waiting for, come on boys, what're you waiting for.'

Around her a group of self-conscious, sniggering men had gathered. Morrison, against his will and appalled at her, the men, and himself, had joined them. She was naked to the waist when the police got there.

When he rose to say good-bye Louise asked him, as if it was a matter of purely academic interest, whether he thought she would ever get out.

On his way out to the car it struck him that he loved her. The thought filled him like a goal, a destiny. He would rescue her somehow; he could pretend she was his cousin or sister; he would keep her hidden in the apartment with all his dangerous implements, razors, knives, nailfiles, locked away; he would feed her, give her the right drugs, comb her hair. At night she would be there in the sub-zero bedroom for him to sink into as into a swamp, warm and obliterating.

This picture at first elated, then horrified him. He saw that it was only the hopeless, mad Louise he wanted, the one devoid of any purpose or defence. A sane one, one that could judge him, he would never be able to handle. So this was his dream girl then, his ideal woman found at last: a disintegration, mind returning to its component shards of matter, a defeated formless creature on which he could inflict himself like shovel on earth, axe on forest, use without being used, know without being known. Louise's notebook entry, written when she had surely been saner than she was now, had been right about him. Yet in self-defence he reasoned that his desire for her was not altogether evil: it was in part a desire to be reunited with his own body, which he felt less and less that he actually occupied.

Oppressed by himself and by the building, the prison he had just left, he turned when he reached the main road away from the city instead of towards it: he would take his car for a run. He drove through the clenched landscape, recalling with pain the gentle drawl of the accommodating hills east and south, back in that settled land which was so far away it seemed not to exist. Here everything was tightlipped, ungiving, good for nothing and nothing.

He was halfway to the zoo before he knew he was going there. Louise had said it was kept open all winter.

Not much of the day was left when he reached the entrance: he would be driving back in darkness. He would have to make his visit short, he did not want to be caught inside when they locked the gates. He paid the admission fee to the scarfed and muffled figure in the booth, then took his car along the empty drives, glancing out the side window at the herds of llama, of yak, the enclosure of the Siberian tiger in which only the places a tiger might hide were to be seen.

At the buffalo field he stopped the car and got out. The buffalo were feeding near the wire fence, but at his approach they lifted their heads and glared at him, then snorted and rocked away from him through the haunch-deep snowdunes.

He plodded along the fence, not caring that the wind was up and chilling him through his heavy coat, the blood retreating from his toes. Thin sinister fingers of blown snow were creeping over the road; on the way back he would have to watch for drifts. He imagined the snow rising up, sweeping down in great curves, in waves over the city, each house a tiny centre of man-made warmth, fending it off. By the grace of the power plant and the gas plant: a bomb, a catastrophe to each and the houses would close like eyes. He thought of all the people he barely knew, how they would face it, chopping up their furniture for firewood until the cold overcame. How they were already facing it, the Koreans' fishes fluttering on the clothesline like defiant silver flags, the woman downstairs shrilling 'Whispering Hope' off-key into the blizzard, Paul in the flimsy armour of his cheap nationalism, the landlady holding aloft torchlike her bar of soap stuck with artificial flowers. Poor Louise, he saw now what she had been trying desperately to do: the point of the circle, closed and self-sufficient, was not what it included but what it shut out. His own efforts to remain human, futile work and sterile love, what happened when it was all used up, what would he be left with? Black trees on a warm orange wall; and he had painted everything white. . . .

Dizzy with cold, he leaned against the fence, forehead on mittened hand. He was at the wolf pen. He remembered it from his trip with Louise. They had stood there for some time waiting for the wolves to come over to them but they had kept to the far side. Three of them were near the fence now though, lying in its shelter. An old couple, a man and a woman in nearly identical grey coats, were standing near the wolves. He had not noticed them earlier, no cars had passed him, they must have walked from the parking lot.

The eyes of the wolves were yellowish grey: they looked out through the bars at him, alert, neutral.

'Are they timber wolves?' Morrison said to the old woman. Opening his mouth to speak, he was filled with a sudden chill rush of air.

The woman turned to him slowly: her face was a haze of wrinkles from which her eyes stared up at him, blue, glacial.

'You from around here?' she asked.

'No,' Morrison said. Her head swung away; she continued to look through the fence at the wolves, nose to the wind, short white fur ruffled up on edge.

Morrison followed her fixed gaze: something was being told, something that had nothing to do with him, the thing you could learn only after the rest was finished with and discarded. His body was numb; he swayed. In the corner of his eye the old woman swelled, wavered, then seemed to disappear, and the land opened before him. It swept away to the north and he thought he could see the mountains, white-covered, their crests glittering in the falling sun, then forest upon forest, after that the barren tundra and the blank solid rivers, and beyond, so far that the endless night had already descended, the frozen sea.

# W. D. Valgardson

WILLIAM Dempsey Valgardson was born in Winnipeg, Manitoba, in 1939. Although his father is of English and Icelandic descent ('In *Njal's Saga*, which was written somewhere around 1280, there is a Valgardson. I am tied to an old tradition'), the Nordic element in much of Valgardson's writing he attributes to his having grown up in Gimli, in northern Manitoba, a town that was once known as Nya Island, or New Iceland. He received his B.A. from United College in Winnipeg in 1961, his B.Ed. from the University of Manitoba in 1965, and an M.F.A. from Iowa in 1969. After Iowa he taught high school in Winnipeg for a year, then taught at Cottey College in Nevada, Missouri, for four years. Since 1974 he has been teaching creative writing at the University of Victoria.

Valgardson's first book of stories, *Bloodflowers*, appeared in 1973, and since then he has written two more—*God Is Not a Fish Inspector* (1975), the title story of which has been made into a film; and *Red Dust* (1978), from which the following story has been selected. His first novel, *Gentle Sinners*, was published in April, 1980.

In an essay entitled 'Personal Gods' (in *Essays on Canadian Writing* #16, 1980), Valgardson writes that 'A Place of One's Own' is 'about the need of someone to have a place of his own, to have that place recognized, sanctified by society, to overcome the role as outcast.... I am also aware that the pedlar, with his echoes of the Wandering Jew, is not universal as the result of there having been wandering Jews throughout history but because both the pedlar and his antecedents represent the fear of all of us of being displaced.'

# A PLACE OF ONE'S OWN

THE SOUND of the bell came all at once, as though the clapper had been held and then suddenly released. The sharp, unexpected ringing startled Angela. She stopped picking strawberries, looked about the yard and, seeing neither her father nor mother, rose to her feet and ran toward the road with a peculiar, flat-footed shuffle.

When she reached the gate, she climbed the horizontal boards of the white fence and leaned precariously forward. To her left, at the bottom of a rutted gravel road that descended to a swamp, then rose southward until it topped a gravel ridge thick with scrub brush, she saw a black horse pulling a flatbed wagon. Set upon the wagon was a high, narrow shed with a peaked roof. The outside of the shed had been shingled. A small window had been set in the front wall. A stove-pipe jutted like the tip of a finger toward heaven. The driver, instead of riding, was walking beside the horse with the reins in his left hand.

Angela watched for a minute, her short blonde hair gleaming with a reflected halo of light, then, cautiously setting one foot on the ground, climbed down and hurried back to the strawberry patch.

She was kneeling on the path between two rows of plants when her mother appeared at the corner of the house and called, 'Who's coming?'

'The pedlar,' Angela replied without stopping work. She didn't bother to look up.

Her mother, a heavy-set woman with a waxy pale face, stayed in the shade cast by the eaves. She cupped a hand to her forehead. In her other hand she held a ladle that dripped strawberry jam.

'What's going on?' Angela's father shouted from the doorway of the barn. Harry Fedorchuk was twenty years older than his wife. He was a swarthy man with a body so narrow that when he stood still he could easily be mistaken for the trunk of a maple tree. Although his eyesight was good enough for him to shoot pigeons from the barn roof, he claimed his hearing was so poor that he could only make out what was being said on television when the volume was turned to maximum. However, if anything was said that was private or interesting, he could hear it all the way across the yard.

'It's the pedlar,' Sophie answered. 'With the tattoos.'

He cupped his hand to his ear and screwed up his face.

'What's wrong?' he called. His words, drawn out so that the vowels were multiplied three-fold, faded gradually, like the sound of a horn.

His wife, for all her sturdy appearance, suffered from emphysema and her voice was weak. Raising her voice exhausted her. A month before, she would have appealed to Angela to repeat the message or to run across the yard to answer her father's question, but she knew it was no use. He no longer spoke to his daughter, refusing to acknowledge anything she said. When he had first realized what was wrong, he had beaten her with his razor strop, chasing her around the yard, into the house, in and out of rooms, her screaming with every blow and him threatening and demanding until, at last, she had crawled under her bed and curled into a corner. For the next week he had never quit questioning her, demanding the answer to one question over and over, even waking her in the middle of the night to try and catch her off guard.

At the end of seven days, when she still would not tell him what he wanted to know, he turned away from her, matching silence with silence. Since then, when she passed before him, his eyes looked through her and his lips set one against the other like the edges of a press used for crimping metal.

His daughter's condition was only the last of a series of blows. For three years in a row, there had been bad crops. One year, it had rained too much. The next year, it had snowed early. Now, the stunted grain was ripening with half-filled heads. Only two months before, his best cow had squeezed through the fence and been run down by a car. Because he was afraid of being sued, he had denied that the cow was his and so did not even get to keep the meat. He hadn't paid his taxes in two years.

He slopped across the yard in a pair of boots five sizes too big. He loved bargains and regarded anything that was cheap as a bargain. Only after arriving home did he stop to consider the object's appropriateness. His rubber boots had been on sale for a dollar because they were a size twelve. He took a size seven. However, rather than admit that he had made a mistake, he fitted them with three insoles and stuffed crumpled newspaper into the toes.

When Sophie told him the news, he went directly to the gate. She followed him and stood, her arms crossed, her ladle firmly clenched. The two of them looked as if they were preparing to repel an attack.

The pedlar's wagon was so old that it had high wheels with wooden spokes and iron rims. The upper section had been constructed with meticulous care so that, painted brown, the shingled exterior looked like nothing so much as an old fishing shed. On the sides, various large items hung from black hooks—galvanized tubs, rakes, shovels, even some loops of electrical wire and small farm equipment.

The pedlar walked with the steady, unhurried gait of someone who has walked a long distance and still has a long distance to go. He was tall and thin and he wore a hat with so wide a brim that it seemed like a miniature umbrella. His long hair was tied back with a shoelace. His beard was reddish brown and lay on his chest in carefully combed waves. His face was narrow and the bones lay close to the skin.

As the mare's head came even with the Fedorchuks, the pedlar tightened the reins and the horse stopped.

'We got no money to buy nothing,' Fedorchuk said, his gaze passing the pedlar to run quickly over the goods hanging on the caravan.

The pedlar remained motionless, not looking at them but to the left of them as though someone else was there whom only he could see. All at once, he looked directly into Fedorchuk's eyes and said, 'My horse needs watering. May I use your well?'

It was a request that could not be denied. There had been no rain for weeks. The ditches were dry, their bottoms silvered with foxtail. What water was to be found in the sloughs that lay between the Fedorchuks and the next farm was brown and stagnant and completely unfit for drinking.

'We don't need nothing,' Fedorchuk said. Reluctantly, he lifted the latch and swung back the gate.

With a click of his tongue and a barely discernible flick of his wrist, the pedlar started the horse into the yard. The black mare stopped and nuzzled the pump. The pedlar took a pail from a hook and filled it with water. Fedorchuk followed right behind the pedlar.

'We didn't expect you back so soon,' he said.

The horse began to drink noisily. The pedlar, instead of replying, held one hand over the spout and worked the`handle until water flowed over the top of the casing. He knelt, put his lips against the spout and bent his palm so as to make an opening for the water. He drank greedily until there was no water left, then worked the handle and drank again. When he stood, he took a deep breath, clutched his beard and squeezed the water from it.

'It's a hot day,' Fedorchuk said, eyeing a cream can he could make use of.

The pedlar nodded his agreement. He wore a plaid shirt, blue jeans and thick-soled boots that laced up past his ankles.

Sophie was standing three feet behind her husband, watching the pedlar so closely she might have been afraid he would, through some magical sleight of hand, steal the pump before their eyes.

'You needed thread the last time I was here,' the pedlar said. 'I've got lots of it this trip.' As he spoke, he watched Angela out of the corner of his eye. She had her head bent so that her face was hidden. Her basin of strawberries gleamed white and red.

'Purple?'

'I think so. I'll have to look.' In an attempt to be friendly, he added, 'I'll give you a spool in exchange for the water.'

Neither Fedorchuk nor his wife approved of people not brought up in the area. Of the pedlar, they were particularly contemptuous because he had no place of his own and, therefore, no trustworthy identity. Like all people who live on the very edge of having nothing, a place of one's own was very important to them. Divorced from the land, constantly travelling, appearing and disappearing without explanation, the pedlar was no better than a gypsy. Although he had come to their farm frequently during the past three years, he had never offered his name and they had never asked for it.

All through the Interlake, there were rumours about him, many of which were contradictory. Some said he had been a criminal; others that he was a defrocked priest; still others that he had been involved in unsavoury politics. Some adhered to the theory that he was the cast-off son of a noble family. When he had first appeared in Eddyville, he worked as a day-labourer, going wherever he was needed, moving from farm to farm and camp to camp. He never talked about his past and, according to the postmaster, never received any mail.

It was while he was harvesting for a farmer south of town that someone saw him washing and discovered that his chest and back and arms were sprinkled with tattoos. That made him the object of intense curiosity for no one in the district except a Ukrainian who had survived Auschwitz had a tattoo and his was only a number. People even went so far as to drive to where the pedlar was working and to ask him to take off his shirt. He had refused and his refusal had caused some resentment.

The pedlar, although at that time he was not yet called that, had made it a habit to stop at the parlour every Saturday night for a beer. Usually, he came in, ordered two draft and contented himself with sitting and nodding to the people he knew. It was during his second summer in the Eddyville area that a group of rowdies who had had too much to drink had surrounded his table and asked him to take off his shirt. He had shaken his head, then ignored them. When they insisted, he tried to leave. They had overpowered him and ripped his shirt into strips. All that was left were his cuffs. It was right after that that he disappeared. Everyone thought he had left the district until one day when he reappeared with his wagon and stock of goods.

Since then, he avoided crowds and towns, sticking to back roads, selling his goods at farms and camps. Sometimes, when there was a wedding or a funeral or even a bingo game, he would park his caravan on the road and watch from a distance but, if any notice was taken of him, he would drive off.

'My horse,' he said to Fedorchuk, 'is favouring her right foot.'

He bent down. Grasping the mare's leg, he gently raised it up. Fedorchuk crouched to inspect the hoof but he kept his distance. He had once been kicked by a horse and still bore the scar on his chest. Gingerly, he reached out and grasped the shoe.

'That shoe's no good,' he grunted. 'It's a wonder she's not lame.'

The pedlar poked and pulled at the shoe. 'It needs a new one,' he admitted. 'I can do the work. Have you any equipment?'

Fedorchuk sucked on his teeth and said nothing.

'I'll give you that cream can for the use of your equipment,' he said. 'I don't want anything for nothing.'

Before, the pedlar had taken his time about answering. Now, it was Fedorchuk's turn. He strolled to the pump. Even without socks, his feet were sweltering. He took off one boot, held his left foot under the spout and pumped water over it. The pump clashed and banged so much that there was no use trying to talk. When his foot was cool, he took off the other boot and rinsed his right foot. His ankles were thin and hairy and looked like two-inch planks with knots. His feet were mottled purple and white.

'I'll need to see what I've got,' he said at last.

With that settled, the pedlar turned to Sophie. 'I'll get that spool of thread,' he offered. He disappeared into his caravan. When he reappeared, he had an armload of boxes. 'I'm not very well organized,' he apologized. 'I'll need to look until I find it.'

Sophie didn't want her husband to think she might buy something so she didn't step forward but stretched her neck until she appeared to be trying to see over some high obstruction. As the pedlar opened the first box, there was the acrid smell of stale smoke. The box contained a tumbled assortment of narrow silk ties. He dipped in his hand, raised the scarlets, indigoes, and oranges to the sunlight, then let them slide shimmering into the box.

'We got no use for neckties,' Sophie said. 'Harry's got one.'

'There's no harm in looking,' the pedlar replied. 'It don't cost nothing.'

He set the box aside and opened another that contained a pile of tiny handkerchiefs all marked with the initial M. Some of them were charred around the edges but none were so badly burned that they couldn't be used.

The pedlar's goods were constantly changing. No one, not even the pedlar himself, knew from one trip to the next what he would be bringing. He purchased his stock not from a wholesaler but from a salvage company hidden among the slaughterhouses and factories that had sprung up on the edge of the city.

Sometimes he managed to procure bankrupt stock, but more often he bought fire-damaged goods. He gathered these on regular but infrequent trips to the city and stored them in an abandoned church, which he rented for thirty dollars a month. His customers had long since grown accustomed to tea and sugar and chocolate that tasted as if they had been hung for a time over smouldering sawdust. They didn't complain. The pedlar's goods were cheap and they were delivered to the door.

One after another, the pedlar opened the boxes, spreading them over the rear of the wagon. When there was no room left, he began a second layer. There were items of every kind, the debris of ambition and greed and miscalculation and bad luck gathered indiscriminately together by misfortune—crocheted doilies, small mesh hats covered with velvet flowers only slightly crushed, white gloves, women's underthings (when he displayed these last items, he delicately looked away into the distance), needles, pins, cards filled with barrettes, brooches, and earrings.

As he searched through his goods for the thread, he was silent. His face, what showed of it above his beard, was long and sad, the face of someone who has waited a long time for something and then been disappointed.

The door on one of the outbuildings banged. Fedorchuk strode across the yard on his mottled feet. His green workpants were rolled nearly to his knees. His pale legs were narrow as a goat's. He stopped near the tailgate, surveyed all the open goods, twisted up the corner of his mouth in disapproval and said, 'I got everything you need except coal.'

The pedlar nodded gravely. 'I guess,' he said, 'I could make it to the next farm.'

Fedorchuk pretended to be looking at a box of toothbrushes but his eyes were fixed on the cream can. In his own mind, he already owned it and now that he was in danger of losing the can, he felt as though something was being stolen from him. To have it given to his neighbour who already had two cows and three pigs more than he had was nothing less than a personal injury.

'I can,' he volunteered, swinging his eyes fiercely toward the pedlar as if to challenge him to combat, 'get you some coal first thing in the morning.'

At this offer the pedlar gave a short, formal bow as though he had just been introduced to someone of consequence. The pedlar opened one more box. It was filled with spools of thread. He held it out so that Sophie could pick what she wanted.

The pedlar made his supper from sardines and bread and drank water from a small saucepan. When he had finished, he smoked his pipe for half an hour, then went to the back door of the house. Fedorchuk came to the landing and stood on the opposite side of the screen like a priest waiting to hear confession.

'Since I'm going to stay until tomorrow, I thought you and I might make a few dollars out of it.'

At the mention of money, Fedorchuk turned his head to one side in the attitude of someone listening to the sound of distant thunder.

'You could phone your neighbours,' the pedlar suggested, 'and tell them I'm here. They can come and, whatever I sell, you get five percent.'

Fedorchuk brushed his lips with his upraised index finger, looked over his shoulder into the kitchen to see if his wife had overheard the conversation, then let himself out. He caught the pedlar's arm and led him half-way across the yard. The sun sat above the barn, a circle slightly flattened at the top and bottom, so that it looked complacent like a fat banker who is resting after a profitable day.

When they were half-way between the house and the barn, Fedorchuk said, 'They'll dig up my lawn with their cars.' He pressed his small, monkey-like face close to the pedlar's.

The pedlar glanced at the hardpacked dirt that was dotted with islands of quack grass. 'You could make a little extra,' he suggested, 'by serving food.'

'Someone,' Fedorchuk replied as his mind searched the nooks and crannies of profit, 'might back into my fence. Anyways, how do I know I'll get anything out of it?'

'You've got to have faith. Other people have done okay.'

'That,' Fedorchuk answered, barely restraining a sneer, 'was when things were more prosperous. Times have changed.' All at once, his face, which had been full of anticipation, grew as still and cold as if he had seen a vision of his own death. 'I don't want anyone coming around here,' he declared. He swung his head back and forth like he was searching out a hidden enemy.

'Seven and a half percent,' the pedlar countered. 'You might make twenty, twenty-five dollars just off my sales.'

Just then, the sun flared up, turning the horizon white, so that it seemed the sun was rising, not setting, but right after that, the light faded sharply.

'That would be a miracle,' Fedorchuk said. He governed his life by the supposition that there was nothing that would not be worse shortly. 'I've got trouble with my neighbours,' he complained. His face worked with emotion, his muscles disturbing the skin like a turbulent current roiling the surface of a stream. He clamped his lips shut, drew his head into his shoulders and stared over the garden into a grove of stunted oak where shadows were rapidly gathering. 'Someone,' he said at last, his words tightened to a whisper, 'let his scrub bull in with my cows.'

The pedlar stooped and dug a stone from the dirt. He rubbed it clean, then taking careful aim, threw it into the air. The stone rose in a high arc and looked, for a moment, as if it would follow the sun over the horizon. Instead, it dropped in a tangle of weeds. 'Someone not coming might tell you something. Someone who comes and acts suspicious might tell you more. Maybe if you found out who it was, you could make a deal with him.'

Fedorchuk did not appear to hear the suggestion. He gazed blankly toward the grove where his cattle moved through the shadows like great mythic beasts. It was as though he had turned back inside himself. His emotion was so great that his left arm jerked twice.

'I'll kill him,' Fedorchuk whispered.

'Maybe,' the pedlar began.

'It's a deal,' Fedorchuk snapped. 'Seven and a half.'

'In that case, let's have a drink.' The pedlar lifted two folding chairs from the roof of the caravan. Then he brought a gallon jug of homebrew and two glasses. They mixed the liquor with water from the well.

Without any discernible change, the grey of the sky became gradually darker until it was a deep, impenetrable black. A full moon of beaten brass rose with a stately, formal air, silvering the eastern sides of trees and buildings.

'You're very lucky,' the pedlar said, his voice heavy with tiredness. When Fedorchuk looked up, a miniature moon was reflected in each eye. 'To have a place of your own, I mean. To be able to stay in one place.'

After this, he fell into a reverie that lasted until Fedorchuk said, 'Riding on that seat must be pretty hard on your kidneys.'

The pedlar refilled their glasses. The night air lay on their skins like warm water. Framed in the kitchen window, Angela might have been a delicately painted water-colour. Her skin glowed softly. Her face was enclosed by the curve of her yellow hair. The pedlar had set his chair at an angle so that by looking over Fedorchuk's shoulder, he could watch Angela without appearing to do so.

'Everyone,' the pedlar sighed, 'gets worn down after a while.' They had both faded until all that was visible of them were their outlines. 'I'm thinking of buying Grebon's store.'

'It's a good business,' Fedorchuk replied. Normally, he loved to gossip, gathering up scraps of information like a caretaker spearing gum wrappers on a pointed stick. It was a measure of his resentment and anger over his daughter's condition that he didn't try to draw out the pedlar. 'I'll have to tell my wife!' he suddenly exclaimed. 'She'll have lots of food to prepare.'

When Fedorchuk woke at four, the sky had already begun to soften. He kept some money buried in a tobacco tin and his sleep had been haunted with images of someone digging up his yard. Still in his nightshirt, he crept outside and inspected the ground. Then, like a ghost, lifting his bare feet high so as not to stub his toes, he flitted from outbuilding to outbuilding, checking the padlocks. The pedlar's caravan he circled twice, as though to cast a spell upon it. Finally, he returned to the house, dressed, and sat in the window, brooding.

The morning sky was empty and vast. When the pedlar stepped down from his wagon, he glanced about and, seeing no one, took off his shirt. Fedorchuk had already returned with the coal. He hid behind the shed door. Angela peeked from behind the blind of her bedroom window. The pedlar's body, from the edge of his pants to his neck and along his arms to his wrists, was solidly covered with tattoos. In the morning sun, his body glistened blue and red. There did not appear to be one piece of skin free of pictures.

All through the Interlake he was known as the pedlar. Although no one called him that to his face, substituting *you* and *hey, there* for his name or avoiding calling him anything at all. Once he had been called the pedlar, his first identity, that fragile endowment from parents whom no one had ever met, whose existence and place in society no one ever confirmed, was swept away. If anyone had come to town and had asked for him by name, no one would have recognized who was wanted.

While many people spoke of him, it was seldom that they actually had anything to do with him. In any case, he was hard to find, for he never stayed long in any one place. Whatever his reason for coming to Eddyville, he had never settled. That robbed him of any chance of becoming respectable. In spite of the fact that most of the villagers were seasonal workers and regularly moved back and forth from town to fish camps or joined the freighting outfits for the winter season or disappeared into the bush to cut pulp, they all had a place of their own.

As soon as the pedlar had buttoned his shirt, Fedorchuk appeared, showed him the coal and the equipment and gave him some horseshoes that had been left from years before.

He watched the pedlar work, then asked in a disinterested fashion, as if it was of no consequence, 'Have you ever thought of marrying?'

The pedlar was pumping a pair of hand bellows. He stopped as suddenly as if he'd touched a hot coal, then started again. His face had taken on the watchful look of a hunter hearing a piece of deadfall snap.

'I've thought of it,' he admitted.

'Where do you come from?'

'East,' he answered vaguely.

Fedorchuk lingered another minute or so but he asked no more questions.

When he entered the kitchen, his wife and daughter were making long rows of egg sandwiches.

'Spread the filling thinner,' he ordered. He studied his daughter. All that revealed her pregnancy was the way she walked and that, he knew, would not mean much to an inexperienced man. 'That pedlar,' he said to neither of them in particular, 'is not a bad fellow. He's buying a store for himself and settling down.'

'He's got pictures all over himself,' Sophie countered.

'His wife wouldn't need TV,' he said. His eyes were fastened on his daughter's waistline. She was wearing a smock so he couldn't see if she had begun to thicken over her hips. 'People do worse things to their bodies.'

There was the sound of a hammer beating on steel.

'Tell her to take him some coffee,' he ordered. 'We're in business together.'

With the doors open to the morning sun, the thick shadows of the shed had been forced back into the corners. The pedlar bent over the forge, his body enveloped by early-morning light. The air was pungent with the smell of steam and burning coal.

Angela appeared in the doorway with a white mug and hesitated on the threshold, pausing with the slender grace of a startled fawn. The pedlar, upon realizing who it was, stopped working and waited for her to approach. When she still held back, he went to her and accepted the cup. After drinking from it, he asked, 'Will you dance tonight?'

'Dance?' she replied, uncertain of what he was asking.

'There'll be music.'

Her eyes searched the corners of the shed as if seeking a shadowed place to hide and her face, which normally was smooth and fragile as the wild rose's that bloomed along the roadside, was drawn. Her cheeks were still pink, her nose still touched with a careless spray of freckles, but now the skin was pulled tightly at the corners of her eyes and mouth. Her eyes seemed deeper set and the flesh around them delicately bruised.

'There'll be lots to do,' she said.

As she turned to go, he said, 'I'm thirty-two,' but she made no sign that she had heard him. After she was gone, he remained where he was, watching the place where she had been.

When the horse was shod, he let it loose. He hated to see it tied and, if it began to stray, relied upon no more than a short, sharp whistle to bring it back. He leaned into his caravan and drew out a violin. The heat, as on the day before, lay over everything, silencing the fields. Here and there, a sparrow bathed in the dust. Occasionally, as if a child had released a spring, grasshoppers fluttered toward the sun then, before their leap had carried them more than a few feet, fell back.

Fedorchuk's house sat primly among a few scattered maples. It was white with blue trim and a blue roof. Although quite small, it looked a lot larger than it was because the front had been extended three feet on both sides. In the front yard, blue-and-white javex bottles hung from the trees. They had been cut along the sides and the resulting flaps bent outward so that, in the slightest wind, they turned in constant circles. In the fall, when the wind was strong, the trees appeared ready to rise from the ground and shoot into the heavens.

An upended bathtub enclosing a plaster Mary and Joseph watching the Christ child faced the road. A sheet of glass had been set over the tub to protect the figures from the elements. At the moment, three dahlia bushes obscured the crèche; in the fall, however, they were cut back. On the twenty-first of December, in a yearly ritual he broke for no one, Fedorchuk set out all the decorative figures he had collected over the years so that they staggered over the snow-drifts toward a star of Christmas set directly above the crèche—wise men leading a mixed parade of pink flamingoes, dwarfs, deer, frogs, skunks, and rabbits. Overhead, surrounding the star, he hung birds he had painstakingly carved and painted—robins, geese, bluebirds, jays, doves—and intermingled with these were a dozen handmade Messerschmitts and Spitfires.

The pedlar tested the violin strings with his thumb. The sound of each string, as it was plucked, fell into the silence as precisely as a single drip of water striking the surface of an empty and resonant barrel. Satisfied, the pedlar began to play. He didn't play complete tunes but parts of many, some sad, some happy, some fast, some slow, as though he was remembering songs he had nearly forgotten.

Angela was sitting at the kitchen cupboard wrapping sandwiches in wax paper.

'Do you think many people will come?' she asked.

'The world is full of fools,' her mother replied.

'I'll stay in my room if you want.'

Her father was listening at the door. 'She'll help serve,' he said. 'She's not there, people will talk. If they aren't already talking.'

Angela's hands trembled so much that she was unable to fold the paper. 'They don't know from me,' she said, her voice husky with emotion.

Angered by the justice of her remark—in his first fury he had gone from house to house, drunk, seeking information—he spit out, 'Tell! Who needs to tell? That's been done for you. Do you think men keep secrets? He'll be bragging in the beer parlour every night.' He beat his fist twice on the wall.

'She can't go out,' Sophie said.

'She'll serve,' he screamed. Rather than provoke him further, they both bowed their heads. He jerked around, stamped down the stairs and flung himself outside.

The pedlar's wagon sat directly before the window. It had large wheels, the spokes of which were the colour of weathered bone. The upper part sat well forward, so that there was about five feet of empty wagon bed at the back.

Sophie said, 'He plays well.'

'He's covered his body with pictures,' Angela retorted.

After he had tried out various tunes for half an hour, the pedlar put away his violin. The plainness of his caravan was deceptive. He had, with the care and expertise of a master carpenter, constructed the caravan to perform a double duty. He unhooked the catches on the wall facing the house. As he swung the wall up, two long sticks unfolded in sections, and these he set into the sides of the wagon to form a canopy. He lifted up his bed and by setting it on its side with the bottom facing outward, he formed a counter. His goods he arranged in racks that pulled out from the walls.

Fedorchuk appeared, carrying a sawhorse under each arm. He put them down and went back for more. When he had six set out, he laid three sheets of plywood across them to make tables that were low enough for blocks of stove wood to be used as seats.

Angela arrived with an armload of newspaper, which she was to staple over the plywood. As she worked, the pedlar could not keep from glancing at her.

'Why did you come here?' she asked, without looking at him.

'I sell to all the farms,' he replied. 'My horse has a loose shoe so I had to stay.'

She spread a layer of newspaper and tacked it in place. Her top, which fitted closely under her breasts and then flared outward, pulled up as she reached across the makeshift tables, baring a handspan of lightly tanned skin.

'Will you dance with me tonight?' he asked.

'I'm expecting someone,' she answered confidently.

'I'm buying Grebon's store. I can pay half.' He said it intensely as though it was of great importance.

'How come you've got pictures all over?'

He opened another box. 'Would you like to see them?'

She stopped stapling and stood up. She had a spray of three anemones tucked behind her ear. While she watched, he undid his shirt and took it off. She came up close to study the crowded pictures.

'Why'd you do it?' she asked.

He put his shirt back on. 'It's been a long time since I've shown those to anyone.'

'You're like a picture-show,' she said.

The pedlar chopped a block of wood into kindling. He crumpled some paper, set the wood around it, then hauled six cordwood sticks from Fedorchuk's pile. He laid these in a circle with one end of each log set on the kindling.

Fedorchuk came rushing over. 'What're you doing?' he demanded.

'This is for the bonfire.'

'What bonfire? You never said anything about a bonfire.'

The pedlar clapped his hand to Fedorchuk's shoulder. 'Leave this to me,' he sighed. 'I know what people like. A bonfire is good for another hundred dollars' worth of sales.'

Just before six o'clock the cars began to arrive. Fedorchuk had called every house within ten miles. He wanted to be certain that as many people as possible came. He was skeptical about their making any money but the pedlar's suggestion throbbed in his head. His determination not to have a grandson who was a bastard sat inside him like the tough, knotted root of an oak.

A crowd quickly gathered around the caravan. The pedlar did a brisk trade.

'What you need,' Fedorchuk said as the pedlar was frantically trying to make change and keep track of sales, 'is a wife to help you.'

As the pedlar had predicted, provided with food, liquor, and company, nearly everyone stayed. Angela, under her father's watchful eye, wound her way through the crowd selling drinks and sandwiches. Over her white dress with its sprays of violets, she wore an apron with large pockets to hold her change. People were civil but the men held back, giving her no more than a nod or a curt hello. After she passed, their eyes followed her legs and buttocks speculatively. For her part, she kept her face as still as if it had been glazed with a fine layer of porcelain. Her eyes, however, never ceased to roam the edges of the crowd.

As darkness fell, the pedlar climbed down from his wagon and lit the bonfire. He wandered through the crowd, selling the last of his homebrew. Then, without anyone seeing him do so, he took up his violin and, standing well back in the shadows, began to play. To those lounging about the yard, the music seemed to rise from the ground. Then, slowly, as though he moved in a dream, the pedlar strolled into the light of the bonfire. He stood for a time, playing a high, wailing lament but then, before the last sounds had died, he broke into a wild, throbbing *kolamayka*. From out of the darkness, a farmer, his face beaming, appeared with an accordion and, without waiting to be asked, joined in. Another farmer brought a guitar and still another rose from the table and, fitting two spoons between the fingers of each hand, began to beat out a steady rhythm.

The pedlar, turning this way and that as he played, was alternately exposed to the light of the bonfire and obscured by the shadows. His eyes glittered, then filled with pools of darkness, and his teeth, even and white, flashed.

Gradually, the crowd formed a wide circle around the hub of fire. An open, grassy space lay between the crowd and the flames. There was only one break in this rim of bodies and that was where it met the caravan. The pedlar climbed onto the back of the wagon and stood above the crowd. The other musicians joined him. As the music grew louder and more insistent, a huge woman in a purple dress laughed out loud, grabbed a short, bald man standing beside her and whirled him into the cleared space.

Others followed until there was a solid mass of bodies moving around in an endless stream. The band, caught up in the excitement of its own music, didn't stop between numbers and, even when Fedorchuk urgently came forward to speak to the pedlar, the musicians went on.

'What's the matter?' the pedlar shouted above the noise.

'We're out of food. Have you got any?'

The pedlar shrugged and climbed into the caravan.

'That's it,' he said when he returned. He handed over the better part of a case of canned sardines and kipper snacks and three loaves of bread.

When all the pedlar's food was sold, Angela came to sit on the steps of the caravan. The pedlar gave up his violin to a windburnt man in a white shirt and climbed down to join her. His face was flushed with exertion. Sweat ran down his face and disappeared into his beard. Angela didn't turn her head but sat staring straight ahead, her legs tucked back so she would not be stepped on.

'You don't dance,' the pedlar observed.

Angela's face was pale and pinched and she looked as though she might cry. 'There's time yet.'

He nodded slowly and his face became heavy with sadness as though by his long isolation he knew exactly what she was feeling. He lifted his hand tentatively toward her cheek but lowered it without touching her.

The dancers whirled by, oblivious to everything but the music, their clothes creaking and rustling like sails in a high wind.

The dancing stopped at midnight. Within fifteen minutes the last car was gone, the yard silent. The fire had been reduced to embers. The pedlar moved about, picking up empty boxes and squares of wax paper and foam cups. From time to time, he dropped these onto the coals and, briefly, bright flames shot up, imitating the fire that had burned earlier. Angela had not moved from the end of the wagon. The dancing had been carried on without her and, now, she sat by herself.

When, at last, her father passed close to her, picking up papers, she said, in a plaintive, bewildered voice that made her sound like she was no more than twelve or thirteen, 'No one would dance with me.'

'You fool,' her father cried, grabbing her arm and flinging her toward the house so that she stumbled and looked, for a moment, like she might fall. 'They'll ask you to dance, all right. But it won't be where anyone can see.' He followed after her, making an obscene gesture by forming a circle with his thumb and finger and shoving his index finger through it. Savagely, he called, 'Come here. Come here. Let's go to the car.'

She fled to the house. The door slammed. Fedorchuk stood with his back to the fire, his body twitching and jerking. The pedlar stood at the corner of his caravan. He waited until Fedorchuk had composed himself, then carried an armload of paper to the fire. With his foot, he pushed the few remaining ends of wood onto the coals, then added the paper.

'Come and have a drink,' he said. 'I've kept a little. We can finish this in the morning.'

He filled Fedorchuk's glass. Together, they squatted like savages around the fire, silent, brooding. The earlier gaiety pressed upon them like a heavy weight.

'We did well today,' the pedlar said. 'You must have made two hundred dollars gross and I've sold four hundred dollars' worth of goods. That's thirty dollars for you.' He took some bills from his pocket. 'It's ten dollars for the food I gave you.' He counted out twenty dollars. 'It's hard work,' he said, holding out the money. 'I'll be glad to be settled in one place.'

Fedorchuk watched the pedlar with the corners of his eyes. He looked away into the darkness with the intensity of someone searching the sea for a sign of survivors.

'You'll need a wife,' he said slyly. 'You need two to keep a store open. You can't get no hired help that's any good today.'

The pedlar shrugged his shoulders indifferently, but his face smoothed with expectation. 'I've been careful with my money but if I'm to start a business ... ' His voice trailed away. 'She would have to be an asset.'

Fedorchuk thought of the tobacco tin and the five hundred dollars he had secreted in it for emergencies. In other circumstances, the pedlar would have been unthinkable as a son-in-law. Now that no one else would have his daughter, he was all that was available.

'You've been here a lot of times this year,' he said.

'I pass this way when I go for supplies.'

'No other reason?'

'I'm thirty-two. I don't want to spend the rest of my life alone.'

Fedorchuk tossed a wad of paper into the ashes. It smouldered, then burst into flame.

'I have a daughter,' he said, 'who's ready to marry.'

'A wife's expensive.'

'It takes two to run a store.'

'Getting started . . . ' the pedlar protested but there was no force in his voice.

Fedorchuk waited, letting the silence of the night settle between them. He had bought and sold a lot of cattle and he knew it wasn't wise to appear too eager. At last, when the only sound was the occasional tearing of grass as the black mare browsed invisibly beside them, he said, 'I've got three hundred dollars put away. Instead of paying for a wedding, it could be a present.'

The pedlar did not reply. Instead, he went to his caravan and lifted a pail from inside. The pump rasped and squealed and the water shot out like blood from a severed artery. He came to the grey patch of ashes and poured out a thin stream of water. Sparks and ashes flew up and the embers hissed and cracked and the air was filled with the bitter smell of drenched coals. When the fire was out, he said, 'I'll tell you before I leave.'

They concluded their agreement in the morning. The pedlar didn't speak to Angela. He and Fedorchuk shook hands and Fedorchuk gave him a hundred dollars. The pedlar returned directly to town, had a blood test, applied for a marriage licence and concluded the purchase of Grebon's store. He gave them an extra hundred dollars to be out in five days.

At nine o'clock in the morning, eight days later, Mr and Mrs Fedorchuk appeared with Angela seated between them. They parked in front of the Legion. A judge was in town to hear cases too serious for the local JP. He took less than five minutes to perform the ceremony.

Afterward, Fedorchuk led them to the Sunset Café. They all sat in one booth and watched a group of boys try to cheat a pinball machine. Angela and the pedlar, whose name, on the licence, was John Crestyin, ordered hamburgers and french fries. Mr and Mrs Fedorchuk had chicken in a basket.

'People are talking about your buying Grebon's store,' Fedorchuk said with a good deal of satisfaction. He had brought a mickey of homebrew in his jacket pocket and had added a little of it to their soft drinks.

'I'm going to put in a gas pump and go-karts,' John replied.

Fedorchuk nodded his approval. 'Kids got lots of money today.'

When they were finished, they went to Fedorchuk's car and John transferred Angela's suitcase to the back of his truck. Fedorchuk handed him a white envelope covered with silver stickers in the shape of bells.

John waited until his in-laws' car had disappeared, then gently touching Angela's arm, said, 'Let's go home.' He held the truck door open and helped her in.

Except for her responses when they were married, Angela had said nothing.

Instead of leaving, he sat and waited, working up enough courage to speak. In a few minutes, a Grey Goose bus pulled up beside them and the driver got off and went into the café.

'I came to your farm as often as I could,' he said. 'I never went to anybody else's as many times.'

'I know,' she murmured.

He opened the envelope Fedorchuk had given him and counted the money. There was one hundred and fifty dollars. He took out his wallet and counted out the other hundred. He put the money on the seat so that it lay half-way between them.

'That's your wedding money,' he said.

His store was five minutes from town. It sat on the corner of a crossroads facing the church where he stored his goods. On the other corner there was a community hall and an outdoor skating rink. The store was not large but it was large enough to make a living for a family. In the back there was a living space. In the small bedroom he had already set up a crib.

They lived together until the baby was born, then one day while he was behind the house feeding the black mare, his wife disappeared. The bus stopped for anyone who waved. He had heard it stop but had thought nothing of it, for passengers often stood on the corner. When he went inside, the store was empty, the child gone from its crib. His wife's suitcase and the wedding money, which she kept in a chocolate box on a closet shelf, were gone.

He stayed in the store for six months. Twice a day, when the bus went by, he stood at the window, watching to see if it would stop and, if it stopped, whether or not his wife would climb down. He kept the crib ready and left the house exactly as it had been when Angela left.

In the spring, he closed the store and went to the city for two weeks, wandering the streets all day and most of the night. When he returned to Eddyville, he sold the store at a loss to a retired farmer and disappeared for a second time. In a week, he reappeared, driving his caravan. There were only two differences: he no longer stopped at Fedorchuk's, and on the lobe of each ear he had a miniature daisy tattooed.

# Matt Cohen

MATT COHEN was born in Kingston, Ontario, in 1942, but lived in Ottawa until 1960, when he entered the University of Toronto. After graduating he spent some time in Europe, where he began a novel that was accepted by an English publisher. In 1963, however, Cohen withdrew (and later burned) the novel and returned to Canada to attend graduate school. In 1969, after the publication of *Korsoniloff*, he moved to a farm north of Kingston and began his next novel, *Johnny Crackle Sings* (1971). Since then he has written four connected novels—*The Disinherited* (1974), *The Colours of War* (1977), *The Sweet Second Summer of Kitty Malone* (1979), and *Flowers of Darkness* (1981).—and two books of short stories—*Columbus and the Fat Lady* (1972) and *Night Flights* (1978). For the academic year 1979-80 he was writer-in-residence at the University of Victoria.

Cohen's strength is his ability to experiment within the traditional forms of fiction without destroying them, recreating them in much the same way that myth, history, and tradition (like Christopher Columbus) can penetrate contemporary reality. As he told Graeme Gibson in an interview included in Gibson's *Eleven Canadian Novelists* (1973), the following story 'is also about science and the rational world that succeeded the medieval world. Reason existing as flight from chaos, both in the obvious chronological way, and in the sociological way, the new middle class who were interested in reason and science gained some sort of stability and freedom. But Columbus becomes a victim of his own flight. There's no way out for him. . . . he can just suffer in an interesting way.'

# COLUMBUS AND THE FAT LADY

HE MOVED aimlessly through the fairgrounds, letting the August sun warm him, filter through the dust and fill the gaps in his time. A tall man in his early forties, he wore a vaguely Spanish costume: tight black pants and an embroidered silk shirt. He had a sharp bearded face and large dark eyes. Despite his lack of direction he moved carefully, like a cat sensing its path. Occasionally he stopped and rubbed his hands across his ribs. They had never healed quite properly and he was aware of his body pushing out against them.

'Christopher.' Rena, the Fat Lady, waved him toward her. She was sitting out behind her tent, her dress hitched up over her enormous thighs. He went and sat down beside her in a lawn chair. He took off his shirt and stretched himself out to the sun. A scar in the shape of a cross had been burnt into his chest. 'Help yourself,' she said, meaning the bourbon that was standing in the shadow of her chair. He drank directly from the bottle and then passed it to her. Her face was rippled like a pile of bald pink tires. 'Praise the Lord,' she said when she had finished. She wiped her mouth and put the bottle back on the ground. They sat and contemplated the taste of the bourbon. Christopher took another drink and passed the bottle to Rena. 'Praise the Lord,' she said each time she drank. And then, shaking out the last drops, 'I know you're not supposed to drink in the sun.' She giggled. 'Yes,' she said, 'I surely know you're not supposed to drink in the sun. They say it makes you talk too much. At least it makes me talk too much. It makes me *want* to talk too much. Lord yes.' She had a voice that was thin and husky at the same time. 'Christopher,' she said, 'sometimes I believe you myself. Yes I do. But do you believe me?' She looked at him earnestly, across a half-empty bottle. He nodded. 'Yes,' she said, 'it's real for sure.' She took a handful of her face and shook it. 'It's all real. Took me ten years.' She traced out the scar on Christopher's chest. 'Yes,' she said, 'I do believe it's real. It must have smelled something awful.' Her finger had filled the gouge the iron had left. At first the scar tissue had been bright red but now it was dull and tough. He was tanned from his mornings in the sun. Felipa didn't like to come outside with him. She stayed pale and cool.

He stood up. The bourbon had made him dizzy but not drunk. 'It's time,' he said. He kissed her hand and put on his shirt.

'Oh,' Rena said. 'You have such beautiful manners.' He kissed her hand again and then started on his way. He had spent months on the ocean, but he didn't have the sailor's rolling gait; he walked like an ocelot sensing its path. He waved at the candy-floss man, at the foot-long-hot-dog booth, at the man who had a new gimmick that was guaranteed to open cans in three seconds; worked his way through the games and gadgets until he came to the midway. The crowds were beginning to fill up the spaces between the tents. Some of the barkers had already started, advertising their three-breasted women, their dwarfs and talking animals. He came to his own tent and signaled to a man wearing a striped shirt and a straw hat. He was sitting on the stage with Diego, showing him how to cheat at cards.

'He learns quick,' the man shouted to Christopher. Diego pocketed the cards and went to stand beside his father.

'Come on,' Christopher said. 'We'd better go inside.' The man dusted off his pants and ground out his cigar. He cleared his throat. He spat on his hands and rubbed them together. He climbed onto the platform in front of the tent, cleared his throat once more, whistled loudly into the microphone, and began:

'Ladies and gentlemen, step right up, yes—'

On either side of the tent were large crude posters showing a trio of old-fashioned ships tossing in a storm at sea.

'Step right up and see the world's most amazing freak of time, right here, ladies and gentlemen, come right in, only twenty-five cents, see Christopher Columbus and his ships, hear him tell about his famous voyage, see the man who found America, ladies and gentlemen, the world's strangest freak from time, see the cross they burnt onto his chest, hear about the women he left behind him, the man who met kings and princes, Christopher Columbus, only twenty-five cents, you have to see it to believe, it's absolutely true, ladies and gentlemen, bring your children, bring your friends, this is the world's only living history, hear him tell about the Santa Maria. . . . '

Water slopped across the deck of the ship, leaving flecks of foam and seaweed in its wake. Columbus was hunched into his coat, scanning the strange shore and estimating how much longer he could go without sleep. His hand moved in his pocket, seeking the familiar shape of the bottle. Fatigue had permeated him. It was like having a sliver in his nervous system. He uncorked the bottle: it wasn't working for him any more, it might have been thin wine or water. His tongue and throat were so immune it just drained down into the bowl of his stomach.

In his dream he was on land, and that, as he came to consciousness, was the first thing he was aware of. 'Christopher,' the boy was saying, 'Christopher.' He was making the name into an incantation. He opened his eyes. He was lying in a room lit by a lantern.

'Don't worry,' Columbus said. He closed his eyes.

'Don't worry,' a woman's voice echoed as he was falling back to sleep. He thought again that they must be on land. He felt the boy's lips on his hand. Tears. The water slid along the polished surface of his skin. They had tied him to a giant wooden wheel and were rolling him slowly through the village. When his cousin had died on the rack, he had stayed outside all night watching constellations slip off the edge of the earth. The priest's face was covered with tiny pouches, his eyes grey and certain. He walked along the Spanish coast with Columbus, one night when the clouds were layered into prayers. Columbus knelt down on the grass to confess. He closed his eyes and saw flesh being ground between millstones.

'You will feel better,' the priest said. 'A man does not have to carry his sins.'

'Yes,' Columbus said. Another cousin had been taken during a storm. He had seen him lose his balance, start sliding across the wet wood. He had dived flat across the deck to save him and had cracked his ribs. Afterward, still in the rain, they had bandaged him tightly while he drank to distance the pain. He remembered the man's wife. She had long black hair that had crackled in his hands.

'We only ask you to believe,' the priest had said, looking pointedly at Columbus, raising the question.

'Yes,' Columbus had said. While they bandaged him, he kept seeing the widow crossing herself over an empty grave.

The stone walls were seamed with damp lichen. They had given him a wooden bench to sit on. From the next room he could hear the meshings of clockwork gears mingled with the screams of heretics. But, every morning and every evening, he knelt and rested his head on the wood. He didn't dare use words any more. He just closed his eyes and held Felipa in his mind. When the image was clear, she could move around and whisper to him.

When they brought him in, the priest was there, his hands clasped in front of his grey robe. 'You will feel better,' the priest said. 'A man does not have to carry his sins.' Columbus nodded. He kissed the priest's bony hands. The skin caught in his teeth and moved around loosely.

With his compasses and sextant he had searched for God on the open sea. When he stumbled on the new world he half expected to find Him, sitting on a great carved throne, unsurprised that He had finally been discovered by mortals. The skin caught in his teeth and moved around loosely. He clamped his jaws; blood vessels popped open like grapes in his mouth.

Felipa caressed him as he slept. She drew her hands across the muscles of his back and plied his spine. Each day, the water had been different. He would stand on the deck and try to read its moods, calculate the margin of its mercy.

In his dream he was on land, and that, as he came to consciousness, was the first thing he was aware of. Felipa was holding a steaming bowl of soup out to him. He sat up and took the bowl. He smelled it and circled the strange aroma with his tongue. Diego was sitting beside the bed, watching him eat. 'You hurt your elbow,' Diego said. 'It's all swollen up like an egg.' Columbus set the soup down and slid his hand along his arm. The lump was big but not painful.

'There's a reporter here to see you,' Felipa said. 'She said you told her to come today.'

Columbus sat up straight. They had a cot for him, backstage, for when he fainted. He could see the sun setting through the yellowed plastic window of his tent. 'It's getting better,' he said. 'This time I was still conscious when I hit the floor.'

'No,' Felipa said. 'It's not good.' She frowned. 'The doctor said you mustn't do it any more.' The reporter had come in and was taking notes.

'I can't help it.' He saw the reporter. She had crouched down and was taking his picture.

'I'm going to Rena's,' Diego said. 'I guess I'll sleep there.' He looked sadly at the reporter and his father. 'I'll see you tomorrow.'

'What made you decide to discover America?'

Columbus lay back on his cot and closed his eyes. 'I'm sorry,' Felipa said. 'He's not very good at giving interviews.' She stood between Columbus and the girl. The girl put away her notebook and snapped her camera into its leather case.

'I don't mind,' she said. 'I just wanted to meet him.'

'Maybe some other time. He's very tired.' She edged the reporter out of the tent. When she came back in, Columbus was brushing his hair. 'Don't worry,' she said. 'Everything's going to be fine.'

He nodded. Lying on the cot, he had suddenly been reminded of rows of men in cells waiting for time to pass. The memory made him uncomfortable. His finger traced the scar on his chest. 'Is there time for a drink?'

'Yes there is. But *please*, it won't be bad tonight.'

'I know,' he said. 'If we could just settle somewhere, I would get my bearings.'

'I'm sure they're going to give you the job. The professor was very interested. He even invited us to dinner.'

'I don't mind this,' Columbus said.

'It's not healthy. Every time you tell the story, you faint.'

That evening, they went through the usual interrogations. His heart and pulse were checked. They shone lights into his eyes and poked at his ribs. They had a tape recorder and asked him questions about the Spanish court.

When they were finished, they left Christopher and Felipa in the dining room while they retired to deliberate. Professor Andras was the first to come out. He looked puzzled.

'Well?'

'They won't hire you but they will pay you a small fee to stay on if you will let them question you. You would be welcome to live here but my wife—' he shrugged his shoulders. 'I'm sorry, Mrs Columbus.'

'It doesn't matter.' When they were back in their hotel room, they lay on their bed in the dark listening to the breeze breathe through the curtains. He still remembered the man's wife. He had met her only once, by accident, at the edge of the forest.

'I don't want him to go,' she had said. Then she had drawn him back into the trees and embraced him. 'Forgive me,' she had said, 'make him stay.' The impact of his body had snapped the railing. It had been impossible to hear him above the storm, but they had seen him fighting hopelessly in the water.

'Yes,' Felipa said. 'This is how it was, before.' She gestured broadly, including everything in the sweep of her hand: the redwood trees, the long sandy beach, the Pacific Ocean stretching toward the Orient. Diego was already splashing and swimming in the water but Christopher and Felipa were sitting under a tree by a small stream that fed into the ocean.

'It's very beautiful,' Christopher said.

'Yes.'

'It seems a strange kind of ocean.'

'Maybe we could sell the truck, get a job on a freighter or something.'

'No,' he said. 'I'm tired of the sea.' They stood up and walked back to the truck, to get food and their bedrolls. Rena was waiting for them there, talking with a strange girl. The girl had a camera and was taking pictures of them as they came toward her. She had arrived on a motorcycle; it was parked beside the truck. There was a dead snake beneath the rear wheel. She put down her camera and took out her notebook.

'Hello,' the girl said. 'I followed you.'

'What do you want?'

'I want to do something different,' she said. 'You know, what kind of person you are, how are you with your wife and child. That kind of thing. For example, you could tell me who your favourite pop star is.'

'I was born in Genoa in 1450,' Columbus said. 'When I was nine years old I was apprenticed to a weaver.' He hadn't thought about that for a long time, the rhythms of wool and patterns, the miraculous transformation of single strands into shawls and blankets.

'What made you decide to discover America?'

Columbus sat down on the sand beside the truck and closed his eyes. 'I'm sorry,' Felipa said, 'he's not very good at giving interviews.'

'I don't mind,' the girl said. 'I just wanted to meet him.' She put away her notebook and snapped the camera into its leather case. 'I took psychology at college. Last week I interviewed a guy who thought he was Jesus Christ.'

'Maybe he was.'

'Oh, yes,' the girl said. 'I've always believed in reincarnation. My grandmother was Queen Elizabeth the First. I had to curtsy and kiss the hem of her dress every time I came into the room.'

Rena had her lawn chairs and her bourbon. She pointed the bottle toward the girl and motioned her to sit down. The girl was wearing tight white shorts, rolled up as far as they would go. 'Have a drink,' Rena said. She handed the bottle to the girl. The girl unscrewed the cap, wiped the neck of the bottle carefully, and took a delicate sip. She coughed. 'Praise the Lord,' Rena said. She took a long swallow. 'Praise the Lord,' she said again and handed the bottle back to the girl. The girl shook her head. 'Come on, it won't hurt you.' The girl accepted the bottle, took another delicate sip. This time she didn't cough. 'Praise the Lord,' Rena said. 'What's your name?'

'Laura Nimchuk,' the girl said.

'I'm pleased to meet you, Laura. That's Christopher Columbus down there and this is his wife, Felipa Moniz de Perestrello. And the boy on the beach is Diego, their son. Praise the Lord.' She threw the empty bottle past Laura into the back of the truck. 'It took ten years,' Rena said. 'I never stopped eating. I had to borrow money from the bank. It was a business investment. At the end I got a contract; I had to gain fifty pounds in the last two months and it nearly killed me.'

'God,' the girl said.

'And it's all real, too. Here, feel it.'

'I don't know,' Columbus said. 'I said I was going to India but all along I knew I would discover America. I guess I finally did it because I had to.' The girl was stroking Rena's arm. She spread out her fingers and plowed her hands through the flesh. 'It was a very hopeful thing to do. I felt we needed a new beginning.' He got up and paced as he talked. 'I thought there must be some place untouched by time.' The girl was still discovering Rena. It was like exploring a huge geography of lukewarm spaghetti.

'It's real,' Rena said. 'It's not a fake at all. People used to accuse me of wearing pillows and falsies, all sorts of things. But it's all real. It was hard work, too. Don't believe what you hear about glands. I have a picture of myself when I was a girl. I was just as thin as you.'

'I believe you,' Laura said. 'You've really accomplished something.' Her hands scooped up loose flesh around a shoulder and shaped it into a vase.

'They didn't want me to go.'

'I ate twenty-five apple pies in three days.' They had broken him of course. He had written endless pages of confessions, lists of heresies and failures to believe.

'It's not your fault,' the priest had said. 'Perhaps you are possessed. I've heard of such cases.' His face was covered with tiny pouches, his eyes grey and certain. 'Especially since your cousin regained his faith at the end. We could try to help you, to purge you of these things.'

'Or?'

'A man does not have to carry the burden of his sins,' the priest said. 'Not in this life.' After his confessions they gave him a wooden bench to sit on. Twice a day, in the morning and the evening, Columbus knelt and rested his head on the wood. He didn't dare use words any more. From the next room he could hear the meshings of clockwork gears.

'Jelly rolls, ice cream, chocolates—they're not any good at all. The best you can do with those is get flabby. You need something that will give you a good firm base. People don't understand that. They try to put it all on at once. Bourbon and beer, they're very good for after, pass me my purse, Laura, they feed the flesh, but what you need to begin with are grains and molasses.' She giggled. 'I know it sounds silly about the molasses but I believe it, it sticks it all together. Feel that: it's quite firm underneath. A person doesn't want to cover themselves with goop. Like you take the lady before me, she was disgusting. Praise the Lord. She was just a slob. People don't pay good money just to see a slob. It's a science, really. Without discipline it's almost impossible to get above three hundred pounds. Of course you have to have the talent, too. I guess you're just born with it. Praise the Lord. My father taught me everything. He used to be able to put it on any part of his body at will: an arm, or a leg, or even his head. He could never get it on everywhere at once though, so he couldn't get steady work. He used to make bets with people. In one week he could double the weight of any part of his body. It's science, really, but it's not the kind of thing they teach in school, Lord, I am thirsty, getting dehydrated is the big danger, yes, feel that: it's nice and moist, I make sure to keep it that way, yes.'

They had burned the cross into his chest to make sure he would carry his faith to the new world. 'A man can protect himself by the sign of God upon his body,' the priest had said. He had waited until Columbus regained consciousness and had gently wiped his face with cold water. It was weeks before he could move comfortably. 'My own sign is chastity, but that is given to very few.' He squeezed the cloth over the wound. When Columbus screamed, the priest slapped his face. 'We are not trying to punish you. That is what you have to understand.'

'If you want my secret in one word, I guess it was porridge.'

'I don't think of myself as a hero,' Columbus said. He had eaten dinner with the Queen of Spain. When she sent for him, the priest smiled, satisfied that he had had his audience first. Laura was sitting on Rena's lap. She had her notebook out again and was taking it all down in shorthand.

'Because of what happened, time doesn't exist for me,' Columbus said. A tall man in his early forties, he wore a vaguely Spanish costume. He had a sharp bearded face and dark eyes. He was leaning against the truck again. 'I don't know why it's real for anyone. There are always gaps, unexplained moments.'

'You dream,' Laura said. 'At night and sometimes during the day you dream.'

'I dream about my father,' Rena said. 'He was always changing his shape. The only part of him that stayed the same was his feet. He could never do anything with his feet. He said it saved him a fortune in shoes.'

Columbus got up and went down to the beach. Diego had found some wood and had started a fire beside the stream. Felipa was there too, rinsing off clams and preparing to cook them in a cast-iron kettle. Two men had held him when they taped his ribs. He had met the man's wife only once, by accident. She hadn't wanted him to go. He had a knife and helped Felipa by prying open the clams. 'Do you dream?'

'No,' she said. 'I just have pictures. Trees and castles and lakes and things like that. But no one ever talks. In real dreams people talk. Last night I saw a white rabbit.'

'Sometimes you have to make a sacrifice,' the priest had said. 'It might be someone or something very close to you, something that is felt as a great loss. Or it might be something that you aren't even aware of. In such cases it can take years to discover what has been given.'

'There must be something constant.'

'God's love.' The clams hissed as they were plunged into the boiling water. When he had dinner with the Queen he remembered his manners and didn't talk with his mouth full. But she ate carelessly, tearing the fowl apart with her fingers and throwing the remains over her shoulder.

'Yes,' Rena said. 'I believe everything he says, even the part about the Queen asking him to bring back souvenirs.' She was washing her clams down with bourbon and whole wheat bread. The girl still had her notebook but had lost her pen. She was curled up in the firelight, her head on Rena's lap. Rena stroked her hair and played cards with Diego.

'Let's play strip poker,' Diego said.

'Lord,' Rena laughed. 'You're too young. The sight of me would kill you.' Her voice was thin but husky. 'But I will if Laura does.'

'Are you really his son?' Laura asked later.

'Yes.'

'Really?'

'Yes.' Her shorts lay on the beach, flashing in the moonlight.

'And you were with him the whole time?'

'The whole time,' Diego said. He ran his tongue down the inside of her arm. The moon had laid a superhighway across the ocean.

'What was it like?'

'It was fun. But the food wasn't very good.'

'I wish I'd been there.' She went to the ocean and dipped her foot in the water. She stood ankle deep, looking at herself. Diego came and stood beside her. He put his arm around her. 'I don't really wish I'd been there,' she said. 'I can hardly stand up.'

'You get seasick easy?'

'I never have before.'

There was noise near the fire behind them. Rena came running and tripping toward them, a blanket wrapped around her, her flesh bouncing out in all directions. 'Beware the Spanish Infidels,' she was shouting, 'beware the Latin Lechers.' She rushed up to them and dropped on her knees in front of them. 'Save me, Diego,'' Rena cried. 'Save me, I beg of you.' She kissed his feet suppliantly. 'Save me from your father and anything I have is yours.'

'You know I can't interfere,' Diego said. 'I'm sorry.'

'Laura, you'll help me? Please?'

'Of course I will,' Laura said. She began leading Rena back toward the fire. 'What happened?'

'It's too horrible.'

'Now, now,' Laura said. 'I'll protect you.' She waved good-bye to Diego, the ocean, her tight white shorts, the highway to the Orient.

'Good night, Laura,' Diego said.

'Good night, Diego,' Rena called. 'Keep your eyes on the top card.'

Diego walked along the shore until he found Columbus. He was sitting on the beach, drawing maps with a stick. Diego squatted down beside him. The maps showed a clear route from Spain to India. 'This is the way it should have been,' Columbus said. 'All the rest was a mistake.'

'Yes.'

'Who won your card game?'

'Rena.'

He moved aimlessly through the fairgrounds, letting the sun warm him, filter through the dust and fill the gaps in his time. He had a sharp bearded face; his skin was burnished from the summer. Felipa was not with him. She stayed indoors, pale and cool, preparing for winter.

'Christopher.' Rena, the Fat Lady, waved him toward her. She was sitting out behind her tent. He went and sat down beside her in the lawn chair that was beside her own, that she had placed there for him. He took off his shirt and stretched himself out to the sun. A scar in the shape of a cross had been burnt into his chest. 'Help yourself,' she said, meaning the bourbon that was standing between their chairs. He drank directly from the bottle and then passed it to her. 'Praise the Lord,' she said after she drank. She wiped her mouth and put the bottle back on the ground.

'It's warm again,' he said.

'Indian summer. You could have been the first man to see an Indian.' She laughed. 'The first white man, I mean. It surely would have been something.' She laughed again. Her face rippled like a pile of pink tires. 'I guess you missed your chance.'

There was a taste in his mouth that he'd never noticed before. He didn't know where it had come from. 'I guess I did.'

'Yes,' Rena said. 'You surely did pick a strange time to discover

America.' She tipped her bottle up high. 'Praise the Lord.' Laura came out of the tent. She was wearing a dressing gown and carrying a cup of coffee. She rubbed her eyes and blinked.

'Diego's just getting up too,' she said. The priest used to like to bring him supper and watch him eat. He would sit beside him on the bench and watch him as he searched the soup for hidden messages. Diego was ready; he stood at the door of the tent, waiting.

'It's time,' Columbus said. He kissed Rena's hand. Then he and Diego set out together, walking around so they could come across the midway from the inside, as if by accident. The barker was waiting for them. He wore a striped shirt and a straw hat. They stood beside him for a moment, conferring about details that had been decided a hundred times, and then went inside, ready to begin.

'It's absolutely true, see the world's strangest freak from time, he's right here, yes, ladies and gentlemen, step right up here, it's absolutely true, see Christopher Columbus and his ships, hear him tell abut his famous voyage, see the man who found America, ladies and gentlemen, the world's strangest freak from time, see the cross they burnt onto his chest, hear about the women he left behind him, the man who met kings and princes, yes, Christopher Columbus, and it's only twenty-five cents, you have to see it to believe it, it's absolutely true, ladies and gentlemen, bring your children, this is the world's only living history, hear him tell about the Santa Maria. . . . '

'Yes,' Columbus said, 'it's absolutely true.' He stood on the stage in his tight black pants and embroidered silk shirt. He winked at the ladies in the audience. When the tent was jammed full the lights would go down. Felipa would come on stage, clicking castanets and singing a throaty Spanish ballad. While Columbus traced lines on the map and told his story she remained on stage, sitting on a velvet cushion. 'We had sighted the coast. I had been standing on the bridge of the ship for three days, hoping for land. It hadn't rained for a week. Suddenly a great storm came up. The winds blew the ship around like a matchstick—' he gestured expansively with his hands. His voice was beginning to tremble. 'And then, there was a flashing light, a clap—' His arms outstretched, his mouth open, he suddenly stopped. There was a sound like an

aborted cough. His arms dropped to his sides. He fell over, unconscious. Felipa knelt beside him. She pulled a scented handkerchief
from her bodice and gently stroked his head.

'And then,' she said, 'he was rescued. He and his son, Diego.
They were brought to my house in the middle of the night. The
ship was utterly destroyed and there were no other survivors.' She
signaled Diego. They dragged Columbus's body off into the wings.
'And now,' she said, 'I will sing one more song; it is the lament of a
widow who has lost her husband at sea.'